THE WHITEHALL CONSPIRACY

TRACY GRANT

The Whitehall Conspiracy

Ebook ISBN: 9781641971997
KDP POD ISBN: 9798831434293
IS POD ISBN: 9781641972208

NYLA Publishing
121 W 27th St., Suite 1201, New York, NY 10001
http://www.nyliterary.com

For my mother, Joan Grant, with whom I wrote and with whom I first discovered the fascinating history of Queen Caroline's trial. And for my daughter, Mélanie Grant, who is now writing herself and was an inestimable help brainstorming and proofreading in the writing of this book.

ACKNOWLEDGMENTS

As always, huge thanks to my wonderful agent, Nancy Yost, for her insights, support, and brilliant eye for editing cover copy. Thanks to Natanya Wheeler for shepherding the book expertly through the publication process and once again working her magic to create a fabulous cover that captures Whitehall, the mood of the story, Mélanie Rannoch, and the masquerade ball that is central to the novel, both in terms of plot and theme. To Sarah Younger for superlative social media support and for helping the book along through production and publication. To Kate Collier for a great set of quote cards. And to the entire team at Nancy Yost Literary Agency for their fabulous work. Their creativity and dedication make all of them a dream to work with. Malcolm, Mélanie, and I are all very fortunate to have their support.

Thank you to Eve Lynch for the meticulous and thoughtful copyediting. I love sharing the Rannochs with you and so appreciate your care for getting their story right when it comes to everything from historical usage to series continuity.

Thank you to Kristen Loken for a magical author photo taken in one of my favorite places, San Francisco's War Memorial Opera House, on one of my favorite occasions of the year, the Merola Grand Finale. Your brilliance never fails to amaze me, Kristen!

I am very fortunate to have a wonderful group of writer friends near and far who make being a writer less solitary, even— or especially—during the pandemic. Thanks in particular to Lauren Willig for guest hosting a wonderful virtual book party and conversation about the series—and for sharing the joys of historical research and the challenges of juggling life as a writer and a mom. To Penelope Williamson, for sharing adventures, analyzing plots from Shakespeare to *Scandal*, and being a wonderful honorary aunt to my daughter. So glad we are able to travel together again. Thank you to the #momswritersclub on Twitter for bimonthly chats that are energizing and inspiring, and especially to Jessica Payne for starting it and to Jessica and Sara Read for their wonderful #MomsWritersClub YouTube channel on which Mélanie and I had the fun of doing a guest interview.

Thank you to the readers who support Malcolm and Mélanie and their friends and provide wonderful insights on my Web site and social media, and especially on the Goodreads Discussion Group for the series.

Thanks to Gregory Paris and jim saliba for creating and updating a fabulous Web site that chronicles Malcolm and Mélanie's adventures.

And thank you to my daughter Mélanie, for brainstorming *Whitehall Conspiracy*, proofreading, and supporting me all the way through the process. One of my proudest moments was when she said "Can I borrow your computer? I want to type the story I'm writing." I am so proud that my website now includes "Mélanie's Corner" for her stories, starting with her wonderful series *Talea's Mysteries*. From the time she could touch the keys, Mélanie has contributed something to each of my books. This is Mélanie's contribution to this story – "I ADORE MUMMY'S BOOKS SO MUCH!!!!!!!!!!!!!"

DRAMATIS PERSONAE

*indicates real historical figures

The Rannoch Family & Household

Malcolm Rannoch, MP and former British intelligence agent
Mélanie Suzanne Rannoch, his wife, playwright and former
French intelligence agent
Colin Rannoch, their son
Jessica Rannoch, their daughter
Berowne, their cat

Laura O'Roarke, Colin and Jessica's former governess
Raoul O'Roarke, her husband, Mélanie's former spymaster, and
Malcolm's father
Lady Emily Fitzwalter, Laura's daughter from her first marriage
Clara O'Roarke, Laura and Raoul's daughter

James Fitzwalter, Duke of Trenchard, Laura's first husband's son

Gisèle (Gelly) Rannoch Thirle, Malcolm's sister

Andrew Thirle, her husband
Ian Thirle, their son

Valentin, footman

Alexander (Sandy) Trenor, Malcolm's secretary
Elizabeth (Bet) Simcox, his fiancée

Alistair Rannoch (Alexander Radford), Malcolm and Gisèle's putative father, Elsinore League founder

The Davenport Family & Household

Lady Cordelia Davenport, classicist
Colonel Harry Davenport, her husband, classicist, and former British intelligence agent
Livia Davenport, their daughter
Drusilla Davenport, their daughter

Edith Simmons, classicist and former governess

Archibald (Archie) Davenport, Harry's uncle, MP, and former French intelligence agent
Lady Frances Davenport, his wife, Malcolm's aunt
Chloe Dacre-Hammond, Frances's daughter from her first marriage
Francesca Davenport, Frances and Archie's daughter
Philip Davenport, Frances and Archie's son

The Mallinson Family

Julien (Arthur) Mallinson, Earl Carfax, former agent for hire
Katelina (Kitty) Velasquez Mallinson, Countess Carfax, his wife, former British and Spanish intelligence agent

Leo Ashford, her son
Timothy Ashford, her son
Guenevere (Genny) Ashford, Kitty and Julien's daughter

Hubert Mallinson, spymaster, Julien's uncle
Amelia Mallinson, his wife

David Mallinson, MP, their son
Simon Tanner, playwright, his lover

Lady Mary Laclos (former Duchess of Trenchard), Hubert and Amelia's eldest daughter
Gui Laclos, her husband
Marie Louise, their daughter

Lady Lucinda Mallinson, Hubert and Amelia's youngest daughter

The Lamb Family

*Emily, Countess Cowper, patroness of Almack's
*Harry, Lord Palmerston, Secretary at War, her lover
*George Lamb, her brother, playwright
*Caroline (Caro George) Lamb, his wife
*William Lamb, Emily's brother
*Lady Caroline (Caro William) Lamb, his wife

*Henry Brougham, MP, Queen Caroline's lawyer, Caro George's former lover

The Blayney Household

Edmund Blayney, journalist
Philippa (Pippa) Langdon Haworth, his fiancée
Danielle Darnault, opera singer and agent

Pierre Ducroix, journalist, her husband
Ilia, their daughter

The Smythe Family

Humphrey Smythe, Lord Beverston, Elsinore League member
Barbara Smythe, Viscountess Beverston, his wife
Benedict (Ben) Smythe, their younger son
Nerezza Russo, Ben's fiancée

The Talbot Family

Frederick Talbot, Marquis of Glenister, Elsinore League member
Viscount Quentin (Quen), his elder son
Aspasia, Quen's wife
Lord Valentine (Val) Talbot, Glenister's younger son

Honoria Talbot Atwood, Glenister's niece and ward
Carlisle Atwood, her husband

Evelyn (Evie) Mortimer Cleghorn, Glenister's niece and ward
Max Cleghorn, her husband

Others in London

Major George Chase, former agent and Cordelia's former lover
Abigail (Abby) Clifton, his mistress

Thomas Thornsby, classicist
Lady Shroppington, his great-aunt

Rupert, Viscount Caruthers, MP and former British intelligence agent

Timothy Drummond, former gamekeeper

Anne Forbes, former agent

Hugo, barkeep at Les Trois Amis
Joseph Eden, agent
Étienne Lémieux, assassin

Sofia Vincenzo Montagu, wife
Kit Montagu, her husband
Selena Montagu, Kit's sister

Jennifer Mansfield Smytheton, actress
Sir Horace Smytheton, her husband, former Elsinore League member

Jeremy Roth, Bow Street runner
Hopkins, Bow Street patrol
*Sir Nathaniel Conant, chief magistrate of Bow Street
*Lord Sidmouth, British home secretary

*Robert Jenkinson, Earl of Liverpool, prime minister of the United Kingdom

Contessa Montalto

Bianca Falconetti

*George IV, King of the United Kingdom of Great Britain and Ireland
*Caroline, his wife

Marriage is a matter of more worth
Than to be dealt in by attorneyship
—Shakespeare, *Henry VI, Part 1,* Act V, scene v

PROLOGUE

*H*ubert Mallinson sat back in his chair and looked at the man across from him in the shadows of the coffee room in a nondescript inn off the Dover Road. The sort of inn suited to couples looking for an anonymous place for an illicit tryst. Or to spies looking for a location for secret discussions. Which were often best conducted in prosaic settings.

Of all the unusual conversations he'd had in the course of his career as a spymaster, he wouldn't have predicted this one. And yet perhaps it was inevitable. "I assume you have your reasons for risking this."

"I'm not risking a great deal," Alistair Rannoch said. "No one's looking for me. And you won't make this public."

"You seem very sure."

"You don't want to force it into the open any more than I do." Alistair leaned back and took a sip of wine. "It doesn't really make sense that we're enemies, you know."

"Doesn't it?" Hubert regarded his opponent across the single candle and the bottle of wine on the table between them. "I'd have said that that's one of the few things that does make sense."

Alistair pushed a glass across the table towards Hubert. "We're aligned on most important issues. And we could accomplish a great deal more as allies."

"Assuming I had any desire to help you accomplish anything."

"You've always been a pragmatist. Surely it would depend on what I have to offer."

Hubert reached for his glass but did not take a drink. Much as part of him wanted to toss the wine in Alistair's face and stride from the tavern, he had to ask the inevitable question. "What do you have to offer?"

"A profitable alliance that will benefit us both. You have much more in common with me than with Malcolm. And, god knows, more than with O'Roarke."

"Malcolm's a very good agent. So's O'Roarke, if it comes to that."

Alistair grimaced. "I suppose I can't deny that. But that doesn't make you allies. You can't deny O'Roarke stands against everything you believe in."

"Oh, yes. So does Malcolm. But I don't have to worry about their stabbing me in the back."

"I should think St. Juste would give you enough to think about in that regard."

Hubert took a drink of Bordeaux. A good vintage; he'd give Alistair credit for being a good judge of wine. And other things. "You have a point there."

"Not to mention Mélanie Rannoch. She can't possibly be as domestic as she appears."

"I think Mrs. Rannoch would rake you over the coals for suggesting she even appears anything of the sort."

Alistair gave a short laugh. "She certainly pulled the wool over Malcolm's eyes. And apparently continues to do so, considering the fact that he's still living with her."

"That might signify that he knows her very well indeed."

"In what way?"

Hubert shifted his glass on the tabletop. "Malcolm's a number of things, and god knows I've been known to bemoan his impossible delusions about the human race. But I wouldn't discount what's between him and his wife. Or his determination to preserve a marriage that means a great deal to him."

"At what cost?"

"You'll have to ask him that." Hubert pushed his spectacles up.

Alistair twirled his glass between his fingers. "I'd assume you think him a fool. But you don't sound that way."

"I wouldn't necessarily play the situation as he's done. But recent events have perhaps given me an appreciation of why a man might see the value in preserving his marriage."

Alistair gave a grunt. "Some marriages can't be preserved."

"Very likely." Hubert took a swallow of wine. It had a sharper bite now. Perhaps with the realization that his own marriage might be one of those. "The Rannochs' isn't one of them."

"You sound very sure of that."

Hubert tugged the left earpiece of his spectacles more firmly behind his ear. "I'm sure of few things in life. But oddly, I think I am sure of that."

"She married him to spy on him."

"And managed to deceive all of us. It was ably done. Among other things, Malcolm appreciates her talents. And Mélanie, I rather think, values having a husband who appreciates her."

"You sound as though you admire her."

"I do," Hubert said, for once speaking the unvarnished truth. "And not in the way most men do. It doesn't mean I trust her. But I'd rather have her at my back than you."

A shadow flickered across Alistair's face. He took a drink of wine. "I thought you said you were interested in what I had to offer. Or was that all a hum?"

"Oh, I'm interested. It wouldn't be prudent not to explore all options."

Alistair leaned forwards. "I can help you secure the king's case. There's a lot to be said for a grateful monarch. It will ensure the

Whigs and Radicals retreat and give them no chance of turning the royal divorce to their advantage."

The new king's dogged determination to divorce his long-estranged wife was a farce. It also threatened to bring down the government and had normally orderly citizens demonstrating in the street in ways that called up memories of France in the nineties. Hubert took a measured sip of wine. "I'm listening."

"You can send that upstart Brougham packing with his tail between his legs."

Hubert grunted at the mention of the Queen Caroline's attorney general. "Brougham has a tendency to bounce back like a rubber ball. But go on."

"It will let you consolidate your power against Castlereagh and Sidmouth and anyone else who's been encroaching."

Hubert stretched his legs out under the table and cupped his hands round his glass. "I wasn't aware that anyone had been encroaching. I must be slipping."

"You know damn well you're not slipping. But you can't deny certain people have been taking advantage of the recent changes in our circumstances."

Hubert's hands tightened round the wine glass, though he flattered himself no one could tell. "My power never rested on being Lord Carfax."

"But you turned being Carfax to your advantage. You're good at turning things to your advantage. I'm offering you the chance to do so again."

Hubert took a deliberate drink of wine. "And in exchange?"

His companion reached for the bottle and refilled their glasses. "I want what Fanny got for O'Roarke and Mélanie. I want a pardon."

"For what?"

"For everything."

"I don't even know what everything is."

"No, that's true. You don't."

Hubert scanned the other man's face. He was good at reading clues in an expression. An agent had to be. But his companion was a master at hiding things. "It's asking a great deal."

"If the king gets what he wants it will be worth a great deal."

"To him."

"And to you if you bring it about."

Hubert twisted the stem of his glass between his fingers. "You could of course be setting all this up to ruin me. You've tried to enough in the past."

"That's because you were trying to destroy us. If you join us you wouldn't be an enemy anymore. After all, isn't joining us what you always wanted?"

"Joining you?" Hubert laughed at the thought of ever having been part of the Elsinore League. "I wanted to stop you from wreaking havoc on Britain and the Continent. Just like O'Roarke and Malcolm and their Leveller friends."

"Are you sure it wasn't jealousy of your brother?"

The word lingered in the air. "I never paid enough heed to my brother to be jealous."

Alistair leaned back in his chair. "Can you really say you wouldn't have joined us all those years ago if we'd asked you?"

"Oh, I daresay I would have done. To keep an eye on you. I daresay O'Roarke would have done for the same reasons."

"You're talking about O'Roarke as though he's a friend."

"He is, after a fashion. I'm not particularly pleased that you've tried to have him killed."

"You've done the same yourself."

"Possibly. With better cause. I wouldn't do so now unless things change drastically."

"Things have a way of changing, don't they?" Alistair took a drink of wine. "Given our current circumstances, I'd have no reason to move against you. Not if I could secure your cooperation."

Hubert held his companion's gaze. "Unless you wanted to destroy me for the same reason you wanted to destroy O'Roarke."

Alistair returned the gaze like a duelist returning fire. His hand remained steady on the wine glass, but Hubert fancied it cost him an effort to keep it so. Because the one thing Alistair, Hubert, and Raoul O'Roarke shared was a connection to Arabella Rannoch, who had been Alistair's wife and Hubert's and Raoul's lover. "In your case it was a mission," Alistair said. "In Arabella's too."

"Difficult to tell sometimes where the mission leaves off. I imagine Mélanie could tell us something about that. And I imagine Malcolm and my wife could tell us something about whether or not it's being a mission negates the impact on others involved."

Alistair's gaze hardened. "Don't make the mistake of confusing me with Malcolm, who for all his apparent coldness is entirely too likely to dwell on the emotions involved. O'Roarke has always been my opponent. Our tactics could never align. Yours and mine could. That's all it comes down to."

"There's rarely any 'all' anything comes down to." Hubert tugged at his right earpiece. "And while I agree it's a tiresome waste to dwell too much on emotions, I think one ignores them at one's peril. I'd never make the mistake of assuming you were entirely rational."

"I think I should be insulted by that."

"Don't be. I don't claim I could be entirely rational if you'd seduced Amelia." Hubert's fingers froze on the frame of his spectacles.

"No," Alistair said. "That never occurred to me. Proof perhaps of my own rationality in such matters."

"Or of the fact that you can deceive even yourself." Hubert took a drink of wine, gaze steady on the other man's face. "Take it from one who knows."

"You're talking like a fool, Hubert."

"We're all fools at times." Hubert continued to watch the man who had been his opponent for so long. The man whose wife had briefly been his mistress. "For what it's worth. I can imagine Arabella upsetting a man's best laid plans. She'd be worth it."

Alistair's fingers tightened round his wine glass.

"That isn't what she meant to me," Hubert said. "Or I to her. But I liked her. And there aren't many people I'd say that about."

Alistair tossed down a drink of wine and drummed his fingers on the table. "You're very good at prevaricating. Which I admit can be a useful talent. But this is a business proposition. I wouldn't attack you or O'Roarke or anyone else simply for personal reasons. Do you want what I have to offer? If not, I'll make other arrangements."

Hubert sat back in his chair and took a slow, deliberate drink of wine. Because what he said could change everything.

CHAPTER 1

The Palace of Westminster, London
Tuesday, 3 October 1820

*S*candalous. *Shocking. Impressive. Never thought I could feel sympathy for* her. *Remember the evidence about the bedsheets? Whatever else one thinks, he can hold a room's attention. Didn't he run off to Italy himself with someone's wife?* Non mi ricordo! *What's sauce for the goose is fit sauce for the gander.*

The fragments carried through the crowd on the stairs outside the White Chamber in the Palace of Westminster, which had been the Court of Requests and currently served as the House of Lords chamber, thick as a flurry of autumn leaves, bouncing off bonnets and cravats, walking sticks and reticules, ruched skirts and padded coats, half boots and Hessians.

"What's more exciting?" Cordelia Davenport asked over the patter of voices and footfalls. "Having your words spoken onstage at the Tavistock or in the House of Lords?"

Mélanie Rannoch tightened her grip on her son Colin's hand as they negotiated the crowd on the stairs outside the House of Lords. "Those were hardly my words just now."

9

"Some of them were," Laura O'Roarke said, keeping pace beside them, holding her daughter Emily's hand. "I can attest that you and Malcolm spent hours editing Brougham's speech. I made two pots of coffee while you were at it."

"We maybe sharpened it a bit." Mélanie righted her bonnet as someone jostled into her and dug an elbow into her spencer. Parliament was as crowded today as the Tavistock or Covent Garden on a first night. Perhaps not surprising given the drama playing out in the chamber, though it would be difficult to say if it was tragedy or farce. Henry Brougham had just given the opening speech for the defense in the trial before the Lords in which George IV, the new, as yet uncrowned king, was attempting to divorce his long-estranged wife, Caroline of Brunswick.

"Where's Aunt Kitty?" Colin asked, looking round at the crowd pressing past.

"We're here." Kitty Mallinson and her elder son Leo slipped between two men earnestly debating the merits of Brougham's speech. The four women had each brought their eldest child to hear the opening of the defense. Mad as the events unfolding in London now were, they were shaping history, and it seemed important for the children to see it unfold.

More people were spilling onto the stairs from the chamber. Mélanie caught Emily's hand in her free hand while Cordelia and Kitty joined hands, and the four of them and the children tried to stay close together. It was harder than trying to keep a group of fighters together in a skirmish in foggy terrain. As Mélanie could attest from personal experience.

They turned a corner and were halfway down the last flight of stairs when the crowd stopped abruptly. A dark-coated man in front of Mélanie surged backwards, knocking into her. Her half boots skidded on the step. Emily clutched her hand.

"That man fell!" Colin yelled.

Mélanie could see a man's bootlegs sprawled a few steps down. Someone screamed. Mélanie cast a quick glance at Laura. Laura grabbed Colin's hand. Mélanie pushed forwards and dropped down beside the man who had fallen. He had tumbled on the steps at a haphazard angle. She tugged off her gloves and went still at the sight of his familiar features. But there was no time to focus on that. His blue eyes were open but already glazed. She put her hand to his chest to check for his pulse and felt something damp and sticky. Blood was seeping through the side of his waistcoat. She pulled off her spencer and pressed it to his chest. "Can you hear me? Try to stay with me."

He shuddered. "Cor—Cordelia." His eyes were clouding. She could feel spreading dampness through the velvet of her spencer. Someone else screamed. She pressed her hands to his chest, heard him gasp, saw the light go from his eyes. She looked up to see a circle of people gathered round and met Kitty's gaze, though Kitty could not possibly understand the full implications. "He's dead."

Cordelia pushed forwards beside Kitty. She'd gone completely still, as though she was looking into a gaping chasm. "George."

"For someone used to weapons, I'm coming to appreciate the power of the spoken word." Julien Mallinson, now Earl Carfax and one of the newest members of the House of Lords, leaned his sleek blond head close to Malcolm Rannoch to make his voice heard in the crush outside the Lords chamber. "I don't know how it seemed from the gallery, but you could have heard a pin drop on the floor."

"In the gallery as well. But it won't be enough. Not on its own." Malcolm scanned the crowd. Probably fruitless to try to catch sight of Mélanie, Laura, Cordy, and Kitty and the children in the throng. He'd told her he'd see her at home later tonight, since he'd be caught up in the endless Whig strategy discussions at Brooks's after today's session.

"They're all good at navigating chaos," Harry Davenport said, reading his thoughts. "Better than we are. This is nothing to the crush at a first night or a successful ball."

That was true. And no need to worry, Malcolm told himself. London was on edge, but it seemed excessive to fear violence inside the Palace of Westminster. So far the protests had been confined to the streets. And it was the Tory opposition and people like his former spymaster, Julien's uncle Hubert Mallinson, who worried about the protests, while Malcolm was inclined to think they were a release of very understandable frustrations by a populace suffering from high corn prices and unemployment after years of war. But recent events had left Malcolm on edge.

"A lot of long Tory faces." Raoul O'Roarke, Malcolm's father, slid through the crowd to join them. "At the risk of sounding small-minded, I confess it's quite satisfying."

"Nothing wrong with that," Malcolm said. "But however dour they look, we haven't won anything unless they change their votes."

Harry clapped Malcolm on the shoulder. "Take your victories while you can. Our side has at least won the day. And you and Mélanie helped hone the winning speech."

"Just round the edges," Malcolm said.

The crowd had eddied enough to allow them to inch forwards. Julien was slightly in the lead. He went still suddenly, nearly making Malcolm stumble. "Did you hear that?"

"What?" Malcolm asked. Julien had catlike senses.

"A scream."

"Probably Tory frustration," Harry said. "Though it's difficult to tell the Tory screams of frustration from Whig shouts of glee."

"No." Julien was frowning with a seriousness he rarely showed. "I don't know if it was a Whig or a Tory, but someone shouted murder."

CHAPTER 2

" $\mathcal{D}$ rink this." Kitty put a glass of brandy into Cordy's hand in the sitting room the parliamentary staff had hurried them into.

Cordelia stared into it. "Will it help?"

"There's always the hope."

Cordelia gulped down a sip and glanced towards the end of the room where Laura had gathered the children with the lemonade and biscuits the staff had produced.

"You didn't know George was in London?" Mélanie asked.

"Of course not." Cordelia's fingers whitened round the glass. "You can't think I wouldn't have said something."

"Probably not. But I can't be sure of myself in similar circumstances so I can't very well claim to be sure of you."

Cordelia shuddered. Her blue velvet bonnet was slipping back, caught round her throat by its azure satin ribbons. Her blonde hair was slipping loose from its pins, tendrils clinging to her forehead and cheeks. Her eyes were smudged darker than the blue velvet. "I haven't heard from him since Waterloo." She tugged the brim of her bonnet into place. "A part of me has always known I'd see him again. Has dreaded his showing up. I've played out a dozen scenarios in my head. But I never thought—"

"One never does," Kitty said.

The door opened and a brisk purposeful figure strode in, coat-tails whipping about him.

"Jeremy. Thank god." Mélanie moved to the door as Jeremy Roth came forwards.

"I was in the gallery." Roth crossed to her side and gripped her hands. An uncharacteristic lack of restraint for him, especially on duty. Roth, a Bow Street runner, was usually very conscious of his role, for all he had become a personal friend. "We were worried about trouble today, though this wasn't what we had in mind. I'm sorry you stumbled across this, but also relieved to have you involved." He glanced at the end of the room where Laura was sitting with the children, then looked back at Mélanie, Kitty, and Cordelia. "Do you know who the victim is?"

"George Chase," Cordelia said. She had tightened the ribbons on her bonnet and was gripping her brandy glass in steady hands. "Major George Chase."

"You know him?"

"I grew up with him. I hadn't seen him since just after Water-loo. He'd been seconded to Malta. I had no notion he was back in England." Cordelia tossed down the remainder of her brandy, glanced at the children again, drew a breath. "You'll hear all of this, it's common gossip, and you need to know. George Chase was my first love. We wanted to marry but neither of us had a feather to fly with and my father refused his consent. George married an heiress, Annabel Lovell, bought a commission, and went off to the Peninsula. I married Harry. Who was the right person for me, but I married him for all the wrong reasons. When George came home on leave, he and I tumbled into an affair. When Harry learned of it, George and I ran off together. Harry joined the army and went off to the Peninsula. Actually, living with George I quickly realized it wouldn't work. When we

14

learned his wife was pregnant, I sent him back to her. But a part of me was distinctly relieved to see him go." Cordelia had also been pregnant at the time, but that fact, and the fact that George might be father of her eight-year-old daughter Livia, who was now across the room nibbling biscuits and listening to the story Laura was telling, was too much for her to share. Mélanie quite understood. Though at some point Roth might have to know.

"Your candor is admirable, Lady Cordelia," Roth said. His gaze was neutral but at the same time kind. "That was the last time you saw him?"

"No." Cordelia held her glass out to Kitty. "Do you mind? I think I'm going to need more." She folded her hands together and turned back to Roth with the gaze of the woman Mélanie remembered from when they had first met in Brussels, the gaze of a woman determined to stare down scandal and society's censure. "I saw George again in Brussels just before Waterloo. And after the battle. Things were over between us, but George didn't quite accept that."

"He wanted to resume the relationship?"

"Yes." Cordelia accepted a refilled glass of brandy from Kitty and smiled at her. "Thank you." She took a sip of brandy. "But there was no question of George's and my relationship resuming. I knew that even before I learned he'd murdered my sister."

Roth, who had seen all sorts of human depravity and rarely displayed shock, drew in and released a harsh breath. "That was proved?"

"Mélanie and Malcolm proved it and George confessed it to all of us. But there was no evidence to convict him. We also learned he had killed a ward of Lord Carfax—the former Lord Carfax, Hubert Mallinson—several years earlier."

Roth kept his gaze steady, though Mélanie saw the story's impact in his gaze. "Does Carfax—Hubert Mallinson—know that?"

"Oh yes. So does Wellington. They packed George off to

Malta." Cordelia took another drink of brandy, holding the glass with both hands. "I always knew he'd come back some day, though sometimes I could forget about him for days at a time."

"Has he ever tried to contact you?"

"No. For years I lived in dread that he would. I'm friends with his sister Violet. But she's always careful not to mention him round me."

"You have no idea why he was back in England?"

"No." Cordelia's fingers tightened round the glass.

"But he likely came back to England to see you?"

"Not necessarily."

"So he accepted what was between you was over?"

Cordelia's shoulders tightened as she drew in her breath. "He —As I said, he hadn't tried to contact me in five years. It's difficult to imagine he could have believed there could be anything between us after what I knew. Even if I weren't happily married. Though George always had the ability to delude himself."

Roth nodded and pulled his notebook from his coat. Unusual for him not to have used it before now. "It sounds as though Carfax—Hubert Mallinson—had considerable reason to dislike George Chase. I can't see his lightly letting a man who had killed his ward go free."

"No." Kitty pushed a tawny side curl behind her ear. "Nor can I."

"To own the truth," Mélanie said, "I kept expecting to hear George had had an unfortunate accident. You should also know that George was an agent."

"Military intelligence?" Roth asked.

"Yes, but he worked directly for Carfax—Hubert Mallinson."

"Like a number of us," Kitty said.

"Did you know him?" Roth asked Kitty.

"I met him once or twice in the Peninsula," Kitty said.

Cordelia stared at her.

"There seemed no reason to tell you." Kitty looked at Cordy, her green gaze at once direct and compassionate. The gaze of an agent but also of a friend. "By the time I met you, I realized all it would do is stir up unfortunate memories."

"You're kind," Cordy said.

"Or a coward. I often have difficulty telling the difference."

"Did the victim"—Roth drew a breath. "Did Mr.—Captain—"

"Major," Cordelia said.

"Major Chase say anything before he died?" Roth asked.

Mélanie shook her head. "He was barely conscious when I got to him. I was so focused on doing what I could for him I scarcely registered who it was. I don't think he even recognized me. Though he did look at Cordelia. I think—"

"He knew me," Cordelia said. "He said my name. I have no idea what that means. It certainly doesn't address the question of who killed him."

"Do you think he came to the House of Lords looking for you?" Roth asked.

"I don't—" Cordelia swallowed. "It seems a very odd place to try to find me. And if he could have found me in the crowd, he couldn't have counted on any private conversation. In fact, private conversation would have been almost impossible, even if I'd been willing to talk to him."

"You might have had a hard time getting away from him in the crowd," Kitty said. "And you wouldn't have wanted to make a scene. But I still don't see how he could have counted on much intelligible conversation."

"I haven't seen the body yet," Roth said. "He was stabbed?"

"In the side," Mélanie said, keeping her voice brisk. "Probably with a thin blade."

"It's the sort of thing my husband used to be known to do," Kitty said in a cool voice. "But Julien was still in the chamber when Major Chase was killed. And Julien wouldn't. Not now. Not without cause, anyway. Not that—" She looked at Cordelia.

17

"Whatever threat Major Chase represented, Julien would know it would only complicate things for you more."

Roth nodded. He knew Julien enough now not to question either.

"His pockets were bare of identifying information," Mélanie said. "I searched them before the staff hurried us away." She'd forced herself to do so rather than turning to Cordy, though she'd been keenly aware of Cordy's stricken presence behind her. Cordy would understand, but the memory still scraped against her throat.

"I can get you another look at the body," Roth said. "We thought about closing the doors to the palace, but it would only have led to panic, and by then the killer was almost certainly long gone."

"Quite certainly," a familiar voice said from the door.

Julien was standing there, having entered with his usual soundlessness. Malcolm pushed past him and came forwards to grip Mélanie by the shoulders.

"We're all right, darling," Mélanie said, closing her fingers on his elbows, aware of their son Colin watching them from across the room. "He died just after I got to him. The killer was gone."

"We were in the wrong place at the wrong time," Cordelia said, looking round to meet Harry's gaze, as he and Raoul followed Julien and Malcolm into the room. "But we—" She looked at Harry. "It was George."

For a moment Harry went still. The reality settled in his eyes like a lead weight. Mélanie had seen men who'd received a bullet react the same way, the realization following on the actual shot. Harry crossed to his wife in two strides. His hands closed over hers.

"I had no notion he was in England," Cordelia said.

"Of course not." Harry drew her closer. His gaze shot to Livia and lingered for a moment, then went back to Cordelia. "Did he—"

18

"He died just after we got to him."

"So he didn't have a chance to say anything."

"Not really." Cordelia swallowed. "He said my name."

Harry gave a quick nod. "I'm sorry, sweetheart."

"You're—"

"My god, Cordy. It must have been hell."

Cordelia looked up at him with a bright determination that conjured memories of the days in Brussels when their every interaction was layered in artifice. "It was a shock."

"I understand Major Chase had been an agent," Roth said, with the care of one intruding on a private scene. "None of you knew he was back in England?"

In the brief silence that followed, Mélanie could feel Malcolm, Raoul, Harry, and Julien all hesitating just a fraction of a second over what the others might have known. As any self-respecting agent would. "No," Malcom said.

"I only heard a few rumors about him after Waterloo," Julien said.

Malcolm nodded. "After Waterloo—"

"I told Jeremy," Cordelia said. "About my past with George and George's killing Julia and Amy Beckwith."

Harry's arm went round his wife's shoulders.

"We've got the body isolated," Roth said. "I don't have a doctor yet. But I could use an experienced eye."

"I'll go," Julien said in an easy voice.

"Do you want me to?" Cordelia turned in the circle of Harry's arm.

"Do you want to see him?" Roth said.

"No. I—saw him. On the steps. That was enough." She shuddered. "I don't think I could really help if I looked at him again. But I will if you think it could help."

Julien squeezed her hand. "Let me first and see what I learn. If I think you should see him, I'll let you know."

Cordelia gave him a grateful smile. "You're splendid, Julien."

"Are you all right, Mummy?" Livia ran over to Cordy as Julien and Roth left the room.

Cordelia turned from the circle of Harry's arm and bent down to hug her daughter. Her gaze went to Harry's. Oddly, Mélanie was reminded of the moment Harry had met Livia when she had watched both parents pick their way through what to say to their young daughter with no time to talk it through. "I'm fine, darling." Cordelia stroked Livia's hair. "But I knew the man who was killed. A long time ago. We grew up together. I hadn't seen him in years. But it's still a shock."

Livia's gaze remained on her mother's face. "I'm so sorry. You lost a friend."

Cordelia's arms tightened round Livia. "We hadn't been friends for a long time. But yes, it's hard."

"You'll have to Investigate," Colin said, running over to his parents. The spell that had held the children with Laura was broken.

"Malcolm and Julien can't." Emily followed Colin and slid her hand into Raoul's. "They have to save the queen."

Laura got to her feet and followed the children, Leo beside her. Leo ran to Kitty. Colin tucked his hand into Mélanie's. He looked up at her, asking her again to Investigate, but in a very different way. Now he wanted her to fix something he couldn't even articulate. She squeezed his hand.

Roth turned to Mélanie. "Do you know any of Major Chase's —" He broke off as the door burst open again to admit Hopkins, one of the Bow Street patrols who worked with him.

"I'm sorry to barge in." Hopkins pushed his fair hair back from his face and glanced round the company. He had always struck Mélanie as quite matter-of-fact, but now his blue eyes were wide with shock. "But there's been an unexpected development. To own the truth, sir, I'm not sure what to make of it. But I think you'll have to send for the prime minister."

Hopkins drew a breath. His gaze darted round the group,

taking in the various people he was more apt to encounter in Mayfair, the children clinging to their parents. He generally darted in with messages for Roth in this crowd, rather than delivering them himself.

"It's all right," Roth said. "You can say whatever it is in front of this group."

Hopkins gave a quick nod. "One of the staff came up to me. He said he didn't know who the dead man was, but that the man had come up to him earlier in the day. Shoved a note into his hand. Asked him to get it to the PM's staff. Said he'd be paid handsomely if he did. The staff member says the man moved on before he could ask questions. He stuffed the note in his pocket to look at later. Didn't think about it until he saw the dead man and realized it was the man who'd given him the note." Hopkins reached inside his coat and held out a crumpled paper.

Roth spread the paper out, scanned it, and then handed it round to the others.

I have important information that will assist the king's case. I'll be in the back room at the Three Kings in Russell Street at midnight tonight.

The note was written in a trained hand with no signature.

"That's George's hand," Cordelia said, in a ruthlessly level voice. "What in god's name was he up to?"

"There were no papers on him," Mélanie said. "And I got to him within seconds. I don't see how the killer or anyone else could have taken anything off him. So if he was trying to barter information, he didn't have written evidence with him."

"But he's been away," Cordelia said. "What could he—"

"The queen was out of the country too, until recently." Raoul was scanning the paper, analyzing ink and stains and anything else that might be a clue.

"But George wasn't in Italy," Cordelia said. "He was in Malta."

"We don't know for a certainty where he was," Harry said. "Or what he might have stumbled across. George was an agent."

"I take it he wasn't likely to still have been working for Carfax?" Roth said. "Hubert Mallinson, that is."

"It seems extremely unlikely," Malcolm said. "But I wouldn't put using anyone past Hubert."

"Nor would I," Kitty said.

Roth nodded. "If Chase had information about the trial, it's a motive." He looked at Malcolm. "You must know the prime minister."

"A bit," Malcolm said. "But Raoul knows him better."

Roth turned to Raoul with a look of surprise. Understandable, given that Raoul was a known revolutionary who had worked to overthrow governments in France and Ireland.

"Years ago." Raoul looked up from the note. "But we were unlikely allies then. In this case I think I can at least apprise him of the situation." He looked across the room and met Laura's gaze briefly, then touched Malcolm's arm. "The rest of you can get on with the investigation."

"You think he'll agree to see you?" Roth asked.

Raoul, spymaster and former Bonapartist agent who had worked against the British government for years, moved to the door. "I'm not sure. But I have no intention of giving him the choice."

CHAPTER 3

*R*aoul found Robert Jenkinson, Earl of Liverpool, Prime Minister of the United Kingdom, in a small, nondescript sitting room off one of the passages in the Palace of Westminster, giving directions to two secretaries and scanning a document at the same time.

One of the secretaries noticed Raoul first. "Here, you can't be in here."

Liverpool's head snapped up. His gaze settled on Raoul across the room. For a moment, Raoul could see him weighing the situation. Then he folded the papers and glanced from one secretary to the other. "Leave us."

"Sir—" the first secretary protested.

"Now."

Neither secretary protested further.

Liverpool watched the door click shut behind his secretaries, then shot his gaze to Raoul. "How did you get in here?"

"Relied on my instincts and acted as though I had an unassailable right to go where I wanted. That's usually half the trick."

Liverpool grunted. "I would have thrown almost anyone else out."

The words spoke to their complicated history. Raoul and Robert Jenkinson, now Lord Liverpool, had crossed paths in Paris over thirty years ago. Even then they'd been political opponents but they had been united in their efforts to rescue a young actress named Louise Doret from an abusive lover. Who happened to be the Duke of Trenchard, who a few years ago had been scheming to push Liverpool out and be made prime minister himself. Trenchard had been murdered before he could carry his plan out. Liverpool and Raoul had had little contact since their alliance assisting Louise, but the PM had shown tolerance and even support for Raoul from afar, including through events that could have led to Raoul's arrest for treason.

"I appreciate that you didn't," Raoul said. "And I suspect you will too."

"I assume it's something to do with the unfortunate man who was killed. My secretaries were just updating me. If you're going to tell me he was a foreign agent—"

"He wasn't. But that doesn't mean it isn't complicated." Raoul surveyed the prime minister. Liverpool had been a boy of less than twenty when they first met. Raoul hadn't been much older, but he'd already been an agent and involved in the intrigues of the Revolution in France. The difference in their experience had stretched wide. In the intervening years, Liverpool had arguably achieved more. At the very least they were on the same level now. "How much have you heard about the murder?"

"That a man was stabbed on the stairs. I was hoping it was the act of a madman. Have they identified the victim?"

"Yes. It was Major George Chase."

Liverpool's brows snapped together. "Wasn't he the one just after Waterloo—"

"Yes. He was sent off to Malta."

"Some sort of scandal. I know there was that business with Cordelia Davenport, but—"

"It was more than that. He was responsible for Julia Ashton's death. But it couldn't be proved."

"Good god." Liverpool was a man who believed in order. "Does Wellington know?"

"Wellington knows. So does Hubert Mallinson."

"And they let him—"

"A trial still takes some sort of proof. And no one wanted the scandal."

"I can see that. But he had the temerity to show himself in England now? In the House of Lords?"

"Apparently he gave this note to one of the parliamentary staff and offered remuneration for getting it to your staff." Raoul held out the note. They had made a copy in case they didn't get it back from Liverpool.

Liverpool frowned down at the paper. "What the devil was he going to show me?"

"We don't know. He didn't have any papers on him. But he was a former agent."

"You think he was working for someone?"

"I'm not sure." Raoul scanned Liverpool's face. "No one had reached out to you lately?"

Liverpool grimaced. "The city is engulfed in protests, the king is more demanding than ever, the queen is threatening to set up a rival court, my foreign secretary had to go abroad because he's too allied to the queen. Name me a day someone hasn't reached out to my staff with some sort of crazy proposal or possible theory. But I had no notion that anyone was going to do so today."

"The fact that Chase was killed suggests someone was trying to stop him from reaching you. Which suggests whatever he had to offer may have gone beyond crazy."

Liverpool's brows tightened. "If he had substantive information to offer, it's fairly obvious who or at least which side in the trial would have had the strongest motive to stop him."

"The most obvious motive, perhaps. The fact that I'm bringing this information to you should support that I don't believe anyone I'm close to is behind this."

"And you're interested in learning who is?"

"Aside from the fact that I don't generally favor allowing killers to run free?" Raoul regarded the man who had once been his ally and who opposed nearly everything he stood for. "Yes."

"You said Chase was an agent. Was he working in intelligence abroad?"

"Possibly."

"Did he—"

"He didn't work for me." Raoul met Liverpool's gaze. It was the closest he had ever come to acknowledging to Liverpool—or anyone officially in the government—that he'd been a French agent. But he had a pardon now. "His brother was selling information to the French before Waterloo, but we have no reason to believe George Chase was. As to whether he might be working for someone now. It's possible. He's the sort who would take something on for the fortune."

"So you can't say which side he might be working for?"

"No. Especially not given the seemingly infinite number of sides we have. A number of people might claim to have information relating to the royal divorce to extract money or simply create a stir."

"Yet this one ended up dead."

"Quite."

"And he's a former agent of some skill, known to be unscrupulous."

"Precisely."

Liverpool's mouth tightened. "Malcolm and his wife are looking into this?"

"Mélanie was on the stairs when Chase was stabbed. She got to him just before he died. They've sent for Bow Street."

Liverpool nodded. "The Rannochs are close to the Davenports. To Colonel Davenport and Lady Cordelia."

"Yes. Cordelia was there when Mélanie found Chase as well."

"Good god. That must have been—"

"Unspeakably awful. But Cordelia and Harry aren't strangers to investigating in difficult personal circumstances. They'll assist the Rannochs."

"So the Rannochs will investigate."

"I doubt they could be persuaded not to."

"Good. We need answers. Quickly."

EDMUND BLAYNEY TUCKED his pencil behind his ear and slid his notebook inside his coat. He had come to Westminster today because he was a journalist and the divorce trial of Queen Caroline was news that could shake a nation. Whatever else was going on in his life, he couldn't *not* be there, as his lost love and (remarkably, amazingly) present betrothed Pippa Langdon Haworth had pointed out. The complications of their life, how they were going to manage an improbable marriage and make a family with her two daughters, could wait, Pippa said. The events of the day wouldn't.

But in coming to cover the opening of the defense, he had stumbled upon a different story. Or rather, he hadn't been near enough to stumble on it, but he had heard the rumors running through the crowd packed tightly on the stairs and in the corridors that a man had been stabbed. So far he hadn't been able to discover the man's name or any other details. But he'd be a poor excuse for a journalist if he didn't try.

He was intent on slipping through the crowd when a hand closed on his sleeve. He turned round to meet an anxious blue gaze.

"Mr. Blayney?"

Blue eyes, winged brows, a heart-shaped face with a pointed chin. It was Abby Clifton, he realized. An opera dancer at the

Haymarket. He'd interviewed her for a story about the lives of those who worked in the theatre the previous spring.

"Is it true?" Abby asked. Her bronze-green bonnet had slipped back, hanging from its ribbons round her throat. Her bright gold curls tumbled in disarray about her face. "A man was killed?"

"I know no more than you." Edmund scanned her intent face and desperate gaze. "Or perhaps less."

Abby's hands came up to grip his arms. "I'm afraid—Do you know the dead man's name?"

"No. It sounds as though no one does." He watched her a moment. "Do you?"

"I'm not sure." Abby bit her lip. "I need to see him."

JULIEN STUDIED the dead man lying on top of a polished oak table in another sitting room. His hair was starting to thin a bit. His eyes were clouded. No one had closed them. There was a smudge on one of his cheeks, probably from where he had fallen on the stairs. It was undoubtedly the face of George Chase, the agent Julien had known in the Peninsula and more recently abroad. And the rascally, high-spirited boy Julien remembered from before his own exile. He'd had a wicked cricket arm.

Julien unbuttoned George Chase's waistcoat—striped silk, not the best quality, but in style—pushed it back, and tugged up his shirt. Good quality linen. The lethal wound small and precise. "This was done by a professional. It takes a lot of skill and training to hit at just the right point to kill that quickly and efficiently." Memories flashed before his eyes. An Austrian colonel in the Place de Grève, a Royalist courier who'd threatened Josephine Bonaparte, a double agent in the Argentine when the woman who was now his wife was at his side. "If he—or she—was good enough to do this, they'd have been lost in the crowd by the time the victim fell. Mélanie wouldn't have glimpsed anything even if she'd been looking."

"And the weapon?" Roth asked.

"Thin. Tucked away. It wouldn't have been that bloody, not if it was wrapped up or tucked under heavy clothing. Time enough to dispose of it later. The killer wouldn't have been obviously bloody. Whoever it was went looking for George Chase specifically and had good reasons—however they defined those reasons—for targeting him."

"Could a woman have done it?"

"It would have taken finesse, not strength. Leaving aside that some women are stronger than some men. So yes."

"How many people could have pulled this off?"

"It's an elite group, as one would expect with any highly specialized skill. I can't give you a number. But I doubt there are that many in London." Julien drew George Chase's shirt down over his wound. "And like most specialists, those who can do this would charge a lot. So whoever hired someone to kill Chase presumably had vast resources and very strong reasons for wanting George Chase dead."

He looked round as the door opened and Mélanie came into the room with Edmund Blayney and a young woman with guinea gold ringlets spilling out from a fashionable bonnet.

"Oh god." The woman froze for a moment, then ran to the table. "Eddy?" Her hands went to George Chase's shoulders. Then she looked up from Roth to Julien. "Who did this to him?"

CHAPTER 4

a bigail Clifton blew her nose and took a drink from the glass of brandy Kitty had poured from the same decanter she had used for Cordelia. The drinks table in the sitting room, probably intended for members of the Lords seeking refuge from debates, was proving helpful. "His name was Edward Hartley," Miss Clifton said.

Mélanie flashed a look at Julien, but none of them apprised Miss Clifton that the name had been an alias. Edmund Blayney met Mélanie's gaze as though he understood. Mélanie had only met Edmund a few days ago in the course of their prior investigation, but she had had great respect for his keen understanding. And she had begun to consider him a friend.

"How long had you known him?" Roth asked.

"A fortnight—maybe a few days longer. He came round to the green room. I'm a dancer at the Haymarket." Miss Clifton glanced at Edmund. "That's how I met Mr. Blayney. He interviewed me for a story."

"And you and Mr. Hartley had become well acquainted?" Roth asked.

Miss Clifton tossed her head. "You needn't waste time on

politeness. Not with all this. He wasn't keeping me. It hadn't progressed that far. But I think it might have done if things had gone on. He was different from most men in the green room."

"Where did he live?" Roth asked.

"He had rooms in Wardour Street. He hadn't been in London long. He'd been abroad on a diplomatic assignment."

"So that's what they're calling it now," Julien murmured.

"What?"

"Sorry. Not relevant. Did he tell you what bought him to London?"

"He had family, but he was estranged from them. He was trying to work out how to approach them."

"You knew Mr. Hartley was here today?" Malcolm asked.

"Yes. I knew what he meant to do. I was supposed to meet him afterwards at the King's Arms across the way. I was waiting there when someone came in talking about a murder, and I was terrified."

"Why?" Julien said in a kind but steady voice. "Why jump to the conclusion that your friend might have been killed?"

Abigail Clifton's fingers tightened round her glass. She was still wearing her lemon-colored gloves. There was a smear of blood, probably George's, on one of the fingers. "He wouldn't admit what he was doing was dangerous. But I knew it was. I'd have been a fool not to see the risks."

"What was he doing? "Mélanie asked.

"Delivering a warning. He said he had to."

"A warning to whom?" Malcolm said.

"The prime minister. He said someone had to know, someone at the top. It was too important to trust it to someone else."

"Did he say what it was?" Malcolm asked.

"Someone was trying to intervene in the trial. He'd overheard something. At his lodging house. It could impact the outcome of the trial, and he said it was his duty to share it."

Mélanie met Cordy's gaze. George had always wanted to cast

himself as a hero, even in the midst of his most reprehensible actions.

"Did he say what this thing was that could impact the trial?" Malcolm said.

"Only that it could damage the government. He said he couldn't share it all with me but that he'd stumbled into something he'd never thought to be involved in."

"What?" Malcolm asked.

"He didn't say. He wouldn't trust me with those details. I think he only told me anything at all because he needed someone to talk to. And perhaps because he wanted to impress me."

"That sounds like George," Cordelia said.

"Who?" Miss Clifton said.

"Time for that later," Cordelia said.

"Where are his rooms?" Roth asked.

"Number 18 Wardour Street."

Roth turned to Malcolm. "We need to get there and search immediately."

"Do you want me to come with you?" Malcolm asked.

"No, I want you to go for me. I think I need to stay here and manage the situation."

Malcolm nodded. "Harry, if it's all right with Cordy, will you come with me?"

"Of course it's all right," Cordelia said.

Harry pressed her hand.

Malcolm looked at Mélanie. "There'll be plenty to do here," she said. "And we don't know what Raoul may learn from Liverpool. You need to get to Wardour Street. Before anyone else does."

"JUST WHAT WERE you afraid I'd do?" Harry asked as he and Malcolm negotiated the crowd outside the Palace of Westminster. Protesters with white cockades in support of the queen, hawkers selling oranges, coffee, bawdy sketches, and more cockades. Members of the Lords and well-dressed spectators trying to get back to their carriages and to Mayfair.

"It wasn't so much what I was afraid you'd do as that I thought you'd do better doing something."

"Cordy's the one who'll be in shock. But I don't think I can do anything for her. Not right now. In fact, it's probably better I got out of there. I think she'll be better off talking to Mélanie and Kitty and Laura."

Malcolm shot a look at his friend. "That's very insightful."

Harry shrugged, gaze on a piece of rotting orange peel on the cobblestones. "When Kitty re-appeared, whom did you find it easier to talk to at first—Mélanie or me?"

Malcolm was on such good terms now with his former lover and her new husband that it was hard to remember the shock Kitty's reappearance in his life had brought little more than a year ago. "Point taken. I knew I needed to talk to Mel. But sharing my thoughts—"

"And you hadn't left Mélanie for Kitty."

Protesters, prosperous tradesmen and clerks by the look of it, had surrounded a carriage up ahead, and were pounding on the crested panels. The coachman whipped up the horses and they surged through the crowd. Two of the protesters fell into the dirt. Malcolm and Harry started towards the downed men, but the other protesters were able to pull their friends to their feet and the men looked unhurt. One of the protesters hurled an orange at the departing carriage. Pulp splattered on the glossy green paint.

Of one accord, Malcolm and Harry turned down an alley to escape the crowd.

Harry fixed his gaze on the glow of a charcoal brazier at the corner and the three young boys gathered round it, roasting potatoes. "Cordy's mourning George and she won't want to admit it. She wouldn't admit it to me. I only hope Mélanie can get her to admit it. So she can at least talk." He shot a look at Malcolm. "Wouldn't you mourn Kitty, whatever she'd done?"

Malcolm drew and released his breath. "I confess to mourning my brother, at times, despite knowing what he did. Or if not mourning him, mourning the person I thought he was. So yes." Malcolm drew a hard breath. "And it took me months to admit it."

Harry fished a half crown out of his pocket and dropped it in a cup beside the three boys. One of the boys flashed a grin at him. "George was a part of her life for far longer than I've been."

"Yes, but—"

"George was in our marriage from the first. He's never really been gone. Not completely. And don't you dare tell Cordy I said that."

"My dear fellow. I'm more than capable of mistakes, but not of that magnitude. At least, I hope to god not."

"He was the first man Cordy loved. He'll always be that. She won't let herself think about it. She won't let herself grieve, because of everything he did. But that doesn't mean she won't mourn him. And I can't—" Harry stopped walking in the archway out of the alley and slammed his hand against the stone support. "Sorry."

"You have every right to smash everything within sight," Malcolm said.

Harry rubbed his hand. "You didn't when Alistair returned. Which was probably worse."

The reappearance in their lives of the man Malcolm had grown up calling Father still threatened to upend all Malcolm cared about. With everything that had happened since the night Alistair had suddenly appeared in the Berkeley Square library, Malcolm hadn't fully been able to grasp the implications. But— "I'm not sure about that. My wife was never in love with Alistair."

Harry gripped the archway, fingers white round the moss-covered stone. "I'd have given anything to spare Cordelia this. To spare Livia it. But I wouldn't—"

"Of course not," Malcolm said.

"I'm not sure it's 'of course' to Roth. He wouldn't be a good investigator if he didn't wonder."

"You couldn't have killed George. You were with me."

"I could have hired someone."

"You wouldn't."

"Don't talk rot about my being too honorable not to face George myself."

"No, you'd be too aware of the risks. Anyway, George's being dead doesn't make the problems go away."

"Far from it."

Harry walked forwards, bleak profile etched against the smoke-stained gray of the buildings. "There's so much Cordy and I've never talked about. Somehow we managed to be happy. We haven't so much confronted the past as managed to ignore it and found that it's retreated."

"My dear fellow. Don't you think there are any number of things I don't talk to Mel about? Still?"

Harry shot a look at him. "You've always had a far more equable temper than I do. And your coping skills never fail to amaze me."

"That's not what I meant. But you have to know—"

"I know how Cordy feels about me. I believe it, more than I ever thought I could. We'll get through this. I'd give anything to help her through it. But at the moment I think I'm better suited trying to work out what the hell George was up to."

They said little more for the rest of the walk, for there was little more that could be said. Number 18 Wardour Street, where George Chase had lodged, was a tall, narrow house built some time early in the last century, with slightly faded paint. Harry surveyed it. "George had finer tastes when I knew him."

"He probably wanted to be anonymous," Malcolm said. "And I doubt he has a great many resources. Unless he's working for someone."

The porter, at first not inclined to admit them, thawed at Malcolm's card. At the news that the tenant he knew as Mr. Edward Yardley had met with an accident, he seemed mostly concerned about possible scandal. "Kept to himself," the porter muttered. "Agreeable gentleman."

He conducted them up a worn but clean staircase. A door clicked shut at the front of the first floor and Malcolm caught a glimpse of skirts in a shimmering green. "That's our only other lodger," the porter said. "Keeps to herself as well. Always been a quiet house."

He unlocked the door of the rooms George had occupied. They were sparsely furnished. A bed and chest of drawers. A shaving kit and dressing case stood atop a writing table. A brass-bound trunk in worn bottle green leather was at the foot of the bed. With the ease of many shared missions, Malcolm and Harry divided the work without speaking. They went through the trunk and then Harry moved to the writing table while Malcolm pulled apart the chest of drawers. The trunk contained the expected clothes, expensive, well cut, but a bit worn. Even Malcolm, whose valet deplored his lack of interest in fashion, could tell they were several years out of date. No books—George, as Malcolm recalled, hadn't been much of a reader, but a code book would have been helpful. No notebooks or scraps of paper or sheaves of foolscap or anything that might contain secrets George had been trying to barter to Liverpool.

Malcolm pulled out the top drawer, reached beneath a stack of shirts and cravats, felt along the back of the drawer. Nothing. He tried the second, which contained waistcoats, then the third, which had two pairs of trousers, a pair of silk knee breeches, and a pair of pantaloons. He tugged the drawer off its tracks, shrugged off his coat, got down on his knees, and reached into the frame. He had to lie flat on the floor to reach to the very back. A splinter of wood jabbed into his palm. He reached further and felt a tell-tale crinkle of paper. He wedged his shoulder into the open space, reached still further, and tugged carefully, easing the paper out from the wood it was wedged between, bit by bit so as not to tear it. Finally it came loose with only a corner frayed.

Malcolm eased his arm from the opening, tearing his shirt cuff, and rolled to his knees on the dusty floorboards. His discovery was a scrap of paper that looked like it had been torn from a bill or other document. It had a single word scrawled on it. "Any idea why George would have the word Fortinbras written on a scrap of paper tucked in the back of a drawer?"

Harry turned from the chest of drawers. "He discovered a love of Shakespeare in his exile. Or, like a number of other spies, he found Shakespeare a good source of codes."

"Quite. But this one just happens to come from the same play as Elsinore."

Malcolm's fingers tightened on the scrap of paper. Shakespeare had been his private joy almost from the moment he had learned to read. His actual father, Raoul O'Roarke, had fostered his interest in Shakespeare, and it was something he and Mélanie had shared from the first. Even when they were enemy agents working for opposite sides. One of the many things that had galled him when he learned Alistair Rannoch, the man he had grown up thinking was his father, had founded a secret organization of wellborn men dedicated to advancing their own interests, was that Alistair, who had never seemed to have even a passing interest in Shakespeare, had appropriated the Elsinore League's name from one of Malcolm's favorite plays.

"Do we have any evidence that the League used other Shakespeare references?" Harry asked.

"Aside from the caves full of bawdy murals that I have to erase from my mind whenever I think of *Twelfth Night, Othello, Midsummer Night's Dream, Troilus and Cressida, Romeo and Juliet,* or *Merry Wives of Windsor*?" Malcolm shuddered at the thought of the rooms, in caves below Dunmykel, the estate he had inherited from Alistair. They were as troubling for how they perverted Shakespeare as for their explicitness. Mélanie had been much more matter of fact about them than he was. But then Mel was much more matter of fact about a number of things. "We've never run into their using the names of Shakespeare characters. Which doesn't mean they didn't. Don't. If this Fortinbras notation is nothing to do with the League, it will feel a bit coincidental. To put it mildly."

Harry pulled a razor out of George's shaving kit. "George didn't have anything to do with the League, that we know of."

"No. Of course, when we investigated Julia's murder in Brussels, we hadn't heard of the League yet." And Malcolm hadn't known his own wife was a French agent. Not to mention he hadn't yet officially known Raoul O'Roarke was his father. And at that time, Alistair Rannoch, his putative father, hadn't yet apparently died only to prove still to be very much alive. It didn't seem so very long ago and yet so much had changed. "George has worked for Carfax," Malcolm said. "For Hubert. If George wanted to reinstate himself, it wouldn't be surprising for him to be looking for information about the League. To barter with Hubert or the League or the government."

"But he wanted to see Liverpool. And the League don't have anything to do with the trial." Harry set down the razor.

"That we know of." Malcolm pushed himself to his feet and walked over to the writing table.

Harry was examining George's shaving kit. "Does the name Timothy Drummond mean anything to you?"

Malcolm went still. "He was the gamekeeper at Dunmykel when I was a boy."

"There's an address in Clerkenwell written next to his name." Harry held the paper out.

Malcolm stared down at it. A chill dropped round his shoulders. Not entirely odd, but it was a strange time for it, with everything that had happened today. With everything that had happened this week. "It's as though George had his talons into everything to do with our family. And by family, I mean all of us."

Harry made no protest or overt acknowledgement. At this point it was a given that they were all family. "Not surprising, perhaps. George's life was inextricably bound up with Cordy's from childhood. And he'd worked for Hubert. I'm not sure in his own mind he could envision a life that didn't involve all of us. If he wanted his past back, he'd have wanted Cordy."

Malcolm set the scrap of paper on the writing table, gaze trained on Harry. "He has to have known he didn't have a prayer of getting her."

"I think you're underestimating George's ego. Or his conception of what was between him and Cordy. He could always convince himself he wasn't to blame for his most egregious actions, so it's not surprising he believed he could convince Cordy of it as well." Harry pulled a washleather bag of razors from the shaving kit and reached beneath it. He went still, the taut lines of his back speaking volumes. Then he held out his discovery to Malcolm. An oval gilt-framed miniature. Cordelia, golden curls falling about her face, a frothy white gown slipping from her shoulders, blue eyes blazing with life, lips slightly parted.

"As I said," Harry said, with a light irony that probably took roughly the same effort as his final charge at Waterloo.

"Cordelia moved on with her life," Malcolm said. "George didn't."

Harry stared down at the miniature. "Difficult to move on from Cordelia. I should appreciate that. I don't know if it will make her feel better or worse to know he had this."

"Neither do I. But you need to tell her about it."

"Yes. Even in my admittedly far from rational state, I can grasp that." Harry stared at the miniature a moment longer and then pocketed it. He reached back into the shaving kit and tugged at the lining. He grabbed the scissors and cut with surgical precision, then tugged up the lining and held up a small paper-bound book.

"George was good at hiding his secrets, but not entirely unconventional."

Malcolm moved to Harry's side and they flipped through the book in the light from the windows. Instead of more names or cryptic Shakespeare references, a jumble of letters and numbers met their gaze.

"And like any good agent, he kept the real secrets in code." Malcolm said.

Harry nodded "George Chase was a lot of things. But he was no fool. And he wasn't a bad agent. So if he was investigating and writing things down in code—"

Malcolm stared from the notebook to the paper with Timothy Drummond's direction while his mind spun with what a visit to Drummond might reveal. "Quite."

CHAPTER 5

"You're telling me his name wasn't Yardley at all?" Abigail Clifton looked round the circle in the sitting room at the Palace of Westminster, which had become a sort of investigation headquarters. They were all gathered there, including Edmund Blayney, whom Roth hadn't asked to leave and who Mélanie thought was an asset to the investigation. The staff had brought in tea, probably produced, like the lemonade and biscuits, from Bellamy's refreshment rooms in the palace, which served everyone from members of both the Lords and Commons to journalists, messengers, and strangers from the galleries.

"It was George Chase," Cordelia said. "He'd left England in disgrace, so I imagine he didn't feel he could use his real name."

Miss Clifton's gaze fastened on Cordelia's. Her blue eyes were a shade less gray than Cordelia's. Her hair a slightly darker blonde, her chin a fraction less pointed. But a casual observer might have trouble telling one from the other. "And he was in love with you," Miss Clifton said.

Cordelia's fingers tightened on the cup of tea she was drinking in place of the brandy. "A long time ago. We grew up together."

Miss Clifton's hands curled round her own cup. "If that isn't just like a man." She took a sip of brandy-laced tea. "He told me he'd always liked golden hair."

"I imagine he did. George could be flowery. I'm sure he appreciated you on your own."

"Did Mr. Yardley—that is, Major Chase—mention anyone else he'd seen recently?" Roth asked Abigail Clifton. "Do you know the names of any of his friends?"

"He said he'd fallen out of touch with his friends in London." Miss Clifton spoke carefully, but she seemed to have decided there was at least some advantage to being on their good side. "If we went out to a pub, he liked to sit at the back where it was shadowy. Mostly we didn't go out much at all." She took another sip from her cup. "But there was one man I saw once outside his lodging house whom I recognized. Because I'd seen him about the theatre. He writes plays."

For a horrible moment, Mélanie wondered if their friend Simon Tanner could be caught up in this. Then Miss Clifton said, "It was Mr. George Lamb."

Mélanie shot a quick look at Cordy. George Lamb, brother of Malcolm's friend William and her own friend Emily Cowper. One of the least political members of one of the most prominent political families in the land.

"Was Mr. Lamb there to see Major Chase?" Mélanie asked.

"No. They didn't speak at all. But I'm quite sure George Lamb was watching the house. I asked Eddy—Major Chase—about it and he told me not to worry. But I could tell he'd recognized Mr. Lamb and it meant something to him."

Roth turned to Cordelia. "How well did Major Chase know Mr. Lamb?"

"We all more or less grew up together," Cordelia said. "But I wouldn't have called them friends. I'd be surprised if George Chase told George Lamb, of all people, that he was back in

London. If George Lamb did find out somehow, I'd be surprised if he called on George Chase. And even more surprised if George Lamb was following George Chase. Unless George Lamb is an agent and we don't know it?"

"Not that I know of," Mélanie said. "Though I wouldn't necessarily know." She looked from Julien to Kitty.

"Stranger things are possible," Julien said. "But if so, he's under very deep cover."

"I saw him," Edmund said. "George Lamb. Earlier today. He was going into the King's Arms after the house broke up. Just before I heard about the murder."

Mélanie reached for her bonnet and set it back on her head. "I don't know him well, but I am a fellow playwright. God knows when Malcolm will be back, and Raoul's still with the prime minister." Dear heaven, what had they come to that Raoul was meeting with the prime minister?

"Go," Julien said as Mélanie tightened the ribbons on her bonnet and went over to kiss Colin. "We'll manage things here. I think this investigation is running even more quickly than others."

"COULD you introduce us to the other lodger?" Malcolm asked the porter when they emerged from George Chase's rooms in the house in Wardour Street. "She might have seen something."

The porter hesitated. "She keeps to herself."

"We don't want to importune her. But it's a matter of some urgency. I suspect she would rather speak with us than with Bow Street."

The porter glanced from Malcolm to Harry, shifted his weight from one foot to the other, then gave a curt nod, walked to the end of the passage, and rapped at the door.

"I'm not receiving visitors," the lady said. The voice that carried through the door panels had a faint Continental accent, though the English words were clear.

"Begging your pardon, ma'am, but there's been an accident."

The door eased open. Malcolm found himself looking into a pair of bright eyes, set beneath cautious, carefully plucked brows.

"We don't mean to trouble you," Malcolm said, "but your fellow lodger, the man who calls himself Mr. Yardley, has met with an unfortunate accident."

"Good heavens. I hope he does not have a bad injury?"

"I'm afraid he's dead."

Her hand went to the cameo on a black velvet ribbon round her throat. "How dreadful."

"My name is Rannoch, Malcolm Rannoch." Malcolm held out a card through the gap in the door. "My friend Harry Davenport. We are associated with Bow Street. If we could come in and speak with you, it might spare you a visit from a Bow Street runner."

The woman hesitated, fingered the card, then gave a nod and tugged the door open. She stepped back quickly into the shadows as though to avoid too much contact with them. Only one brace of candles was lit in the room, diagonally across from her, and the light from the windows was at her back. But she was a slender woman, slightly above average in height, with hair that could be any shade from dark blonde to medium brown, dressed in a loose Grecian knot and ringlets that fell about her face. Beneath the ringlets, her features appeared delicate. Her eyes might be brown or blue or green or gray. Her gown was dark blue or gray—difficult to tell in the slanting, cloud-filtered light—and was cut modestly with full sleeves and a filmy tippet at the neck. But Malcolm, careless as he was of his own clothes, could recognize the cut and lines of a gown crafted by an excellent modiste, probably trained in Paris.

"I scarcely knew Mr. Yardley," the woman said. She had a low, slightly husky voice. "We only passed once or twice in the passage. I'm staying very quietly in London."

"You're visiting from abroad?" Malcolm asked.

"From France. My late husband was a soldier and he left business in London I need to see to." She hesitated a moment, fingering a fold of her skirt. "My husband was Captain Thomas Egerton."

"I was in the army in the Peninsula and at Waterloo." Harry, who had decidedly mixed feelings about his military experience, could be expert at evoking it in the service of an investigation. "What regiment was your husband with?"

"The 73rd. We met when he was in Paris before Waterloo. He fell at Waterloo."

"My condolences, Mrs. Egerton. I barely survived myself and am forever grateful that I did. Rannoch saved me." Harry cast a glance at Malcolm that was quite genuine and yet still part of the investigation. "I lost many friends that day."

She clasped her hands together, fingering what Malcolm realized was a wedding band. "It seems hard to have had so little time together. I thought I might feel closer to him in England, but it is a strange country and it is difficult to be a woman alone. I have mostly been staying in my rooms while I wait for my husband's lawyers to complete the paperwork."

"Did you hear Mr. Yardley come and go?" Malcolm asked.

"Occasionally. It was none of my business where he went or whom he spoke to. He was very polite, but it would not have been appropriate for me to engage him in prolonged conversation."

"Did you ever see Mr. Yardley have visitors?" Harry asked.

Mrs. Egerton hesitated. "There was one young woman. Very pretty with golden hair. I had the sense they were—well acquainted. I didn't hear her name."

"I believe we did," Malcolm said. "Miss Abigail Clifton."

"If you've met her, I'm sure she can tell you more than I possibly could." Mrs. Egerton hesitated. "If Mr. Yardley met with misfortune, do you think I need to be worried?"

"I very much doubt it," Malcolm said. "He appears to have been targeted specifically. But it is possible there will be attempts to search his rooms. We'll speak with the porter and have a Bow Street patrol watch the house."

"Oh dear. Is that necessary? I don't like the thought of any notoriety."

"The patrols are very discreet. Meanwhile, if you recall anything else about Mr. Yardley—"

"Of course I'll let you know."

The porter was far more accepting of the idea of a patrol watching the house than Mrs. Egerton had been. "If you ask me, it's her own behavior Mrs. Egerton is worried about," he said. "She does live quietly, but her lawyer calls on her quite often. At least she says he's her lawyer."

"Bow Street are only interested in the investigation," Malcolm said. "Not in anyone else's secrets."

"But secrets have a way of coming out, don't they Mr. Rannoch?"

"They do indeed," Harry said.

~

"Sensible man, the porter," Harry said, as he and Malcolm started down Wardour Street. "Mrs. Egerton definitely wasn't eager for Bow Street's presence. It may just be because of something she had every right to keep to herself. But I'm quite sure there wasn't an Egerton who was an officer in the 73rd. And I'd have sworn her accent was Italian, not French."

"So would I. And while I'm sure there are Italians in London at present who have nothing to do with the trial, it's difficult not to wonder. Especially as George claimed to have information that could shake the trial." Malcolm stopped and glanced towards Westminster. "We need to get the codebook to Mel and Raoul and Julien and Kitty. But I should talk to Timothy Drummond and see if Chase had contacted him."

"I'll take the codebook. Drummond's more likely to talk to you without me. Don't worry, I won't hover over Cordy."

"My dear fellow." Malcolm gripped Harry's arm. "I can't imagine your hovering if you tried."

CHAPTER 6

"*M*élanie." George Lamb looked up from the pint he was nursing in a shadowy corner of the King's Arms, situated within a short arrow's flight of the Palace of Westminster. "What are you doing here?" He pushed himself to his feet. "This is no place for you."

"Stuff, George." Mélanie put a hand on the shoulder of George's well-tailored coat (Italian superfine, judging by the smooth texture and glossy finish that gleamed in the lamplight) and pushed him back into his seat, then dropped into a seat on the high-backed bench across from him. "I'm not a Mayfair hostess anymore, I'm a playwright. I get to follow your rules, not Emily's."

"Yes, but you're—"

"A woman? I've never let that get in my way." Mélanie smoothed her sarcenet skirt. She had had to discard her spencer and there were bloodstains on her skirt, but the cherry-and-white stripes helped disguise it. She knew George Lamb far less well than she did his sister Emily Cowper, who had become a close friend, or his brother William, who was a friend and colleague of Malcolm's and married (if not happily) to Cordy's friend Caro. But since she'd begun writing, she and George had discussed plays. He'd been quite complimentary on her first opening in January. And she could sympathize with his need to find something of his own in the midst of a political family.

George settled back into his seat, though his shoulders were set with wariness. "I suppose Malcolm's in a committee room in the palace or at Brooks's. Consumed with the trial. In Brougham's inner circle and all that."

"Hardly. He's in the Commons and at the trial merely as an observer."

"Not behind the scenes. William said you and Malcolm wrote half of Brougham's speech today."

"If William said that, he's exaggerating or misinformed, neither of which sounds like him. We did a bit of editing. Brougham's an excellent writer and a first-rate speaker."

"But the trial isn't settled."

"Far from it."

"In fact, it's an uphill battle still. At least that's what William says and what I gathered today in the gallery. I'm only an observer. Haven't even been in the Commons since March. Busy with my Catullus translation lately. Must talk to Davenport about that." George had briefly been an MP for Westminster but had turned back to literary pursuits lately. "Still, a bit odd with his being my godfather."

Mélanie regarded George's flushed face in the lamplight. The former prince regent, now George IV, was not only his godfather, he was rumored to be George's biological father. If he wasn't, the other likely candidate was the king's brother William, the Duke of Clarence. "I can imagine that," she said.

George grunted. "Father's relieved to be excused from the trial on account of his age. Lucky escape."

That referred to Viscount Melbourne, George's putative father. Who was almost certainly less close to him biologically than King George IV, whose marriage was being contested before the House of Lords. Family bloodlines in Mayfair were far more tangled than anything she could dare put in a play.

George sat back against the dark wood of his bench. "So what are you doing here?"

Mélanie folded her hands in her lap. "A man was killed outside the chamber just after the Lords rose."

George's gaze shifted to the side. "Yes, I heard. Terrible. The violence seems to keep getting worse in London over this, but I never thought it would actually get inside the Lords."

"This wasn't to do with protesters. At least not directly."

"But you're investigating it?"

"Malcolm and I and some of our friends are assisting Bow Street as we can. The victim seems to have been killed by an assassin who was targeting him in particular. The man who was killed was trying to take information to the PM, but we're not quite sure what information."

George's hands curled round his tankard. "Mélanie, I may not have William's brains, but it's starting to sound like you're interrogating me. I can't figure out why else you'd want to talk to me just now, with the country on edge and a man murdered outside the House of Lords. But I also don't see what I could have to do with this. I didn't even know anyone had been killed until I heard gossip in here after the Lords rose."

Mélanie met George's gaze. The guilt of moments when she hadn't taken George seriously washed over her. He was the fourth son in a brilliant family and the one most on the fringe of the politics that was the core of his family's existence. "The murdered man was George Chase."

George Lamb's fingers froze on the tankard. "Good god. What was he doing back in London?"

"That's one of the pertinent questions."

"One?"

"As I said, he claimed to have evidence of interest in the trial. He was trying to offer it to Liverpool."

"Evidence about what?"

"We don't know."

A waiter stopped by the table, a confused look on his face. Mélanie ordered a pint of stout. The waiter blinked, then inclined his head. Really, once one stopped worrying about blending in and the possible impact on one's husband—who couldn't care less about blending in—it was much easier to make one's way in London. George's sister Emily would be horrified. And perhaps envious. No doubt she would question Mélanie about it later. And not be best pleased with Mélanie's interrogation of George. "We do know George Chase had been in London for a matter of weeks and had taken rooms in Wardour Street. He'd struck up an acquaintance with a young woman named Abigail Clifton, who is an opera dancer."

George's ruddy skin flushed deeper. He stared into his tankard. "Mélanie—"

"Oh, for god's sake, George. At this point you should be used to my being about the theatre. This is no time for missishness. In any case, Miss Clifton is employed at the Haymarket. She'd met you or at least seen you. And she says she saw you outside George Chase's lodging house in Wardour Street."

"What?" George's gaze shot to Mélanie's face. He sounded genuinely shocked. "I didn't know George Chase was in London. And even if I had done, I had no reason to seek him out. We were never what you'd call mates. I thought the whole business with Lady Cordelia was dashed ungentlemanly. Both to George's wife and to Cordelia."

"You have a point." Mélanie kept her gaze steady on George's face. "Have you been in Wardour Street?"

The floorboards creaked as though George had dragged his boot toe over them. "I don't see what that's to say to anything if—"

He broke off as the waiter returned and set a pint of stout down in front of Mélanie. Mélanie lifted the tankard and took a deliberate drink. It was a rich, smooth brew, with a tang of sharpness underneath. "Go on."

George picked up his own tankard and gulped down a swallow. "I don't see what I have to say to anything if I didn't see Chase. Even if it was the same house."

"Was it?"

"How the devil should I know?"

Mélanie curled her hands round her tankard. "So you were there."

"Damn it, Mélanie. You're just like Malcolm. He has the most detestable way of running rings sound a fellow." George's gaze shot to the side, then back to her. His eyes were bleary and shot with red. It occurred to Mélanie that she'd rarely seen him when he wasn't dipping deep, in ballrooms, green rooms, boxes, or drawing rooms. "I didn't go there because of anything to do with George Chase. I had no notion George Chase was anywhere near London."

"So why did you go to Wardour Street? Miss Clifton said you seemed to be watching the house."

George huffed in and released his breath. "You probably don't understand, Mélanie. Married to Malcolm. Probably never have a moment you wonder about your life. Oh, I know people say you and Malcolm aren't affectionate, that he's not affectionate, but it's fairly obvious how he feels about you. What a thing it must be not to have doubts."

Mélanie took another drink of stout to cover a desperate urge to laugh. She could see Malcolm's gaze, raw with torment, when he'd confronted her in the Tavistock Theatre about her betrayal. "I think we all have doubts about the people we love. How could we not? One can never know what another person is thinking and feeling. Not completely." Particularly not if one was an enemy agent under deep cover, married to a man one had married to spy on. For a moment it was eight years ago and she was saying wedding vows to an enemy agent, believing she could walk away once the mission was over. Or a few years later, in love with her husband but convinced their marriage would be over if he learned the truth.

"Yes, well, it's a damned sight harder when your wife runs off to bloody Italy with bloody Henry Brougham. And then she comes back and after she does you scarcely even talk about it. You scarcely talk about anything. Polite conversation over the breakfast dishes. Over the dinner dishes. In the carriage on the way to or from a rout or a musicale or a deadly family dinner. In the box before a play. During a dance, on the occasions you still manage to dance together. And every time she goes out, you can't but wonder. Can't but tote up how long she's gone, can't but look for clues when she comes back to if she's actually been where she said. Did she really order something new from her modiste? Was she really at Gunter's with her cousins or a china warehouse with one of her other friends?"

"Of course she might have been wondering the same about you," Mélanie said. She had heard the gossip, both in the green room and in Mayfair ballrooms, about George's affairs and the fact that even though he and Caro were childless, he had more than one illegitimate child.

George folded his hands round his tankard. "That doesn't stop one from asking questions."

"No, I suppose not." Certainly her own betrayals, though not romantic, had not stopped her from asking questions about Malcolm.

George took a deep swallow from his tankard. "So it was probably inevitable that at some point I followed her."

"To Wardour Street."

George gave a curt nod. "Couldn't imagine what she was doing there. Not a place any of her friends live. Aside from the fact that she'd told me she was going to her dressmaker's, which is nowhere near. She was wearing a veil, but I had no doubt it was her. And then he appeared."

"He?" Mélanie asked, though she was quite sure she knew.

George met her gaze. "Brougham. Caro met him outside that house in Wardour Street. I could scarcely believe they'd be so brazen. Then they went into the building together." George glanced away, his jaw tightening. "You can imagine my thoughts. I trusted her—or no, I didn't, or I wouldn't have been following her. But I didn't believe she would go so far. Not openly, blatantly. In the middle of the afternoon."

George's wife, Caroline, had run off to the Continent with Henry Brougham, Queen Caroline's attorney general, four years ago. Mélanie had been in Paris with Malcolm and had scarcely known the Lambs and their set at the time. But since she and Malcolm had moved to Britain, she'd heard the story from George's sister Emily, who had gone to Italy to convince her sister-in-law Caro to come home. "Do you know what actually transpired between Caro and Brougham the day you saw them in Wardour Street?" she asked.

"God, Mélanie. I'm sorry, I don't mean to be crude with a lady, but what do you think, considering what they'd been to each other?"

"It seems an odd place for them to have met if that was their intention."

"An anonymous lodging house makes a fair amount of sense."

"Where there would be other lodgers and probably a landlady or landlord or porter?"

George blinked. "What on earth else would they have been doing there?"

"Calling on someone?"

George blinked again. "This is to do with your investigation."

"George Chase lodged in that house."

"Surely you don't think Caro and Brougham were calling on George Chase."

"I have no reason to suspect so. But it is a coincidence. George

54

Chase claimed to have information about the trial. Brougham is certainly at the heart of the trial."

"I thought you said Chase wanted to talk to Liverpool. That hardly makes him a likely ally of Brougham's." George frowned. "Do you think that's it? Chase was trying to blackmail Brougham over Caroline?"

"I don't think that sort of blackmail would hold much weight with Brougham."

"No, I suppose not. Fellow's damned brazen."

Mélanie liked Henry Brougham, who had become a good friend of Malcolm's and of her own as well. She had no doubt of Brougham's ambition, but also no doubt that he genuinely wanted to achieve change. He saw supporting the queen as a way to bring about that change. But having dined with him and spent late evenings strategizing speeches and editing them with him, she also was quite sure he cared about the queen as a person and wanted to do his best for her. "George Chase was a shrewd judge of situations. I can give him that, if nothing else. I doubt he'd have thought anything to do with Caro and Brougham would be enough to get Liverpool's attention."

George flushed. "You mean everyone knows the scandal and it's old news."

"I wouldn't say that. But it's not enough to overset plans."

George took a drink from his tankard. "This must be hell for Cordelia and Davenport." He set the tankard down and wiped a trail of moisture from the side. "Odd. You'd have thought their marriage had been smashed far more than ours. I mean, it's not as though Brougham had been the love of Caro's life from childhood. But now Cordy and Harry are smelling of April and May, and Caro and I can barely put together half a dozen sentences that aren't colorless. What the hell does that mean? I know we weren't love's young dream when we married, but then neither were Cordelia and Davenport."

"No." She wasn't betraying Cordy and Harry to say this much, as both of them would admit it. "They weren't then."

"But they fell in love later? What is that even supposed to mean?" George scraped a hand over his hair. "I write about love. You write about it. It makes sense on paper. The characters say the right things, the story ends tied up in a neat bow. But I'm damned if I see what it has to do with life."

"Has Caro talked to you about Mr. Brougham?"

"Good god, no." George stared at Mélanie across the scarred tabletop. "What would she say? But I know she still follows his activities. I know she's aware of the trial. How could anyone in London not be? I didn't know she was sneaking off to meet him."

"Do you know now that she was sneaking off to meet him?"

"They went into the building together, Mélanie. Even if they had happened to bump into each other on the street—which is a coincidence both of us would know better than to use in our plays —I can't come up with circumstances where they would have decided to go into a lodging house together."

"But you haven't asked her about it?"

"Good god, no. A fellow can't—As I said, Caro and I haven't talked about much of anything of substance since she came back. I'm certainly not going to ask her about Brougham." George stared into his tankard. "It could upend everything. And I'm just not ready for that."

"I can understand that."

His gaze shot to her face. "Can you, honestly?"

God, the conversations she had put off having with Malcolm because she feared what they might reveal or where they might lead. "I think there's always ground in a marriage the partners hesitate to tread on at times. So you don't think Caro and Brougham could have been calling on George Chase?"

"Why on earth would they? I mean, I have no idea if Brougham knew him well, but Caro didn't. We were all more or less in the same circles, had been all our lives, but she certainly wasn't well acquainted with him. That is—" George's hands tightened round his tankard. "I suppose I can't claim to know Caro that well. I certainly had no idea she'd run off or that she'd go off with Brougham again after she came back. So I suppose she might have been concealing a closer relationship with George Chase for some reason." His brows drew together. "Or I suppose I might just not have been paying attention. But I don't see why she'd go see him with Brougham."

"George Chase claimed to have information that could impact the trial. He was trying to present it to Liverpool."

"Then I don't see why he'd have been talking with Brougham."

"Unless he'd been making a deal with Brougham and Brougham turned on him."

"And Brougham brought Caro with him while he was making this deal?" George stared at her. "If Brougham had a falling out with Chase, or if Chase in some other way got information on the trial he was taking to Liverpool, that makes Brougham a suspect, doesn't it?"

Mélanie's throat tightened. You'd think at this point she'd be used to her friends being suspects. "It gives him a motive. Almost certainly not the only one we'll find."

"Damnable time for it. You'd think I'd be happier to see Brougham in trouble." George sat back in his chair, fingers rigid round his tankard. "You're going to have to talk to Caro, aren't you?"

"I'm afraid so."

"Damnation."

Mélanie subdued an impulse to touch his hand, as though he were one of her children. "Are you afraid of what our talking to her may reveal?"

"No. Yes." George downed another swallow from his tankard. "I'm afraid it will provoke her into leaving me again."

CHAPTER 7

"Oh god." Cordelia stared at the group left in the sitting room in the Palace of Westminster with stricken eyes. Edmund Blayney had escorted Abigail Clifton back to her lodgings after Mélanie left in search of George Lamb, but Kitty, Julien, Laura, and Roth were still there. Kitty recognized the symptoms of shock settling in Cordelia's gaze. "Annabel." Cordelia looked at Roth. "George's wife. She's been living in Derbyshire with the children. At least, that's the last I heard. I wonder if she knows George is back in England. She almost certainly doesn't know he's dead. I've—always felt guilty about Annabel. More later than I did when George and I ran off, which isn't at all logical of me."

"Does he have other family?" Roth asked.

"His parents are dead now," Cordelia said. "His sister Violet is in London. She's married to John Ashton."

"Ashton?" Roth asked. "Is—"

"Yes, Johnny was married to my sister Julia. He and Violet married after Waterloo. They're raising his and Julia's son and they have two more children of their own now. They don't know that George killed Julia. But they're careful not to talk about George in front of me. George and Violet's brother Tony died at

Waterloo. But Tony's wife Jane is in London with their children. She's married again to Captain Will Flemming."

"Was Chase close to any of them?"

Cordelia hesitated. "We all grew up together. So Jane's known George since we were children. I don't think she has a very high opinion of him, though she doesn't know the full truth about his actions. But—those ties endure."

The door opened on her words and Raoul slipped back into the sitting room. Kitty, who was itching for something to do, saw the light of a successful mission in his eyes. Lucky. She'd give a great deal even to be able to interrogate someone just now.

"Were you able to see Liverpool?" Roth asked.

Raoul nodded. "He says he hadn't heard anything from George Chase, and I'm inclined to believe him. He's always been very straightforwards in his dealings with me, and while he's certainly capable of lying to me in the right circumstances, I don't see why he would about this." He glanced round the room. "We seem to have lost a number of our party."

"I'll update you," Laura said.

Roth looked at Julien, as Raoul and Laura moved to the side and Cordelia went to sit with the children, who were playing cat's cradle with a length of twine Julien had produced. "Who else?"

"Who else what?" Julien's voice was light and easy, but Kitty caught the sharpness in it. He guessed what Roth was getting at even before she quite did herself.

Roth's gaze stayed steady on Julien's own. "Who else in London, besides you, could have done this? There can't be that many assassins with that level of skill in the city."

"No, I wouldn't think so," Julien said. He was leaning against the sitting room wall, legs crossed at the ankle.

"So surely you can locate some of them."

Julien raised an ironic brow. It was, Kitty knew, one of his best defenses. "We aren't a club. We don't discuss the finer details over port or write percentages down in a betting book. And we aren't a guild that organizes in a town hall."

"No." Roth's gaze remained level. Not judging, but not giving way. "But you must know names of others. An agent of your calibre."

Julien pushed himself away from the wall. "I've been out of that business for a long time. At least it feels like a long time. But you're right. There are inquiries I can make."

"Do you want me to come with you?" Kitty asked. Even as she said it, she realized how unhelpful it was, but she couldn't shake the feeling that she was like Leporello watching Don Giovanni pulled down into hell.

Julien gave a twisted smile. "I always do. But I think a loving wife, however ruthless an agent, might not be the best asset if I'm trying to appear a hardened agent myself. Also"—he cast a glance towards the children—"I'd rather one of us was with Leo. And perhaps I'd rather not have you see me step into my past. Which is probably folly, considering how well you know it."

Kitty reached up to kiss him, heedless of the others. "This is probably folly to say to you, especially in these circumstances. But be careful."

Julien gripped her shoulders for a moment and returned the kiss. "If I wasn't careful, I'd have been dead before I turned sixteen. But I appreciate the concern, my love."

MÉLANIE SLIPPED between a stout man in a frock coat and an equally stout woman in a poke bonnet, sober citizens by the look of their clothes, shouting vigorously in support of the queen. At another time she'd have been interested to observe the crowd and learn more, but now she was bent on getting back to Cordelia and the others as quickly as possible. She inched through the crowd of protesters towards the Palace of Westminster and had almost broken free when a hand closed on her arm.

She jerked away, thinking it was one of the protesters, and found herself looking into the incisive dark gaze of Lord Beverston, Elsinore League member and now something of an ally against Alistair Rannoch.

"Good," Beverston said. "Glad you're here. I assume you and Malcolm are looking into this?"

"The death of the man on the stairs just now?"

"George Chase. No need to prevaricate. I know it was he. Come inside where we can talk."

Anything Beverston had to say about the murder was definitely worth hearing, so Mélanie took his arm without objection and let him lead the way through the crowd, past mounted members of Horse Guards, into the palace, and down several winding passages to a small sitting room.

"I heard you got to Chase right before he died." Beverston closed the door and spoke without preamble. "Did he say anything to you?"

"He said Cordelia Davenport's name."

"Humph." Beverston strode across the room. He always moved with brisk purpose. "Might have known it wouldn't be anything useful."

"Lord Beverston." Mélanie regarded the viscount. She didn't know him nearly as well as Malcolm did, but she had a healthy respect for his acumen. And for all he'd been an ally at times of late, she was far from trusting him. "Did you know George Chase was in London?"

"Did I?" Beverston turned in front of a narrow window that let in murky light, conveniently at his back. "Oh, of course I did. He was working for me."

Mélanie was used to surprises. Particularly when it came to the League. Particularly in the midst of an investigation. But —"Working for you? George Chase was part of the League?"

"I wouldn't say that." Beverston tapped his fingers on a pier table. "The other members didn't know about him. And I'm more on the outs with the League now than ever. Chase was gathering information for me personally."

"For how long?" Past events raced through her mind. "In Brussels before Waterloo?"

"Good god no. He worked for Carfax—Mallinson—damn it, too many Mallinsons we all know, just have to call him Hubert—in those days. Chase got in touch with me a few months ago offering information."

"About whom?"

"Some of my rivals in the League." Beverston frowned at his fingers and brushed off dust from the table. "Then three weeks ago he stopped me coming out of Brooks's. At first I didn't recognize him. Then I did but saw no reason to speak to him. But he insisted he had more to offer, and I thought it made sense to at least listen to what he had to say." Beverston's brows snapped together. "Don't look at me like that, Mélanie. I don't believe we've ever addressed it directly, but surely you realize I know the truth about you. Surely you're too sensible and too good an agent to feign shock at my talking to Chase. I imagine you'd have talked to him as well if he'd buttonholed you—or the equivalent—outside Almack's."

Mélanie bit back the obvious retort. "I rarely go to Almack's these days. But all right—if he'd suddenly appeared before me claiming to have information, I'd probably have listened to what he had to say to find out what he was up to. So I could thwart him and protect my friends. But I wouldn't have employed him."

"You're loyal to Davenport and Cordelia. I understand that."

"Yes, I'd be thinking of Cordy and Harry. But I'd also know better than to trust George Chase."

"Oh, I didn't trust him. I wouldn't want him anywhere near my daughters or Roger and Dorinda or my grandchildren or Ben and

Nerezza or Barbara or anyone else I care about. But he was useful."

"Whom did you have him gathering information on?"

Beverston studied the pattern his fingers had left in the dust on the table. "He was looking into Alistair."

The chess board that their life had become shifted beneath her feet once again. The game they had been playing ever since they had walked into their library to discover that the man Malcolm had grown up calling Father wasn't dead, as they had believed for three years. "George knew Alistair was alive."

"He'd seen Alistair in Italy. He seemed to think he could barter the information. He was playing a lot of games."

"What did he want?"

"To reinstate himself in England. And I think he was willing to play all of us against each other to get that. But as long as he was going to be looking into all our dirty linen, I thought I'd rather have him doing it for me, so I could at last keep an eye on him and possibly learn something in the process." Beverston stared at the pattern in the dust for a moment longer, then tugged a handkerchief from his sleeve and wiped it over the table. "He claimed to have information about Alistair and Trenchard and what they'd been doing three years ago trying to get Trenchard made prime minister. He said he'd been working for Alistair after Alistair went abroad."

"After Alistair faked his death?"

"So George claimed. George had acquired a lot of information on a lot of people. Have you found his papers?"

"Malcolm and Harry have gone to where he was staying in London."

Beverston gave a curt nod. "I'm not fool enough to ask you to turn anything you find over to me. I wouldn't, in your shoes. But for god's sake, get everything you can, and take care to lock any papers up." He hesitated. "George said he was investigating Alistair. That he might have information that would let me take Alistair down, if he was right."

"Did he say what the information was?"

"No, damn it. He wasn't going to tell me until I paid him, and I wasn't going to pay him until he had proof to give me. But he asked me about a night at Dunmykel, twenty-some years ago. What I knew about it. Which wasn't a lot."

"Why that night in particular?"

"I'm not sure. Save that it was the night Cyril Talbot accidentally shot himself."

"Glenister's younger brother?" Lord Glenister was Malcolm's godfather and had founded the Elsinore League along with Alistair Rannoch, but Mélanie only vaguely knew about Lord Cyril Talbot. That he had died long before she came to England, leaving a daughter who was Glenister's ward. And who might have become Malcolm's wife had Mélanie not married him on a spy mission. But that was beside the point. "Cyril Talbot was a League member?"

"Yes, though not nearly as involved as his older brother."

"But he died at a League house party?"

Beverston rubbed the dust from his fingers. "You could call it that. A dozen or so of us were there. And then the ladies arrived unexpectedly."

"Ladies?"

"Lady Frances—Dacre-Hammond then, Davenport now. And her friend Louisa Mitford. They arrived in the middle of the afternoon and said they'd had no notion anyone else was in residence and just thought to stop the night because it was Frances's sister's house. But I'm quite sure they came deliberately to try to see what the gentlemen were up to."

"That must have been awkward."

"To say the least. Alistair managed to smooth it over on the surface. We had a dinner that was much more restrained and organized than our usual affairs. At least at this particular house party there were no other females in attendance."

"I'm sure Fanny wouldn't have minded dining with a Cyprian."

"No, but Alistair wouldn't have wanted her to."

"It amazes me how gentlemen will tumble anyone in skirts, but still try to draw these distinctions."

Beverston didn't shirk from her gaze. "I won't argue with you, Mélanie. I confess my own thoughts on the subject have undergone something of a revolution in recent years. In any case, after dinner Alistair complained a bit over the port and then we joined the ladies in the old drawing room. For tea and coffee and more strained conversation. As I don't find much interest in being a witness to others' peccadilloes, I retired to bed fairly early. But Cyril was already dead drunk at that point. I heard the ladies coming upstairs not long after I retired. I think I fell asleep for a few hours before I was awakened by screams and running feet and general commotion. I went out to see what had happened, to learn that Cyril had accidentally shot himself trying to shoot a card off the drawing room mantel."

Given what she knew of the League, it was not a wholly unbelievable story. And yet—"Are you sure it was an accident?"

Beverston frowned. "I'm rarely sure of anything when it comes to the League. But I've heard no suggestion it was otherwise."

"Could he have been murdered?"

"By whom? Alistair?"

"Possibly, if George thinks this would be enough to destroy Alistair. Who saw it happen?"

"Alistair and Glenister and Archie Davenport. Glenister was disconsolate. I can still see him on the library sofa. Couldn't stop crying and looked as though he was staring straight into hell. Archie and Alistair were making the arrangements. I did my best to help. Fanny came down and was quite helpful organizing the servants to see to details."

Mélanie frowned. She'd never heard Archie, who was Harry's

uncle and now married to Frances, who was Malcolm's aunt, mention the incident. Or heard Frances mention it. Not that they would. Another reminder of how much and how deep the history of her husband's family and close friends was before she had even set foot in Britain or met Malcolm or Raoul. And how much of it she still did not know. In many ways, she lived her life like a play she had come into in the third act. "Did Glenister seem to blame Alistair for his brother's death?"

Beverston frowned, seeming to genuinely be sifting through his memories. "As I said, Glenister looked like a man who was seeing into hell. But he didn't appear to blame Alistair." Beverston's brows knotted tighter. "In fact, Alistair was rather kinder towards Glenister, and Glenister rather more accepting of Alistair's help, that night than in the general run of things. Perhaps more so than at any other time in my memory."

"What happened next?"

"Glenister insisted on leaving that night to see Cyril's daughter. Honoria. She was in the nursery at Alford."

"Malcolm's grandfather's house?" The scholarly Duke of Strathdon had always seemed removed from the details of the League.

Beverston nodded. "Arabella was there with Malcolm and Edgar, and Fanny and Louisa had been staying there with their children. Cyril had left Honoria there on his way to Dunmykel." He watched Mélanie for a moment. "All the families have always been intertwined. Perhaps more so then than now. I forget you've married into the family comparatively recently."

And you're an outsider. Beverston didn't say that, but his gaze said he understood.

"Did Glenister go to Alford that night?" Mélanie asked.

"Yes. Fanny and Alistair tried to talk him out of it. Given his condition, we were afraid he'd break his neck. But he wouldn't be dissuaded. And he returned safely the next day. We all stayed for Cyril's funeral."

"There was no inquest?"

"It was an accident, with witnesses. And Alistair was the local bailie, in any case. Given that he had been there at the time, he'd have no reason to seek out other witnesses."

"How much of this did you tell George Chase?"

"None of it. I said I'd been asleep when Cyril died and knew no more than the public accounts. If Chase had further information on it, I wanted to hear what he had, not anything built on what I could offer."

"Did Alistair know George Chase was in London?"

"Not according to Chase. He most definitely did not want Alistair to know. But if Alistair had learned of it, he would certainly have had motive to get rid of George."

"George claimed to have evidence that could influence the trial. He was trying to see Liverpool when he was killed."

Beverston's gaze flickered. "That's interesting. He didn't mention that to me. He probably was trying to barter it to someone else. Our sovereign's failed marriage is hardly at the top of my list of concerns and I tend to think the outrage of the populace is less volatile than many fear. It also may be something Chase stumbled on later. He was certainly good at ferreting out information, I'll give him that. And evidently something he ferreted out got him killed."

"Precisely," Mélanie said. "The question is what?"

CHAPTER 8

Timothy Drummond lived with his daughter and her husband who had a pub in Clerkenwell that adjoined the brewery they also ran. Malcolm had looked in when Drummond first came to London and had returned a few times since, but not in recent months.

The pub was crowded, mostly with clockmakers, jewelers, and printers from neighboring businesses, it appeared. Fragments of talk Malcolm caught as he made his way through the common room said the queen's case was the overwhelming topic, not surprisingly. He saw a number of white cockades, and more than a few flyers with tankards of beer leaving damp stains on them. But Meg Tompkins, Drummond's daughter, recognized Malcolm and took him into a back room, brought him a pint, and said she'd send her father in.

Drummond came in with his usual exuberance. He was a big-boned, sandy-haired man. A trifle grayer and thinner of hair and a trifle broader round the middle than Malcolm remembered, but essentially still the same. "Mr. Rannoch! Good to see you. I've been hearing all sorts of things about you."

"You're kind, Mr. Drummond."

"I don't think so. Got the ear of Mr. Brougham, they say."

"Brougham's a friend. I admire what he's doing."

"Hope he can show the king he can't always have it his way." Drummond drew a breath. "Begging your pardon, Mr. Rannoch."

"No need to do so. I quite agree with you."

"Not sure whether to be sorry or glad to be in London to see all this. I expect you were in the Lords today?"

"I was. Which is why I'm here, in a roundabout sort of way." Malcolm told Drummond quickly about the murder. "An associate and I just went through George Chase's things," Malcolm concluded. "And we found your name written down. Had he written to you or called you? He might also have been using an alias. Perhaps Edward Yardley."

Drummond's fingers stilled on the pint his daughter had left for him. In the light from the windows, his face suddenly looked gaunter, his ruddy skin touched with ash, the lines more deeply scored. "I didn't know. I didn't have the least idea he—the man who called himself Edward Yardley—wasn't who he claimed."

"Of course not," Malcolm said. "You couldn't have done. What did he say? That he was a friend of mine?"

"No. That he was a friend of Master Andrew's. Young Mr. Thirle."

Malcolm sat back in his chair. Andrew Thirle was married to Malcolm's sister Gisèle and his own parentage had come into question with the revelations of a few days ago. "What did the man who came to see you say his name was?"

"Edward Yardley, as you said. Said his family had sent him to Edinburgh for his education. He said he'd gone into the army and then had lived abroad, but that he'd lately heard rumors people might be trying to dig up information to Master Andrew's disadvantage."

Malcolm took a deliberate sip from his pint. "What sort of information?"

Drummond shifted in his chair. "He asked me about when

Master Andrew was born. If Mrs. Thirle had gone away when Master Andrew and Miss Maddie were born. If Mr. Rannoch—your father, sir—had been at Dunmykel then. I couldn't quite make sense of what he was getting at. I do remember Mrs. Thirle went to stay with relatives for her lying-in, but I didn't see why that should be remarkable. And I also didn't see why it was any business of this gentleman. Mr. Yardley, as he called himself. So mostly to whatever he said, I said I didn't know or didn't remember. It's been years, after all." Drummond studied Malcolm's face. "Didn't do wrong, did I?"

"On the contrary," Malcolm said. "You'd have been pardoned for saying more and considering it unexceptionable, but it's all to the good you didn't tell him more. I don't think Yardley—Chase—meant Andrew any good."

"So nothing I said to him led to Mr. Yardley—Major Chase's—death?"

"Almost certainly not. But the questions he was asking—and why he was asking them—may well have done."

Drummond took a drink from his pint. "What does it have to do with Master Andrew?"

"I'm not sure. What do you remember about his birth?"

Drummond frowned. "Mrs. Thirle went away, like I said. Thirle went to join her before the birth. They came back a few weeks later with the twins—Master Andrew and Miss Maddie. I remember calling to see them and offering my congratulations. They seemed happy, if the household was a bit overwhelmed with two little ones. Mr. Thirle saw me out. I mentioned that two must be twice as challenging, and he said yes, they hadn't anticipated it and it was a bit of a surprise, but they were happy and wouldn't have it any other way. I said, 'Of course not, they're your children.' And he got a sort of odd look on his face, almost as though he'd had a surprising revelation, and said, 'Quite right, they are.'"

Malcolm took a drink from his pint. "Was Alistair Rannoch about?"

Drummond's head jerked up. "Oddly, yes. Odd because he didn't own Dunmykel yet. But a bit after the Thirles came back with the babies I saw him at the Griffin & Dragon." Drummond's elder brother had run the Griffin & Dragon in Dunmykel village and now his nephew Stephen did. "I was surprised, as his cousin wasn't in residence, and I thought it was odd he was there without staying at the main house. But of course I didn't ask him. Didn't converse with him at all, except to nod my head. He acknowledged me, but I didn't think he was best pleased to see me. Not that he was ever particularly friendly. Begging your pardon, Mr. Rannoch."

"No need to do so. That's an excellent description of Alistair Rannoch."

Drummond met Malcolm's gaze, friend to friend. "I'm sorry, Mr. Rannoch. He can't have been an easy father."

"He wasn't." Malcolm took a drink from his pint and let the malty ale linger on his tongue. "Which is why I was vastly relieved to learn he wasn't my father at all."

~

MÉLANIE RETURNED to the sitting room that had become Roth's headquarters to find Harry updating the others.

"Malcolm will be back soon," Harry said. "He's gone to visit a former gamekeeper at Dunmykel whom George had notes about. Meanwhile, we have what appears to be a codebook. George was apparently gathering information."

"George was bent on returning to his old life," Cordelia said. "And gathering information to do it."

"He was working for Beverston," Mélanie said. "And he claimed to have been working for Alistair." She updated them about her interview with George Lamb and then with Beverston.

"Henry Brougham was calling on George?" Cordelia said.

71

"We don't know that necessarily," Kitty said. "George Lamb just saw them going into the building, apparently."

"Exactly," Mélanie said. "But it's hard to imagine it doesn't have anything to do with George's claiming to have information that could influence the trial."

"It doesn't mean Brougham had anything do with George Chase's death," Laura said. She'd joined the others when Mélanie came back from the King's Arms, while the children played cards by the fire.

"No," Mélanie agreed. "But it raises a lot of questions. Much as she liked Henry Brougham, she knew he was someone willing to go to great lengths. She could recognize it because she was much the same herself.

"It's hard to imagine Caro George going into a house with Brougham in broad daylight," Cordelia said.

"That was my thought as well," Mélanie said. "Which makes me inclined to think it wasn't a tryst." She looked at Cordy for a moment. It was painful territory, but Cordy was a key source of information when it came to George Chase. "How well did George know either of them?"

"Not well at all. I mean, as far I knew. Obviously there was a great deal about George I didn't know at all." Cordelia folded her arms and gripped her elbows, but her gaze remained steady. "For all I know, George Chase could have been Caro George's lover too, save that everyone, including Caro herself, seemed so surprised when she ran off with Brougham that I have a hard time crediting it. But if she had been George Chase's mistress, I can't imagine why on earth she'd have called on him with Brougham. And if George was bartering information to Brougham about the queen's case, I can't imagine why Brougham would have taken Caro with him to meet with George. George Chase, that is. In fact, I can't imagine why Caro and Brougham would have gone into that lodging house at all if they'd had the least inkling George or anyone else who would recognize them was there. Even if they weren't bent on a tryst—which I agree seems unlikely—they'd have to have known what anyone would think seeing them together. Whatever they were doing, why on earth did they do it in broad daylight? I mean, there are plenty of—" She broke off, flushing. "Oh god. I'm all too well versed in such matters."

"No need to apologize," Harry said, in a level, friendly voice that was like steady boards overlaying a chasm. "It's a valid point."

"Beverston didn't seem to know anything about George's having any information about the trial," Mélanie said. "Not that he'd necessarily have told me if he had done, but he was bent enough on cooperating to share a lot. And he was very concerned about what other information George might have had. He mentioned George's asking about the night Cyril Talbot died, as though that had a connection to Alistair. But I think we need Malcolm to ask more about that." She hesitated a moment, aware that many of those in the room perhaps knew more about Cyril Talbot and his death than she did herself.

Raoul met her gaze for a moment. "I wasn't anywhere near Dunmykel then. And Fanny's never talked about it to me. Neither has Archie."

"It was not long after I went to live with Archie," Harry said. "I remember his coming back from that trip. At least, I think it was that trip, piecing it together from what I know now. I'd hardly say he confided in me, but he was very quiet when he got back. Eventually he apologized to me for his abstraction and said that someone he knew had died. I was surprised by the news and surprised that he talked to me so directly. My parents never did anything of the sort. I asked him if the man who died had been a good friend. He said not precisely, but it had still been a shock. He didn't offer more details and it wasn't the time to ask for them. But I've always remembered that exchange because he treated me like an adult. Or at least as though I deserved honesty and was capable of understanding."

"That's more than I heard about it from Archie," Raoul said.

Archie Davenport had been reporting to Raoul both on the League and on intelligence relating to Ireland and France at the time. And Archie, Harry's uncle, was now married to Fanny, Malcolm's aunt, who had also been at Dunmykel at when Cyril Talbot died. "But it never seemed connected to any of our work, so I didn't press him. We should talk to both Archie and Fanny, but we should see what Malcolm knows first. Meanwhile, we can see what we can do with the codebook."

"We should get the children home," Mélanie said. She looked at Roth.

Roth smiled. "I know where to find you. I have a feeling we're going to be talking a lot in the next few days."

CHAPTER 9

A slender woman with ashy brown hair twisted up in a simple knot answered the door in response to Julien's ring. She had a toddler girl with curly fair hair in her arms (about twenty-two months, Julien judged, based on his own Genny) and an older girl of four or five clinging to her skirts. The woman wore brown spotted muslin. It was unlike anything he had seen her in before, as was her hairstyle. But the high cheekbones, sharply angled brows, and clear gray eyes were indelibly the same.

She went still, gaze locked on Julien's own. "Well. I always wonder if the past will appear on my doorstep, but this isn't the form I expected it to take. You'd better come in." She stepped backwards and touched her older daughter's hair. "A friend of mine from a long time ago, *petite*. Hetty!" She called.

A maidservant with red hair and a friendly smile appeared from the back of the house and took the children. Julien's friend conducted him into a sitting room with faded upholstery and a cheerful chaos of toys and books. "Do sit down," she said. "It seems past ridiculous to stand on ceremony."

"I'm not even sure what to call you," Julien said as he moved to a chintz-covered chair.

"And yet you found me."

"I'd heard you were in London. I'd made some inquiries. But I saw no reason to bother you." Not then, anyway.

"My husband calls me Anne. So do the friends I've made—and there are a surprising number of them, considering I didn't used to believe in friendship. Those who know me less well call me Mrs. Forbes. Which is a name I couldn't even have imagined pronouncing a few years ago."

"We've all changed. I now go by—"

"I'm quite well aware of who you are. Lord Carfax. I read the papers. Unlike me, you've hardly sunk into the woodwork. I've heard the gossip. Considering you make no secret of having been Julien St. Juste, I assume you aren't trying to hide your past."

"Not most of it. I'd have to give up too many of the parts I don't want to lose." Julien regarded Anne. When he had known her, she'd gone by Antoinette Leblanc. One of the more fascinating courtesans in Paris. Also a skilled agent who'd been deadly with a variety of blades. The same face that could go hard with mockery or blend effortlessly into a crowd had beguiled with angelic sweetness. And the hair that now appeared a cool brown had been bright gold.

Anne moved to a set of decanters, poured two glasses of amber liquid into small glasses, and gave one to him. "Sherry. My husband gave me a taste for it." She dropped onto the sofa, sage velvet draped with a flowered shawl, and took a sip from her own glass. "I knew you were in London before you became Lord Carfax. I caught a glimpse of you once at Les Trois Amis."

Les Trois Amis was a tavern favored by French émigrés, particularly agents. "I remember." Julien took a sip of sherry. Dry but faintly nutty. It stirred memories of afternoons by the fire after a ride through misty countryside. "We exchanged glances, as I recall."

"You had your hair darkened and you were bent on talking to one of Fouché's former agents. I assumed you had no desire to be recognized. Like me. I rarely go there. I'd gone to meet a friend who'd just arrived from France and was in need of help." Which was more or less code for had escaped the White Terror. "For a while after that, though, I couldn't go anywhere in London without expecting to see you. I'd walk in the park with my children or sit at the theatre with my husband and imagine I could feel your eyes staring into my back. But lately I've thought you were as happy to be lost as I am."

"I wouldn't call it lost. But I am happy." Odd to say it. He'd have laughed at the word as recently as a year ago. Even as he smiled at Kitty across the pillow or watched Genny asleep in his lap or played chess or lottery tickets or catch with the boys and realized he was content in a way he'd once never have been able to imagine.

"I wondered if you were undercover at first, when we learned you were Carfax. But I couldn't imagine how you could have set up something quite so elaborate. Or what you were playing at."

"Life is always a sort of cover. But I'm probably less undercover now than I ever have been in my life."

Anne twisted the gold locket round her throat on its chain. "I could say the same. Oh, I liked the more glittering parts of my life. At the time. But they began to pall. I met my husband just before Waterloo. Not on a mission. Not precisely. That is, I wasn't spying on him. And he knows now that I was an agent. He knew when he asked me to marry him and come to England. I don't think he believed I'd say yes. He seemed rather stunned. Even asked me why. I said that in addition to the fact that I cared for him in ways I hadn't thought possible, I could see the appeal of a quiet life. Of course, my life here is very different from yours."

"In some ways. I could do with mine being quieter at times. But I understand the appeal."

Anne settled back amid the fringed sofa cushions and took a sip of sherry. "So why come see me now?"

"A man was killed today. Outside the House of Lords."

Her brows rose. "The protests turned violent?"

"No. He was stabbed on the stairs with a thin blade. The killer was gone before he fell to the steps. It was a precise strike. Only a handful of people could have done it."

"I didn't."

"I didn't suggest you did."

"But you're here. Which I assume means you didn't do it yourself."

"I happened to have been with friends at the time. Which hasn't stopped people I know well from sending inquiring glances at me. Including my wife."

Anne regarded him for a moment, head tilted to the side in a way that conjured a memory of her with ringlets spilling over her shoulders, sparkling earrings instead of simple pearls, and a frothy bodice slipping from her shoulders instead of demure brown-spotted muslin. "I saw you with your wife once at the theatre. The Tavistock. You were in a box. She's very lovely. And her taste in clothes is exquisite. None of which is surprising in any woman you married. But when I turned my opera glasses to look at you—which I freely confess I did—I caught you looking at her. I confess I went still at the look in your eyes. I don't think I've ever seen you look at anyone that way before."

Julien and Anne had only been lovers on a few occasions. Not from lack of enjoyment, but that had never been a defining element in their relationship. And both of them were more likely to sleep with subjects of a mission than with fellow agents. "I can't speak to the look in my eyes, as I don't generally go about with a mirror—unless I need to look behind me. But I know I've never felt about anyone else the way I feel about Kitty. She changed a number of things for me. At a time when I was changing in any case. But without her I wouldn't be here. Not because she wanted to be Lady Carfax, but because if she hadn't been willing to make the sacrifice of being Lady Carfax, I'd have run off with her as far away from my so-called heritage as I could get."

Anne smiled. "For what it's worth, I also saw her looking at you. I'm quite sure your feelings are returned." She settled back amid the cushions. "You aren't the only one who's married. Or the only one who loves your spouse. I like my life. Once, I'd have thought it would bore me to tears, but I like the quiet. I like not having my nerves on end every moment. I like the familiarity. I like seeing the same people every day. I like caring what happens to them. I like having children. They're so much more interesting than I'd ever thought. And yet so much more in need of protection."

"Quite," Julien said.

She met his gaze. "My husband would laugh at the idea that he needs protection, but he does, for all he survived the Peninsula and Waterloo. Which is another reason I wouldn't run such a risk. I don't expect you to believe that."

"I don't have enough data to believe it or disbelieve it. But I'm inclined to believe it. Especially having seen you with your daughters. Which leaves the question of who did do it."

Anne shifted on the cushions. "It's not even as though it's something I did very often. I mostly dealt in papers. I happened to have learned how to protect myself rather well, and I made use of that talent on occasion. It wasn't the sort of thing I was engaged to do, like—"

"Like I was," Julien said in an easy voice. That scraped just the slightest bit against his throat. "True enough. But you have the capabilities to have done this. I remember your dispatching an assassin sent by the Austrians outside the opera. I had cause to be grateful to you that night. I can only think of a handful of others who could have managed this so skillfully, and none of them are in London, that I know of. Of course, contrary to what my friends believe, I'm not personally acquainted with or even knowledge-able of every assassin on the Continent. But I do have a fair range of connections. This was carefully planned. Has anyone tried to hire you lately?"

Anne took a sip of sherry. The lack of a quick denial spoke volumes.

Anne met his gaze. "Oh, poison. If I wanted to have a hope of prevaricating convincingly, I should have denied it immediately. Which probably means I didn't actually want to prevaricate at all." She took another sip of sherry, got to her feet, refilled her glass and then Julien's. "I was walking in Green Park with the girls. They'd run to investigate a robin's nest and a man approached me. At first I thought he was simply making a tiresome proposition—which is an odd thing to do to a woman with two young children in tow, but I do rather push the boundaries by going about without a maid, and I'm often taken for the girls' nurse. But he stopped and murmured that he was searching for someone with my talents. It took me far longer than it should have done to realize what sort of talents he meant. And then I went cold, in a way I don't think I ever did in all my missions. Because the girls were right there, just feet away. I told him he must have mistaken me for someone else and I had no talents beyond passable piano and watercolors and making a cherry pie —I'm not sure where that came from, I've never baked a cherry pie in my life."

"Did that send him off?"

"No. He mentioned a very large amount of money. I simply opened my eyes wide and pretended not to understand what he was talking about. I didn't want to go home and risk his following me, so I simply said as a respectable married woman I couldn't afford to be seen talking to a man I hadn't been introduced to. He moved away but stayed watching us for the longest time. Finally, when I was quite sure he'd moved off, we went home by the most roundabout route imaginable. Lizzy kept asking me if we were lost and Janie, after trudging along far longer than I've ever asked her to before, simply turned me and held up her arms and insisted on being carried the rest of the way home. Eventually we did get home. I'm quite sure we weren't followed and I don't think either of the girls guessed how frightened I was, both of which I count as minor triumphs."

"Did you see the man again?"

"No. And you must believe I've been wary. I debated with myself over and over that night if I should tell Teddy. I'd certainly want him to tell me if there was any risk to him or our family. But I'd know how to respond to it if there was. He really doesn't. He fought in a very different war that has no place in these games in London." She looked at Julien. "And I wondered if I should tell someone else. But I'm not like you—or at least I don't have what I think you have. I don't have a network of former agents. I've cut myself off deliberately. If I'd gone to Bow Street or the home office, I'd only have exposed myself and my family to danger. And I had no way of knowing who the target of the supposed plot was."

"Understandable," Julien said. "One always asks questions after the fact. But I'm quite sure they'd have continued in their aims in any case. What did this man look like?"

Anne frowned in a way Julien knew meant she was conjuring the memory. "Middle years—late thirties, early forties. He had his hat pulled low but his hair looked to be light brown, possibly dark blond. Average height. Medium build. Blue eyes, I think. Difficult to tell again with the hat. His clothes were sober and anonymous —tan coat, buff breeches, boots. The kind one would pick for a mission on which one didn't want to attract attention and might have to elude followers. He took care to keep the sun at his back too."

"Accent?"

Anne's brows drew together. "British. I'd swear it was his first tongue, but then I'd have sworn French was yours when I first met you."

Julien leaned back in his chair and stretched his legs out in front of him. "My mother liked to speak French to me. So in a way it was. Education?"

"An Oxford or Cambridge sort of voice. I didn't understand that when I first met you, but it makes more sense now. I can't judge public schools. But I suspect he went to one as well. But he wasn't—" She frowned a moment longer, gaze in the distance, and Julien could see her considering possible scenarios, the way he'd once seen her evaluate possible escape routes with enemy agents surrounding a box at the opera. "I don't think he was doing this on his own account. That is, he had the accent and bearing of a gentleman, but I had the sense that he was seeking an assassin at someone else's behest. This wasn't on his own account." Anne smoothed her hands over her lap. "It's odd. I actually thought I'd put it behind me. Oh, I still looked over my shoulder, and I accept that I always will. But I thought I was just protecting my family. I didn't think I'd be caught up in intrigues." She stared at a loose thread in her cuff. "I didn't think I'd feel responsible for someone else's safety. Or the lack of it. Someone I didn't know."

Julien met her gaze. There were some things only a fellow agent could understand. "It bothers me more now than it used to. Or perhaps it's that if I'd let myself think about it at all in the past, it would have totally paralyzed me."

"I've been thinking like a mother and wife. I can't do that. Not entirely." She pressed down the loose thread. "Do you know who it was who was killed?"

"His name was George Chase. He'd been a soldier and agent. He was not a very admirable person. To put it mildly."

"I suppose that should be a relief. But I still don't much care to think that if I'd behaved differently, he might still be alive."

"Nor do I. Rather to my surprise. Though I will say that he knew the dangers of the game he was playing."

"Did he have children? Funny, I never used to think that about people who were killed. Now it's my first question."

"He did. But I don't believe he'd seen them in some time."

"Still. They'll grow up without him now. Not easy, whatever sort of person he was."

"His death will in some ways make life easier for some of my friends. Which paradoxically has them more concerned and causes its own problems."

"Do you think the man who tried to hire me will come back?"

"I honestly don't know. It partly depends on how much he believed you, and partly on why Chase was killed and if that's ended things. You'll have to make your own decision if he does. But I'd appreciate it if you'd let me know. For a number of reasons."

"It seems this isn't a time to work alone. And it also seems I'm working again, to a degree."

Julien nodded. "Where did you think he'd have gone next?"

"I don't know. Honestly. Like you, I don't know of anyone else in London with those skills. But if I had to hazard a guess, I'd say Les Trois Amis."

Julien sighed and pushed himself to his feet. "That's what I was afraid of. Wish me luck."

CHAPTER 10

"*M*ummy." Jessica Rannoch ran down the stairs to the hall in the Berkeley Square house and flung her arms round Mélanie's knees. "You've been gone for ages."

"I know." Mélanie bent down to scoop her daughter up. "I'm sorry, *querida*. Today got complicated."

"Bet's been telling a story," Jessica said, as Drusilla Davenport and Timothy Ashford ran down after her, followed by Bet Simcox, who was carrying Genny and Clara. "About a prince who marries a peasant girl. Dru thinks the peasant girl's really a princess, but I said that would spoil it."

"I quite agree," Mélanie said.

Kitty hugged Timothy and took Genny from Bet. Raoul took Clara. Drusilla had run to Harry and Cordy. Berowne, the family cat, bounded after them.

Jessica tugged at Mélanie's pearl necklace. "Colin got to go with you."

"You can go when you're older," Colin said.

"There won't be a trial when I'm older. Not like this. Not ever again. Daddy said."

"Well, probably not again." Mélanie settled Jessica on her hip.

"What went wrong?" Jessica asked. "Was someone killed?"

Livia gasped. "Who said something to you?"

"No one." Jessica leaned back, gripping the puffed sleeves of Mélanie's gown. "That's usually why Mummy and Daddy are late."

"We have another investigation," Mélanie said. Then she turned to Bet. "Thank you for staying with the children."

"We had fun," Bet said. "I love playing with them. And we're so happy to be here." Bet cast a quick glance at her fiancé Sandy Trenor, who had just emerged from Malcolm's study.

Sandy had recently become Malcolm's secretary. Recently as in days ago, when his betrothal to Bet, his mistress, who had been born in St. Giles, had caused his parents to end his allowance. Malcolm had offered Sandy the post, and Sandy and Bet had moved into the Berkeley Square house.

"I've got the notes for tomorrow," Sandy said. "Will Malcolm—"

"He'll be at the trial tomorrow," Mélanie said. "I think much of the investigation will fall to the rest of us."

Jessica tugged at Mélanie's sleeve. "Stay safe?"

Children didn't ask much, did they? Mélanie touched her nose to her daughter's. "Like always."

JULIEN STEPPED into the shadows of Les Trois Amis. The oil lamps were the same as in English coffeehouses, but something about the air always smelled distinctly French. A combination of dark coffee, brewed well, bread and pastries made with fresh butter, herbs and seasonings used with a light hand. And then there were the sounds. It was months since he'd heard so much French. French and an undercurrent of secrets. Les Trois Amis wasn't just popular with émigrés. It was popular with émigré agents, and the White Terror had made Britain an unlikely refuge for many of them.

He hadn't changed his clothes, but he realized he was walking differently. With a slight slouch and a languid gait. For once without consciously trying to. He hadn't realized how much the way he walked and moved had changed—since he'd settled in England? Since he'd become Carfax? It was not a comforting thought. But at least on some level he still had a spy's instincts.

He sauntered up to the bar without trying to attract notice, but also without trying to avoid it, which could be the worst way to draw attention. Hugo, the barkeep, met his gaze with recognition. Six years ago, Hugo had worked in a tavern in Lyons that had been one of the most active places to exchange information currency. He'd been mostly trustworthy then. You couldn't survive long in that role if your clients couldn't trust you.

"Didn't think we'd see you here again."

"I haven't changed that much."

"Changing to a lord from—whatever you were. Hard to imagine much more of a change." He regarded Julien through narrowed lids. "Wouldn't imagine you'd have need of anything here."

"Then you have less imagination than I credited. I may have a different name. I haven't changed in essentials."

Hugo put his elbows on the bar. "What do you want, my lord whatever-you're-calling-yourself-now?"

"Information. What else?"

"Talk's all about the trial. But I'd think you'd know more, seeing as you sit in the chamber that's deciding it."

"You'd be surprised. But it actually isn't to do with the queen's case. Not directly. Was someone here recently trying to hire for a particularly skilled job?"

"A lot of people come here hiring for jobs. Or seeking them. What sort of job?"

"The sort I might once have been hired to undertake myself."

Hugo's gaze locked on Julien's own. "What have you heard?"

"Not a lot. That's why I'm here." Julien hesitated, but if he wanted information, he needed to offer some of it. "A man was killed outside the Lords chamber at Westminster today. It would have taken skill. Someone was trying to hire an assassin with those talents recently. I suspect they may have come here."

Hugo dragged a towel over the seemingly gleaming bar. "There was a man asking questions. Not anyone I'd seen here before. Well dressed, English, though he managed to fit in." Hugo reached for a glass, poured brandy into it, and pushed it across the bar to Julien. "He asked if I knew how to reach you."

Cold settled in Julien's stomach. "By name?"

"No, but it was clear he meant you."

Julien took a drink of brandy. It was far more welcome than he'd like to admit. "What did you say?"

Hugo poured a glass for himself and took a swallow. "Same as I said to you. That I couldn't imagine why you'd come back in here now."

"Did he believe you?"

"He asked when I'd last seen you. I told the truth."

Julien took another drink of brandy. "So who did he talk to then?"

"It looks as though you're here for the same reason I am," a husky voice said beside him.

Julien turned his head to meet a pair of blue eyes that could hold an opera house in thrall even when she wasn't singing. Danielle Darnault wore a dark blue gown ornamented only with a narrow frill of lace and a plain chip straw bonnet, but she would be striking in any setting.

"It looks as though you've learned what you can from Hugo," she said.

"I shared what I could," Hugo said. "It wasn't much."

Danielle nodded. "Then pour me a glass of something. I need to talk to Julien."

Hugo complied with a smile and no effort to disguise his relief at his part in the conversation being done.

"You might have shared the fun," Danielle said, dropping onto a highbacked bench across from Julien in a quiet corner.

"I was trying to be considerate of the fact that the man I recently learned is your husband is recovering from life-threatening wounds, and you are trying to take care of him and your very young daughter."

She grinned and took a sip from the glass of wine Hugo had given her. "Such thoughtfulness from you. But you know I'm used to juggling. I wouldn't have stayed alive this long if I couldn't. And if I'm going to continue to stay alive and protect my family, I'll need to continue to do so."

"This isn't about you."

"Not directly. It's difficult to tell how things are tangled up." She smiled at him over the rim of her wineglass. "And I might also feel the need to assist newfound friends who've been kind to me. I expect that sounds maudlin."

"No. Or perhaps, but I understand the feeling. How did you find out? Edmund Blayney?" Danielle's husband Pierre was a journalist and currently recuperating in Edmund's rooms above his printshop. Edmund had helped Danielle smuggle him out of France and away from Royalist authorities.

Danielle nodded. "He came back today full of suppressed excitement. He's putting a story out, but only what he learned on his own, separately from the Rannochs. Pippa Haworth, who is quite remarkable, is sitting with Pierre, and her daughters are playing with Ilia." Danielle shifted her shoulders against the back of the bench. "I suppose you've talked to Anne—it's Forbes now, isn't it?"

"How did you know what she was calling herself?"

"I've been focused on Pierre, but I haven't wholly lost touch with my friends. I don't think she did this."

"She says not, and I'm inclined to believe her. I didn't either, by the way."

"Edmund said so. He said you were with Malcolm at the time."

Danielle tilted her head to one side. "How long could a victim continue walking after a wound like that?"

"Not long enough for me to have got through the crowd and back. And before that, I was sitting in the House of Lords. Along with all the men who are now my colleagues, god help me."

Danielle gave a faint smile. "I actually don't think you would have, in any case."

"Thank you." Julien stretched his legs out under the table. "So who do you think did?"

She hesitated a moment. "Did you know Étienne Lémieux?"

"I met him a few times. And I know his reputation." Lémieux had been an agent for Fouché, the minister of police, who had survived Napoleon's fall but was now in exile. "What's he been doing since Fouché's downfall?"

"Freelancing, like most of us. But rumor has it he left for England a fortnight before I left France. He often used cruder weapons, but he could have done this."

"Yes." Julien's hands curled round his own glass. "I believe he could have done. The question is who hired him?"

"That," said Danielle, "is the interesting part."

CHAPTER 11

*C*ordelia stared at the brown-leather-covered book on brown-veined marble table in the Berkeley Square library as though it might bite her. "I wouldn't have the least idea of what codes George might have used. I didn't even know he was an agent. Which I suppose means I didn't know him at all really."

"Not precisely." Mélanie touched her arm. "One can know a person very well and not know anything at all about their being an agent."

Cordelia flashed a look at her. "You and Malcolm knew each other far better than I ever knew George. Malcolm always knew the person you were. He says so. I didn't know the real George at all. Or I never could have loved him."

"The real person can be a complicated idea," Kitty said. "I'm not at all sure I understand the real me, let alone the real anyone else."

Harry moved to the table beside Cordelia, not quite touching her. "You may not know George's codes, but you have more insights than any of us into how his mind worked."

"But do we need that? It may just all require mathematical calculations. In which case we need Allie."

"Perhaps," Harry said. Malcolm's cousin Aline was brilliant at

90

codes. "But George wasn't a mathematician. Or particularly adept at codes, from what I saw. If he wanted something he could decode easily, he's more likely to have used something he could code and decode based on keywords. You have far better insights than the rest of us into what keywords he might have chosen."

Cordelia turned to her husband as though he'd just suggested she was working for the enemy. Or possibly something worse, Mélanie thought with bitter acknowledgement.

"Don't you dare say he'd have used my name," Cordelia said to her husband. "I can't imagine he would have. Not recently."

"I can." Harry's gaze was steady. "I didn't want to make too much of this, but he had a miniature of you in his shaving kit."

"Oh god." Cordelia glanced away. "I remember that. I remember—sorry—I remember giving it to him."

"Understandable," Harry said.

"It was silly. At a time when I was silly. He probably just hadn't got rid of it," Cordelia said.

"He was keeping it close to hand. But he might not have been so obvious as to use your name as a code word. He'd have known a number of people would think of it."

Cordelia frowned. "It's not like with Malcolm and Mélanie or you. I can't say he loved Shakespeare or fifteenth-century history or the Julio-Claudians. But—George was fond of his horses. And his dogs. Odd that. To think of his being kind to horses and dogs when to people he—" She shook her head, memories dancing in her eyes like shards of glass from a smashed mirror. "Try Faversham. He was George's favorite horse."

"It shouldn't take me long to do a table," Mélanie said.

With her, Raoul, Harry, and Kitty working, and the aid of a pot of coffee, it didn't take long. They stared down at the decoded papers. Which came down to a list of names, with no identifying details.

"It doesn't all fit together," Cordelia said. "These people aren't connected. Are they?"

"Not that we know of," Raoul said. "But they're powerful."

"We know he was offering information to Beverston," Harry said. "But this is more. George seems to have been putting together information on powerful people. Information that could give him an advantage. Probably because he wanted to reinstate himself."

"It seems to be a theme just now," Mélanie said.

"George couldn't have got pardoned," Cordelia said. "Could he?"

"I doubt it," Raoul said. "But he'd also never been formally accused of anything. He might have thought that if he could get Hubert and Wellington to take the pressure off, he could come back to his old life. Or something resembling his old life."

"Hubert wouldn't—" Cordelia swallowed, not quite able to say it. "I mean, George murdered his ward."

"It's hard to imagine Hubert letting George go." Kitty's gaze narrowed as though she was surveying shifting terrain. Which was a good way to describe Hubert Mallinson, her and her husband's and Malcolm's and George's former spymaster. "But I could imagine his making use of George."

"You think that was his aim?" Cordelia said. "Because some of these names relate to the League. So George could have been doing this for Beverston, couldn't he? Or before that, for Alistair?"

"He could," Mélanie said. "But he was trying to see Liverpool, and he told Beverston he had information that could bring Alistair down. Of course, he could have been playing both sides. Or he could have been a double agent with Beverston, and he was actually working for Alistair. He could have been trying to see Liverpool for Alistair."

"There's a certain logic in his and Alistair's finding each other," Cordelia said.

"Which makes one wonder where Trenchard fits in," Laura said in a cool voice. Her gaze went to her former lover's name on the list. "Was it his ties to Liverpool long ago? Or his schemes with Alistair a few years ago? Or his crimes in India? Or all of them?"

Raoul slid his hand round Laura's. "We still don't entirely understand Trenchard's scheme to make himself prime minister. Or Alistair's role in it. But Trenchard's hatred of Liverpool seems to have been part of it."

"Cordy," Kitty said. "Could George have been part of the League?"

Cordelia stared at her friend, gaze bruised. "Beverston told Mélanie he wasn't."

"He wasn't, as far as Beverston knew. And that's assuming Beverston was telling Mélanie the truth."

"He's the wrong age," Cordelia said.

"To be a League member," Mélanie said. "But he's much the same age as Tommy Belmont and John Smythe, who were employed by the League. And he—"

"Has the temperament to have fallen for it," Cordelia finished with resignation. "In fact, he's just the type they sought out. Young men from the beau mode with a talent for spycraft and no particular morals or loyalties."

"That could have described Julien," Kitty said.

Cordelia gave a faint smile. "I don't think so. Not really. Julien would never have done what he did with the *Unicorn* if he hadn't had very clear morals and loyalties. But I should have added young men from the beau monde with a talent for spycraft and no morals who are clever enough to carry out missions but not so clever that they cause problems."

"And the League did try to recruit Julien," Kitty added.

Cordelia was frowning. "George never gave any hint he was involved with the League. But then at that point I'd never heard of the League. And I wasn't used to investigating. So I'm not sure I'd have picked up on anything if he had let out any information. There was so much about George I didn't understand."

"We didn't know about the League then either," Mélanie said.

"But there was nothing in anything we discovered that connected to the League, even in retrospect. You'd think there might have been. Although it's certainly possible we missed it. It would explain how he went to work for Alistair later, assuming Beverston is telling the truth."

"Or Alistair or his allies in the League could have recruited George after his disgrace," Harry said. "In fact—" He checked himself.

"The fact that George was connected to me and that I'm married to you and close to Mélanie and Malcolm might have encouraged them to do so?" Cordelia said.

"Yes."

Cordelia nodded. "It makes sense. Of course, we have no way to be sure."

"If he was working with the League," Laura said, "was he reaching out to Liverpool on their behalf or to spite them?"

"An excellent question," Raoul said. "And if it was to spite them, it gives us a very plausible murder motive."

Cordelia rubbed her arms. "Where it comes to George, I don't think murder motives are in short supply."

THEY WERE STILL DEBATING George Chase's possible links to the League a quarter hour later when Malcolm arrived in Berkeley Square.

He stared at the codebook. "You've broken George's codes."

"He seems to have been amassing blackmail information," Mélanie said. "On a number of powerful people with no obvious connection. And Beverston told me George was working for him and had been working for Alistair."

"We're debating if George had been working for the League in the past," Cordelia said in a cool voice. "And if he was still working for Alistair."

"I don't think so." Malcolm drew up a chair beside Mélanie. "He'd been to visit a retired gamekeeper from Dunmykel. Timothy Drummond. With questions about Alistair." He hesitated, and Mélanie suspected those questions had to do with the recent revelations about Gisèle's husband Andrew, which Malcolm hadn't yet shared with the others.

"Abby Clifton told us she'd seen George Lamb watching the lodging house in Wardour Street where George Chase lodged," Mélanie said, to change the subject and because it needed to be said. "I found George Lamb at a tavern near the House of Lords. He claims he was in Wardour Street because he followed Caro. He says he saw her go into the lodging house with Brougham."

Malcolm already looked tired and worn, but at that his eyes widened. And then narrowed, as she saw the implications sink in.

"George Lamb thought they were bent on a tryst," Cordy said. "But Mélanie and I doubt they'd have been so obvious."

"I tend to agree," Malcolm said. "And put together with the fact that George Chase claimed to have information about the trial, one can't but wonder if he got it from Brougham one way or another. I can't see Chase's being stupid enough to think Liverpool would be impressed by the news that Brougham and Caro George were sleeping together again. Even if it was true. Which makes me think he either overhead something or Brougham told him something and turned on him. Either way, it gives Brougham motive."

"It doesn't mean he killed him, Malcolm." Cordelia sounded shocked, for all that had already happened that day.

"No," Malcolm agreed. "Of course not. But I need to talk to him—"

"But he's—" Cordelia trailed off.

"A friend. And because he's a friend, I know just how committed he is to his cause. For his own sake. And perhaps for the queen's as well. Which makes him all the more determined to go to whatever lengths it takes to win."

"Surely you don't think he'd go to these lengths."

"I don't know," Malcolm said. "That's the honest truth. But then we never know how far someone will go. Even those close to us. Even ourselves. Not until we face a situation. My father taught me that." He looked at Raoul.

Raoul inclined his head. "It doesn't mean Brougham did do anything of the sort. It doesn't mean he even knew that Chase had whatever information he had. But you should talk to him."

Mélanie reached for her husband's hand. "Beverston also said George asked him about the night Cyril Talbot died." She hesitated, then pushed forwards with a steady gaze. "I didn't realize he'd died at Dunmykel. Or that it had been an accident with a gun."

Malcolm squeezed her fingers. "It's not something I like to dwell on. I suppose—there seemed no point in going into details about a past tragedy that didn't have anything to do with us."

"It's all right." Mélanie returned the pressure of his hand. "There's still a lot we don't know about each other."

Malcolm met her gaze, his own steady, but both their pasts hung between them, as they always would, however many bridges they had crossed, however far they had come. Then he glanced at the others. "It seems it may have more to do with the present than I thought." He looked at Raoul. "Did Aunt Frances ever mention Cyril's death to you?"

Raoul shook his head. "I was in Ireland at the time. I remember hearing about it, but I barely knew Cyril. I had no notion Frances was there. Though her deciding to surprise Alistair at Dunmykel doesn't surprise me."

Frances and Alistair had seemingly disliked each other, but in fact, Mélanie had learned, at the same time Malcolm learned it, had been lovers off and on for over two decades. While apparently still cordially disliking each other, at least on the surface.

"Which would undoubtedly have caused a disturbance,"

Malcolm said. "Though it's difficult to see how that could have led to Cyril's death." He looked at Harry.

"I knew Archie was disturbed by Cyril's death," Harry said. "I didn't know more. But it sounds as though Archie may have done."

"Fanny couldn't have been—" Cordelia bit the words back.

"Cyril's mistress?" Malcolm finished for her. "Not that I know of. But I'm not sure I would know. More to the point, I'm not sure how that would get us to Cyril's ending up dead in some way that implicates Alistair."

"It would if Alistair killed him in a fit of jealousy," Kitty said. "But then, Glenister and Archie would know. I can't see Archie's not telling. Not if—"

"Not if what?" Julien asked, strolling into the room.

"You have a knack for returning at the right moment, darling." Kitty got to her feet and went to his side. "Was it very dreadful?" She slid her hand through his arm.

"No, but I haven't anything concrete to report, save that someone definitely was trying to hire the right sort of assassin. And possibly did hire Étienne Lémieux for the job. Danielle Darnault's helping us. She learned about it from Edmund, and she's checking with more sources."

"But Pierre—" Cordelia said.

"I know," Julien said. "I was impressed Danielle offered her services. Pierre's mending, and Edmund and Pippa are looking after him. I think it's partly that Danielle feels a debt of gratitude and partly, to be honest, that she misses the game. Meanwhile, perhaps someone would catch me up on whatever you were talking about."

Mélanie told him about her talk with Beverston and his revelations about George Chase.

Julien whistled. "I suppose it shouldn't be a surprise George was working for Beverston. Or for Alistair." He folded his arms.

"If Cyril's death was more than it seemed, I wonder if Uncle Hubert had anything to do with it."

Mélanie looked at Julien. "That's right. Cyril's wife—"

"Was Hubert and my father's sister. My aunt Susan. I didn't know her well. She died when my cousin Honoria was born. Cyril's and her only child."

"Yes," Mélanie said, before she could think better of it. "We've met."

"Of course," Julien said in an easy voice that told her he knew perfectly well why she was disturbed. "Honoria has all the family talent for espionage but no outlet to put it to use. And rather fewer morals than I possess." He looked at Malcolm. "I always thought she had her claws into you."

Malcolm gave a wry smile. "She paid rather more attention to me than made any sense, given my complete lack of dash. If I'd shown the remotest interest, she'd have tired of me within months. Fortunately, she found Atwood."

"Oh, I don't think she'd have tired of you," Julien said. "She has the brains to recognize your understanding. But she wouldn't have been able to mold you, which would have driven her to distraction. And you'd have been too loyal to stand up to her. Which is a receipt for disaster. All things considered, it's a good thing you married a French spy first. Much higher chance of success."

"Thank you," Mélanie said.

"Only pointing out my cousin Honoria's drawbacks."

Honoria Talbot—Honoria Atwood now—had once haunted Mélanie as just the type of girl Malcolm should and would have married had he not stumbled across her, and had she and Raoul not made use of that encounter. Honoria was lovely, accomplished, impeccably British, but clever enough not to bore Malcolm. She knew just what to do and say, but with an insouciance that kept her from being stuffy. She could have expertly guided the social side of Malcolm's political career without boring him. At least so it had seemed to Mélanie.

"She'd have bored Malcolm silly," Kitty said. "Sorry, but I think it makes sense that I have an opinion."

"Point taken," Malcolm said. "And you're absolutely right. Though Honoria's had a difficult time of it."

"Honoria is a viper in Parisian fashions and Asprey jewels," Julien said. "Trust me, it takes one to know one. I can appreciate her talents, but she's not honest enough about the games she plays. I never could stand hypocrisy."

"Was Carfax—Hubert—Honoria's guardian when her father died?" Kitty asked.

"No, Glenister was," Julien said. "But Hubert had influence over her fortune, thanks to my aunt Susan's marriage settlement. I was gone from England before Cyril died, but I've heard bits and pieces. Honoria may have set her sights on Malcolm, but I rather think Aunt Amelia wanted her to marry David. But then there are a lot of girls Aunt Amelia wanted David to marry." Julien frowned at his fingernails. "I can't really see Uncle Hubert's being overly concerned if Alistair killed Cyril, all things considered. I don't think Uncle Hubert was particularly fond of Cyril. On the other hand, if Hubert had learned something about Cyril, I can imagine Hubert's having him killed. Especially if he didn't think Cyril had treated Aunt Susan well."

"How?" Kitty said.

"Presumably because Aunt Susan wasn't happy."

"No, I mean how could Hubert have had Cyril killed? According to Beverston, only Archie, Alistair, and Glenister were there when Cyril died. Do you think one of them was acting for Hubert? Or that Hubert somehow got an assassin into Dunmykel and no one knew?"

"Stranger things are possible," Julien said. "Especially as we don't yet have an account of Cyril's death from anyone who was actually there. We don't know if Alistair or Archie or Glenister saw it. And while I refuse to suspect Archie—with a trust I would have once thought not possible in me—and my imagination fails as to how Hubert could have got Glenister to kill his own brother, I can imagine Hubert and Alistair's being in on it together in some way. But then, I can imagine Uncle Hubert's doing just about anything."

"With cause, dearest," Kitty said. "But don't let your prejudices get the better of you."

"We need to talk to Aunt Frances and Archie," Malcolm said. "And I suppose we need to talk to Honoria too."

Julien gave a reluctant smile. "I'd say better you than me, save that I can see through her better. You're too chivalrous."

"Believe me, I've always seen through Honoria."

Julien smoothed his coat. "There's seeing through her and seeing through her. You might have ended up married to her just because you felt you owed to it to her to lend her your protection."

"I like to think I'm a bit better able to defend myself now," Malcolm said, "but I need to see Brougham. It's complicated—"

"Don't waste time on explanations," Julien said. "Kitty can catch me up. I'll call on my poisonous cousin. But you owe me." He grinned at Malcolm but also flashed a quick look at Mélanie. Mélanie smiled back.

Julien reached for Kitty's hand. "And you'd best come with me. No one should have to take Honoria Talbot on alone."

Kitty reached for her bonnet. "I wouldn't dream of letting you go into battle alone, darling."

Mélanie looked from Cordelia to Harry. "I can go with you to talk to Archie and Frances."

"Yes," Cordelia said. "Please."

Normally Frances and Archie were part of every investigation the group undertook. But this was the first time they'd ever gone to ask them for details of a death that might be murder.

CHAPTER 12

*K*itty cast a glance at her husband as they descended the steps of the Berkeley Square house. A breeze had come up, stirring the branches of the plane trees in the square garden. "Do you want to talk about this?"

"What part of it?"

"Any part. But I was thinking of the fact that someone who was practically copying you killed George Chase."

"Not much to say about that." Julien scanned the street ahead. "You do believe I didn't kill him, don't you?"

Kitty tucked her hand through his arm. "You're good, Julien, but you don't have supernatural abilities."

"That's my Kitty. Hackney or walk?"

"Walk." Kitty put a hand to her hat. At least it was a particularly stylish one, the brim lined with green satin that matched the piping on her spencer. That was the sort of thing Honoria would notice. "With the crowds about these days, it will be faster and we could both use the air." Of course, Honoria was also likely to raise her brows at walking, like Caroline Bingley with Elizabeth Bennet.

"Right." Julien squeezed her arm against his side. "Let's go see my poisonous cousin."

"Isn't that a bit much for someone who was a toddler when you left Britain?"

"Some things were clear when she was a toddler. But I did get reports on what was happening at home. And I may perhaps have paid rather more attention to them than I let on." He adjusted the angle of his hat with his free hand. "Anyway, you've met her. You can't tell me you like her."

"Not precisely. But then she obviously sees me as an interloper. As most ladies in the ton do."

"Which is reason enough for me to dislike her."

"You're much too clever to waste your energies on something so commonplace, darling," Kitty said, in a light voice designed not to let Julien see quite how much such slights stung. They were minor, after all. A small thing to put up with beside the life they had. "There's nothing Honoria can do to hurt me. Though I rather think Mélanie has a few more qualms about her."

"Yes," Julien said, scanning the street ahead. "So do I. Foolish. But I do think Honoria had her claws into Malcolm rather more than he'd admit."

Kitty hesitated, because open as they all were, there some things about Malcolm it was better not to discuss with Julien. Even if he knew them. And yet there were things Julien needed to know. "Honoria visited Lisbon with your uncle and David and Lord Valentine Talbot. Perhaps you know that?"

"Yes, as it happens. Though I wasn't there at the time. Did she say anything spiteful to you?"

"Oh, no. I scarcely saw her. But I gather she made a rather insistent effort to secure Malcolm."

Julien grimaced. "That's not surprising. I told you he was the one she wanted for a husband. Girls like her play those sorts of games."

"Yes, but they don't generally hide in the gentleman's bed."

Julien stopped walking and swung round to look at her, gaze narrowed against the golden autumn twilight. "Is that what Malcolm told you?"

"Not precisely, not in so many words. But I could piece it together. I'm quite sure nothing actually happened between them."

"No, I wouldn't think it would have done. Though Honoria certainly—"

"Julien. I'm sure it didn't. When Malcolm and I—I'm sure nothing had happened with Honoria."

Julien's gaze settled on her face for a moment. "Point taken. I'm rather slow. But that makes sense."

"I'm sorry. I didn't mean—"

"Sweetheart. It's nothing to do with me. Save that in this investigation it happens to offer rather helpful insights. I do appreciate the confidence."

Kitty met her husband's gaze. "You're rather remarkable, Julien."

"I have a remarkable wife."

Julien was silent for a moment as they turned and cut through a mews. But she could feel him weighing something. "I never knew you knew George Chase," he said.

"Cordelia didn't either. There was never any need for any of us to talk about him since I've come to Britain. Cordelia's made the occasional comment, but it always seemed best simply to listen sympathetically."

Julien nodded. "I quite understand." His gaze was mild and shaded by the brim of his hat. "Did you work with him?"

"On a couple of simple missions." Kitty lifted her gown as they skirted a pile of manure, gaze on the green satin rouleaux on the moss-colored sarcenet. "I was getting information on a Portuguese colonel, whom Carfax thought might be selling information to the afrancesados. Which he was. George was my contact." She released her grip on her skirt and smoothed the folds.

"Kitkat?" Julien continued walking steadily, but she felt his gaze on her. "I imagine you worked closely with him."

"During the mission. And then later we worked together to retrieve some papers from a Portuguese general for Carfax." Kitty turned to face her husband in the shadows of the close-set buildings. The light from the street beyond the mews spilled between them. "It never amounted to much. I was bored. Edward was impossible. George Chase seemed amusing." Her fingers curled inwards and she felt a stitch give way in her glove. "I confess now I know what he had already done and what he did later, I shudder at the thought that I ever let him touch me. By the time I met Cordelia, George was off in Malta, and he was out of Cordelia's life and mine. There seemed no need to tell Cordy and dredge up those memories."

"No. Obviously not."

"And as for telling you—"

"My darling." Julien lifted a hand and tucked a curl beneath her hat. "We've always agreed we wouldn't tell each other everything. If we recited the names of everyone both of us had been entangled with, it would only be tedious. And Chase seemed to be in the past."

"But now he isn't."

"No." Julien paused at the end of the mews and turned to face her. "Had you heard from him since he went to Malta?"

"No." Kitty stared at him. "You do believe me, don't you?"

"I don't see any reason not."

"That's my Julien. Don't make declarations when rational calculation will do."

"Don't make declarations the other person wouldn't believe."

Kitty scanned her husband's face. "Did you work with George Chase?"

"Once or twice as well." Julien tucked her arm closer to his, and they started walking again. "Or perhaps I should say our paths crossed. The first time I was in disguise as a *guerrillero* and working for the French. The second time I was myself and handing off some information I'd acquired on the French that I'd agreed to give to Carfax. Uncle Hubert. And no, we didn't. I don't think he'd have been interested. Though I confess I didn't ask."

"I don't know whether I'm relieved or envious that you don't know what it is to feel my distaste."

"I confess there are lovers in my past I think back on unhappily. I wouldn't be happy to have been entangled with Chase."

"Precisely." Kitty studied his face from the side. "Had you heard from him recently?"

"I saw him once in Naples not long after I got back from the Argentine. But we didn't work together." Julien returned her gaze. "I was with Malcom when Chase was killed, Kitkat. I was the one who heard the shout of murder. I can do a lot, but I don't see how I could have got from the House of Lords chamber, stabbed someone in the crowd on the stairs, and got back to Malcolm by the time Mélanie reached the body. Which can only have been seconds."

"No. I know, dearest."

"But you wonder."

"Because you could have done it. And not many people could. And because, I suppose—"

"You wonder even if I didn't, if I might have done."

"He's a beastly threat to Harry and Cordy."

"True enough. I wouldn't have been happy if I'd known he was back in Britain. To put it mildly." Julien's gaze stayed on her face, unwavering as a sword's point in the candlelight. "And yes, I'd have wanted to protect Harry and Cordy. It seems to be my impulse when it comes to my friends. Odd in a man who until a couple of years ago would have denied even the idea of having friends. But now that I admit to having them, I confess to being distinctly protective. Though as to what I'd have done, how far I'd have gone—I can't really say. George Chase's death doesn't seem to have solved things, it seems to have raised new problems."

Kitty tightened her grip on his arm. "I love you."

"But you aren't sure."

"Would you really expect me to be? If I was sure, it would mean I didn't really know you."

"A fair point, sweetheart." Julien stopped walking and pressed a kiss to her forehead beneath the brim of her bonnet. "Neither of us may be sure of my possible actions, but I'm quite sure Harry wouldn't kill George Chase. No matter the circumstances. Not unless Chase was about to kill someone else."

Kitty pictured Harry Davenport's face every time George Chase was mentioned. The ironic twist of his mouth, the deliberately matter-of-fact tone of his voice. The careful effort to hide roiling emotions that even a master of sarcastic control like Harry Davenport couldn't quite pull off. "Can you really be sure of that, Julien? If we've learned nothing else, haven't we learned we can't be sure of anyone?"

Julien tugged her hat into place where he'd knocked it askew. "Perhaps not. But I seem to have come to the remarkable point where I at least have to believe in my friends."

Honoria Talbot Atwood lived in an elegant cream sandstone house in Upper Brook Street. The liveried footman recognized them at once and showed them upstairs to Honoria's drawing room without first taking up their cards.

Honoria got to her feet as her footman showed Kitty and Julien into her drawing room. She was, as always (or at least all the times Kitty had seen her), impeccably gowned, today in a blue cashmere wrapping gown that just matched her eyes, fastened with pearl clasps over a paler blue silk slip. Pearls gleamed at her ears and round her throat. Her smooth, pale gold hair was dressed simply, with ringlets escaping round her face. The overall effect echoed the classical medallions embossed on the pale blue walls of the room.

Kitty had met her husband's cousin a handful of times. At their first ball when they moved into Carfax House last summer, on an outing to Somerset House, at the theatre, once when Honoria called and Kitty had to receive her without her husband. Once more in this house when Kitty had returned the call. She might be her own type of Lady Carfax, as she had warned Julien, but she played the social game to a degree.

"Julien. Kitty." Honoria walked forwards with her hands extended. "I despaired of seeing you until the trial was over. Do tell me you've come to share some diverting news."

"I'm sure you have more of the latest news than we do, cousin." Julien took Honoria's hand and kissed her cheek. "News always moves faster in Mayfair than in Westminster or Whitehall."

"Not these days." Honoria sighed and made a moue of frustration. "Atwood left for Westminster this morning before I had even finished my chocolate, and he hasn't so much as sent word about what happened, odious man. He's bound to be at Brooks's until the small hours. Husbands are so provoking."

"Being a husband now myself, I refuse to be drawn in."

"Don't be a wretch, Julien. You must have been in the chamber today."

"I was. And Kitty was in the gallery."

"You're so intrepid, Kitty," Honoria said with a smile that was at once self-deprecating and also managed to imply that Kitty was willing to step over lines no true lady would cross. Which was probably true. Depending on how one defined "lady."

"How much have you heard about what happened today?" Julien asked, as they all seated themselves by the unlit fireplace.

"Scarcely anything." Honoria reached for the teapot that already stood on a Wedgwood tray on the sofa table. "I've been home all day, and as I said, Atwood didn't send news and my only caller was Corisande Ossulston, who knew no more than I did. Was Brougham's speech as impressive as expected?"

"It was impressive," Julien said. "How many minds it changes remains to be seen. But we've come about something else. A man was murdered outside the chamber just after the House rose."

"Good god." Honoria's fingers froze on the delicate porcelain handle of the teapot. "Do they know who he was?"

"Yes, and you do as well. It was George Chase."

Honoria's blue eyes widened. "But he's in Malta."

"He was." Julien's voice was surprisingly gentle. "He'd come back."

"What a horrible tragedy." Honoria poured tea into the cups, snatched one up, and took a swallow. "Had Cordelia seen him?"

"She was there when he died," Kitty said. "So was I. Mélanie tried to save him, but it was too late."

Honoria set the cup down. "Mélanie—"

"She got him on the stairs. She has medical training. But he died within seconds."

"Do you know why he'd come back to England? I should have thought the scandal—" Honoria picked up a teacup as she spoke and held it out to Kitty, seeking refuge in the familiar ritual.

"We don't know precisely." Julien accepted a second cup of tea from Honoria and settled back on the sofa beside Kitty. "But he was asking a lot of questions. Among other things, about your father's death."

Honoria clunked her cup back in its saucer. "Why on earth—"

Julien took a sip of tea. "That would seem to be the question."

Honoria's eyes narrowed. "Julien, are you suggesting my father's death was other than what it seemed?"

Julien settled his cup in its saucer. "Do you have reason to think it was?"

"Of course not. I was a child at the time. And no one's ever suggested to me that it was. But you must have reasons for asking questions about it."

Julien took a drink of tea. "I'm sorry." His voice again turned uncharacteristically gentle. "I wouldn't have dredged it up if it weren't tangled with the murder."

"Darling Julien. Are you asking me to believe you, of all people, are solicitous?" Honoria dabbed at the tea spattered in her saucer.

"Perhaps it's for Kitty's benefit, though I didn't think the two of you played those games."

Julien shot a quick smile at Kitty, barely the slightest softening of his gaze. "We don't. But I don't much care for dredging up someone else's nightmare. I didn't even at my most cynical."

Honoria reached for the blue paisley shawl draped over the back of her chair and drew it round her shoulders. "Malcolm sent you because he thought you could get me to talk more easily, didn't he?"

Kitty held her tongue. There was no reason to think Honoria knew about her own relationship with Malcolm. Although the woman certainly had the instincts of a spy.

Julien set down his teacup and leaned forwards. His gaze was level and direct and disconcertingly kind, the way it could sometimes get. "We're cousins. There are all sorts of reasons you'd be more likely to talk to me."

Honoria glanced away. "It was so long ago. I wasn't anywhere near Dunmykel when it happened. Papa had left me at Alford. Malcolm was there too, along with Edgar, and Lady Frances's children, and Louisa Mitford's as well. Lady Arabella was there. Lady Frances was too, for a bit, but then she and Lady Mitford went off somewhere."

"They went to Dunmykel, as it happens," Julien said.

"Did they? I never knew that. But then, I wouldn't have done. No one talks to children about those sorts of details. In any case, Papa had left some time before."

"He left you a lot," Julien said.

Honoria reached for her tea and took a sip. "I don't mean to be an undutiful daughter, but yes. As parents do. I don't think he had the least idea what to do with a baby when my mother died. Not that my mother necessarily would have done either. I mean, one does tend to rather leave that sort of thing to the nursemaids, doesn't one? They know so much better."

"I wouldn't know," Kitty said, squeezing lemon into her tea. "I had to get by without nursemaids for so long."

"You poor thing. I don't know where I'd be without my nursemaids. Thank goodness you have a proper staff at Carfax House now."

"Quite," said Kitty, who still didn't have a nursemaid and kept the children next to her and Julien's room rather than in the Carfax House nursery that was upstairs and seemed miles away. She was redoing it as a sitting room for the staff.

"I suppose in a way I don't want to talk about it," Honoria said. "I'm prevaricating, which isn't like me. In any case, I was far away when Papa died, and the first I knew that anything had gone wrong was when Uncle Frederick arrived in the middle of the night."

"The night your father died?" Julien asked.

"Yes. He got my nursemaid to wake me up and bring me into the day nursery. I can still remember Uncle Frederick kneeling in front of me and hugging me as though he'd never let me go. I remember being very confused because Uncle Frederick had never paid much attention to me. Even when he told me my father was gone, I didn't entirely understand it. I just stood there and then I started crying and my nurse had to take me away. Uncle Frederick kept saying he'd take care of me. The next morning, he was gone and it almost seemed like a dream. My nurse told me my father was dead, but it scarcely seemed real. Eventually Uncle Frederick came back and took me to live with him. My nurse went with us, so my life didn't change that much. Except that I had to put up with Quen and Val." She looked at Kitty. "Uncle Frederick's sons. And then he brought Evie to keep me company."

"Evie?" Kitty asked.

"Evelyn Mortimer, my cousin. Her mother is my father and Uncle Frederick's sister. She—my Aunt Georgiana—made an unfortunate marriage and had a passel of children, so Uncle Frederick took Evie in, to help his sister out. And to give me company, I suppose."

"That must have made things less lonely in the Glenister House nursery," Kitty said.

"Oh, yes. It was kind of him. Though Evie and I aren't much alike. But we rubbed along."

"As I heard it, Evie was quite good at running your errands," Julien said.

Honoria smoothed the fringe on her shawl. "Evie is sweet. She just never had my taste for society. She's quite happy now, I think, married to her clergyman in the wilds of Northumberland."

"I thought I heard it was Durham." Julien reached for his cup.

"Just as remote either way. They're in London now to see his parents. Evie came to see me yesterday and we talked about the past, because we have so little in common in the present."

"Did Glenister ever talk about your father's death?"

"I was three."

"Later."

Honoria drew her shawl up about her shoulders. "Actually, he seemed to go out of his way to avoid it. For a man so given to scandal, he's always been quite protective of Evie and me. It was years before I fully realized what had happened. I vaguely thought Papa had fallen off his horse and broken his neck, I suppose because one hears about riding accidents, though it didn't make sense that that happened in the middle of the night. Eventually Val let slip it had been an accident with his gun. I suppose they were playing some sort of horrid shooting game and were all three sheets to the wind. At least, that's what I always thought." She looked between Julien and Kitty. "If not that, what? I know you all investigate murders now, but surely you don't think my father was murdered. I mean, there were others there when he died. Uncle Frederick was there, and Alistair Rannoch and Archie Davenport, I think."

"Were they actually in the room?" Julien asked.

"Well, they must have been. If they were playing a shooting game, Papa wouldn't have been alone."

"But do you actually know they were playing a shooting game?" Julien asked.

"What else could it have been? He was shot in the middle of the night at Dunmykel. I know you were an agent, but surely you don't think someone broke into the house and killed my father. And if they had, why keep it a secret? Uncle Frederick was devastated. I remember that clearly enough from childhood. If someone had killed Papa, I'm sure Uncle Frederick would have wanted to find out who."

"But you don't know that your uncle saw your father die?"

Honoria's brows drew together. "Not for a certainty, no. I told you, Uncle Frederick didn't like to talk about it. I mean, I can't imagine talking about such a thing with my children. One wants to shield them. I may not fuss as a mother, but I do want that. The truth is I scarcely knew Papa. He was away much of the time, and when he was in the same house he didn't do more than make a daily visit to the nursery. If that. It's not expected of fathers the way it is with mothers. I always go up after breakfast, but gentlemen don't do that sort of thing. Uncle Frederick seems far more like my father now."

"Understandable," Julien said. "He raised you." He took another careful drink of tea. "Did George Chase ever ask you about your father?"

"George Chase? Good heavens, I scarcely knew him. I danced with him a few times, but he'd hardly have been so ill-bred as to ask me about my dead father. Or so unkind. George certainly had his flaws. But he was never unkind. That is—"

"I know what you mean," Julien said.

Honoria smoothed her shawl over her shoulders. "I'm sorry. I wish I could help you more. I confess I'd quite like to assist in an investigation. But even though it's my father, it's really very little to do with me."

"I understand," Julien said. "Do tell us if you remember more."

They left the house shortly after, after finishing their tea, asking after Honoria's sons, and replying to questions about their own children. As they descended the steps outside, Kitty tucked her hand through Julien's arm. "It's understandable she doesn't have a lot of information to share. She was only three and Cyril Talbot doesn't sound like a very engaged parent."

"No," Julien agreed.

"But I can't help but feel—"

"That Honoria's holding something back?" At the base of the steps, Julien turned his head and met Kitty's gaze. "No, neither can I. The question is what?"

CHAPTER 13

$\mathcal{M}$ alcolm first sought Henry Brougham at Brooks's, but William Lamb, whom he met on the stairs, said Brougham wasn't at the club and was probably with the queen.

"Is it about the murder?" William asked. "I heard it was George Chase."

"News travels fast. Yes, it was. We still don't know what he was doing in England." Malcolm thanked William and hurried off, without delving into the fact that William's brother had been watching the house where Chase was staying and had seen his wife and Brougham going into it. Time enough for that when he had some answers from Brougham.

Queen Caroline was staying at Brandenburgh House, a villa on the Thames in Hammersmith. The government had not granted her a royal residence when she returned to England in June. Richard Keppel Craven, who had briefly been one of her chamberlains, had persuaded his mother, the former Lady Elizabeth Berkeley, to give the queen the use of Brandenburgh House. Lady Elizabeth was no stranger to scandal herself. She had lived at Brandenburgh House with her second husband, the Margrave of

Brandenburgh Anspach, after she was divorced from Keppel Craven's father. She was also a playwright, like Malcolm's own wife.

Malcolm had been to call on the queen with Brougham several times, but he more than half expected to be denied admittance when he gave his card to the footman. However after only a short interval, he was shown into a sitting room where the queen was closeted with Brougham.

Caroline of Brunswick, the uncrowned, unhappy Queen of England, greeted Malcolm with a smile. She wore a gray gown with a high ruff and her dark hair tumbled over her shoulders. Her color was high beneath her the bright rouge on her cheeks. "Mr. Rannoch. I understand I owe you and your clever wife a great deal for Brougham's prowess today."

"Ma'am." Malcolm bowed. "My wife and I were happy to help, but the credit for today goes to Brougham. He was masterful."

"No need for flattery, Rannoch. Time enough for it later." *If we win*, Brougham's gaze said, though he didn't say it in front of the queen. "I still have to finish my opening tomorrow."

"Mr. Brougham has a way with words. But so does your wife. Brougham gave me her play to read. I wish I could have seen it performed. She has a keen understanding of the nuances of marriage. And of what a woman gives up."

"She'll be pleased to hear you say so, ma'am. I am eternally grateful she was willing to give up what she did to marry me." And the queen could not know the half of what his French-agent wife had given up, not to marry him but to stay in the marriage.

The queen laughed. "The world would be a better place if more husbands had your self-knowledge, Mr. Rannoch." Her eyes narrowed. "You didn't come here just to pay compliments or bask in reflected glory. I've heard about you. I suspect you know something about this unfortunate man who was killed at the end of the day's proceedings."

"News travels fast."

"I may not have been an expert at the game of public life when I married, Mr. Rannoch, but the years have forced me to acquire at least some expertise. I've heard about the unfortunate gentleman. A tragedy. I deeply regret that it happened on a day that had anything to do with me, little as I wished this trial to take place. I understand he was a gentleman known to Mr. Brougham and I suspect to you? A Major Chase?"

"Yes. He had been living abroad."

"As many of us have."

"In Major Chase's case, his exile from Britain was driven by his own actions."

The queen's brows heavily penciled brows drew together. "And that got him killed?"

"We aren't sure yet what got him killed."

"I trust it was nothing to do with my case. I never met the man."

"These days ma'am, your case has obsessed a number who have never met you."

"To many of whom I am very grateful. But I would not wish—" Queen Caroline drew a brisk breath. "You and Mrs. Rannoch are investigating this?"

"My wife was there when Major Chase was stabbed. We're assisting our friend Jeremy Roth of Bow Street."

"I would say how very unfortunate for Mrs. Rannoch, save that I suspect it is a very good thing for the investigation that she was there. Your children—"

"Our son was there. He's fine, as are our friends' children who were present. They didn't see anything too frightening. But for a number of reasons, we want this resolved as soon as possible."

The queen nodded. "I suspect you need to speak to Brougham in private. By all means, don't let me stand in your way."

Brougham flashed a quick smile at her, though Malcolm could see the tension that shot through him. "We won't be long, ma'am."

"Take the time you need. You've done what you can for today.

And for the sake of this poor man and the country in general, not to mention my case, this murder needs to be solved."

Brougham led Malcolm through a door in the white-and-gold paneling to a smaller sitting room with a writing desk overflowing with books and papers. Probably where he worked while visiting the queen. He closed the door with an audible click.

"What the devil is going on, Rannoch?"

"I'm sorry, Henry. I wouldn't have interrupted today of all days were it not urgent. But all other concerns aside, the murder investigation could become a distraction when we sorely need public opinion on our side."

"Granted." Brougham relaxed, leaning against the closed door. "And I should have said I realized you wouldn't interrupt without good cause." He folded his arms. "It's the devil of a thing to have happened. I thought Chase was in Sardinia. Or was it Sicily?"

"Malta. So did we all. But apparently he'd been in London for several weeks at least. And when he was killed, he was trying to get a message to Liverpool."

Brougham's gaze sharpened the way Malcolm had seen Raoul's do at a rustling or stir of movement in enemy terrain. "What about?"

"Important information relating to the trial, he claimed. There were no papers on him and we couldn't find any papers relating to the trial in the rooms he'd rented. They were in Wardour Street." Malcolm paused, studying Brougham's face for a reaction. He thought he caught a telltale trace, but Brougham was skillful enough it was hard to be sure. Brougham was a politician and lawyer, after all.

"Does Wardour Street mean anything to you?"

"I think I've been to a pub there. They had a decent brown ale. Other than that—no. Should it?"

"You were seen going into the house where George Chase had lodgings."

Brougham's brows snapped together. "The devil I was. Who said so?"

Malcolm hesitated, but there was no way to keep names out of this. "George Lamb. He was following his wife. Who was with you."

Brougham spun away, stalked across the room, and slammed his hand down on a pier table. A silver vase thudded to the floor, spilling water and Michaelmas daisies onto the floorboards and carpet. "Damnation. For a man who is seemingly bloodless with his wife, he can be like a ferret with jealousy. I wouldn't have guessed he'd go so far, though."

"What were you and Caro doing in Wardour Street?"

"What the hell do you think?" Brougham snatched up the daisies and jammed them back in the vase. "Damn it, Malcolm, I'm not going to say more. There's a lady's reputation at stake. It was stupid. It was unpardonable, in fact. But I've always been fond of Caro. It's been hell these past weeks. No rest from the trial. Sometimes one just wants a few moments of escape with someone who understands and won't pressure you about witness or strategy or who did what to whom when. As a gentleman, that's all I'm going to say."

"Why Wardour Street?"

"A friend had rooms there he wasn't using. He gave me the use of them."

"The porter said there was only one other lodger."

"My friend's been in the country for months. Probably the porter doesn't count him as a lodger. It seemed an anonymous place to go."

"In the middle of the afternoon?"

"Don't turn Puritan, Rannoch. In the middle of the afternoon Caro could say she was going to her dressmaker's."

"But you walked in together in broad daylight."

"We didn't think anyone was following us."

"Did you see George Chase?"

"Of course not."

"What about the other lodger in the house? A soldier's widow, recently come from France. Or so she claims. She sounded more Italian to Harry and me."

Brougham tugged a handkerchief from his pocket, threw it on the spilled water, and rubbed it over the floorboards with his foot. "We didn't see anyone. If we had, I'd have been more on my guard."

Malcolm folded his arms across his chest and regarded his friend and colleague. "That's a good story, Henry. On the spur of the moment, from a non-spy. It has the ring of truth, and it's clearly rooted in truth. And I don't believe a word of it."

"You jump at shadows, Rannoch. You're too much of a spy."

"If I jump at shadows, it's because I'm used to moving in them. And finding things there." Malcolm studied Brougham. "The truth has a way of coming out, Henry. And I can do more to help you if I know now."

Brougham snatched up the sodden handkerchief, stared at it, and stuffed it in his pocket. "I didn't kill anyone."

"I never suggested you did."

"And if I did, you'd be the last person to help cover it up."

"That's very true. Though not exactly reassuring."

"Damn it, Malcolm." Brougham moved forwards, hands clenched at his sides. "You know what's at stake. We got a step closer today. But it's still a long fight. We can't afford distractions."

"I'm trying to head off a distraction."

"You might be making it worse. Surely there are things you don't even trust Mélanie with."

"Any number." Malcolm kept his voice light. Brougham knew him well, but he didn't know Mélanie had been a French agent.

"Then accept there are things I can't trust you with. For your own sake."

"Forgive me if I don't think my sake has anything to do with this. Or should."

Brougham held Malcolm's gaze, then shook his head. "You aren't going to let it go, whatever I say. You aren't going to believe me, whatever I say. Even if I just told you the truth."

"The one thing I'm sure of," Malcolm said, "is that you just told me a lie."

～

"To think I thought London had had enough scandal." Lady Frances Davenport set down her teacup. "Not to mention that we'd had enough drama in the family and had enough things to worry about. I suppose there's something to be said for outside drama offering a welcome distraction."

She looked from Mélanie to Harry to Cordelia to Raoul. They had all called together on Frances and her husband Archie, Harry's uncle. Archie, who was an MP, had been in the gallery for Brougham's opening, but had left to return home before the news of George's death had spread through the palace. They had heard through one of their footmen, who had it from the underhouse-maid across the street, that there had been a murder but did not yet know who the victim was.

Mélanie reached for the tea Frances had poured, aware that they were all existing for a few moments in a make-believe world where this was some sort of outside danger and scandal. Some-thing to be investigated, something perhaps tragic, but not personal to them. She took a sip of the delicately scented tea and then told Frances and Archie about the man being stabbed and falling in front of them, and how she'd tried to save him. Cordelia added the fact that it was George, as though that was something she needed to say for herself.

"Oh, my dear." Frances reached across the table to squeeze Cordelia's hand. Archie gave Cordelia an encouraging smile. He was Harry's uncle, but he'd been very supportive of Cordelia during the time she and Harry were apart.

"Thank you," Cordelia said. "It was a shock. But it's got even more complicated."

They went on to describe the rest of the day's revelations, as quickly and succinctly as possible. Until they got to Beverston's revelation that George Chase had asked him about the night Cyril Talbot died.

Fanny's hand closed on the silver filigree locket she wore on a blue velvet ribbon round her throat. Her faced stilled as though her features had turned to marble. Archie continued to lean back in a corner of the sofa, but his eyes, the same piercing blue as Harry's, held the weight of a revelation. As though a lid had been ripped off to reveal the truth beneath. And what had settled in the depths of his gaze wasn't so much shock as the acknowledgement of a reckoning long coming.

Fanny turned her head and met her husband's gaze. "We haven't talked about it."

"No," he said. "We weren't on terms to do so at the time. And it seemed to be in the past. Foolish to think that about anything."

"I still remember arriving at Dunmykel that day with Louisa," Fanny said. "It was a mad start, but we were bored at Alford and we wanted some sort of diversion. And I wanted to see what Alistair was getting up to. I didn't understand what the League were at the time, but I knew these house parties were secret. I confess I more than half expected to find Cyprians lounging about in various states of undress, or a full-fledged orgy in progress."

"You might have, on another occasion," Archie said.

"Yes, so I gather. Instead, the gentlemen were playing billiards or drinking port in the library. The same dull activities my husband got up to. Considering how commonplace it all was, it was odd how shocked Alistair appeared to be to see us. He looked daggers at me, but of course it was my sister's home and he couldn't very well turn us away. We were shown to rooms, and as I dressed for dinner I was already regretting the excursion. Instead of titillating, it was proving tedious. I said that to Louisa before we went downstairs. Yes, I know that sounds horrid considering what happened, but I had no idea of what the night would hold. It was an awkward dinner, to say the least. But I don't remember Frederick and Cyril quarreling, particularly. Any more than the usual between brothers. They were both dipping rather deep. Everyone was. But Cyril in particular could barely stand straight when Louisa and I left the drawing room to go upstairs."

"It happened much later," Archie said. "After you'd gone to bed."

Fanny stared at him. "Somehow I never thought—Of course, you were there. But I didn't realize how much you'd seen. And we never—"

"We never talked about it," Archie finished for her. "As we said, we weren't lovers then. We weren't confidants. We weren't even close friends." He stretched out his bad leg, the one that made him need a walking stick, though it didn't really slow him down when it came to action. "I haven't ever told anyone, as it happens." He looked at Raoul. "You were in Ireland. Arabella was worried about the situation in Ireland. Worried about you. And it seemed—it was personal, from all I could tell. Which is an odd thing to say about anything to do with the League. I suppose—it seemed like a betrayal of Glenister's confidence. Which I realize sounds absurd, considering I was spying on him."

"If you think spies don't worry about betraying the people they're spying on, you haven't been listening all these years," Raoul said.

Archie's gaze locked on Raoul's for a long moment. The two had been allies for decades, against the League and in the service of revolutionary forces in Ireland and France. "A point. In truth, I think part of the reason I never spoke of it was that it was so hard to make sense of the events of that night. Fanny's right, we were all dipping deep. And Cyril more than any of us. He always liked his claret and brandy—anything with alcohol in it—but I'd never seen him toss drinks back quite so steadily. It wasn't particularly pleasant to observe. Like Fanny, I began to find the whole evening rather tedious. In truth, for a long time I'd found League events tedious, but there seemed little likelihood I'd uncover any information of interest that night. Which would have been the only reason to stay up, and the only thing to keep me engaged. I took a book and went upstairs."

"Who was still up when you left?" Mélanie asked.

"Alistair, Glenister, and Cyril. Beverston had already gone up. So had Trenchard."

"I might have known he'd have been there too." Raoul's fingers whitened round the arm of his chair. For all his control, his temper came close to snapping at any mention of Laura's former lover, who had blackmailed her for years and kept Emily from her.

"He was usually at League gatherings in those days," Archie said. "I never cared for him, though I didn't have the reasons I now do to loathe him. Harleton was there too. And Dewhurst."

"All the usual suspects," Harry said.

"Quite." Archie nodded at his nephew. "As I recall, I went to my room and started a letter to you. It wasn't much more than half an hour later that Alistair came hammering on my door and insisted I come downstairs. He said they needed a third man if it was to have even the vaguest trappings of an affair of honor."

The words settled over the room, shifting the image of what had happened at Dunmykel the night Cyril Talbot died into an entirely different key.

"Archie, are you saying Alistair shot Cyril in a drunken parody of a duel?" Fanny demanded.

"No," Archie said. "Alistair was one of the seconds. I was the other. Glenister shot Cyril."

CHAPTER 14

"Good god." Fanny's fingers froze on the handle of her teacup. "I mean—I'd never have said Glenister and Cyril were particularly close, but they never—What on earth was the duel over?"

"I don't know," Archie said. "Alistair didn't offer details. He took me out on the lawn where Glenister and Cyril were. I can still see it. Arabella's flower gardens were spread below in the moonlight. Glenister's face was white with rage and his hands were fisted at his sides. Cyril could barely look him in the eye."

"Who issued the challenge?" Raoul asked.

"Glenister," Archie said. "Alistair was his second. I was Cyril's. I went over to Cyril and said surely we could put an end to this. Couldn't he just apologize to his brother. Cyril was swaying on his feet, but he looked at me quite steadily and said no apology could atone for this." Archie's gaze clouded with the memories. "I said something like, 'My dear fellow, don't be so dramatic, he's your brother.' Cyril said, 'That's the problem.'"

Archie gave a long sigh, gaze on the blue medallions in the carpet as though they were a portal to the past. "I can't tell you how many times I've wondered what more I could have done to stop it. When I couldn't make headway with Cyril, I tried to remonstrate with Glenister. He dealt me a right hook and gave me a bloody nose. I wrapped my cravat round my nose and told Alistair we couldn't let them do this. Alistair said they weren't going to let it go, and it would be worse if we simply left them to it. He was checking the pistols at the time. He showed them to me. I checked them, because that's what one does. God, the idiocy of thinking we shouldn't interfere with an affair of so-called honor. I'd have said I knew how hollow that was. But a part of me still followed instincts that are more ingrained than I'd admit."

"Castlereagh and Canning risked their careers over a duel," Fanny said. "When they were secretary of state for war and foreign secretary. I suppose we shouldn't be surprised Glenister and Cyril risked their lives, especially drunk."

"When they turned and started pacing, I realized they were actually going through with it. I tried to run between them," Archie said. "Alistair pulled me back. I told myself they wouldn't actually shoot each other. Cyril deloped. Glenister's arm was shaking. I'm still not sure if he meant to shoot Cyril or not. But Cyril fell. Glenister rushed over and dropped down beside Cyril. I ran after. When I got to them, Cyril was saying, 'Take care of her.' And Glenister said, 'Of course I will.'"

"Who?" Mélanie asked.

"I don't know, but I assume Cyril meant his daughter."

Fanny looked at Archie. She'd been studying him throughout his account of the duel as if he were a familiar book that she had suddenly discovered contained a code. Mélanie had gut-twisting memories of Malcolm's looking at her in the same way when he first learned she'd been a spy. "What did Alistair say about it?" Fanny asked her husband after a moment.

Archie's gaze moved over Fanny's face. In his blue gaze, Mélanie could see the spouse warring with the spy. The constant struggle they all faced. "That it was Glenister's tragedy and we should stay out of it. Glenister would punish himself enough. Oddly, it's one of the few times I've had the sense Alistair was telling the unvarnished truth. He looked—shaken. I don't think I've ever seen Alistair shaken from his moorings before or since."

"I remember the commotion," Fanny said. "I heard it and woke and went out in the passage and then down to the hall. Everyone was milling about. Glenister was demanding a horse to go see Honoria. All Alistair would say to me was to give him time."

"Do you think Alistair knew what the duel was about?" Raoul asked.

"Yes," Archie said. "I'm quite sure of it. I almost had the feeling he felt he'd let things go too far."

"Odd," Fanny said. "I felt as though he blamed himself as well. He didn't want to talk about it, which isn't surprising. But I could tell how disturbed he was. I said something about how he couldn't blame himself for Cyril's drunken idiocy and he snapped, 'You don't know the half of it.' Then he said he was sorry, he was in no fit state to talk about anything. Which was also surprising. Alistair didn't often apologize. In fact, I'm not sure I can think of another time he apologized to me."

"Alistair seduced Glenister's wife," Harry said. "And got her with child. A child who is Glenister's heir. And Glenister didn't challenge Alistair to a duel. In fact, he kept up the appearance of being friends with Alistair for decades. So one rather wonders what pushed him over the edge with his brother."

"There can be a lot of baggage between brothers," Raoul said. "Glenister may have been driven by more than whatever set him off that night."

"Frederick and Cyril were always rivals," Fanny said. "The way many brothers are. Not—"

"The way Edgar and Malcolm were?" Mélanie asked. She knew enough now to say that about her husband and his late brother, though it still felt as though she was treading on ground that wasn't hers. "At least, not on the surface."

"No," Fanny agreed, without evading the painful past. "Malcolm and Edgar wanted different things in life. Frederick and Cyril both wanted to be the best. At riding, at driving, with cards. With women." She hesitated.

"I'd never ask," Archie said, "but—"

"With both of them, briefly," Fanny said. "Hardly enough to give me insights."

"Could you be—" Mélanie swallowed. Even in the midst of the investigation, even as frank as all of them were, she couldn't quite say it.

"I very much doubt it," Fanny said. "It wasn't serious enough with either of them for them to have quarreled over me. One can never know what is in another's mind, but I'd be shocked if I mattered more to either of them than a passing fancy."

Mélanie thought of herself as broadminded and of her own past as scandalous, but she would never fully understand the depths of the Glenister House Set's or Devonshire House Set's intrigues. Perhaps she was far more commonplace than she tended to think.

"So," Cordelia said. "What was the duel about? And how did George think it could bring down Alistair?"

Archie shook his head. "I can't answer either one. One could say Alistair should have stopped it. But if not stopping one's friends from dueling could bring about a person's downfall, half the League would be disgraced. I came in at the end. The quarrel was most definitely between the two brothers, from what I could see. Alistair was a spectator. And not happy about the quarrel, from what I could tell. And as I said, genuinely concerned for Glenister. Which from Alistair is saying a lot."

"Why do you think he chose you as the other second?" Harry said.

Archie met his nephew's gaze. "I've asked myself that. Because even then I wouldn't say he completely trusted me. But I think perhaps he trusted me to keep quiet about this. Trusted me not to gossip about personal tragedy."

"Which argues that it was personal," Harry said.

"Quite. Of course, I suspect he also thought I was the least drunk of all the other League members in the house."

"Did he say anything to you about it afterwards?" Mélanie asked. "Did Glenister?"

Archie shook his head. "Alistair came over to Glenister and me when we were bent over Cyril. He looked at me and said, 'Cyril had an accident with his gun.' I nodded. When we left the lawn, there was a tacit agreement we wouldn't speak of it again." He looked at Fanny. "Did he say anything to you?"

Fanny took a quick drink of tea, as though to fortify herself. "Only once. Louisa and I stayed to help with the funeral details and to see Cyril buried the next day. Glenister was back by then, but he seemed to have retreated into himself. When I offered my condolences, he looked as though I'd tormented him somehow. Which makes sense, now I know what happened. That evening, Alistair and I—spent the night together."

"Understandable, in the circumstances," Archie said in an easy voice.

"We didn't talk much at all. But at one point I said something about the tragedy and he said, 'I couldn't have stopped it. I'm quite sure I couldn't have stopped it. But I should have seen it coming.'"

"So he knew what it was about, as Archie thought," Raoul said. "And it was something that went back a long time."

"Yes," Fanny said. "But they'd all known each other since university."

"A quarrel about a woman they were rivals for?" Cordelia asked. "But I don't see why it would have suddenly provoked a fight that particular night. Unless Glenister had learned something new."

"Precisely," Fanny said. "But when Alistair was so insistent that he couldn't have stopped it—I'm quite sure that on some level he thought he should have been able to."

"I still don't see why that would make George think the truth could destroy Alistair," Cordelia said. "I doubt it would even destroy Glenister if the truth came out. Not after all these years and not without proof. Though it would be very painful for him. And for Quen and Val and Evie and especially Honoria."

Frances set down her tea. "Has anyone talk to Honoria?"

"Julien and Kitty are there now," Mélanie said.

Frances picked up the teapot. "That's good. Julien's much more clear-eyed when it comes to Honoria than Malcolm is." She began to refill the teacups. "You have no cause for alarm, my dear. I think a part of Malcolm is quite aware of Honoria's games. But he's too chivalrous to fight back. Raoul was afraid he'd marry her once."

"Not precisely," Raoul said. "I didn't think it would go that far. But if it did, it didn't seem likely to make either of them happy."

Mélanie took a careful sip of tea. "In this, she's nothing but a victim." Which of course would only make Malcolm more concerned for her.

AFTER TAKING an inconclusive leave of Brougham and a more cordial leave of the queen, Malcolm went from Hammersmith to Clarges Street, where his former spymaster, Hubert Mallinson, once Earl Carfax, now lived. An elegant terrace house, but far smaller than Carfax House from which Hubert had orchestrated British intelligence operations for a quarter century. Including the years Malcolm had worked for him. To Malcolm's shame. Carfax House now belonged to Julien since his resurrection from being thought dead. Leaving aside the fact that Hubert had known he was alive the whole time and had been blackmailing Julien into spying for him.

A great deal had changed, but Hubert's centrality to British intelligence had not. With everything that happened this day, Malcolm was afraid he wouldn't find Hubert at home, but not only did he find Hubert in his study, Julien was already there as well.

"Oh, Malcolm, good," Hubert said. "We were wondering when you'd get here."

"I was afraid I wouldn't find you here. I almost went to White's."

"Why on earth would I have gone to White's?" Hubert asked. "I'd only get caught up in a lot of analysis with no substance and too many jokes in poor taste. I have better ways to spend my time."

"I just got here as well," Julien said. "Though I almost looked for Uncle Hubert at Westminster."

"I left immediately after the closing. But you think I've slipped more than I truly have if you think I wouldn't have heard about the murder immediately."

"You're more dangerous than ever, Uncle."

"I heard the news before I got home, but I thought it would be easiest for you both to find me here."

"Did you know George Chase was in London?" Julien asked.

Hubert sat back in his chair. "If I had, don't you think I'd have warned all of you?"

"Not necessarily." Julien pushed aside a stack of papers and perched on the edge of his uncle's desk. "Especially if he was working for you."

"God in heaven, Julien. The man was responsible for Julia Ashton's death. And for Amy's. Can you imagine I'd employ him or even converse with him, after what he's done?"

Julien moved a silver paperweight onto the ink blotter. "Yes. You're the ultimate in putting the objective before personal considerations."

"There are limits, even for me. And more to the point, Chase wasn't to be trusted. Morals aside, neither of you would have employed him either."

"A fair point," Malcolm said.

Julien inclined his head. "Granted. Which brings us to the next question. Did you have him killed?"

Hubert pushed his spectacles up on his nose. "I won't pretend I haven't wished George Chase dead any time these past five years. I won't even deny I've considered arranging his death. More than once. But why in god's name would I wait all this time only to suddenly do so now?"

"Because of whatever bought him to London." Malcolm advanced into the room, hooked a chair with his foot, and dropped down in front of the desk.

"Which is what?" Carfax inquired.

"We were hoping you could tell us."

"I had no notion Chase was in London until I heard he'd been found dead. If I had known—" Hubert tugged at one of his spectacle earpieces. "Killing in revenge can be satisfying, but it's an unproductive indulgence that doesn't really resolve anything. Eliminating a potential threat on the other hand is sometimes necessary. If I'd known Chase was in London and what he was up to, I might have been behind his death. And I'd probably admit it now, because there isn't a great deal either of you could do, and I doubt either of you is sorry enough he's dead to try to bring me to justice. But I didn't know he was here."

"He was trying to see Liverpool," Malcolm said. "He claimed he had information that could impact the trial."

Hubert's brows snapped together. "Did he?"

"Not on him. But a young woman who'd become his mistress claims he actually had the information."

Hubert frowned. "He might have done. Chase had gone to Italy."

"You were having him watched," Julien said.

Hubert spread his hands on the tooled leather ink blotter. "Obviously. From the moment he left Brussels. He was a threat. Not because of Lady Julia's and Amy's murders. Though a man who's killed twice might do so again. Because he was a former agent with no need to be loyal any longer, and very little left to live for."

"He appears to have been trying to restore his reputation," Malcolm said. "And using blackmail to do so. He was also working for the League." He updated Hubert on their discoveries of the day. Almost all of them, which was unusual.

Hubert listened with the same neutral gaze with which he'd always assessed Malcolm's intelligence briefings. "Interesting. Not surprising he tangled with the League, though I confess I didn't see it."

"You were watching Chase but didn't know he was working with Alistair?" Julien said.

"Obviously." Hubert sat back with his hands on the desk. "I didn't know Alistair was alive until a few days ago."

"So you've told us," Julien said.

"Don't waste time seeing conspiracies that aren't there, Julien," Hubert said. "We have enough real conspiracies to confront."

Malcolm sat forwards in his chair. "What does Fortinbras mean to you?" He'd kept the word back until he could use it on its own, for maximum effect.

Hubert's fingers froze reaching for the coffee cup beside his ink blotter. "Where did you hear that?"

"I saw it on a piece of paper in George Chase's rooms."

Hubert took a drink of coffee. "Interesting."

"So you have heard of it?" Julien said.

"It's a code name."

"For someone in the League?" Malcolm asked.

"I don't think so." Hubert set the cup down and curled his hands round the arms of his chair. "It's an agent who goes back to far before the League. To before I was active in intelligence. It's a code name from the 1760s. For a highly placed British agent."

"Who?" Julien asked.

"I told you, I don't know. It was before I was active. Desolated as I am to disillusion you, Julien, I wasn't running intelligence networks at Harrow."

"I wouldn't put it past you. But more to the point, agents don't simply stop being agents," Julien said. "As we have cause to know. What was this Fortinbras doing by the time you were active in intelligence?"

"Not reporting to me."

Julien slapped a hand down on the stack of Hubert's papers he'd moved earlier. "Don't give me that, Uncle. I don't believe there was a moment once you had even dipped a toe into intelligence when you didn't have everyone's networks at your fingertips."

"Then you vastly overrate me. And underrate the creaky complications of intelligence. When I began, Benjamin Howland was running military intelligence along lines that might have worked a quarter century before. My first goal was to build up my own networks along lines I thought would be effective in the modern world. I was more focused on doing my own work separate from Howland and staying out of his way so he couldn't interfere with my networks than on learning the identities of his prized agents."

"So Fortinbras was a prized agent," Malcolm said.

"Apparently. Supposedly Fortinbras uncovered a French agent. Also long before I was in intelligence."

Malcolm calculated the dates. "But that would have been—"

"Well before the Revolution. In case you'd forgot, Britain's quarrels with France go back centuries before the Declaration of the Rights of Man."

"Who was the French agent?" Malcolm asked.

"I don't know that either."

Julien folded his arms across his chest. "There's a lot you conveniently don't know."

"My dear Julien. Sooner or later, you're going to have to grow up and see me for what I am."

"Ha."

Malcolm leaned forwards, hands resting on the desk. "George Chase was interested in Fortinbras now. Why?"

"Excellent question." Hubert tapped his fingers on the carved arms of his chair. "Chase tended to be interested in things that could benefit him. And presumably that was his point here. Especially given that he seems to have been gathering information on powerful people from what you say."

"If Fortinbras was a British agent and is no longer active, why would his identity be of such interest now?" Malcolm asked. "Are you sure there isn't a connection to the League?"

Hubert leaned back in his chair. "Much as you and your wife and your father and the rest of your friends may like to treat Shakespeare as your own private code, his plays have inspired numerous works of art and no doubt numerous agents."

"Point taken. Still."

"Fortinbras is an outsider who comes in and cleans up the mess everyone else leaves," Julien said. "Just saying."

"Not everyone may appreciate the nuances of the Bard's works so well," Hubert said. "But it's a point."

"It's an interesting code name," Malcolm said. "I always gave some thought to the ones I took. Even if it was just an effort to mislead people."

Hubert adjusted his spectacles. "The question then would be what Fortinbras was trying to mislead people about?"

"Who has Benjamin Howland's papers?" Malcolm asked.

"He apparently had the sense to burn them. I made inquiries after his death."

"Could there be anything official still left?"

Hubert shook his head. "God knows. The official army records are a mess. Which makes it hard to find anything. But also means things are written down that never should have been, and things that were written down and should have been burned are probably still moldering somewhere without anyone's having the wit to know how dangerous they are. Part of why I was happy to be able to separate my own operations from military intelligence. The Carfax title had its uses."

"You're welcome," Julien said.

"Don't be cheeky, lad. I'm better off being more anonymous now, for any number of reasons."

"So there could still be evidence about Fortinbras somewhere," Malcolm said.

"Possibly. But for god's sake, don't go off on a tangent after Fortinbras. Just because George Chase got it into his head Fortinbras is relevant doesn't mean he is. Fortinbras was already antiquated when I started in intelligence."

"Antiquated things can still be dangerous, Uncle." Julien picked up the silver paperweight and tossed it in his hand. "Some would call your whole worldview antiquated. And look at the damage it's done."

Hubert leaned back in his chair with an equable smile. "Or look at the damage it's prevented."

"You won't be able to turn the clock back forever. But that isn't the point of debate now." Julien clunked the paperweight down on the stack of papers he'd moved. "What do you know about Cyril Talbot's death?"

"Very little. I wasn't anywhere near Dunmykel at the time."

"You didn't have doubts? It was an Elsinore League party."

"And so Cyril's shooting himself in a drunken game made a great deal of sense."

"It wouldn't be the first time you've questioned the seemingly obvious explanation," Malcolm said.

Hubert picked up his pen and grimaced. "Cyril didn't make Susan very happy."

"Noticed that, did you?" Julien said.

Hubert shot a look at his nephew. "I may not put the emphasis you would like on the finer feelings, but I am not entirely deaf and blind to them."

"You've always been good at judging feelings when they can suit your purpose," Julien said. "Though you badly misjudged David for a long time. But I thought you were too busy saving the country from whatever or whomever you were afraid of at the moment to worry about anything as trivial as a sister's happiness."

Hubert turned the pen in his hands and frowned at the black streaks of ink on his fingers. "I'm not a complete monster, Julien. I may have paid far too little attention to my sister's marriage—and certainly I didn't pay enough to my daughters'—but I was aware of the complexities."

"Did you know Cyril was a League member when he married your sister?" Malcolm asked.

"I suspected it." Hubert dropped the pen and tented his hands together. "I confess I saw that as an advantage. Just as, to my shame, I later saw Mary's alliance with Trenchard as advantageous. I never suspected what the marriage would actually mean to either Susan or Mary. I like to think that if I had, I'd have intervened."

"Think?" Julien asked in a taut voice.

"My dear Julien. Surely you of all people realize we can never be entirely sure what we'd do in a hypothetical situation."

"My father says that same thing," Malcolm said.

"Not the first time O'Roarke and I have agreed. Or the last, I suspect."

"Susan," Julien said.

"She seemed happy about the marriage. In the way girls generally do. I remember watching Alistair and Glenister at the wedding breakfast and trying to get wind of what they were talking about. But all I got was some speculation about which opera dancer at the Haymarket had the best ankles and which horse to back at Ascot. I didn't see Susan again until some time after the wedding, but when I did, she seemed—subdued. Even then, I didn't give it a great deal of thought until—" Hubert broke off, frowning with uncharacteristic bemusement.

"What?" Malcolm said.

"A month or so before Honoria was born. I made some remark about remembering when Amelia and I were expecting our first. And Susan said she hadn't realized how rare what Amelia and I had was until she realized not all couples had it. I made some awkward brotherly remarks about how I was sure Cyril cared for her, and she just shook her head and said she'd never have Cyril's heart. She understood that now." Hubert tugged at the right earpiece of his spectacles. "I suspected Cyril had mistresses—I'd heard the talk—but something about the way Susan said it disturbed me more than I'd have expected. I kept wondering if I should say more to her. But I didn't see her alone again before she died giving birth to Honoria." He drew in and released his breath, gaze on the ink blotter. "I saw Cyril less after that."

"And when he died?" Malcolm said.

"I wondered what the hell they'd been up to at Dunmykel that night. I did wonder if it was possible someone else accidentally shot Cyril. But my imagination failed me at its being more."

"Did you ask Arabella?" Malcolm asked.

Hubert shot a look at him.

"It was when you were lovers," Malcolm said. "Julien knows. No reason to be squeamish."

Hubert settled back in his chair. "Arabella said she couldn't be sure what Alistair got up to at his League parties. But then she said when she saw him, he seemed more genuinely shaken than she'd have expected. Cyril wasn't a major player in the League or I might have asked more questions."

"You didn't get rid of him yourself, did you?" Julien said.

"I was in London. And there were witnesses."

"I thought you might have made an alliance with Alistair."

"Alistair and I have been opponents from university. And at the time, I was sleeping with his wife, as Malcolm so thoughtfully reminded me."

"That wouldn't stop you."

"It might have stopped Alistair."

"Did he know?" Malcolm asked.

"I'm not sure. But Alistair Rannoch is one of the few people I would not have considered an alliance with. As it was, I was less worried about how Cyril had met his death than worried about Honoria. Cyril had appointed Glenister her guardian, and I couldn't intervene, though Amelia and I did offer to take her."

"Watching Honoria grow up in the same household as Mary would have been interesting," Julien murmured.

Hubert gave a grunt of acknowledgement at the reference to his eldest daughter. "Given Glenister's lifestyle, I thought he might be quite pleased not to add to his nursery. But he was adamant that he owed it to his brother to raise Honoria. Amelia was horrified at the thought of Honoria's growing up in Glenister House, but I have to say Glenister seemed to take his responsibility to Honoria, and then to young Evie, quite seriously. She visited us, along with Evie, and I made sure to remind Glenister that I had to agree to any marriage Honoria made."

"According to everyone, Glenister was particularly devastated by Cyril's death," Malcolm said. "If Cyril was shot accidentally by someone else, do you think it could have been Glenister?"

"It's entirely possible," Hubert said. "Whatever they were all up to. Men in their cups have no business playing with guns. But that doesn't explain why George Chase was so interested. Even if he could have proved Glenister accidentally shot Cyril, no one would prosecute Glenister. I can't even see Glenister's paying to keep it secret."

"What if it was Alistair who accidentally shot Cyril?" Malcolm said. "What if that's why he decided he had to disappear?"

"Over twenty years later? Alistair wouldn't have paid for it any more than Glenister would. It wouldn't have cost more than embarrassment. Glenister's the only one who might have wanted to avenge Cyril, and Glenister presumably knew what happened." Carfax reached for his pen. "So does Archie Davenport, I would think. He's the one you should talk to."

Unease settled over Malcolm at the thought of what Mélanie and the others might have already learned. "We will."

CHAPTER 15

*C*ordelia pressed her hands to her eyes. "I'm a mess."

Mélanie moved to her friend's side and wrapped her arms round Cordelia's shoulders. They were back in Berkeley Square, where they had found Kitty returned from her visit to Honoria while Julien had gone to see Hubert Mallinson. Raoul and Harry had taken the children into the square garden. Partly because their parents would be out all evening, partly, Mélanie suspected from the look Harry had given her, so Cordelia could talk to her friends.

"It's no wonder," Mélanie said. "I'd be worried about you if you weren't."

"Yes, but I have to pull myself together for the children. Or else I have to tell them something's wrong." Cordelia turned in Mélanie's arms and dragged her hands from her face, leaving streaks of blacking below her eyes. "I don't know what's worse. Their knowing how bad things are, or my trying to keep it from them and their suspecting something's wrong."

Mélanie bit back a desperate laugh. "If you knew the times I've wondered that. And for a long time, before Malcolm learned the truth, I couldn't tell Colin and Jessica anything at all. I had to pretend everything was all right. I had to try to make myself believe it. Which actually worked some of the time. But I don't think it was very good for my health." She'd needed Raoul desperately to talk to in those days, but she wasn't quite ready to say so now.

"I tried to hide things from the boys when they were little," Kitty said from the sofa. "As they got older, I found myself telling them more and more. I never tried to hide my relationship with Julien, thank goodness. It would have been fiendishly hard to do. And probably pointless, because they always do seem to sense so much more than we tell them. But of course there are limits to what one can say."

Cordelia turned away, hands gripped together. "I have so many images running through my head. Julia lying dead in that cart. George the last day I saw him, claiming he'd done it—killed Julia and everything else—so we could be together." Her fingers closed on her elbows, digging into the blue lustring of her gown. "But then I remember other things. George helping me clamber up a tree. George picking strawberries for me. George asking me to waltz. George the night —"

"It's not surprising you're mourning him, Cordy," Mélanie said.

"But I hated him. I saw him for what he was *years* ago. What I felt for him was a sham. I hate myself for ever caring for him. What's left to mourn?"

"The person you thought he was," Laura said in a soft voice. She was sitting beside Kitty, both of them giving Mélanie and Cordelia space. They were all friends and had shared a great deal, but the bond between Mélanie and Cordelia went back to Waterloo, forged in the hell they had lived through during and after Quatre Bras and Waterloo itself.

"And maybe the person he actually was, at times," Kitty said. "To a degree. Just because you saw through him doesn't make those memories go away."

"I'll confess there's a way I mourned Trenchard," Laura said. "And I was never in love with him the way you were with George."

Cordelia dashed a hand across her eyes. "You'd think I'd have mourned him when I learned the truth."

"But now you know you'll never see him again."

"I never wanted to see him again."

"But this is more final," Kitty said. "It's different. He was such a part of your life it would be a wonder if you didn't mourn him."

Cordelia straightened her shoulders and folded her arms across her chest. "I can't let Harry know."

"Darling," Mélanie said. "I'm sure Harry knows. He's far too acute a judge of feelings. And he knows you far too well."

"It's one thing for him to know. It's another for me to admit it. After everything I've put him through—in some ways, I think he's only just actually begun to believe I love him as much as—more than I loved George. Oh, I know he knew I cared for him and we were happy. But I don't think he quite believed I could love him as freely as I loved George."

Images shot through Mélanie's mind. Raoul. Kitty. Arabella Rannoch. Laura, who was sitting by quietly. "I'm sure Harry realizes there are different types of love."

Cordelia turned to her with a gaze bruised within the smeared blacking. "Yes, but I don't think he believed mine for him was unconstrained. Perhaps not that I'd have been with him if it weren't for Livia and Waterloo and a hundred other things. There was no way for me to convince him. I was wise enough to see that. You know how ruthlessly dispassionate Harry is when it comes to looking at data. That extends beyond classical texts. But lately, I'd sensed something had shifted. That we'd moved beyond George. Now he's pushed his way in the middle of our lives again."

"It's beastly," Mélanie agreed. "But I do know that pretending George's death doesn't affect you will only make it worse. It won't convince Harry of anything and it will make you sick bottling everything up inside."

"Pot calling the kettle."

"What?"

Cordelia regarded Mélanie with a faint smile. "You've been bottling everything up inside for years."

"Well, yes, but I had to."

"Define 'had.'"

"I couldn't let Malcolm learn the truth."

Cordelia's gaze locked on Mélanie's own, filled with understanding but also fear. "And I don't want Harry to see this."

"I'm all for the idea that no one should have to share things they don't want to," Kitty said. "With anyone. And in my first marriage, keeping things from Edward was no problem." She frowned. "In fact, it would have been a distinct challenge if I'd wanted Edward to understand what I was feeling. But now that I'm in a more coherent marriage, I can say that Julien has a way of understanding things whether I want him to or not."

Cordelia tore her gaze away from Mélanie and looked at Kitty. "So you're saying there's no way I can escape this?"

"I'm afraid there isn't any escape for any of us."

Laura got to her feet and moved to the decanters. "Raoul frequently tries to sort things out in his own mind before he tells me. Which I understand. Between political secrets he can't share and past histories I wasn't a part of, it makes sense that he has to work out how much to tell me." She picked up a whisky decanter and poured four glasses. "But when he's deluding himself that I don't have the least idea of what he's wrestling with, and I'm trying to go along with the charade that I'm deluded, I often think it would be much simpler if he'd just admit what he was going through. At least the emotions involved, if not the facts."

"Point taken," Cordelia said, as Laura gave her a glass of whisky. "I just don't want to hurt Harry."

"Silence hurts," Mélanie said. "I've learned that the hard way."

"Harry's an adult," Kitty said. "If—"

She broke off as the door opened and her husband and Malcolm came into the room.

"Are we interrupting?" Malcolm asked. "Raoul and Harry are involved in a game of tag, but they said you were here."

"And desperate for news," Cordelia said with a bright smile.

"I'm afraid we don't have much." Julien moved into the room and sat beside Kitty. "Fortinbras is apparently a code name."

He and Malcolm explained Hubert's information about Fortinbras, and then Mélanie, Cordy, and Kitty recounted their interview with Fanny and Archie. By the time they finished, Raoul and Harry had joined them, while Bet took the children to the kitchen for a snack.

Julien whistled. "Well, that explains the secrecy about the duel. But it makes even less sense that the truth could hurt Alistair."

Malcolm was frowning, and Mélanie could tell moments with his own brother were echoing in his mind. "We need to talk to Glenister. I actually find myself grateful we agreed to attend the Beverston masquerade. We have a number of people to talk to, and most of them will be there."

Mélanie took sip of whisky and held her glass out to her husband. "As I often say, society has its uses, darling. We need to talk to Caro George."

"She'll be at the Beverstons' tonight," Cordelia said. "Emily told me—yesterday, I think. It seems a century ago. Which I suppose means we should all be there."

"We can handle it if you don't want to go," Kitty said.

"You mean because everyone will be looking at me and talking behind my back?" Cordelia flashed a smile at her. "Fortunately, I'm quite used to that. And I used to have to do it without Harry." She looked at her husband, meeting his gaze like a soldier charging into fire. "That is, if you're willing."

"How could I not be?" Harry took her hand and lifted it to his lips in an uncharacteristic gesture. "For once, a ball seems precisely where we should be."

HUBERT PICKED his way through the tavern. The sort of place in Covent Garden where gentlemen entertained the actresses and opera dancers they had in keeping. Or where stage folk gathered before or after a performance. Presumably. Hubert wasn't familiar with the activities of the theatre set. Simon Tanner, who lived with Hubert's son David, might frequent a place like this. So might Mélanie, come to think of it. But both of them were going to the Beverston masquerade tonight. In the early evening the tavern was fairly empty. A few people, both male and female, who seemed to be studying scripts. A few with heads close together over some sort of gossip. A few more tossing dice. A flyer proclaiming support for the queen was tacked to the wall, he noted, and beside it a scurrilous cartoon depicting the new king with his mistress, Lady Conyngham, and the queen with her supposed lover, Bergami, both engaged in salacious activities with their backs to each other. Really, it would be easier to keep the monarchy stable if the monarch would behave with a bit more discretion.

Alistair Rannoch was at a table at the back of the tavern. Hubert dropped into a seat across from him. "It's getting harder to meet. Soon you won't be able to hide anymore."

Alistair picked up the bottle of wine on the table. "Soon I hope I won't have to."

"You're very confident."

"Things are going favorably at present." Alistair poured a glass and pushed it across the table to Hubert.

Hubert took the glass and let himself appreciate a sip of Bordeaux. "I found myself telling Malcolm and Julien I wouldn't make an alliance with you. And they believe me. But it was true. Then."

Alistair refilled his own glass. "We both know the board changes. Why did you want to see me?"

"Malcolm and Julien were asking questions about Cyril Talbot's death. Apparently, George Chase was looking into it."

Alistair set the bottle down with a steady hand. "That's interesting. But it's old news. Scandalous, and the full truth might still destroy Glenister. But I was on the fringe of it."

"Yet you were there." Hubert held Alistair with his gaze.

"Did you wonder about it then?"

"A bit. As I told Malcolm and Julien."

Alistair took a drink of wine. "You've never asked me about it."

"It didn't seem relevant. If you accidentally shot Cyril Talbot because you were drunk, or even if you turned on him in a fit of temper, it was little loss to the world and no concern of mine."

"What's changed?"

"George Chase. He thought it was relevant. And whatever George Chase was, he was no fool. So there's more to Cyril's death than anything I previously suspected."

Alistair set his glass down. "Interesting."

Hubert watched him. "Whatever happened, I suspect Archie Davenport knows. And now that Malcolm and Julien realize Cyril's death is relevant, they're going to talk to Archie. And I strongly suspect Archie will tell them the truth in the circumstances. Which will give them more information to work with than I have. Unless you choose to confide in me."

Alistair swirled the wine in his glass. "So we're allies now? Despite what you told Malcolm and Julien?"

"It would hardly be the first time I've lied to Malcolm and Julien. Or the first time I've made an unexpected alliance." Hubert picked up his own glass. "The board shifts, as you say. We have to shift with it." He took a drink and settled back in his chair. "Malcolm and Julien also asked me about Fortinbras."

Alistair's hand stilled on his wineglass. "That's an unexpected development."

"Apparently Chase had the name written down. Did he hear about it from you?"

146

"My dear Hubert. I make my mistakes, but I'm not a complete fool."

Hubert set down his glass, aligning it over a knot in the wood of the table. "You didn't have Chase killed?"

"Why on earth would I?"

"Because of where he was digging."

Alistair stretched his legs out under the table. "I have more important things to focus on."

"Chase knew a lot."

"Chase thought he knew more than he did."

"He was a capable agent, whatever else he was." Hubert managed to keep his voice steady.

Alistair watched him for a moment. "I'd have sworn you had him killed."

"Yes, that's what Malcolm and Julien thought. But why now, of all times?"

"Because he was back and within reach. Because of where he was digging."

"He wasn't digging close to me."

"So you say. He must have known a lot from when he worked for you."

"I'm not that sloppy." Hubert reached for the bottle and refilled his glass. "George Chase wasn't a threat to me."

"Your agents aren't a threat because you keep things on them. But Chase may have gone so far he felt he was beyond that." Alistair took a drink of wine. "Of course, if anyone had true motive to get rid of Chase, it was Harry Davenport."

"Yes, I thought of that. My first instinct was that Julien killed him for Harry's sake. But Julien has an alibi."

"Who?"

"Malcolm, O'Roarke, and Harry Davenport himself."

"Don't you think they might all be in on it?"

"I'd wonder, except they were all in the midst of a crowd."

"Easy enough to get lost in a crowd."

Hubert took another drink of wine. "Chase was trying to restore his reputation. Much like you."

"I can't imagine his doing it successfully."

"He was gathering information to barter. He thought he knew things about you. He claimed he could bring you down."

"He was bluffing."

"If Malcolm and Julien are close to Fortinbras, what else could they tumble to?"

"It's a maze. Let them get lost in it."

"Chase also may have been about to discover your information about the queen." Hubert had deliberately withheld this until the end.

Alistair frowned. "How much did he know?"

"I'm not sure. He was trying to see Liverpool. But he doesn't seem to have had anything concrete written down. At least not that Malcolm and Julien found. Or if they did, they didn't tell me."

"My god, you sound bloodless."

"It's not my plan. But that, more than anything, gives you a motive to have got rid of Chase."

Alistair took a long drink of wine. "I might well have done. If I'd known."

"So you say."

"My dear Hubert. Our whole alliance is built on what we say."

CHAPTER 16

*M*élanie watched Colin, Emily, Jessica, and Clara (holding to Emily's and Colin's hands) run upstairs. They had had a late dinner and then Julien and Kitty and Harry and Cordy had taken their children home and gone to change for the Beverston masquerade. Laura and Raoul had already gone up to change. Malcolm was in the study with Sandy.

Bet, who was in the hall with Mélanie, glanced towards the study door. "Sandy was in the gallery today for Brougham's speech. He says he didn't speak to his father. That he had other things to focus on. When I said he's Lord Marchmain's son, he said they have nothing to say to each other right now." Bet watched the door to the study a moment longer, then turned to Mélanie, eyes dark with concern. "This is just what I was afraid of."

"But you decided it was worth it," Mélanie said.

"I had a mad moment where I believed." Bet hugged her arms across her chest. "He smiles at me and I still believe. I'm afraid that makes me a very selfish person."

"Nonsense." Mélanie put her arm round Bet as they moved to the stairs. "You have the wit to take risks for what will make you and Sandy happy. If I were Sandy's mother, I'd be very proud of him."

"If you were Sandy's mother, you wouldn't be speaking to either of us."

"I hate to be uncharitable, but Lady Marchmain strikes me as lamentably lacking in maternal instinct."

Bet looked up at Mélanie and gave a quick, shy smile. "I forget, for moments together, about all the difficulties and I'm so ridiculously happy. Then I think about the future and wonder how on earth we're going to manage."

Mélanie bent down to pick up Berowne who was winding round her ankles. "You're the practical one in the family. Sandy will manage much better with you."

"But we can't hide here with our friends forever."

"We've all been hiding with each other quite successfully for years."

"Yes, but not all the time. And you don't *have* to hide."

"In Italy we stayed to our own devices." And they'd believed they'd never be able to come back.

"You told me once you were afraid you'd go mad."

"Caught. But you're much more practical than I am. You'll do much better. And you won't be so isolated." Mélanie settled Berowne against her shoulder. She could feel his purrs through her gown. "Sometimes it's all right to let yourself be happy. And among other things, the people you love will be much happier than if you're making yourself feel miserable."

Bet smiled. "What an odd way of looking at it, but—Thank you."

∿

KITTY PAUSED in the doorway of the Carfax House study. Her husband was lying across the desk, a drawer pulled open, his head hanging down as he felt along inside the drawer. "Sorry to interrupt, but we're due at the Beverston masquerade in less than an hour and the children will expect to see us in our costumes and offer commentary."

Julien lifted his head from the desk that had once been his uncle's. "They're not going to be happy they aren't coming with us. It seems absurd children aren't invited to masquerades. They'd have by far the most fun."

"I think it's absurd children aren't invited to all sorts of things. It would make our life easier. But perhaps the point of masquerades is that they allow adults to act like children."

Julien pushed himself up on one elbow. "I seem to remember doing distinctly unchildlike things at a number of masquerades."

"My point exactly."

"Yes, but I have no desire to do those things in the shrubbery or in an antechamber on chaises longues that are never long enough. Not even with you. What's the point, when we have a comfortable bed at home?"

"We're going for work. Which is what you used to do at masquerades."

"Yes, well, the time in the shrubbery and antechambers was work. But I put limits on my work now. Don't worry, I can dress quickly. I must say, it's rather novel to have a wife to fuss over me."

"I never fuss, Julien." Kitty moved away from the doorway and stepped into the room. "What are you doing? Searching for something of Hubert's?"

"No, of my grandfather's. Of anything that might explain why Beverston is so interested in him. And what connection he might have to the League. He wasn't a member. He was a reprobate, but I wouldn't have thought he was powerful enough to have secrets that would interest them. If he had a secret fortune, he put it to bad use given that he was chronically in debt and left debts to his son. Which prompted my father to marry my mother. Which was a shame for all concerned, save that if it hadn't happened, I wouldn't be here."

"Which makes me inestimably grateful for it."

Julien leaned over again and reached further into the desk, braced one foot on the chair to keep from overbalancing, and pulled out a crumpled paper. He sat up and spread it out below the lamp on the desk. "No, this is Uncle Hubert's. It actually looks like a bill from his bootmaker. Though knowing him, it may be in code. But it's his handwriting. If it's in code, I'm surprised he missed it when he left the house. Of course, he might have taken anything interesting to do with Grandfather."

"Did you ask him about your grandfather?" Kitty asked. "After I found Beverston trying to steal his snuffbox?" That had been at their ball last June and had seemed significant at the time but had since been dwarfed by a cascade of revelations.

"He claimed not to know anything." Julien opened a side drawer.

Kitty moved to stand beside the desk. "What about your grandfather's love affairs? Love affairs seem to be at the heart of so much to do with the League."

Julien leaned down again, arm stretched into the desk. "I never paid much attention to the gossip about him. There was a quite beautiful actress called Phèdre the Fair, after her most famous role, whom he had in keeping for some time, from what I've heard. Until she moved on to a royal duke. But that would have been before the League were even formed."

"Where did the snuffbox come from?"

"I don't know." Julien sat up again, reached into a side drawer, and took out the snuffbox. He turned it over in his hand and held it out in the light of the lamp. "It looks French, but it could have been bought here."

Kitty studied the snuffbox. It was covered in delicate gold filagree of intertwining roses. "The design almost looks like a seal."

"So it does. But it's not the Carfax crest or anything else I can make out as significant. Yet one more piece of a puzzle that is much bigger than George Chase's murder. I hope we can ferret out at least some of the pieces at the masquerade."

~

"UNTIL TODAY, I'd have said Brougham was a hard man to be sure of," Malcolm said. "But I'm damned sure he was lying to me."

Mélanie shut the night nursery door. Bet and Sandy were entertaining Colin, Emily, Jessica, and Clara who were less accustomed than they had once been to their parents being out for the evening, especially after such an exciting and unsettling day. "I'm sorry, darling."

"Sorry?" Malcolm asked.

"It's not easy to mistrust someone you like."

"I'm used to it."

She picked up the apricot silk gown she had ordered for the masquerade, weeks ago, when life had seemed simpler. Her companion Blanca and Malcolm's valet Addison were away with their baby son, visiting Addison's sister, so she and Malcolm were dressing themselves. "I like him too. I don't particularly like the idea that he's lying. But we all know there are plenty of reasons to lie. It may not mean Brougham has anything to do with the murder. In fact, it likely doesn't. Brougham has all sorts of reasons for keeping secrets right now."

"Quite. But if the victim had information about the trial to take to Liverpool, information that could damage Brougham's case, Brougham has the strongest motive of anyone we know of so far to have killed him."

"Of anyone we know of." She undid the tapes on her gown. "But we know remarkably little about the case at this point. We don't even know he was killed because of the information."

Malcolm tugged loose his cravat. "Mel. He was killed on the stairs outside the House of Lords, on the opening day of the defense, bent on taking information to the prime minister."

"And how often have you said not to jump to the obvious conclusions?" Mélanie regarded her husband, her gown slipping off her shoulders. "More of my influence, I fear."

Malcolm tossed the cravat on the bed. "You aren't any quicker to suspect than I am."

"No, but I've made you jump to the worst possible scenario when it comes to the possible guilt of anyone you care about."

Malcolm moved to her side and set his hands on her bare shoulders. "My darling. When it comes to trust and a whole host of other things, you and Brougham aren't remotely in the same category."

"No, but it's the idea." She squeezed his hands, then slipped out of the gown and tossed it on the bed. "That someone you care about may not be what they seem."

Malcolm undid the buttons on his waistcoat with methodical precision. "You're what you seemed in fundamentals. I just didn't acknowledge who you were properly at first."

"You always accepted me for what I was. That's why I fell in love with you."

"But I never put together what it meant that you're as capable an agent as I always knew you were. And Brougham's certainly what I always thought him to be. I always thought—knew—him to be determined and ambitious and willing to cut corners. And devoted to winning. As so often is the case, it's a question of how far he'd go to win. I'd be a fool if I weren't wondering."

"Which perhaps is a point in his favor. Brougham's too clever to be obvious."

Malcolm grimaced and tossed the waistcoat after the cravat. "Brougham was caught unawares today. He's clever and a good game player, but he's not an agent. He had to make up a story on the spur of the moment."

"But surely if he had hired someone to kill George Chase, he'd have known you'd be likely to question him at some point. He'd have had a story ready."

"Possibly. He might not have known he was seen going into the house in Wardour Street with Caro George. I think his surprise at that was genuine."

"Which could mean it has nothing to do with the murder. If it was to do with the murder, he'd have been much more on his guard when he went to Wardour Street."

"Hopefully Caro George can shed some light on it when you talk to her." Malcolm dragged his shirt over his head, ruffling his dark hair. "Who are we going as tonight?"

The words took Mélanie back to the Congress of Vienna, when each night had seemed to hold a different social engagement, many of them requiring different types of costume from masquerade balls to traditional country dress to a mock medieval tournament. Malcolm had left it to her to arrange whatever they were supposed to wear and had often had only minutes to change into the outfit of a Spanish grandee or a medieval knight when he rushed back from the negotiating table before an evening engagement.

"Beatrice and Benedick." She gestured towards the doublet and hose on the bed.

Malcolm regarded the costume. "I've had to be costumed as worse characters. But given what you reported about your conversation with Frances and Archie this afternoon, the thought of your asking me to fight a duel is rather discomfiting."

Mélanie picked up the ruff that went with her Beatrice gown. "I practiced the church scene once with one of the actors in my father's company. Beatrice is so sensible most of the time, it was hard for me to understand how she was so determined to have Benedick kill a man. Even one as arguably despicable as Claudio in that moment. My father said the key is that it's the only way she can see to right an impossible wrong." She ran her finger over the pleated linen, stiff with starch. "Apparently Glenister was horrified that he'd killed his brother. And yet he fought the duel. So whatever it was over, I rather think it was something that mattered to Glenister tremendously."

Malcolm picked up the doublet. "So do I. But my imagination at this point boggles at what."

∼

CORDELIA ADJUSTED the chain that held her dark red cloak closed over her draped white gown. "Everyone's going to think we're Cleopatra and Antony."

Harry turned from securing his toga. "If they can't tell the difference between Egypt and Rome, more fools they."

"Cleopatra might have worn Roman dress. Antony could have brought it from Rome."

"A good point. But he wouldn't have worn Augustus's laurel wreath." Harry nodded towards the wreath beside his shaving kit.

Cordelia caught the movement in the pier glass and turned to face her husband. She was supposed to be Livia, Augustus's wife. "Or they'll think we're Claudius and Messalina. Which in my case might have been more appropriate."

Harry looked up from adjusting the shoulder of his toga. "Damn it, Cordy—"

"Just stating the obvious. I went to a masquerade as Messalina when we were apart. It seemed better somehow to stare down the gossips."

His gaze lingered on her face, but he seemed to be holding himself in check. "That's my Cordy. I understand the impulse."

She put out a hand, then let it fall to her side, into the folds of her cloak. "I'm sorry, Harry."

"*You're* sorry? My god, Cordy. This is a damnable coil, but it's far worse for you."

Cordy met his gaze across their bedroom. They had spent time with Livia and her younger sister Drusilla when they returned home. Livia, though matter-of-fact, had clearly been shaken by the afternoon, and Drusilla, though she'd played with Jessica all afternoon, had wanted attention and also had managed to hear a surprising amount about the events of the day, which elicited a number of questions. So this was the first chance Cordy and Harry had had to talk alone since George had tumbled to the stairs and died before Cordelia's eyes. "Harry, you can't think I still cared about him. Not after everything we learned. Not after the last five years."

Harry slung his imperial purple cloak round his shoulders. "I think caring is complicated. You can be unspeakably angry at someone and still love them. I never stopped loving you, and I confess to being more than a bit angry."

"Yes, but—" Cordelia swallowed. When she and Harry first reconciled, she'd constantly been aware of potential verbal memory mines, but for so long they'd been comfortable together. Now she was stumbling through shrouded terrain set with explosives. "Harry, I'm not diminishing anything I did and you had every right to be angry at me. But I didn't—"

"Sweetheart, I'm not comparing anything you did with what George did." Harry fastened the metal clasp on the cloak with steady fingers. "I'm saying caring doesn't conveniently go away just because one learns inconvenient truths."

"He killed my sister." She could sometimes go days at a time without thinking about Julia. But the pain was there, underneath the undeniably happy rhythms of her life. A gnawing gap, an ever-present sense that a presence that had been inextricably bound up in her life for more than a quarter century was now gone. Sometimes it was a vague sense of something missing that would remind her of Julia. Others she would be caught up short by how she had gone on with her life and forged new bonds and didn't think enough about the sister from whom she had already been growing apart when Julia was killed. Most recently, the thought that Mélanie and Kitty and Laura knew her better than Julia ever had had brought the guilt crashing down on her more than anything. As recently as this afternoon.

Harry moved to her side and set his hands on her shoulders. "This has dredged up an unspeakable amount."

"For both of us." Cordelia looked up at him. Harry was ruthless about not hiding from facts, but he could hide his feelings as few could.

"George wasn't enough a part of my life for me to feel loss."

"Harry. He's long gone, but he hung over our marriage from the start."

"Well, yes, I can't deny that."

"And—" She couldn't quite say it.

"He may be Livia's biological father." Harry was never one to shy away from harsh facts. "Did he know, by the way?"

"He has to have wondered." Cordelia shuddered and cast a quick glance at the door to the nursery. "All these years. I've told myself he couldn't hurt us. But then I'd remember he was still in the world somewhere. That he could come back. That you and I could handle it, but I couldn't bear what it might mean for Livia. Now he's gone. A part of me is terrified of what may still come out. How the reasons he came back and what he was trying to do may impact us. And a part of me is relieved he's gone."

"You can be relieved he's gone without being responsible for his being gone."

Cordelia nodded, though knowing it wasn't quite the same as feeling it. "He can still hurt us."

Harry's gaze remained steady on her own. "Livia's our daughter. She'll be able to handle anything that may come out. I want to protect my children from anything. But that I also want them to be able to handle anything."

Cordelia put her hands on her husband's chest. "Harry—"

Harry looked down into her eyes. As so often between them, she didn't need to say the rest. "I confess to wishing George at the devil most of the time I've known of his existence. I confess to wishing him dead more than once. But not like this."

"No, of course not."

"But you wondered."

"No! You wouldn't. That is—"

"As Malcolm says, we never exactly know what we're capable of."

"Then you must be wondering about me. I could have hired someone. In many ways, I'm far angrier at George than you are."

"A good point. But I can't see your letting yourself take that way out."

"I can't see your doing it either."

Harry met her gaze, while questions neither could quite voice hung between them. "Then it comes down to trust. As does so much in a marriage."

"You'd think we'd have a hard time with trust. That is, you would think *you* would."

Harry gave a quick, sweet smile that squeezed her heart. "Or that we'd have learned there's no way to go on without it."

CHAPTER 17

"Oh, how clever." Corisande Ossulston stopped beside Cordelia and Harry where they stood with the Rannoch party by the entrance to the Beverston ballroom. "You're Helen of Troy and Paris."

"A few thousand years off," Harry murmured, with an ease that Mélanie suspected only his good friends could see through. "But you're quite right, my wife could launch a thousand ships."

Corisande laughed and moved on. Mélanie glanced round the ballroom. Candlelight glittered off mirrors and gilding and cast shadows off the coffered ceiling. Instead of the customary relative harmony of dark coats and pastel gowns found at most balls, the dance floor was a discordant mix of cloth of silver armor, medieval velvet gowns, frock coats and hoop skirts, eye patches and steeple hats, powdered wigs and flowing hair, ornamental swords and net wings. And masks—velvet, satin, beaded, glittering, jeweled, beribboned.

"It's paradoxical," Frances murmured, surveying the crowd, "but I always feel people are more themselves at a masquerade ball."

"Not in the least paradoxical," Raoul said. "Wearing a costume lets people discard their social armor."

Frances turned to look at him. In her red wig and high-standing lace collar, she had never looked more queenly. "For someone who dislikes society so much, you're fiendishly good at reading it."

"I don't dislike society in the least," said Raoul, leaning on his Merlin staff. "I just dislike social distinctions."

"Society is built on social distinctions, unfortunately," Fanny said.

"It's amazing how you can tell who everyone is," Julien said. "For all the talk about the scandalous things the anonymity of a masquerade allows, most people haven't mastered the rudimentary tricks of moving differently and changing their posture."

"But you're forgetting that those same people probably don't recognize each other's posture or the way they hold their heads," Kitty said. She unfurled the fan that went with her Dulcinea costume. "Difficult sometimes for spies to see the world through civilian eyes."

"A good point." Julien said. "And then the choice of costume can be a giveaway." He adjusted the battered shield on his arm. "I need to go find a windmill."

"The idea wasn't to hide who we are," Kitty said. "If we really wanted to be in disguise we'd have come dressed as footmen. And I like Cervantes. Everyone's likely to guess Mélanie and Malcolm are Beatrice and Benedick."

"Assuming they recognize our costumes as Beatrice and Benedick. Or even Shakespeare," Malcolm said.

"We know. That's what's important." Mélanie unfurled her lace fan. "I need to find Caro George. And she won't talk to me in a crowd."

"Balls are so much more agreeable when they're work," Cordy said with a bright smile.

"Break a leg." Malcolm caught Mélanie's gloved hand as she

moved away and lifted it to his lips. Her gaze caught his own and he smiled. Support. They all needed all they could get right now.

Mélanie circulated along the edge of the ballroom, an eye out for Caro George's delicate frame, brown curls, and diffident way of moving. Despite Julien's assertion about people's not seeing through costumes, she was stopped three times with questions about the murder. But she still hadn't seen Caro when a hand plucked at her sleeve.

Mélanie turned round to find herself looking at a fine-boned woman in a flowing blue Cavalier gown with a lace collar and a plumed hat. Despite the blue velvet mask, it was plainly Caro George.

"I was hoping to see you," Caro said.

"As I was you," Mélanie said. But she couldn't say more at this point, because Caro's sister-in-law Emily Cowper was beside her in a gold Amazon's gown.

"That's a very daring dress, Emily," Mélanie said.

"It really should be bare breasted, but I didn't think I could go quite so far. Despite all the things everyone has been listening to all day in Parliament. Really, when the official proceedings of a government body include evidence about bedsheets, what does scandal even mean anymore?" Emily shifted her arm, which had a shield strapped to it, too delicate to be much use in battle but just the right shape to create a flattering image against the gold silk. "You were there today, weren't you? The rumor is you found George Chase's body."

"The rumor is correct," Mélanie said. "Or almost. He wasn't quite dead when I got to him, but he died within seconds."

Caro shuddered. "I can't bear to think of it. In broad daylight, in such a crowd."

"We don't think it was random."

"I should hope not," Emily said. "George Chase certainly gave plenty of people cause to kill him."

"Emily," Caro said.

"Merely stating the facts, dearest." Emily regarded Mélanie. "You're investigating, don't deny it."

"I won't."

"To think you were so close to something so dreadful," Caro said.

"Oh, it's hardly the first time Mélanie's been close to murder," Emily said. She adjusted her diadem, which was either real diamonds or excellent paste copies. "Don't look at me like that, Caro. It's obvious they're all all right or I wouldn't have said anything." Her eyes narrowed. "You are all all right, aren't you?"

"That depends how one defines 'all right,'" Mélanie said. "Yes, we were in no danger, and you're right, it was unsettling and tragic, but we've been through such things before. Though thank goodness I'll never not be unsettled by seeing someone die."

"I'm dreadful," Emily said. "It's the wretched trial. It's enough to make one cynical about everything. Or perhaps I'm just using that as a defense."

"Before—" Caro twisted her hands together. "Before all this happened, did you—"

"Yes," Mélanie said. "His speech was quite splendid."

Caro flushed and cast a quick glance at Emily. "He's still a friend."

"Yes, dear." Emily squeezed her arm. "I do understand. Truly. Much better you can talk about it. And even I'll admit he speaks well." She glanced at Mélanie, her gaze narrowing. "You're at the ball. And you came looking for us. Well, for Caro, I suspect. When the defense has just opened, your play is about to go into rehearsals, and you're in the midst of one of your murder investigations. And since we know less than you about the trial and have nothing to do with the theatre—what do we have to do with the murder investigation?"

"We can't have anything to do with it, Emily," Caro said. "Don't be silly."

"I wasn't trying to be silly at all," Emily said. "And Mélanie's face confirms it."

"But we didn't even know George Chase was in London," Caro said. "At least I didn't. Did you, Emily?"

Emily wrinkled her nose. "Certainly not. I'd have been horrified if I had done. And I have warned Cordy. I assume she didn't know?"

"No," Mélanie said.

"Does anyone say we knew he was here?" Caro asked.

"No." Mélanie looked from Caro to Emily. "Perhaps we should go into one of the antechambers. Caro, would you prefer to talk about this alone?"

"No! That is, yes, let's go into an antechamber, but I'd much prefer to have Emily there. I haven't anything to hide from her."

That was odd language if Caro and Brougham had indeed resumed their affair. Emily had been the one to go after Caro when she went off to Italy with Brougham and to persuade her to come back home. Of course, perhaps that made it easier for Caro to talk frankly in front of her.

Emily's brows had tightened with concern, but she gave a bright smile and led the way to a small sitting room hung with cherry-striped paper. Emily had an unerring instinct for finding quiet corners in any setting. She snatched two glasses of champagne from a passing waiter on the way, gave them to Caro and Mélanie, and then snatched a third for herself.

Mélanie took a sip of champagne and regarded Caro George. Caro had been born Caroline St. Jules and raised as the ward of the Duke of Devonshire in a household that included the duke, the duchess, and the duke's mistress, Lady Elizabeth Foster (whose sister happened to be married to Lord Liverpool). Most people knew or at least suspected that Caro was in fact the duke and Lady Elizabeth's daughter, but according to Cordy, who had known them all since childhood, Caro George hadn't known until she was grown. She had married into another powerful Whig family, the Lambs. Her husband George was the younger brother of Malcolm's friend and parliamentary colleague William Lamb, and of Emily, Whig hostess and patroness of Almack's. William's wife was also named Caroline, leading to the women being referred to as "Caro George" and "Caro William." It was Cordy's friend Caro William who had always been the scandal, notably in her love affair with Lord Byron, but four years ago demure Caro George had run off to Italy with Henry Brougham. Mélanie had been in Paris with Malcolm at the time and hadn't yet been close friends with Emily, so it was only later she had heard Emily's account about going to Italy herself and persuading Caro George to come home. The romance had apparently faded, perhaps more quickly on Brougham's part, but the two were still on friendly terms. Caro had struck Mélanie as quite interested in the trial. As to her marriage, the most Mélanie had seen between Caro and George Lamb was tepid affection. "She didn't want to marry him," Cordy had said. "She wasn't in love with him, and he's not the most exciting of men. I know that sounds horrid, but at least he isn't from anything I've seen. But I think there was a lot of family pressure for her to be married and settled."

"Settled" was what Caro George seemed, returned to her husband. Mélanie had no particular sense that she would run off again or even that she would stray—quite unlike Emily, who seemingly wouldn't dream of leaving her husband, Peter Cowper, and yet was constantly unfaithful not only to him but to her long-time lover, Harry Palmerston, who might actually be the love of her life. It was, as Emily would freely admit, a matter of appearances. And of not breaking up the social order. Emily's love affairs didn't disrupt the settled surface of her life in the least.

Caro took a long sip of champagne but looked at Mélanie with genuine confusion. "What on earth makes you think I would know anything about poor Major Chase?"

"You were seen in the house where he lodged. A house in Wardour Street."

"But—" Caro went pale. Her champagne glass tilted in her fingers. "That was nothing to do with this. You must believe that."

"We can't be sure."

Caro tightened her grip on the glass. "I went to call on a friend."

"Who do you know who lives in Wardour Street?" Emily asked.

"You don't know all my friends, Emily. This was someone I met abroad."

"When you were with Mr. Brougham?" Emily asked.

"Yes. No. It's nothing to do with Henry. That is, it is, but it's nothing to do with our relationship. I mean, it doesn't mean I'm going to go back to him or anything of the sort."

"That's not what Mr. Brougham says," Mélanie said.

"Oh god." Caro's eyes went wide with horror. "You've talked to Henry?"

"Malcolm did."

"And he said—"

"That you had gone into the house for what might be considered the obvious reasons. Malcolm and I are inclined to doubt that, for a number of reasons."

Caro hunched her shoulders. "I was calling on a lady Henry and I met in Italy. I learned she was in London and dreadfully lonely and she asked me to come see her."

"Was she an English lady traveling abroad?" Emily asked.

"No. She's Italian."

And it was an unlikely coincidence that she was in London for reasons not connected to the trial. "You were talking to a witness?" Mélanie asked.

"No. Yes. I'm not sure." Caroline rubbed her arms. "I think— Henry asked her to come to London. She lived very quietly in Italy."

"And she wanted to live quietly in London."

"She likes to live quietly, but it's Henry who wanted her presence here to be secret. Anna—that's her name—seemed rather distressed that Henry was asking her to stay so out of the public eye. But Henry said it was only for a short time."

"She knows the queen?" Mélanie asked.

"She'd met Princess Caroline—the queen—in Italy. She didn't know her well, but she was quite convinced of the princess—the queen's—blameless character."

"Hmph," Emily said. "She can't be very discerning."

"Not everyone's a cynic, Emily," Caro said, her tone sharper than usual. "I quite like the contessa."

"She's a contessa?" Mélanie said.

"The Contessa Montalto."

"All right," Emily said. "She's a lovely woman and you met her with Mr. Brougham, but why on earth did you go see her now? With Mr. Brougham, of all people."

"Because Henry asked me to."

"Why?" Emily asked the question, so Mélanie didn't need to.

Caro twisted her hands together. "She's lonely, living such an isolated life in London just now. Henry thought it would cheer her up."

Emily took a sip of champagne. "I didn't know you and Mr. Brougham still talked so much."

"We don't, not generally. But I'm still fond of him, and I believe he is of me, and goodness knows we can't avoid each other in London society. But of course I try to avoid seeing him alone. In this case, the contessa asked him to reach out to me, and he most particularly asked me for my assistance. He was quite apologetic about it. But I wanted to help the contessa." Caro lifted her chin. "And I wanted to help Henry."

Emily touched her arm. "I never said you shouldn't. And interesting as this all is, I don't see what it has to do with Major George Chase being killed." She looked at Mélanie.

"Yes," Caro said. "I certainly never met anyone else in the lodging house. If someone happened to be prying and noticed us, I don't see what that has to do with anything."

"Unless Mélanie and Malcolm think he was killed because of something he overheard," Emily said.

"Yes, but he couldn't have—I mean, we only talked about Italy and the weather and quite unexceptionable things."

"Not something you said, necessarily," Emily said. "But it sounds as though her presence in England and her role at the trial were a great secret."

"Yes, but—" Caro looked from Emily to Mélanie. "You can't think Henry would have killed someone to keep his witness secret. The very idea is absurd."

"I don't know that it's at all absurd to imagine people would kill over this case, the way tempers have been flaring. And if anyone was going to kill over it, Mr. Brougham certainly has the incentive."

Caro clunked her glass down on a pier table. "Just because you don't like him—"

"He wants to win. He may even care about the queen."

Caro turned to Mélanie. "You can't think—"

"At the moment, all we're doing is gathering information," Mélanie said. "Did you notice anything when you were at the lodging house?"

"Not particularly. I was focused on seeing Anna. It was a quite ordinary sort of lodging house. She has rooms at the back. We went upstairs and down a passage. We didn't see anyone. We certainly didn't see Major Chase. Oh dear, do you think he saw us? Is that what he wanted to tell Lord Liverpool about?"

"Not if he had any sense," Emily said. "An echo of an old scandal would hardly interest someone as brazen as Major Chase. Far more likely he had information about this contessa of yours."

"But why—"

"If she's a witness in the trial, her testimony would be of interest to the prosecution as well."

"But she's a perfectly ordinary, respectable woman," Caro said. "I can't imagine she could have anything particularly important to say at the trial. She could perhaps be a witness to the queen's good character—"

Emily snorted.

"Don't, Emily. A number of people genuinely believe the queen has been ill used."

"A number of people are fools. She was practically living with Bergami. Go on."

Caro scowled at her sister-in-law. "But other than testifying to the queen's good character, I can't imagine what Anna could have to say. She certainly wouldn't be a witness to shake open the trial."

"And yet Mr. Brougham was at great pains to keep her presence in London secret," Mélanie said.

"Well, yes. It had been very difficult for him to persuade Anna to come at all."

"And he obviously thought it was worth the effort," Emily said. "With everything else he has to do."

Caro frowned, then picked up her glass of champagne and took a sip. "He's willing to do everything possible in the queen's defense."

"Precisely," Emily said.

"He lied to Malcolm about what you were doing in Wardour Street." Mélanie said. "He was so determined not to tell Malcolm about this Contessa Montalto that he let Malcolm believe you and he had resumed your affair."

Caro's eyes opened wide. "I can't believe—"

"And Malcolm is his ally," Emily said. "You'd think he wouldn't have hesitated to share this with him."

"Henry is very careful," Caro said. She took another sip of champagne. "Who saw us in Wardour Street?"

Mélanie's fingers tightened round her own glass. "George."

"George? You mean George Chase?" Caro's eyes widened. "Oh, god, not *my* George."

"I'm afraid so," Mélanie said.

Caro dropped down on the settee. The champagne glass tilted in her fingers.

"Do be sensible, dearest." Emily righted the champagne glass before it could spill all over Caro's blue velvet skirts. "George will see reason when he understands. Don't let this come between you, after you've mended things so well."

"But we haven't mended them at all, Emily." Caro jerked away from her sister-in-law. "We've papered them over. How in god's name did George happen to be there—good god, was he following me?"

"Unfortunately," Mélanie said.

Caro hunched her shoulders, sending her Cavalier collar flopping forwards. "It's even worse than I thought. He's never going to trust me."

"Well, in this case, he had good reason," Emily pointed out.

"But I wasn't doing anything the least bit untoward with Henry. For heaven's sake, Emily, I just told you all about it."

"But you didn't tell George."

"Well, no. I know the construction he'd have put on it."

"Precisely. And Mr. Brougham is making it worse by trying to make Malcolm believe the worst. Really, the man is unconscionable."

"That's exceedingly unfair, Emily. Henry cares enormously about what he does. You have to give him that."

"I give him that he cares enormously about himself."

Caro pushed herself to her feet. "I'm going to have to talk to George and try to make him understand what happened. Oh, I could murder Henry for putting me in this situation."

"That's the first sensible thing you've said all night," Emily said. "Honestly, you'd think Mr. Brougham would have known Malcolm and Mélanie would talk to you. What did he think you'd do, pretend to an affair for his sake?"

"I suspect he was thinking on his feet, trying to come up with an excuse when Malcolm confronted him," Mélanie said. "But I completely agree that doesn't excuse his having so little care for what his words would do to Caro."

"Henry is—he doesn't always think things through," Caro said. "Which is no excuse." She tossed down the last of her champagne.

"So you've finally seen him for what he is?" Emily said. "That might just make all this worth it."

Caro clunked down her glass. "I always saw him for what he is, Em. I loved him anyway. Surely you of all people understand that."

Emily met Caro's gaze in the flickering candlelight. They had known each other since childhood, long before they were sisters-in-law, long before Mélanie knew either of them. But oddly, Mélanie had the sense this was one of the most honest exchanges between the two of them. "Yes," Emily said. "But at a certain point one can't put up with that sort of behavior."

"No," Caro agreed. "And whatever I say to George about the truth, I doubt he'll believe it."

CHAPTER 18

"*M*alcolm. Thank god, I was afraid you wouldn't be here." David Mallinson's voice was unmistakable, as was the set of his shoulders in his black Elizabethan doublet.

"Romeo?" Malcolm asked.

"Hamlet. Simon said I should carry a skull, but I drew the line at that. He's Mercutio." David had lived with Simon Tanner since they were all at Oxford, though officially they were still merely friends who shared a house. Hubert Mallinson, David's father, had seemingly at last given up his efforts to get David to marry with Julien's re-emergence.

"Is it true?" David asked, gaze shifting behind his mask.

"Which part?" Malcolm asked. "George Chase was stabbed on the stairs outside the House of Lords after Brougham's speech."

David looked away and swore under his breath. He'd been in Brussels when they learned George had killed Julia Ashton. And learned that George had also killed Amelia Beckwith, whom David had grown up with.

"You haven't talked to your father?" Malcolm asked.

"I left immediately after Brougham's speech. Teddy has a fever and Amy and Jamie seem to be sickening with it. We were going to stay home tonight, but they all seemed better. Lucinda came round with the story about George. And she said she heard you'd talked to Honoria. Is that true? My sister likes to tell stories, but she has a way of making them overly dramatic."

"Julien and Kitty talked to Honoria." Honoria was David's cousin on her mother's side, as well as Julien's. Malcolm and David had been friends since Harrow, when they found a refuge in each other as fellow misfits. David had been in Lisbon on that visit with Honoria and his father all those years ago. But there were things about that visit Malcolm had never shared with David. Despite their friendship. Or perhaps because of it. Because those secrets could rend their friendship in two.

"Why?" David asked. "Honoria barely knew George Chase. I mean, she didn't know him any better than the rest of us."

"George was apparently trying to reinstate himself."

"How the hell could he expect—"

"I didn't say it was doable. George was never entirely realistic in his thinking. He was amassing blackmail information and asking questions. And some of the questions he was asking were about Honoria's father's death."

"Cyril?" David's brows drew together over his mask. "But that was years ago. And it was a stupid accident."

"So it seems. George thought it was important."

Simon Tanner materialized beside them out of the crowd and dropped a hand on David's shoulder. "George Chase isn't worth the energy we're all spending on him. But Malcolm and Mélanie will learn the truth of it."

"Which is what?" David swiveled his head round to look at his lover. "How much more damage will the truth do?"

"A good point," Simon said. "But however despicable George was, none of us supports people going about murdering people. None of us supports capital punishment, if it comes to that."

"For god's sake, Simon. I'm not suggesting any of us actually killed him."

Simon pushed back the sleeve of his artistically wine-stained crimson-slashed Mercutio doublet. "I imagine Malcolm and Mélanie are wondering if any of us did. They wouldn't be doing their jobs if they didn't."

David looked from Malcolm, his oldest friend since Harrow, to his lover of more than a decade. "Malcolm knows we wouldn't—"

Simon cast a quick glance at Malcolm, then looked back at David. "I don't think good investigators can think they know anyone in an investigation. We aren't characters in a play. Come to that, my own characters sometimes surprise me with what they're willing to do. I don't think Malcolm or Mélanie can afford to think we wouldn't surprise them."

"That sounds very clever, Simon. And obviously there are uncertainties. But we're all—"

"Friends," Simon said. His eyes had turned hard as the jet beads on his mask. "I don't think that can be allowed to make a difference."

"You both look splendid." Mélanie joined them in the silence that followed. Her smile was bright with friendship, her sea-green eyes sparkling with amusement, her dark ringlets tumbling round her face. Malcolm wasn't sure if she hadn't heard the end of the conversation or if she thought it best to pretend she hadn't, but knowing his wife he suspected the latter.

"Can't go wrong with Shakespeare." Simon's lazy smile said he suspected it too.

"I might have known you'd recognize Beatrice and Benedick." Mélanie slid her hand through Malcolm's arm. "Do you mind if I steal Malcolm? I'm afraid I've got something rather important to tell him."

"Whether it's the trial or your investigation," David said, in an unusually hard voice, "you'd best tell him at once."

∾

174

Malcolm cursed, with a fluency and vehemence Mélanie rarely heard from him. "What the hell was Henry thinking?"

"I doubt he was thinking at all, darling." Mélanie edged her husband further to the side, next to a potted palm on the balcony where they had sought refuge to talk. Despite the October weather, a number of guests were outside. More were below in the garden, judging by the murmurs and giggles floating up on the cooling night air. "I think Henry was scrambling to come up with an excuse to explain his presence in Wardour Street, as you said."

"Putting in jeopardy a woman he loved. At least once. A woman he admits to still caring for. Putting anyone in jeopardy to protect yourself is—"

"Malcolm." Mélanie gripped her husband's arms. "This is a murder investigation. People panic. People don't act rationally. I'm angry at Henry too, but that doesn't mean his lies are any more than an attempt to protect himself."

"No. Harry and I already suspected the woman in the lodgings was Italian. Why the hell couldn't Henry simply have told me about her?"

"I don't know. But clearly she's a very important witness to him."

"Clearly. I need to talk to Henry at once." Malcom squeezed her hands. "Thank you, sweetheart."

Mélanie scanned her husband's face behind his jet-beaded mask. "He's thoughtless and stupid, Malcolm. That doesn't mean he's involved in the murder."

"No, but he's hiding something. I'm going to have to learn what."

～

"I do like masquerades," Sofia Vincenzo Montagu said. "They're so much less stuffy than regular balls. Though it's not really like a Venetian masquerade, is it?"

Nerezza Russo cast a glance round the ballroom. Some of the masks looked to have been actually made in Venice. Lady Beverston (who was, hard as Nerezza still found it to believe, her future mother-in-law) had asked Nerezza's advice on the decorations. The draperies were the right shade of Venetian red. But there was something ineffably English about the coldly classical white and gold of the walls. As she and Sofia passed the open French windows to the balcony, Nerezza could feel the cold damp of English air (so different from the damp off the canals) and the chatter of English, even with the words indistinguishable, was so different from the lilt of Italian. "Not remotely like a Venetian masquerade. And somehow it's more restrained and at the same time, people go further."

"Do you miss it?" Sofia asked.

Nerezza unfurled her fan. "I miss Italy sometimes. I don't miss the life I had there. Do you miss it?"

"Sometimes. But I'm going back in a few months. Kit and I've agreed we'll always spend part of the year there."

"And I doubt Ben and I will. I don't really have anything to go back for." Nerezza shook her head.

"I'm sorry," Sofia said. "I didn't mean to bring up something difficult."

"No, that's not it. I'm not upset. I just can't quite get used to saying 'Ben and I.' As though we have a future."

"You do have a future." Sofia tightened her grip on Nerezza's arm. "You always did and now it's official, thank goodness. Just like it is for Sandy and Bet. I wish they'd come tonight."

"I don't think they were invited. And even if they had been, it would have been hard."

Sofia wrinkled her nose. "I suppose so. So soon after the betrothal."

Nerezza stopped walking and turned to look at her friend through her beaded mask. "It's always going to be difficult for them." Nerezza loved Sofia, but scoff as she might at convention,

Sofia, who was the daughter of an Italian conte and the step-daughter of an English baron, would never fully understand what it was like for people who had been born outside society. Nerezza had been able to keep her past more shrouded than Bet, and she and Ben had (amazingly) his parents' blessing, but she still felt the glances shot her way, heard the whispered conversations that stopped abruptly when she got too close.

"It's hard for them right now," Sofia said, "but it will get better with time. Eventually Sandy's parents will come round—"

"There's no guarantee they will. And even if they do, that won't make the rest of society forget."

"My mother and Uncle Bernard lived outside society, but even then all sorts of people socialized with them."

"Sofia, your mother is a marquese's daughter who married a conte and ran off with a baron. Bet was born in St. Giles and sold her services and lived with Sandy as his mistress. No one's ever going to forget that."

Sofia frowned. "Malcolm and Mélanie have. And Raoul and Laura, and Kitty and Julien, and Harry and Cordy. David and Simon—"

"Yes. They have a small circle of friends. They can be happy in that circle. But they'll always be outside society." Just as she and Ben might be on the fringe of it, even with his parents' blessing.

"People forget scandals. For heaven's sake, look at what's being said about the king and queen in front of everyone right now. Look at Cordy. Look at Mrs. George Lamb—it wasn't that long ago she ran off to Italy with Brougham, and everyone knows about that."

"People forget scandals. Or lose interest in them. Though they can come back. You've heard what people are saying about Cordy tonight."

"It's beastly about George Chase for so many reasons."

"Yes. And it shows people don't forget. In particular, they don't forget who people are."

"That's absurd. You know who you are. Bet knows who she is. It has nothing to do with where you were born."

"Not for us. Not for the people we care about. But in this world, it always will define us." Nerezza gestured to the ballroom with her fan.

Sofia's dark brows drew together above the gold edging on her mask. "It's monstrous. I know that, but I don't always realize—"

"It's all right." Nerezza squeezed her friend's arm. "Bet and I are both tough. Neither of us would have survived otherwise. There are worse things than living outside a world you never wanted to belong to anyway." Except of course that she was dragging the man she loved there with her. Ben claimed not to care. But Ben, like Sofia, didn't quite understand what it meant. In fact, though Ben was a few years older than Sofia, he was younger in all sorts of experience. When Nerezza was with him, she could catch his blind belief in the future, like a magical spell that suddenly erases obstacles at the end of a fairy tale. Then there were those other moments when cold reality set in and fears of what they were heading into washed over her. It wasn't that she thought she couldn't handle it. It wasn't even that she thought Ben couldn't handle it. It was what she thought it might do to him in the process.

But she hadn't got this far by dwelling on what might happen. She gave Sofia a smile and said, "Let's find some more champagne."

"Oh, there you are." It was Sofia's young sister-in-law Selena, in a Cleopatra costume that Nerezza was quite sure Selena had managed not to let her mother see before she left the house—at least not in its entirety. "My first proper masquerade. I can't wait to go to one in Venice, but this is quite agreeable. Though I have to say, the boys may look more interesting in fancy dress, but their conversation doesn't improve and they still tread on one's toes just as much."

"Yes, masquerades don't change essentials," Nerezza said. "Though sometimes they free people to be themselves."

"I'm not sure most of the boys I know are particularly interesting when they're themselves. I keep hoping."

"Oh, Nerezza, there you are." Lady Beverston swept up as Sofia and Selena were claimed by dance partners. "I think we're going to need more champagne. Could you be an angel and speak to Wilkins? The Duke of Wellington just came in and I need to talk to him."

"Of course." Nerezza was still not sure what Barbara Beverston thought of her, but the request marked her almost as a daughter of the house.

"Thank you, dear. You've been such a help. I could never have managed the decorations so well without you. I've never been to Italy. Humphrey spent quite a bit of time there a year or so after Waterloo and Benedict did later, but of course gentlemen are of no help when it comes to the color of draperies and the right flowers. You knew exactly what was required. You'll be hosting balls yourself in no time."

Nerezza found Wilkins, the butler, downstairs in the library, which had been given over to smoking. Only after she had spoken with him did Nerezza realize that he too had treated her quite as one of the family. She started to go back upstairs, but the waft of breeze as a couple came in from the garden drew her outdoors. A Mayfair ball wasn't so hard to brazen out—she'd been through much worse—but sometimes she wanted a moment to herself.

You'll be hosting balls yourself in no time. It hit her now she and Ben were betrothed exactly what she had got herself into. She no longer had to worry about what she had thought was the inevitable break with Ben that the future had seemed sure to hold. But she knew now that she was staying in this world—or on the edge of it—forever. Sometimes, much as she loved Ben, that thought drove the air from her lungs as though someone had suddenly yanked on her corset laces.

Lamplight created islands of warmth amid the darkened shrubbery. Laughter came from various corners of the garden, but the fresh air and shadows were comforting. Nerezza walked down the steps from the narrow terrace outside the house and perched on the stone wall that bordered the lawn.

"You look quite at home, my dear. I'd never have thought to see you like this in Mayfair society."

The voice came from the shadows. Nerezza went still. Funny, she'd thought it was hard to breathe a moment ago. Now it was as though she'd been knocked in the stomach and couldn't breathe at all. That voice could scrape across her nerve endings. She knew from Malcolm and Mélanie that he was in England, so she'd known she might see him.

But she hadn't expected Alistair Rannoch to appear in the shadows at a ball in the midst of society that believed he was dead.

CHAPTER 19

*S*he turned to see him in the shadows, leaning against the stone wall a few feet away from her. Had he been there all along? Had she been too absorbed to see him? Or had he emerged soundlessly from the shadows beyond? He was swathed in a black domino, and a black mask covered his face, but she'd know that piercing gaze anywhere, just as she'd know his voice.

Nerezza folded her hands and lifted her chin. That cold gaze had always unsettled her. But there was no reason it should do so now. He was a risk to her friends, but her part in the story was mostly in the past. At least, so she had told herself when Malcolm and Mélanie warned her about him. So she tried to remind herself now.

"I was wondering when I'd see you," she said.

"So Malcolm or Mélanie warned you. I should have guessed they would."

"Yes, you should have done. They're my friends." She tossed the word out like a challenge. Once she had scoffed at the idea of having friends. Now she knew how much support they could lend.

Alistair Rannoch gave a short laugh. "Odd how alliances change."

"You and I never had an alliance."

His gaze reminded her of things that didn't embarrass her but that she didn't care to have done with him. Not knowing the man he was now. Not now that she could imagine such things with Ben. "There are other words for it," he said. "More agreeable words."

The lamp he had insisted on leaving on flickering over the canopy. Roaming hands. Sensations that had not been entirely disagreeable. Which made her skin crawl all the more. She sat on the edge of the stone wall arranging her skirts round her. "You realize I could scream and bring people running out here. And masquerade ball or no, your masquerade of being dead would be at an end."

"It's dark. I'd be out into the mews long before anyone got out here. And you'd have nothing more to say to them than what you already knew."

Ben was teaching her how to play chess. Alistair Rannoch was superb at putting his opponent in check. "I thought you weren't interested in me anymore," she said. "My knowing who you really are is hardly an issue now. As you just pointed out."

"No," he agreed in an easy voice, quite as if he hadn't hired men to try to kill her less than a year ago. "Once the time had come to reveal myself, that at least was no longer an issue."

"And if you want me to use any sort of influence on Bet or Sandy, you have less sense than I credited. They're my friends."

Alistair Rannoch ran his gaze over her as though he was toting up her attributes. Not just her appearance, though that wasn't entirely missing from the look. "Let me guess. You're Juliet and Benedict is Romeo."

She smoothed her full violet skirts. "You should appreciate the irony. It's masquerade, after all. We're supposed to be something unexpected." In fact, it had been Ben's idea. *It's Italian. And Shake-*

speare. You know how the Rannochs are about Shakespeare. And what better for a newly betrothed couple? She could hear his voice now, impetuous and insistent. And though she'd laughed, she'd also been charmed.

Alistair shifted slightly to the side, so he could look more closely at her. "You always had spirit. You've done well for yourself. I knew you'd land on your feet, though I didn't guess you'd land quite so well as you have. My compliments."

She resisted the urge to fold her arms across her laced Elizabethan bodice. "You can't imagine I want them."

He raised a brow. "We're cut from the same cloth, my dear. We're both hard-edged and practical. We know the sort of alliances to make. That's why we always went well together."

"Don't delude yourself. What was between us was work, on my side. Nothing more." She was comfortable, more or less, with her past, but the thought that she had let him touch her made her skin crawl. Especially when she thought of Ben. Who had still not done more than kiss her.

He gave a faint smile. "In that case, let me say you're enthusiastic in your work. But you're right, there's no need to dress these things up with supposed emotions. That's something else we have in common. You're far more hard-headed than most of this group you've stumbled into, whom you now call your friends. As it happens, I don't want to talk to you about Alexander or Miss Simcox. But I thought you might be interested in discussing your betrothed."

Her fingers tightened on the ebony and lace of her fan. "Why on earth would I discuss Ben with you, of all people?"

"Because I assume you care about him."

"That's a strange thing for you to assume if you think I'm like you. Do you care about people?"

"A few, I confess. I don't generally let it get in my way. But inconvenient feelings aside, surely it's to your advantage for you and Benedict Smythe to have the easiest time possible. You've managed to secure a far more eligible match than would have seemed possible even to someone as impressed with your talents as I am. But even marriage can only take you so far into the beau monde."

The sound of a country dance drifted from the ballroom above. The sort of decorous dance performed at a well-bred young woman's coming-out ball. "I don't care about being part of the beau monde."

"But do you want to see your husband ostracized? Even with the support of the Rannochs and their circle, you can only go so far. Malcolm and his wife have ostracized themselves a bit, as it is. More than a bit, between Mélanie's playwriting and O'Roarke's divorce and his and his new wife's barely being married before their child was born."

"Ben won't lose his family. That's the most important thing."

"I wouldn't count on Beverston. He's cut from same cloth as you and I. He changes allegiances as he finds it convenient."

That, Nerezza could not deny, was true. She knew Lord Beverston all too well. Intimately, in fact, which was another complication of which she profoundly hoped Alistair Rannoch wasn't aware. These were the considerations that still kept her awake at night, even if she'd spent the day with Ben in a happy dream of love that might be just as much an illusion as one of Mélanie Rannoch's plays, in which improbable marriages had a way of working out. For someone who claimed to be a realist herself, Mélanie favored happy endings. "I don't deny the challenges. I don't see what concern it is of yours."

"It wouldn't be, in the general run of things. I'm interested in how you progress, but it's hardly my concern at the moment. But given your situation, I think we are both in a position to help each other."

The chill that had been tugging at her nerve endings settled in the pit of her stomach. "Why on earth would I help you, of all people?"

"Because you're a pragmatist. Unlike my putative son Malcolm Rannoch. Or Raoul O'Roarke, who tries to convince people he's ruthless when he's actually more driven by his so-called ideals than anyone, and all too inclined to take personal considerations into account. Or even Mélanie and Julien St. Juste, or whatever he calls himself now, who may have once seemed harder edged but are actually more in O'Roarke's mold than I'd have credited. Unlike them, you understand the value of making alliances to progress in the game. You understand that at times you have to pick which objective matters the most and whom to ally yourself with."

"I'm not sure whether to be flattered or horrified. But surely if I were so hard-headed, I'd know better than to trust you."

"A mutually beneficial alliance can work to the advantage of both of us. I credit you with being clever enough to appreciate how far you can trust me." Alistair Rannoch took a drink from the champagne glass he held in one hand. "Of course, you can take the alternative. You can be as starry-eyed as O'Roarke and all the others he's seduced to his way of thinking. Including Julien, who once seemed to have as keen an edge as his uncle."

"Do you trust Carfax—I mean, Hubert Mallinson?"

"I appreciate his abilities. I think he'd abide by an alliance as long as it was favorable to both of us. Which is why, ultimately, Hubert Mallinson and I are the ones who will win this struggle."

"You're saying you're on the same side?"

"There are far more than two sides, my dear. But Hubert and I will both do well for ourselves. You can either stay with the Rannochs and O'Roarke and their friends, who will end in ruin— or you can work with us, protect your betrothed, whom you appear to love, and be in a position to offer some assistance to the new-found friends who appear to matter to you when the pieces settle back into place. For a woman with your practicality, it shouldn't be a difficult decision to make."

The cold had hardened into a knot deep inside her. Her hands were numb, yet oddly steady. "What do you want me to do? If it's anything to do with separating Bet and Sandy, I warn you it won't work." Nerezza knew just how hard Alistair had tried to separate Sandy, who was his illegitimate son though he carried Lord Marchmain's name, from Bet. "That's my dispassionate analysis. They're my friends, but they love each other far too much, and they're too determined to be together for anything I might do to break them apart."

Alistair Rannoch's smile gleamed in the torchlight. "I appreciate that. I learned for myself that both of them are less easy to manipulate than I believed. I'm not asking you to interfere there."

"So what do you want?" Her fingers were ice through her velvet gown and satin underdress, but she kept her voice level.

"It's quite simple. I want a file of papers your future father-in-law has. He'll have them hidden somewhere, probably in his study or bedchamber. Beverston's good at concealing things. Good enough that I can't hope to find them myself in whatever time I have in this house."

"Meaning you've already looked."

"Possibly. But with easy access to the house, a woman of your talents should be able to unearth them."

"Why do you want these papers?"

"The less you know, the better. Then you won't be troubled by qualms of conscience."

"I thought you didn't believe I had a conscience."

"We all have remnants of one."

"Even you?"

"On occasion. I don't let it get in my way."

The sticks of her fan pressed into her palm. "If I do this, and Ben learns, it could destroy our relationship. Why should I give you that power?"

"Because I'd be a fool to use it."

"Why?"

"Because that would end our alliance."

Her mouth had gone dry. But a bitter taste lingered. "So this is just the beginning?"

Alistair Rannoch smiled. "Very much so."

～

"Ah. Julien." Lord Beverston passed Julien in the passage outside the cardroom. "Glad you're here. I assume it's because you're bent on investigation."

"It was kind of Lady Beverston to invite my wife and me. We had accepted her kind invitation long before today's unfortunate events. I understand you were a great help to Mrs. Rannoch, by the way."

"I don't know about that. I shared information I thought she needed."

"You must have known the trial would be discussed when you planned tonight's entertainment."

"It was Barbara who planned it. As I've said, the trial hasn't been a primary concern of mine."

"Anything that could impact the trial is power. Power is a currency you deal in."

Beverston started to speak, then jerked his head towards a door. Julien followed him into a small sitting room lined with books. Beverston moved to the drinks table, poured two glasses of brandy, and gave one to Julien. "Look, my boy, we both know Rannoch is a threat."

"Which one?" Julien asked.

"Alistair, obviously. Though I'm astute enough to know I'd rather have Malcolm as an ally than the opposite." Beverston took a drink of brandy. "Any information about the League and Alistair is helpful."

"Which is why you were trying to take my grandfather's snuffbox at our ball last June?"

Beverston froze, the glass midway to his lips. "Your wife is an observant woman."

"That's hardly a novel observation. I assume my father was part of the League, though I've never been certain."

Beverston took a drink of brandy. "Hardly a great secret. He wasn't as involved as Alistair and Glenister. Or me. But he was one of the founders. I assume it's neither a surprise, nor something you'll take personally, to say your father didn't have his younger brother's brilliance."

"I don't take offense easily, and certainly not where it comes to my father. Why didn't you want Uncle Hubert in the League?"

"Who says we didn't?"

"Because I'm quite sure he'd have accepted if you'd asked him. Possibly to spy on you, but I'm not sure."

"Well, then. We didn't trust him. Wisely, it seems." Beverston swirled the brandy in his glass. "And Alistair didn't want him."

"Why? It was long before he could have had a resentment over Arabella."

"I don't know. Alistair was never much in the habit of confiding in me, even when we were young."

"Did Alistair get on with my father?"

"As well as he got on with anyone. Alistair found your father useful."

"Because he had a fortune. Or did after he married my mother. Or did the League wash their hands of my father after that?"

"Hardly. It gave your father greater resources." Beverston's gaze settled on Julien, not softer but steady. "Your mother was a lovely woman. In all senses of the word. She deserved better than what she got with your father."

"She did." Julien shifted against the wall. Beverston sounded sincere. He had also managed to shift the conversation away from Julien's original point. "None of this explains why you were trying to take my grandfather's snuffbox. Was he also part of the League?"

Beverston hesitated. For a moment, Julien thought he was debating lying in response. "I could say so—but no. You must understand that anything connected to Alistair, anything that might give me a wedge in this game, is of vital importance."

"So why was my grandfather important? And what does his snuffbox symbolize? Or are you saying my father carved a coded message on it? I might believe it of Hubert, but my father hadn't the wit for it."

"I don't know that your father ever paid much attention to the snuffbox. But the fact that it was your grandfather's is significant."

"How?"

"You're clever, Julien. Work it out."

"My grandfather was a spendthrift and a rake. Much like his eldest son. If he wasn't a League member himself, I hardly see what he had to do with them."

"You might say I'm trying to discover that as well."

"But you know he's important."

"I know Alistair would give a great deal for that snuffbox."

"Why?"

"I'm still trying to tease out the truth. I'm hoping you can help."

"But not enough to share what you know with me."

Beverston tossed down the last of his brandy. "Not quite. Not yet."

CHAPTER 20

*H*enry Brougham was wearing a purple domino and a mask, rather than a specific costume. He probably hadn't wanted to spend the time ordering one. On the other hand, he wasn't one to hide in the shadows. Malcolm found him in the cardroom, not playing cards but standing to the side with a medieval knight and a French troubadour who, as Malcolm got a look behind their masks, appeared to be Rupert Caruthers and William Lamb.

"Rannoch," Brougham said, his voice just a shade too hearty. "Caruthers and Lamb are a bit more confident after today than I am."

Rupert shot Malcolm a sharp glance. He was a former intelligence agent who was part of most of their investigations, and though Malcolm hadn't yet talked to him about this one, he must know, or at least suspect, Malcolm was investigating George Chase's murder.

"I'm more confident about the trial, as well," Malcolm said. "Though I can't say I'm sanguine."

"It's true it was George Chase who was found dead?" Rupert asked.

190

"I'm afraid so."

"A damnable twist, with everything else that's going on," Rupert said.

"George mentioned something about Chase," William said. "My brother George, that is. He seemed concerned."

"It's a concerning situation," Malcolm said. Damn it, George and Caro Lamb's mess was going to spill into the whole Lamb family, who had enough to deal with as it was. "I need to have a word with Brougham about it."

"Not surprising," Rupert said. "Why don't you duck through that door? We'll cover for you."

Which effectively left Brougham without an avenue to avoid talking. Rupert was a good ally. Malcolm shot him a look of gratitude as he and Brougham went into the antechamber.

Brougham tugged off his mask and regarded Malcolm with a mix of wariness and entreaty. "You've learned more?"

"Considerably." Malcolm pulled off his own mask. He suspected it had left the imprint of lines round his eyes. "Caro says you haven't come close to renewing your affair, but that she went to Wardour Street with you to call on a friend you had made in Italy. Who happens to be a witness at the trial."

"Damnation," Brougham said. "I should have known you'd talk to her."

"Yes, you should."

"I just didn't think it would happen so fast."

"Murder investigations tend to move quickly."

Brougham glanced to the side.

"Henry." Malcolm put his hands on the round table in the center of the room. The light from the candelabrum it supported jumped over Brougham's face. "We're trying to solve a murder."

"I'm trying to defeat the King of England."

"They aren't mutually exclusive."

Brougham drummed his fingers on the tabletop.

"We're on the same side," Malcolm said.

"You're the one who's always saying there are more than two sides."

"Fair enough. But I hope you know I'm to be trusted with a confidence."

"In the midst of an investigation?"

Malcolm drew in and released his breath. "You have a point. My father says loyalty is a matter of choices. But out of pure pragmatism, wouldn't you rather tell me than have me poking about?"

"Damn it, Rannoch." Brougham tossed down a drink from his brandy glass. "What did Caro tell you?"

"She told Mélanie. And Emily."

"Oh, Christ. My bête noire."

"Emily won't say anything that will harm Caro's reputation. Or her marriage, which Emily seems to care rather more for preserving than either Caro or George do at times."

"So what did my sweet Caro tell all of you?"

"That she went with you to call on the Contessa Montalto, whom the two of you had met in Italy, and who had come to England to be a witness for the queen."

Brougham took another drink of brandy, stalked to the fireplace, and rested his arm on the mantel.

Malcolm regarded his friend. "Talk, Henry."

Brougham crossed his legs at the ankle, glass cradled between his hands. "The contessa has the potential to give victory to the queen."

"She's an important witness?"

"She could be our star witness. She's a lady of unimpeachable virtue, who can—and will—testify to the queen's good character while in Italy."

"If she's a star witness, she must be able to testify to more than the queen's character."

Brougham drummed his fingers on the mantel. "She can say that the queen confided in her that her—the queen's—intimacy with Bergami was a sham, designed to embarrass the king."

"Do you believe that?"

"It doesn't matter if I believe it. Anna—the Contessa Montalto —believes it, and she gives a believable account that provides an explanation for all the stories about the queen's supposed intimacy with Bergami. All the rumors, all the accounts of what people claim to have seen. They don't have to believe that those accounts are lies, they can accept that they were an elaborate subterfuge by a deeply injured wife seeking vengeance on the philandering husband who had embarrassed her from their wedding night, kept their daughter from her, and now seeks to deny her her rightful place as his queen."

"You're good, Henry."

"I know how to give an account of the information at my disposal. But the story is Anna's."

"How did you find her?"

"Caro and I met her in Italy. Caro must have told you that."

"She did. I want to hear your version."

"I heard Anna knew the queen—even then, it was clear any information involving the queen might be of help—and I went to call on her to get her story and brought Caro with me. I thought having another woman present might be of help. Anna is widowed and living quietly, but she was delighted to receive us. She and Caro got along at once. They shared the experience of having husbands who had made them less than happy. I left them to their confidences, which did a world of good."

"You're a devil, Henry."

"Tell me you've never used Mélanie or other women agents you worked with to obtain confidences."

Mélanie, Kitty, Rachel Garnier in Brussels. It was a fair point. "Acknowledged. Did you bring testimony by the contessa back with you?"

"I brought notes. It wasn't clear yet what we'd need. Or if we'd need testimony at all. As time went on, it became more and more clear that I might need her to testify. And yes, I investigated to verify her story. She passed with flying colors. She was reluctant to come to England, but at last I persuaded her. She couldn't bear to see another woman ill-used by her husband. But you know what will happen if the Tories get wind of her evidence. They'll investigate and find some chambermaid or boot boy to say something against the contessa. The contessa—who is eager to do what is right, but shy of public comment—will decide she can't speak. It's taken the greatest persuasion by Denman and me to convince her to talk. The merest whiff of scandal and she'll be off back to Italy, leaving a cloud of questions and no way to answer them. Which will only make things worse than they'd have been if she'd never left Italy at all."

"You trust her?"

"She's been nothing but genuine, and all her vetting has returned impeccable answers. She has no interest in British politics. She's only talking because she believes it to be the right thing to do. Because she cares about the queen. Which I do, for all I don't deny the political advantage to be won."

"I never said you didn't." Malcolm folded his arms. "Who else knows about the contessa?"

"Denman. One of my clerks. Caro. Not anyone else. Part of the value of her testimony is taking the other side by surprise. And if word got out that she was here, it's more likely people would come looking for her, and she'd get scared off. I've promised to have the greatest care of her reputation."

"But you told Caro the contessa was here."

"Anna was restless. She came to London a few weeks ago— we couldn't be sure how long it would take her to travel or how long it would be before we needed her testimony. She wants to avoid public comment, but living in rooms in Wardour Street is stifling to a woman used to a villa on Lake Como, where she could walk and entertain close friends, or the delights of Milan and Venice, where, though she didn't mingle in society, she could go to the theatre and small parties. Even avoiding society, she is used to a great deal of entertainment. I thought seeing Caro would cheer her up and also help convince her of the importance of her testimony. Caro's always been able to talk to her in a way I wasn't. I never quite realized the value of having a woman as a partner. You must find that a great deal, working with Mélanie."

"In myriad ways. So you asked Caro to go with you to call on the contessa?"

Brougham nodded and took a drink of brandy. "Caro was reluctant, but I assured her no one would ever hear of it."

"Well, that failed. George followed her."

"Yes, that was unfortunate. Obviously, I wasn't expecting it. I mean, it's been years. And I wasn't exactly reluctant for the affair to end."

"It can take more than years to get over a partner's infidelity."

"I suppose so." Brougham kicked the toe of his shoe against the fire basket. "I confess I wasn't at all prepared when you asked me about our visit to Wardour Street."

"So you pretended to an affair that could have ruined Caro's life?" Malcolm could barely keep the edge from his voice.

"You and Mélanie would hardly let it do that. And George was already convinced we were up to no good."

"You could have tried to disabuse him of that."

"Do you really think anything I might have said would have done so?"

"It would have been a start."

Brougham glanced to the side and tossed down a drink of brandy. "I needed time to think. I'd have made sure Caro didn't suffer for it, in the end. You must believe I'm fond of her."

"I do believe you're fond of her. I also know that once damage is done to trust in a marriage, it can be hard to repair."

"Says the man with a perfect marriage." But Brougham regarded him for a moment, and Malcolm felt as though he'd stripped off a mask he had no desire to relinquish. "George and

Caro's marriage was already damaged. You've a right to put that at my door too. But it was years ago."

"This made it worse."

"All right, yes." Brougham kicked the andirons. "I'm a black-guard who puts my own agenda ahead of what might laughably be called the personal relationships in my life. I don't wish Caro harm, but you can justifiably say I used her and didn't protect her. Satisfied?"

Malcolm folded his arms across his chest. "Why the hell not just tell me the truth?"

"I told you. If the Tories get the least whiff, they'll try to discredit Anna."

"Are you telling me with a straight face you believe I'd have said anything to a Tory?"

"Information has a way of getting out. You're an agent. Can you tell me everyone who knows something isn't a liability? That you haven't even kept things from your wife?"

"At times." Largely because his wife had been a French agent and might have competing loyalties, though he'd also kept a considerable amount from her before he knew that. Which hadn't been at all good for their marriage.

"You're in an investigation. I imagine you're talking to Carfax. Hubert. Whatever we're supposed to call him now."

"You can't imagine I'd have told Hubert this."

"It's damned hard to keep things from him." Brougham picked up his glass and turned it in his hand. "You think Chase knew about Anna?"

"We haven't found anything in his papers about her. But he was trying to see Liverpool, claiming to have information that could be vital to the trial. He was living in the same house as the contessa. Difficult to imagine the two aren't connected. How much could he have overhead you discussing with her?"

Brougham took a sip of brandy and seemed to be chewing on it. "I've been asking myself that ever since you came to see me this afternoon. Anna and Caro mostly reminisced about Italy. Talked about the latest fashions and the sort of thing women like to go on about. But on earlier visits, I'd gone over her testimony with her. Even if Chase merely had her name and the idea that I thought she could be an important witness, he could have done damage." Brougham took another drink of brandy. "He didn't talk to Liverpool?"

"No."

"Do you think he spoke with anyone else?"

"About your contessa? Not that I know of."

"That you *know of*." Brougham ran his gaze over Malcolm as though he were evaluating a hostile witness. "What else was Chase up to?"

Malcolm hesitated. But Brougham needed to know this. And he needed to know Brougham's response. "Have you heard of the Elsinore League?"

A flicker of recognition crossed Brougham's face. "Vague rumors."

That in and of itself was interesting. Even two years ago, the League had been much more in the shadows. Malcolm hadn't heard of them himself. "Rumors of what?"

Brougham took another drink of brandy. Malcolm had seen him in court. Henry Brougham was well aware of the value of gesture as theatre. "They pose as a sort of hellfire club, but they are something much more complicated. They prize secrecy. Rather to excess, like many secret organizations. They have both Whigs and Tories in their number. But they don't seem to support either."

"They support themselves. And though they're more driven by personal advancement than belief, their beliefs, such as they are, are to the conservative side. Alistair Rannoch was a founder."

"But you aren't a member?"

It was the first time Malcolm had been asked if he was a member of the Elsinore League. "Need you ask that?"

Brougham set his brandy down on the mantel. "These days I need to ask everything."

"Fair enough. If you know anything about Alistair Rannoch and his attitude towards me, you know he'd have done everything in his power to keep me out of the group. And if you know anything about my beliefs, you know nothing on earth would have prevailed upon me to join them."

Brougham gave a slow smile. "Fair enough. And I hope you can accept the same about me."

Malcolm nodded. And he could. More or less. Brougham was ambitious, but Malcolm was quite sure his beliefs were sincere.

"So, what do the League have to do with Chase and Anna?"

"Chase had been working for Lord Beverston, who's a member of the League. And he'd worked for Alistair Rannoch in Italy."

"Before your father was killed.""

"You know damned well he's not my father. He's also not dead, as it happens."

Brougham let out a whistle. "Where the hell is he?"

"In hiding. He seems to feel he needs a pardon. We haven't worked out why. And George Chase also seems to have been trying to rehabilitate himself."

"Do you think the Elsinore League are interested in Anna?"

"There's a big a split in the League now, with Alistair on one side and Beverston on the other. But both sides are interested in information that can help them gain power."

"They could be trying to discredit her. The Tories would pay a lot for that. If they knew about her."

"Could she be discredited?"

Brougham reached for his brandy. "I told you. She's a lady of unassailable virtue."

"I know what you told me."

Brougham tossed down a swallow. "I'd look a bit of a fool putting up a witness who could easily be cut to ribbons on the stand. We vetted her. Before Caro and I met her in Italy. And even more extensively before we brought her to London to testify."

"Nothing about this trial is easy for anyone. And plenty of people with unassailable virtue have been cut to ribbons. On the witness stand and even more by society. One might say society is particularly brutal on the virtuous."

"That sounds like a line from one of your wife's plays. I hired someone to investigate Anna. Because her value as a witness isn't so much in the facts she relates, which may be questioned; it's in who she is and the impact of her support of the queen. You listen to her and can't imagine her lying. So if her credit could be damaged, so would her value as a witness. Denman and I hesitated to put her on the stand for that very reason. We tried to poke holes in her image to see if it could be done. But neither of us could do so." His brows drew together.

"But you're wondering," Malcolm said.

"How could I not wonder? Especially now she seems to have been compromised."

"Chase didn't go to Beverston with what he knew about the contessa. He was trying to take it straight to Liverpool."

"I suppose that's something to be thankful for."

"That he never got to talk to Liverpool?"

Brougham's head snapped up. "You're wondering if I had Chase killed to stop his talking? No, don't answer that. You're a good agent. A good investigator. You could hardly fail to wonder."

"I have to ask certain questions, whatever my instincts."

"Chase was contemptible. You can say with justice I haven't treated Caro well. But what Chase did to Cordelia was far worse. I can't honestly say I'm the least bit sorry he's dead. I'll own I'm vastly relieved he never got to talk to Liverpool. But I had no notion he was trying to talk to Liverpool. I had no notion he was even in Britain. But I don't suppose you believe that."

"I'm inclined to. I want to."

"But that doesn't stop the questions."

Malcolm met the gaze of his ally and friend, and possible opponent. "It can't stop the questions."

Brougham inclined his head. "Point taken."

"I'm going to need to talk to the contessa."

"I thought you and Davenport spoke with her this afternoon."

"She told you?" Malcolm asked.

"She sent word. She was concerned. Concerned someone who lodged near her had been murdered, and concerned you were asking questions."

"We'll need to speak with her again with the truth in the open."

Brougham regarded Malcolm with a hard gaze "The truth as you know it."

"Just so."

CHAPTER 21

"There you are."

At the familiar voice, Nerezza turned from her perch on the stone wall to see Ben step through the French window onto the terrace with that smile that had turned her heart over ever since she had first met him in Venice. She'd once have laughed at the idea that a heart could turn over. Until she'd experienced the sensation.

Alistair Rannoch had vanished into the shadows. Nerezza had already glanced over, and the torchlight showed enough to convince her he wasn't in hearing range. At least, probably not.

She got up from the wall and walked up the steps to Ben. "I just wanted a bit of air," she said, meeting his smile.

"Balls can be stifling. In more ways than one." Ben crossed the terrace to her side, kissed her, drew back to study her face, then tightened his arms round her. "Are you all right, darling?"

"Of course." Nerezza smiled into Ben's familiar blue eyes. Amazing how well she knew them. Once, lying to Ben was something she'd taken for granted. She had sworn their relationship couldn't work without it. Now he knew and accepted so much, and the lie bit her in the throat. At one point she'd have said she didn't know what guilt was. Now she knew it was a knife point stabbing against her collarbone.

But he'd noticed something was amiss and, as Mélanie said, it was always good to use as much of the truth as possible. "I saw Alistair Rannoch."

Ben's eyes widened. "At the ball? What's he thinking of?"

"I don't know. But it's more risk to him than to me."

Ben's gaze skimmed over her face. "He didn't try to do anything?"

"He tried to play on our past. More fool he. I told him what was between us, such as it was, was business on my side. Even if I would admit to sentiment, I have no sentiments towards him for him to play on."

"It has to have been—uncomfortable."

Nerezza put her hands on his chest. "I can live with what I've done, Ben. If I let the past unsettle me, our lives would be impossible." She reached up to kiss him, perhaps as much to reassure herself as him. "And believe me, the past is in the past."

His arms slid round her. "I don't care about the past as long as we can plan for the future."

"I've never been one to live in the past. The future is much more agreeable." Nerezza took Ben's hand and tugged him towards the house and the ballroom upstairs. "Let's dance."

Ben grinned and pulled open the French window for her. Nerezza went through, steeling herself to the fact that she was now lying to the man she loved more than ever.

FRANCES WAS USED to moving about a ballroom. By time she'd turned eighteen, she'd mastered a sense of moving through a crowd without being caught too long in tedious conversation or being cornered into accepting a dance invitation from a man who'd tread on one's toes or let his hands go where one didn't want them, while at the same time showing one's gown to the best advantage. She hadn't been long married before she leaned to use a masquerade to the best advantage for finding time alone with the right man—or men.

Tonight was different. Because she was married. Because her second marriage was very different from her first one. Because society no longer had the same allure. Because they were in the midst of a murder investigation. And because of the personal turmoil that hovered just on the edge of everything right now. Not really on the edge so much, given the things she and Archie had both revealed today. It shouldn't be a surprise given their age, given the lives they'd lived, that they still had secrets. But it was one thing to know it. It was another to actually confront those secrets in the cold light of day, in front of both their families. Her Queen Elizabeth gown was laced tightly but she didn't think that accounted for how unsettled her insides felt.

"You're a sight for sore eyes, Fanny."

Frances nearly spilled her champagne. It was Glenister, obvious behind his mask, and though there was no reason to think he knew what she had learned from Archie today, his voice did sound a bit overhearty. Fanny smiled into his familiar face, still carelessly handsome despite the lines of dissipation left by three decades of indulgence. Aging was tiresome, but really, they were all managing it better than they had any right to expect.

"Let me guess," she said, surveying his purple-slashed black doublet and breeches. "You're Don Juan."

"That would be a bit obvious, wouldn't it? I'm supposed to be the Earl of Essex. And I didn't even know you'd be Queen Elizabeth, though I should have guessed."

"Archie's Robert Dudley. That makes him your stepfather."

"Odd how a masquerade changes our perceptions. Can I persuade you to dance?"

"You don't need to persuade me, Frederick." Frances gathered up her brocade skirt and stepped into Glenister's arms as a waltz started.

"Did you know Chase was in London?" Glenister asked after the opening twirls and flourishes.

"No. Did you?"

"Good god, no. No reason for him to have sought me out. But I imagine Malcolm and Mélanie and the rest of you are in the midst of the investigation."

"Archie and I always seem to help out round the edges."

"More than that, as I hear tell." Glenister spun her under his arm. "You know he's alive, don't you?"

"Archie? I should hope so. I arrived at the ball with him."

"So you do know."

"If I didn't, Frederick, you'd be risking my fainting dead away on the dance floor."

"You're made of sterner stuff than that. But I was already quite sure you knew. Because Malcolm would have warned you. And because I think he—Alistair—would have tried to see you."

"He did. At another ball. He had illusions he could make use of me. I disabused him." And yet she'd waited to tell Malcolm. And to tell Archie.

"Be careful, Fanny. I don't understand his games. But I'm more aware than ever of how he can slip under one's guard."

"You think he's trying to slip under my guard?" The dance had them side by side, hands twisted together overhead.

Glenister twirled so her back was against him. "I think he'd like nothing better. I don't think he can do it. I doubt he believes he can do it."

"Why did he come back, Frederick?"

"I wish I knew."

"You truly don't?" She spun forwards. "Or perhaps more important, why he disappeared in the first place?"

His mouth was set in the practiced smile she'd known for

three decades. "Alistair's and my friendship was a sham. Surely you know that by now."

"A sham you both got so caught up in, it became real at times. Surely you aren't going to deny that."

They circled round the floor for the length of several heart-beats. "You can't think Alistair confided in me."

"I think you knew him. In ways few people did." In fact, at one point she'd wondered if they'd been lovers, if the whole League had been a front for those sorts of games, though she tended to doubt that now.

Glenister's mouth twisted below his mask. "I may have thought I did once. These days I doubt I knew him at all. I certainly don't know why he disappeared. Or why he chose to inflict himself on all of us again now."

Frances tilted her head back. There was a great deal she wasn't sure about when it came to Glenister. But she was quite sure he was lying.

When the dance ended, Fanny moved towards the supper room. Not because she was hungry so much as because circulating was good for gathering information. It had always been that way, except that now the information was in the service of an investigation rather than in the service of gossip. She was just inside an archway draped in Venetian red when a hand closed on her arm.

Not entirely surprising at a ball where she knew so many people. And yet, perhaps it was Glenister's words, but she knew the touch at once.

"My god, you're mad. This isn't even the garden like last time."

Alistair was wearing a black domino and mask. Like dozens of others who didn't want the bother or expense of new fancy-dress attire. "Masquerade balls are useful. We often found excellent uses to put them to in the past."

"None of which we need now."

"Perhaps not, but we need to talk. And I happen to know there's an agreeable little anteroom through that door."

For a number of reasons, she needed to hear what he had to say. Without acting as though she were in any sort of a hurry, she slipped through the crowd to the door in the paneling that Alistair was holding open.

"I have quite agreeable memories of this room," he said, glancing round at the peacock silk wall hangings. "There's a new settee. I wonder if it's more comfortable than the old one."

"I wouldn't know."

"Or you've forgot."

"I'm sure the room's been completely redone. Barbara Beverston likes the latest things."

Alistair's gaze moved over her through the slits in his mask. Cool, appraising. The gaze of an opponent. And yet the echo of a lover was not completely gone. "I was a fool, perhaps."

"We're all fools, at times."

"It seems absurd for me to say this, but I put too much credence on our past relationship. You'd think I'd be used to double crosses."

"Yes, one would think it." Frances regarded her former lover steadily in the light from the candles on the mantel. "You can't claim you wouldn't do the same."

He reached out and lifted the side curls of her red wig, then let them fall against her cheek. "We always had honesty."

She steeled herself not to respond. "But we didn't share everything. In fact, it was a given that we didn't."

He dropped his hand to her shoulder. "What's between Malcolm and me never concerned you."

Her fingers curled into the folds of her gown. "It should have done. Far more than it did. Malcolm was my responsibility."

"Malcolm could take care of himself at a very young age."

"He shouldn't have had to."

"He had O'Roarke. He had you. I didn't see your association with me turning you against him."

"No. I can acquit myself of that, at least. But I betrayed him by letting myself consort with you. And certainly now the lines are clear."

"I don't think there's a clear line in this whole sorry mess." He watched her for the length of several heartbeats, his gaze sliding over her face through the shadows. She could almost feel his familiar fingers tugging loose the strings on her mask. "Do you remember that inn in Berwick? The proprietress kept glaring at us, the washing water was never really warm, and the bed creaked."

"And the coverlet was an unfortunate shade of yellow. What brought that up?"

"I've been thinking about it lately. The night you lost your earring—"

"It was a comb."

"The hedgerows full of buttercups—"

"It was hawthorn."

"The night you sprained your ankle—"

"It was my wrist. I should think you'd remember what we were doing at the time I sprained it."

Alistair laughed and went still, watching her. She had the oddest sense he was searching for something. "I think that may be the happiest I've been in my life."

Something tightened within her. And she knew how at risk she was. "You obviously still want something, Alistair. You might as well tell me directly."

"I want a great many things that I don't think I ever properly appreciated."

"That doesn't explain the way you've been acting. Not remotely."

"Surely you understand complicated motives. I miss you, Fanny. You can't tell me you haven't missed me."

"Of course I've missed you, you provoking man." The words tumbled from her lips. God, what a relief to speak the truth. "That doesn't mean I trust you."

"I'm not asking for your trust."

"My dear. If there was a saving grace to our relationship, it was that we didn't pretend it was anything it wasn't."

"But are you sure we know what it was?"

She moved to a lyre-backed chair that looked appropriately hard. "You're trying to get round me."

"You like the challenge, Fanny. You like going back and forth and getting round someone. From what I've seen of you and Davenport, you must be bored. He can't challenge you."

Frances spread her hands over the stiff silk brocade of her skirts. "Archie challenges me in ways you couldn't possibly understand."

"I don't like to admit to jealousy. But I'll confess to being jealous of Davenport." He paused a moment. "I don't think you cared for any of the others."

"I hope I'm not quite so heartless. But no, I didn't. Not in that sense."

"Well, then. Are you claiming it's over?"

"A thing can change without being over, Alistair." Her fingers tightened on a fold of her skirt. She could feel the imprint of the brocaded flowers. "I haven't forgot. But I'm not the woman I was."

He held her gaze for a long moment. Something shifted in his eyes. But when he spoke his voice was light. "Oh, well. I'm not the man I was either. I don't imagine any of us is the person we used to be."

"And thank god for it." Frances regarded the man who had been her lover. Who was probably the first man she had ever loved. The first of two, the other of whom she was married to. "What do you want, Alistair?"

"I won't interfere. But I'm going to succeed. I'm going to come back. It's not going to be easy for Malcolm. Or O'Roarke. Or those close to them."

"Which includes me. And my husband."

"As you say. I won't let you stand in my way, Fanny. But I'd like to make this as easy as possible for you."

"You can't imagine I'll forgive you if you hurt Malcolm."

"I don't imagine Malcolm has any desire to keep what's not his."

"No. He'd willingly relinquish it to you now if you asked. I assume you have your reasons for not doing so."

"A good try, Fanny. My reasons are my own. Suffice it to say I have my plan and I don't think it will make Malcolm happy. But I can ensure the fallout for you is less disagreeable."

"I'll take care of myself, Alistair. What's between us is over. But if you want anything to exist between us, you'll realize what hurting Malcolm would do."

"What's between us will never be completely over, Fanny. Not with living ties between us."

A chill spread through her tightly laced bodice. "What do you mean?"

Alistair held her gaze over the flickering candle flames. "You can't think I never wondered."

"I'm sure you've had a great deal to wonder about. And with my life, as you must know, there are any variety of possible answers."

"But only one truth. Assuming one could arrive at it."

"Assuming even I could." Fanny hesitated. "Alistair. What really happened the night Cyril Talbot died?

She saw the start in his eyes. If he'd known George was investigating this, he was a good actor. But then, she already knew that. "What brought that up?"

"Recent questions."

"Connected with this investigation?" He regarded her for a

moment, more intrigued than alarmed. "That's—interesting. You might ask your husband."

"I did. He knows more than I knew. But I don't think he has anything like the full story."

"Don't go there, Fanny. You don't want to. And it won't help anyone."

"I think the question is whom it might hurt?"

"It would hurt people, but not me. It wasn't my tragedy. Do you have other questions, Fanny?"

"Did you kill George Chase?"

His mouth curved beneath his mask. "If I had, do you think I'd admit it?"

"Surely you know enough about George Chase to realize I'm not brokenhearted that he's dead."

"In that case, if I say I didn't kill him, will you believe me?"

"Darling Alistair. I haven't believed a word you've said to me from the day my sister introduced us."

"Hardly a surprise." He held her gaze for a long moment. "But then, as we were saying, people can change."

"I'm too old for some sorts of change."

"My darling." Alistair didn't move, but she felt his presence as though he'd taken her in his arms. "You'll never be too old for anything."

CHAPTER 22

*N*avigating a ballroom while aware that a good portion of the gossip occurring behind fans and champagne glasses was about his own marriage was hardly a novel experience for Harry. Even when he'd escaped to the Peninsula after Cordy ran off with George Chase, he hadn't entirely been able to avoid regimental balls and diplomatic soirées. There'd been engagements in Brussels when he and Cordy saw each other again—most notably the Duchess of Richmond's ball. And in Paris after they'd reconciled, he was quite sure people had watched them dance and gone off to the cardroom to lay bets on how long the reconciliation would last. But people got tired of gossip. In recent years, the looks they'd got had been more bemused smiles when they danced together all evening, or ate supper together, or left early because of their children. His uncle and Frances, or Julien and Kitty, drew far more attention.

Tonight, the looks were back. And the whispered conversations that stopped when he drew too close. Which was a shame because any conversation about George Chase was a possible source of information. He and Cordy were too publicly involved in George Chase's life to be able to effectively investigate his death. Which was damnable, because if Harry had ever needed distraction, he did now. And he was quite sure it was the same for Cordy.

"Davenport."

Harry turned and found himself looking into the friendly, level gaze of Thomas Thornsby behind a white mask. Thomas was costumed as the Emperor Claudius.

"It's good to see you," Harry said.

"With everything going on, I understand you haven't been able to come round to the Classicists' Society. But you're missed."

"You're always welcome to call on us in Hill Street. You know that."

"That's kind of you. I don't get out much myself. I wasn't going to come tonight but Mama asked me to for my sisters' sake." Thomas hesitated. "I heard about what happened this afternoon. I'm sorry. It can't be easy for you or Lady Cordelia."

"Thank you. We're better equipped to handle it than we would have been a few years ago. The investigation is what's important."

"That's why you're here tonight."

"Partly. We'd already promised Edith. She's never been to a masquerade before." Harry hesitated. Edith Simmons had come to live with him and Cordelia after a particularly challenging investigation into the murder of Thomas's brother. Harry had already suspected the feelings between Thomas and Edith, who was also a classicist, but by the end of the investigation those feelings were laid bare. As were the complications that kept them from being together. In the old days, Harry wouldn't have pushed it. But he hated to see anyone make the mistakes he had. "Edith misses you."

He saw the flash in Thomas's eyes and then saw Thomas draw inwards. "Edith has the chance for a life she couldn't have had with me. Even if we could have had a life together."

"And you think seeing you will hold her back?"

"I would never presume. But I think—"

"My dear fellow." Harry put a hand on Thomas's shoulder.

"What you and Edith feel for each other is quite obvious. Edith's had a chance to stretch her wings. But it hasn't made her a different person. I don't think it's changed what she wants." He glanced round the ballroom. "She's Agrippina, by the way. She has a red cloak and a gold circlet."

"I know. I saw." Thomas flushed behind his mask.

"Excellent. Ask her to dance. A good way to spend time together without even needing to talk."

Thomas glanced away. "I can't, Harry. My family situation hasn't changed either. We can't count on Aunt Shroppington. I don't want to count on Aunt Shroppington. In fact, I can't bear the thought of any of her money touching anyone close to me. I know she's here tonight and I'm dreading seeing her." He shuddered, which was understandable, considering they were quite sure his great-aunt had had his brother killed. "But that means the only way to recoup the family fortunes is through me."

Harry cast a sidelong look at his friend. "For someone bent on marrying for money, you are leading a quite retiring life. I'm fortunate never to have had to hang out for a rich wife, but I don't think the Classicists' Society and the occasional outing to the British Museum is the way to do it."

Thomas's mouth twisted in what was half a grimace, half a wry grin. "I came here tonight. I do occasionally accompany my sisters to Almack's. But I tend to dance a duty dance with them, and then once they find partners, retreat to the sidelines and hope I can find rational conversation."

"I am entirely in sympathy. Though it does indicate you aren't working as hard as your sisters."

Thomas blinked behind his mask. "I beg your pardon?"

"At finding a financially advantageous match. If a single man in possession of a large fortune must be in want of a wife, surely the same could be said to apply to heiresses?"

Thomas colored. "My sisters—"

"Enjoy it more. Quite. It's a damnable situation to be in, old

213

fellow. Believe me, I'm sympathetic. But I hope it gives you some sympathy for your sisters. They may enjoy Almack's more, but they may be as likely as you to fall in love with someone without a fortune."

"Do you think I don't know that? It's part of why I'm determined to make a prudent match myself. So my sisters have more freedom. But you're right. I haven't done a very good job of pursuing it."

"Quite understandably, given that you're in love with someone else."

"I don't exactly have a great deal to offer."

"You have a well-informed mind and a great deal of kindness. Both of which should matter a great deal. But you're in love with someone else, which is a bit of a drawback."

Thomas glanced away. "Love isn't supposed to have a great deal to do with it. I suppose I need to find a girl who—"

"Doesn't want to fall in love? That sounds distinctly disagreeable. Of course, I think the reason Cordy accepted me was that she didn't want to fall in love again. But that was beastly. And it only worked out because she—remarkably—happened to fall in love with me. If I'd been in love with someone else at the start, I don't know where we'd have ended up. I don't recommend it."

"You must know I would never—"

"It's not easy. One can think one can do something, can manage anything to get what one wants. But in the end, feelings can be damnably messy. I thought I'd endure anything to have Cordy. I thought nothing else would bother me. I was wrong, no matter where we've ended up. I know your reasons for marrying are different. But you may find your feelings change once you marry."

"Are you saying I should abandon my family?"

"I can't imagine your not being there for your family. Supporting them financially isn't the only way to do it."

"Someone has to support them. Or my sisters will have to—"

"Turn governess like Edith?"

Thomas blanched. "Being a governess wasn't easy for Edith."

"But she survived. I wouldn't romanticize it. Or minimize the horrors for some governesses. Edith was far more fortunate than many. But I doubt she'd have preferred her brother marry for money to save her from it."

"She's never—"

"My good idiot, of course she wouldn't say it to you."

"No, I can see that. But I can't imagine this is the fate you want for your daughters."

Harry felt himself give a wry smile. "I want to protect my daughters from all adversity, as I think every parent does. I also want them to have the tools to cope with adversity."

"I'm not unaware of the hypocrisies and challenges in our world. But it's the world we're living in at present." Thomas looked away. "This case you're investigating. The man killed in the House of Lords."

"George Chase."

"Yes." Thomas shifted his weight from one foot to another. "Is there a connection to the Duke of Trenchard?"

"What makes you ask?" Harry said in an even voice.

"I know he's been involved in all this. In this League you talk about. I overheard some muttering in the cardroom just now about this being the worst scandal since Trenchard's murder."

"Did you know Trenchard?" Harry asked.

"Not really. I met him once or twice. Aunt Letitia knew him."

"I didn't realize." Harry kept his voice even, to cover his quickening interest. Anything to do with Lady Shroppington might be very relevant.

"I remember calling on her once—back in the days when I still called on her—and finding Trenchard there. They went quiet as I came into the room."

"When was this?"

"Before Trenchard died, obviously. Before he was killed. But not too long before. I remember thinking about it when we learned he'd been murdered." Thomas stared at him. "Good god. You don't think Aunt Letitia had something to do with his death too?"

"No. But I think they may have been plotting together."

"Plotting what?"

"Trenchard was scheming to get himself made prime minister at the time he was killed."

"But he's a Tory."

"He wanted to oust Liverpool."

"Why on earth would Aunt Letitia care about that? She knew Trenchard, but I couldn't see her plotting to help him."

"Not him on his own. But she may have thought she or those she cared about could gain from his being in power."

Thomas stared at Harry as though he had just upended centuries of accepted analysis of a Roman imperial dynasty. "You think Aunt Letitia was trying to change the course of British politics?"

"Is that so surprising? Given what we know about her?"

"We know she had my brother murdered." Thomas drew a breath with a scrape like broken glass. "Because she couldn't bend him to her will. She's ruthless and unscrupulous. To a degree I couldn't fathom. But that was about trying to control her family. Which we already knew she did. This is about trying to control the country."

"You don't think her interests extend so far?"

"She's a Mayfair dowager."

"Who committed murder and is far more involved in the Elsinore League than we at first realized."

"But she's not an international spy, Harry. She's—a hostess."

Harry glanced round the ballroom. The decorations, the musicians, the footmen circulating with champagne, the supper room beyond. "Hostessing is no mean feat. But perhaps you're underes-

216

timating the scope of your aunt's abilities. Which may go to our conversation about your sisters. And Edith."

"Aunt Letitia isn't Edith. Thank god."

"By no means. But like Edith, she may have sought a greater scope for her talents."

"Good god, you can't be saying you admire her."

"She's one of the most formidable foes we've faced. But I can appreciate her abilities. And the way she put them to use."

"But why? Uncle Shroppington died before Trenchard. And even if this started while he was still alive, surely she didn't expect Uncle Shroppington to gain anything under a Trenchard ministry. He had no interest in politics. He had no interest in much of anything, as I recall. You can't convince me she had a burning desire to remold the country—or that she'd have seen Trenchard as the man to do it if she had. So what did she have to gain from it?"

"A good question. Influence?"

"On Trenchard? To what end? She wasn't going to run the country herself. I couldn't see her running it through Trenchard—not unless she had some policy she wanted to advance, and that wasn't Aunt Letitia. She wasn't the sort to care about Catholic Emancipation, or the Corn Laws, or electoral reform or abolition."

"So she must have been seeking favor for someone else. Or power through someone else."

"Lewis seemed to be her designated heir. That's why she was so angry he wouldn't make the marriage she wanted. But he was hardly of an age to benefit from a Trenchard ministry. At best, he could have had a very junior position."

"No, that doesn't seem right. Who else might she have wanted to benefit?"

"Uncle Shroppington, I suppose, while he was alive. I think, from things my parents have said, she always wanted to push him to do more in the Lords. But he was never more than a Tory gentleman who was a reliable vote when needed and was happier at his club."

"What about a lover?"

Thomas's brows drew together above his mask. "She—"

"She's been widowed for a long time. Not that being married would be a drawback for many."

"Yes, but—" Thomas shook his head. "I can't see it."

"Not surprising, given that she's your aunt. Something connected her to the Elsinore League."

"You think one of the members—Good god, they're young enough to be her sons."

"And I'm sure most have had mistresses who are twenty years older, at some point in their lives."

Thomas stared at Harry from behind his mask. "It was hard enough to accept what she—what she did to Lewis. But at least that made a certain sense. I knew how she wanted to bend Lewis to her will. This makes her seem a wholly different person."

"It's hard. To face that about someone we think we know. But it's amazing how often it happens."

"But if—" Thomas shook his head as though his whole world had fallen apart.

Harry put a hand on his friend's shoulder. Because Thomas wasn't the only one who felt that way.

"LAURA."

Laura smiled at Edith Simmons, a former governess who now lived with Harry and Cordy and was working with Laura on the school they were starting with the Rannochs and Davenports and Julien and Kitty (impossible to call Julien and Kitty the Carfaxes) for children who couldn't get a good education otherwise. "I'm sorry, I think I owe you curriculum notes, but the day turned unexpected."

"I quite understand. I feel beastly for Cordy and Harry," Edith said. "And of course, asking questions is the worst thing I could do. I haven't even had a chance to tell them—I had tea with Alice today. Lady Wilton. For whom I used to work as a governess." She colored but kept her gaze steady. "Whom Lady Shroppington blackmailed me into spying on."

"Go on," Laura said. Alice Wilton and her husband Sir Toby had been in Italy where he'd been on a diplomatic mission and had got to know Queen Caroline. And Alice had had an affair with Lewis Thornsby and had written him some letters that might have been used for or against the queen. Laura and her husband and the Rannochs and Davenports and Julien and Kitty have been involved in recovering them.

"Alice talks more freely to me ever since we helped get her letters back," Edith said. "But today, perhaps because of the trial, she talked about their time in Italy more than she's ever done. She said with everything being said before the Lords it was hard to believe there were any secrets anymore. Apparently there was another diplomat they knew who was sent to Italy long before the Milan commission. In 1816, I think. A Mr. Sidney Newland. His work was much less official than the commission's was later, but Alice said Mr. Newland hinted to her that he was uncovering evidence of interest. Only then his carriage overturned in a river when he was traveling back to England. Sir Toby was called to the scene of the accident and asked to look into things. Mr. Newland was carrying papers about the queen and our government was very concerned about what might come to light. Alice said—and this would sound even more shocking to me if it weren't for what I've seen in the past year—Sir Toby always suspected Mr. Newland's death wasn't an accident."

Laura gripped her hands together to steady them. She and her late husband James had been in a carriage that overturned in a river. James has been killed and she had been presumed dead. And the Duke of Trenchard, James's father and Laura's lover, had been behind the accident. "Does Sir Toby have any idea of who may have been behind it?"

"Not according to Alice. But she said Sir Toby thought at first that the motive was to take the papers Mr. Newland was carrying about the queen. Mr. Newland's dispatch box was never recovered despite an extensive search. In the end it was assumed to have been washed downriver, but Sir Toby thought that was awfully convenient. He was concerned the papers would be made public in some way, but then when they weren't, he wondered if Mr. Newland had been killed to keep the papers from coming to light." Edith hesitated. "I don't know everything about this new investigation into Major Chase's death. But I can't help but wonder if that has something to do with it."

Laura smoothed the purple velvet of her gown. "Nor can I."

~

"MALCOLM." Lord Glenister's laugh was a shade too hearty. The light from the candle sconces in the cardroom, where Malcolm had encountered him when he left the antechamber after his interview with Brougham, caught glitter in his eyes. "I didn't think masquerades were to your taste."

"I actually prefer them to other sorts of evening entertainments—they're less stuffy."

"They are indeed. Though for reasons I didn't think much interested you." Glenister took a drink from the brandy glass in his hand. His face was flushed beneath his mask. "I suppose you're here to talk politics. Or because of the murder investigation."

"A bit of both."

"Damned odd George Chase was back in London."

"You hadn't seen him?"

"Why the devil would I have seen him?"

Malcolm cast a glance round the cardroom. "Could I have a word with you in private, sir?"

For a moment Malcolm thought Glenister was going to protest. Then the other man inclined his head. "Of course. Though I can't see how it will help."

Malcolm opened the door to the sitting room where he'd spoken with Brougham. It held a set of decanters. Glenister crossed to the drinks table at once, added to his brandy, and held a glass out to Malcolm. "Beverston keeps his better liquor here."

Normally Malcolm would have declined, but it might help the discussion to put him and Glenister on a more friendly footing. "You really hadn't seen Chase since he'd been in London?"

"Of course not. I didn't know him well. His father and I weren't particularly friends, and Chase was the wrong age to have been at school with Quen and Val. Why are you asking?"

Malcolm took a drink of brandy. It was indeed a superb liquor, strong but supple as velvet. "Chase had been asking questions about your family since he'd been back in London."

Glenister froze with his glass halfway to his lips. "What sort of questions?"

"About your brother Cyril's death."

Glenister spun away. "Damn it. He had no business—"

"We talked to Frances and Archie—"

"You—" Glenister turned back to him. Behind his mask, his eyes looked as though the veil of civilization had been stripped away.

"I wouldn't have, under other circumstances. And I don't think they'd have shared the information. But it's now part of a murder investigation."

"It can't possibly have anything to do with Chase's death. Cyril's death was—a quarrel between brothers." Glenister's voice was as rough and raw as the crudest spirits.

"Uncle Frederick." Malcolm regarded his godfather. "I'm a brother myself. I understand quarrels. I don't believe in dueling, but I can imagine doing violence to a brother. I'd have been hard pressed not to do so to Edgar, had he lived."

Glenister's fingers closed round his glass. "Edgar had given you great provocation."

"True. So what did Cyril do?"

Glenister glanced away. "Nothing to rival Edgar's actions. I had a mistress I was rather fond of. An opera dancer from the Haymarket. It was some time since my feelings had been so engaged. I went off to Ascot and came back to find that Cyril had engaged her affections and set her up in a house in Hans Place. I was angry enough at that. Then, when we were all at Dunmykel, I learned he had done it because of a bet with Trenchard. That stirred all sorts of memories of Alistair's and my bet, and Alistair's seducing my wife and the whole sorry mess. I snapped when I heard it. When I challenged Cyril, I think I was half challenging Alistair, as I hadn't dared do when I learned he'd got my wife with child."

That made a certain sense. Alistair's betrayal of Glenister, seducing Glenister's wife and fathering Glenister's heir, had to still be raw. And yet— "Archie said he and Alistair tried to talk you out of it."

"I was furious. In that moment, Cyril's betrayal seemed intolerable. The moment Cyril fell, I saw how wrong I'd been. I can blame it on drink. I can blame it on my anger at Alistair that had been simmering for years. I can say my arm was shaking and I didn't even mean to hit him. But in the end, it was my fault. It's my responsibility. I'm the one who has to live with it. Which I have. Every day since."

The pain in Glenister's voice rang sterling true. But something was still off. Malcolm had great belief in reason and evidence. But sometimes one had to go on instinct. And his instinct was that Glenister was lying about something. He took a sip of brandy to give himself a moment to think. "Uncle Frederick—"

The door burst open.

"Malcolm," Lord Beverston said. "Good. I need to talk to you. Carfax as well, so I've brought him."

By Carfax, he meant Julien, who followed him into the room and sent Malcolm a look that was half apology, half query.

Beverston met Glenister's gaze. "Probably as well you're here too. Odd to think we all sat through the events today in the chamber."

"I'm finding the trial quite interesting." Julien prowled across the room and poured himself a glass of brandy.

"Yes, it's not often parliamentary debates can rival a French novel."

Julien took in the aroma of the brandy with an appreciative sniff. "Most French novels I've read are rather more subtle."

"It's enough to put any man off the idea of trying to end his marriage. Funny how it's one thing to tell stories of one's exploits over the port at White's and quite another to have them debated in the Lords. Of course, at White's one can frame the story." Beverston crossed to the decanters. "Glad to see you've made yourself at home." He poured another glass and took a deep drink himself. "George Chase was working for me. I expect you know that by now, Glenister. Perhaps that's what Malcolm was talking to you about."

"No, Malcolm and I were talking about—the past."

Beverston met Glenister's gaze for a moment and gave a curt nod. "Chase was gathering information for me, but he was interested in information about a number of people."

"He wanted to return to his old life," Malcolm said.

"Exactly," Beverston said. "More fool he. One can never go back. Chase was asking about Cyril Talbot's death, as I told Mrs. Rannoch this afternoon. But he was also interested in the events just before Trenchard's death, and his attempt to get himself made prime minster."

Julien shot a look at Malcolm. "How did Chase know about that?"

"I don't know," Malcolm said.

"He didn't say," Beverston said.

"How much did you know about it?" Malcolm asked.

"More than I wanted to. I wished Alistair at the devil at the time. I never had much use for Trenchard. He was willing to go to lengths that shocked even me."

"Just out of curiosity, wouldn't that make you not want to see him as prime minister?" Julien asked.

"Damn it, St. —Car—can't I call you something else? I can't look at you and think Carfax."

"Nor can I when I look in the mirror. You'd better call me Julien. Carfax makes me gag."

"Malcolm knows damn well—and I think you do too—that I've never had much taste for politics. But the thought of Trenchard as prime minister did give me pause."

"Eventually," Glenister said.

Beverston flashed a look at him. "Eventually's what matters. It gave a number of League members pause. That was what started the rift. I actually was prepared to go to considerable lengths to stop Trenchard. But he was killed first."

"Did George Chase say why it mattered to him?" Malcolm asked.

"He asked if it had to do with why Trenchard was killed," Beverston said.

"Interesting," Julien said. "Did Chase know about the League? Before he went to work for you?"

Beverston gave a curt nod. "Which surprised me. His father wasn't a member."

"What about his mother?" Malcolm asked.

"She wasn't a member either."

"Did she have a lover who was?"

Beverston glanced at Glenister. "Not to my knowledge," Glenister said. "I don't have much memory of her."

"Maria Chase was a pretty woman," Beverston said. "But she didn't run in our set. And she wasn't the sort for dalliance, from what I heard."

"Trenchard's plot was when things fell apart," Glenister said. "For the League."

"I think they started to fall apart when Alistair turned on you," Beverston said.

"Possibly. But not for the wider group. Trenchard overreached with his plot to take Whitehall. And Alistair backed him."

"Alistair did more than back him," Beverston said. "Alistair was ready to be the power behind the throne. And if Trenchard had become PM, I doubt Alistair would have been content to remain behind the throne for long. He always wanted recognition in anything he did." He shot a look at Glenister. "That's why he was so quick to want anything of yours. Your paintings. Your wine."

"My women?" Glenister asked with a raised brow.

Beverston didn't blink. "Just so."

"You appreciate power, Beverston," Malcolm said. "Did you consider allying yourself with them? With Alistair and Trenchard?"

"Only as a very fleeting thought."

"A bit more than fleeting from what I heard," Glenister said.

"I admit their audacity was intriguing. But—" Beverston took a drink of brandy. "I pretend to few morals. Having sat in the Lords the past few days and weeks and months, I can't say I think very highly of my country. But I do feel a certain loyalty to it. Enough not to wish Trenchard on it."

"God, no," Glenister said. His voice shook with unexpected feeling. "And I speak as one who abhors politics."

"My father quite agreed when he heard about the plot," Malcolm said. "And he's hardly an admirer of Lord Liverpool."

"Nor am I," Beverston said. "For different reasons. But Liverpool, for all his faults, isn't going to gobble Britain up whole."

"None of which explains why Alistair had to disappear," Malcolm said. "Long before the plot failed."

Beverston and Glenister looked at each other again.

"If I knew that, I'd understand Alistair," Glenister said. He looked more in command of himself now, his habitual armor settling back into place, a mask behind his mask. "And I don't. I never have. He had secrets. The entire time I knew him."

"The plot was causing unrest in the League," Beverston said. "But it hadn't failed by the time Alistair supposedly died. In fact, Trenchard didn't really set it into place until after Alistair supposedly died. Disappeared."

"Did Trenchard turn on Alistair?" Malcolm asked.

Beverston swirled the brandy in his glass. "I don't think so. But even if he had, why would Alistair have disappeared? He had money and property and position. Why not stay and fight Trenchard?"

"Why indeed?" Malcolm said. "Was Alistair working for the French?"

"What makes you ask that?" Glenister's voice cut with unexpected sharpness.

"He's afraid of being accused of treason. He wants a pardon."

"Your father would know more about that," Beverston said. "Or your wife. Or you." He looked at Julien.

There was a time when those words would have had Malcolm arranging to get his family out of the country. But Mélanie and Raoul had pardons. And he was coming to terms with how much of their activities a number of people knew. "None of them knows of any connection of Alistair's with French intelligence," Malcolm said.

"Assuming they're telling you the truth," Beverston said.

"Always an assumption. And one I know better than to make." Malcolm held Beverston's gaze steadily. "Are you saying you know to the contrary?"

"No. Any moral lapse on Alistair's part wouldn't surprise me. Assuming any of us can even use the word moral. But I would be surprised to find him working for the French. Perhaps, above all, because I don't think he'd have wanted to associate himself so closely with O'Roarke."

"I can see that," Julien said. He was standing to the side, one hand resting on the back of a gilded settee, legs crossed at the ankle. "By the way, I really don't know of any connection of Alistair's to French intelligence. Not that I would know. And not that I expect you to believe me."

"And yet Alistair apparently committed treason," Malcolm said. "Enough that he's set on getting a pardon."

"Enough that he faked his own death," Julien said. "Not something one does lightly. Speaking from experience."

Beverston shot him an appraising look. "Yes, I imagine you do know. Judging by circumstances. Perhaps you'll have more ideas about Alistair than I do."

Julien took a sip of brandy. "Believe me, I've devoted a lot of attention to Alistair. And his motives baffle me."

"What does Lady Shroppington have to do with it?" Malcolm asked.

"Why should she have anything to do with it?" Glenister asked.

"She's been connected to the League from the start. And presumably to Alistair."

Silence gripped the room. Beverston cast a glance at Glenister. "I think it's past time we told them."

"Told them what?" Glenister asked.

"Surely you've suspected. Or perhaps you know."

"Know what?" Glenister's voice was taut.

"The reason for Lady Shroppington's singular role in the League."

"She doesn't have a role. Not really. It's not as though she came to our parties." Glenister gave a rough laugh. "The very idea is absurd."

"I can imagine more absurd things," Beverston said. "And our parties were absurd enough as it was."

Glenister shot him a look. "She may have dallied with Alistair, but she's not the sort for the type of dalliance that took place at League parties."

"I very much doubt she dallied with Alistair." Beverston tossed down a drink of brandy. "Unless this whole business is even odder than it already seems. But she's always been there. Funding expeditions. Drawing the line at certain activities. Reining Alistair in. To the extent anyone could."

"No one could rein Alistair in," Glenister said.

"But you have to admit Lady Shroppington could better than most. I remember her appearing at Oxford when we were all staggering back from a punting expedition that had involved considerably more than punting. She just stood there, with the point of her parasol sticking into the mud on the riverbank, and stopped Alistair dead in his tracks. I think I knew then."

"What?" Malcolm asked. His voice came out sharper than he intended.

"If you're implying that she was his mistress—" Glenister began.

"For god's sake, Frederick, no. I already said so. I'm quite sure Lady Shroppington is Alistair's mother."

CHAPTER 23

*M*alcolm put out a hand and found himself gripping the giltwood chair back. A dozen confused thoughts tumbled in his brain. And yet behind them was the sort of clarity that comes when a code is broken or the theme of a story makes the disparate pieces fall into place. "I don't know why that's surprising," he said. "Given the other stories we have of people's birth. But somehow, I never thought—" He shook his head. "Fatal mistake."

"Hard to imagine a change to something one grows up with as immutable fact," Julien said. "Alistair's supposed parents—"

"He never talked about them much," Malcolm said. "He never talked to me much about anything. And fairly early, I was sure his parents weren't my grandparents. His mother died in childbirth. Supposedly died in childbirth. One more reason I never questioned it, I suppose."

"They must have been planning to pass him off as a twin," Julien said. "And then she died and lost her own baby."

"Yes." Malcolm met Glenister's gaze for a moment, because that was precisely what had happened when Glenister's own sister gave birth to the man who was now married to Malcolm's sister, Gisèle. Save that Andrew's adoptive mother and sister had survived. "I gleaned enough growing up to know he had an isolated childhood," Malcolm continued. "I can see why, if his adoptive father had lost his wife and baby and perhaps didn't regard Alistair as truly his. They lived in a remote part of Scotland. A lonely childhood. I can almost—"

"Rannoch, no," Julien said. "You're the most compassionate person on this benighted planet, but don't start feeling sorry for Alistair. That's too much even for you."

"One can feel sorry for what someone has gone through without making excuses for the man he became," Malcolm said. For a moment, memories of moments from his own childhood chilled him. Curled up with a book in the library at Dunmykel. The rattle of his mother's carriage receding in the distance. And he had been far less isolated than Alistair seemed to have been. "I had Raoul. And Arabella, at least some of the time. You had your mother for six years."

Julien nodded. "I may not have your compassion, but I can at least appreciate it. Who sent Alistair to Harrow and Oxford?"

"His godfather. Sir Ian Rannoch. From whom Alistair later bought Dunmykel. At least, that's the story." Malcolm frowned, dredging up the fragments of information he had about Alistair's past. Bits and pieces he overheard as a child. Careless comments his mother had made. Alistair had never told him anything.

"Lady Shroppington would have been a young wife when Alistair was born, if I'm right about her age," Julien said. "Could Ian Rannoch have been Alistair's father?"

"I don't think so." Glenister spoke up for the first time. He drew in and released his breath. "Lady Shroppington is, in truth, Alistair's mother. He told me as much one night at Oxford, when we'd both drunk enough for confidences without quite being insensible." He drew another breath with the scrape of iron. And perhaps regret. "In the days when we were still friends. She paid

Alistair's school and university fees. Ian Rannoch was a cousin on her mother's side. She sent the money through him. According to Alistair, Ian Rannoch was no more than a go-between. Alistair said Ian Rannoch's tastes ran to men."

"That doesn't necessarily mean they didn't also run to women," Julien said cheerfully.

"No," Malcolm agreed. "Though one would hope if he was the father, he'd have done more than act as a go-between." He turned to Glenister. "Did Alistair know who his father was?"

"He told me not," Glenister said.

"Your father trusted Alistair," Malcolm said to Glenister. He didn't elaborate—Georgiana Talbot's out-of-wedlock pregnancy wasn't something to share with Beverston if he didn't already know about it—but he held Glenister's gaze as he spoke.

Glenister glanced away. "Alistair was clever. Father could appreciate that. And didn't hesitate to make use of Alistair's talents."

"Could it have been more than that?" Malcolm asked. It would make sense of so much. Alistair's jealousy of Glenister, the bond between the two men, the way Alistair pushed against the bond, broke it with betrayal, and yet the two remained twined together.

The gaze Glenister turned to Malcolm was stark with a torment that said he recognized it too. "I don't know," he said in a raw voice. "I wondered. Not at first. But not long after we left Oxford. When I learned my father had employed Alistair to do errands for him. Not even at first with that. But eventually the thought occurred to me. And then it was like being struck in the head or slapped in the face, and I couldn't believe it hadn't occurred to me sooner."

"Did you ask Alistair?" Julien said.

"I danced round it. He claimed not to know. He may have been telling the truth. Though if so, it was one of the few times Alistair ever did. At least when it came to me."

"Did you ever ask your father?" Malcolm said.

"My god, no." Glenister turned a face of horror to him. "My father and I didn't have frank conversations in general. That would have been beyond the pale."

"Did your father know Lady Shroppington?" Julien asked.

"Of course he knew her. They both traveled in London society. He didn't know her well, so far as I know. But then I suspect my father bedded any number of women I have no reason to think he knew well." Glenister glanced into his glass. "I confess I have as well."

"Do you have any reason to think your father supported Alistair?" Malcolm asked. "Aside from hiring him for odd jobs?"

Glenister's brows drew together above his mask in seemingly genuine concentration. "Not that I know of. I confess when I inherited the title, I even looked through his papers for any connection to Alistair. But aside from payments I already knew about or suspected, I didn't find anything. However, there were a number of payments in my father's records that are vague as to whom they were to and what for. I'm quite sure his papers included payments for by-blows. As I mentioned to you once before, Malcolm." Glenister coughed, because that discussion had included Andrew's birth and Glenister's sister Georgiana's illegitimate child, whom Alistair had helped conceal. "My father wasn't sentimental. Not with his children—his acknowledged children. So I don't imagine he'd have been so with by-blows." Glenister tossed down his brandy. "I don't know if Alistair's being my brother would make me feel better or worse about him."

"Understandably," Malcolm said.

Julien looked at Beverston. "You've been very quiet, sir."

"I'm on the fringe of this," Beverston said.

"You aren't on the fringe of anything when it comes to the League. You've been part of it from the first."

"Almost the first. It started with Alistair and Glenister." Beverston nodded at Glenister.

"I heard recently that it started with Lady Shroppington."

Glenister and Beverston exchanged looks. "Alistair suggested forming a club to me," Glenister said. "But later he admitted it had been Lady Shroppington's idea. She gave him funding for some of the first—League events."

"Interesting." Julien leaned against the wall, legs crossed at the ankle. "Considering what went on at those events. Though perhaps her tastes ran that way. Did she attend?"

"Good god, no," Glenister said. "Alistair would have been horrified at the very idea."

"If Alistair knew she was his mother, he couldn't very well have been blind to what she'd got up to. Though I suppose it is different with one's own parents."

"You know damn well it is."

"I always thought Alistair designed the League to get himself ahead in the world," Malcolm said. "But it was Lady Shroppington who wanted that for him."

"Alistair wanted it too," Glenister said. "But Lady Shroppington saw the possibilities. Before Alistair did, I think. She had a great deal she wanted him to achieve."

"Not uncommon in a parent," Julien said. "Though most don't create secret societies with an international reach and a penchant for blackmail to bring it about. From what I've seen of Alistair, I imagine at times he frustrated her."

"God, yes," Glenister said. "That was clear from the first. She had her own ideas about who should and shouldn't be in the League. They didn't always agree with Alistair's."

"What about my father?" Julien asked.

"What about him?"

"Did she want him in the League? Or my uncle?"

Glenister frowned. "She wanted them both, actually. Alistair was reluctant. He went along with your father. He drew the line at Car—Hubert. Said he was dangerous."

"He had a point. Lady Shroppington didn't think he was dangerous?"

"She said it was better to have him on their side."

"She had a point as well. Possibly a better one."

"I only heard rumors," Beverston said. "But the story was she wasn't happy about Alistair's adventures in France in the eighties. Especially the business with Jeanne de la Motte and the diamond necklace."

"I'm not surprised," Julien said. "I should think even a quite ruthless woman would be a bit alarmed at her son's helping bring about a revolution and topple a monarchy. On purely selfish grounds, even if she hadn't a thought for the politics."

"She threatened to cut off his funds," Glenister said. "But by that time, Alistair had enough of a fortune of his own that she couldn't control him." Glenister crossed to the drinks table, refilled his glass, refilled the others' glasses, took a drink. "I don't think Alistair knows who his father is. At least, I don't think he did in those early days. One night, after one of our parties—in the early days—before I was married. Before Alistair had started his games with my wife—when we staggered back to our rooms at Oxford, Alistair dropped his coat on the floor and said it was odd to think one or more of the men there tonight might be his brother."

Malcolm's fingers tightened round his glass. "So he thought his father was the father of another League member? Do you think Lady Shroppington told him as much?"

"I don't know. I asked how he knew, and he said, 'Just a feeling.' Perhaps she implied something to him. Which of course made my own father an option. So I said, 'Do you know—' and Alistair just said, 'I don't know anything at all.' He could shut down a conversation more ruthlessly than anyone I've ever known."

Malcolm looked at Beverston. "If you're asking what I know, I don't know anything," Beverston said. "I wondered, at times. I can't quite say why—the way Alistair would look round the group. The fact that Lady Shroppington had helped put the League together. She wanted men who would help him, that was clear even to me on the fringe. Presumably his brother or brothers would be someone who could help."

"Your father—" Malcolm said.

"Would be the right age," Beverston said. "He wasn't conveniently out of the country at the time of Alistair's conception. I admit to checking the dates. He knew Lady Shroppington in the social sense. I can't say there was any more to it than that. But I also can't be sure there wasn't. Like Glenister, I prefer to know as little as possible of those details about my parents. I never guessed they could be of tactical advantage at some point."

"Alistair tried to help make Trenchard prime minister," Malcolm said.

Beverston tossed down a drink of whisky. "Don't think I haven't thought of that."

"And presumably the plan was for Alistair to be the power behind the throne."

"In Alistair's mind, I suspect," Beverston said. "And in Lady Shroppington's."

"I confess to a distinct lack of interest in the details of the peerage," Julien said. "Talking of things one doesn't realize could be of tactical advantage. Trenchard's father—the late Trenchard's father—"

"Would have been alive when Alistair was conceived," Beverston said. "I can't speak to whether or not he was in London or elsewhere in Lady Shroppington's vicinity at the requisite time. But it's possible."

"And now?" Julien said. "Alistair wants to reinstate himself. Presumably the truth of his parentage isn't the secret that made him flee Britain. But could his parentage be part of his plan to reinstate himself?"

"Alistair's plans have always been a mystery," Glenister said.

Beverston frowned into his brandy. "I agree. But without laying undue importance on bloodlines—which I agree really aren't the issue here—I can't help but think that Alistair's father's identity may be the key to who he is."

CHAPTER 24

*E*dith Simmons turned from a group of friends—or perhaps acquaintances was a better word—and took a step towards the supper room to find herself face to face with Thomas Thornsby.

Thomas hesitated, leaning slightly to one side, which was perhaps discomfort, perhaps an attempt at verisimilitude in his Claudius costume. "It's good to see you."

"It's been a long time."

"I don't go out in society a great deal. There haven't been events to bring us together."

"You could call in Hill Street. You can't think Harry and Cordy wouldn't be glad to see you. You've been friends forever."

"That's not—I can't properly offer you what I should, Edith. So it seemed I had no right to call on you."

"Oh, stuff. That assumes calls are only part of the marriage game. I'm not in the least interested in the marriage game. I'm a teacher now. I have a job, not just teaching, but running the school Laura is starting with the Rannochs and Davenports and Carfaxes. A job I can build on. I doubt I'll ever get married."

"That would—be a waste."

"Of what?"

"Of—Don't you want a family? I mean with someone, not—"

"I'm not sure." Edith fingered a fold of her Agrippina gown. Talk about complicated families. Nothing in the present tangle either of her friends or of the current royal family could rival the Julio-Claudians. "I'm quite busy enough with what I have now. I'm not very patient. I don't want to turn into—"

"I don't want to turn you into anything you aren't, Edith. I never did. If—That wasn't the future I saw for us. Your changing into anything you didn't want to be."

"I know, Thomas." Edith smiled at him. It was like smiling at a bittersweet memory. Except that her throat tightened beneath her gold Roman necklace in a way that was very much in the present and said that Thomas might not be quite as much a memory as she tried to convince herself. She did believe he wouldn't have intended to try to change her. But whether that would have stood up to the habits and training of a lifetime was another question. But hardly a question there was any point dwelling on, given their current circumstances.

"I hate to think of your being alone, Edith."

"Being alone isn't so bad. I quite enjoy the freedom. At times I quite like being alone. That's not to say I never—think of other things."

"Edith—I would give anything for things to be different. But I don't see a way for them to change at present."

"You'll always have your family to think of, Thomas. Nothing's going to change that. I wouldn't want that to change. It's one thing to go against convention like Sandy and Bet. I can cheer that. But it's another to hurt other people. I couldn't forgive myself for being responsible for your family's suffering. Marriage is challenging enough. We could never build our happiness on hurting other people, let alone your family."

Thomas met her gaze for a moment. It was so rare either of

them spoke of marriage. For a moment the possibility, even the denied possibility, hung between them, shimmering with things they couldn't let themselves explore.

Edith drew her red cloak about her. "I should go. It's rather complicated just now. They're in the midst of an investigation. I'm only on the fringe, but even that makes it hard to think of anything else."

"I quite understand," Thomas said. "I—Never mind."

"What?" Edith asked.

"Nothing."

But the look in his eyes told her he might not be as much on the fringe of the investigation as one would think.

ARCHIE COULD STILL ENJOY a good game of cards, in the right circumstances, with the right company. But these days the card-room held less allure than it had for much of his life. The clouds of smoke tickled his nose and made his throat and eyes sting more than in former days, the brandy and port didn't taste quite as good as they once had done. The talk sounded cruder and less amusing. But it was still an excellent location to gather information. And he and Fanny were at the masquerade for the investigation. On their own there were far more convivial ways they could have spent the evening.

He played two hands without gathering more than the expected bawdy gossip about the king and queen, and the debates about what the queen might have got up to on her polacre in Italy versus what the king did regularly at his Brighton Pavilion. Then he excused himself so he'd have a reason to move tables, and went to the console table with the decanter to pour another glass of brandy. As he set down the decanter a soft voice spoke beside him.

"Davenport."

Before he even looked round, Archie knew that voice. For all he'd known this confrontation was coming, he felt himself go still. "Rannoch." Archie turned to look at the figure in the black mask and domino. "You realize I could simply raise my voice and end your masquerade."

"You could. But other than creating a stir, what would be the point? Malcolm would simply have to publicly relinquish his inheritance before it was required."

Archie took a drink of brandy. It gave him time. And, he conceded, it also settled his nerves. "What do you want?"

"A few moments of your time. There's an antechamber next door."

Archie took another drink of brandy. There was no question he was going to agree, but he wasn't going to give Alistair the satisfaction of doing so too readily. Then he inclined his head, topped off his own glass without offering any to Alistair, and then led the way across the room to the adjoining antechamber. A small room with cream and gold hangings in which he had enjoyed more than one tryst. Very likely Alistair had done so as well. And more than likely with the woman to whom Archie was now married.

Archie set his brandy glass down on a satinwood table and turned to face the man who was his wife's first love.

Alistair was standing with one hand on the back of the cream satin settee. "Funny. I never thought you were interested in her in the old days."

Archie took a drink of brandy. Part pose of unconcern, part need of fortification. "I could hardly have failed to appreciate her. I'm not blind. But Fanny had little interest in me. And while I prided myself on taking affairs lightly, I perhaps had a certain reluctance to entangle myself with a woman who was in love with another man."

"You knew."

"I am a fool in many ways, Rannoch. That is not one of them."

Alistair met Archie's gaze. For a moment they might have been facing each other across a dueling field. "So you saw her as off limits?"

"Unlike some, I never cared to intervene where strong emotions existed."

Alistair gave a short laugh. "I've often thought that my life would have been much easier if Fanny had been different. After the first time, I tried to tell myself it was merely a conquest. The victory of conquering a woman who had seemed to despise me. After all, I was—"

"Already in love with her sister."

Alistair shot a look at Archie. "I'd never claim to be so commonplace as to have been in love with my own wife."

Archie held his opponent's gaze. "That doesn't mean you weren't."

For a moment Alistair's gaze was cut raw. While at the same time it damned Archie for his pretensions. "What I felt for Arabella is immaterial. But when the affair went on with Fanny, I couldn't claim anymore to simply be interested in conquest. Even in my own mind. After I went abroad, I tried to tell myself she didn't matter. When I heard of your marriage, I told myself it could hardly concern me. That I'd ended things with her. That almost worked. Until I came back and saw her again." His mouth twisted in what might have been irony or regret. "It would have been so much easier if she'd seemed aged. Dimmed by the conventions of matrimony. Jaded, dull, overdressed. But the moment I saw her in the younger Davenports' garden, it was clear she was still Fanny. Which is damned awkward."

Archie turned his glass in his hand. "Yes, I suppose in some ways it would have been easier for me if I'd wanted out of my marriage by the time you reappeared. But of course it was nothing of the sort."

"You must have known—"

"Oh, yes. When I married Fanny—when I fell in love with

Fanny—I knew full well she'd been in love with you. But it's one thing to fall in love with and marry someone knowing they've loved someone else who is dead and in the past. It's a bit different when that person walks through the door."

"So, not surprisingly, you wish me at the devil."

"For a number of reasons, Rannoch. But not on Fanny's account. If she prefers to be with you, I don't want her. I'm a late believer in marriage. But I have enough respect for it that I don't believe it should be about sacrifice."

"Do you think Fanny agrees?"

"You'd have to ask her."

"I won't mince words with you, Davenport. I want back what I gave up. And part of that is Fanny. Though I can't be sure I'll get her."

"Neither can I."

"Can you be sure you'll keep her?"

"That would assume she's mine to keep. Neither of us thinks that way. If I could be sure of anything about Fanny, she wouldn't be the woman I love." Archie tossed down the last of his brandy. "Was there more you wanted to talk about?"

Alistair regarded him with a steady gaze. "Cyril Talbot's death."

Archie kept his fingers steady on his glass. "What about it?"

"It's going to be talked about. Chase was asking questions. I imagine Malcolm has asked you about it."

"No comment."

"It won't help anyone. It won't bring me down. But it will create endless complications."

"For Glenister? Why would you care about that? Considering you cuckolded him with his wife and left him to raise your child? Rather better than you might have done, from what I've observed, but nevertheless."

Alistair remained unmoving. "I don't suppose it's occurred to you that my feelings might be reparations towards an old friend I badly misused?"

"From you? No."

Alistair shrugged, stirring the folds of his domino. "Have it your own way. But you saw what went on that night. Whatever we may think of each other, I appreciate that you have keen instincts. I think we both know better than to unearth things that can only cause further damage. You've been a spy, Davenport. Isn't part of being a spy knowing which secrets to keep?"

~

"O'Roarke." Liverpool paused in the passage outside the ballroom, where he came face to face with Raoul. "I just saw your charming wife on the dance floor. I am reminded I did not have the chance this afternoon to ask after your family."

"Understandably, in the circumstances."

"I trust they are well."

"We are, thank you. My daughters are growing at a rate that bewilders me."

"My wife and I have not been so fortunate as to have children, but I understand that is often the case. Your marriage appears happy."

"It is. I am beyond fortunate. In ways I could never have imagined."

Liverpool hesitated a moment. "I remember when we first met. When we were helping Louise. I asked you what she meant to you. You said she was a friend and your life was too complicated at present for anyone to be more. And you weren't sure that would ever change. You also said your heart wasn't yours to share."

"Did I really say something so trumpery?"

"It made a big impression on me.

Raoul remembered the conversation. It had been impossible at the time to imagine loving anyone other than Arabella Rannoch, with whom he had already had a child. "And then, a few years later, I risked matrimony after all. With disastrous results. More than anything else, the success of such a venture may have to do with the intricacies of the two people involved. I certainly never thought to find anyone who would put up with me. All the more so after my first marriage."

Liverpool gave a faint smile. "I never thought of my wife's putting up with me, precisely—we were too young. But I'm very fortunate she does."

"I still don't live a life best suited to having a family. But I am somehow managing to do it. And I am inestimably grateful for the opportunity."

"You seem—different."

"In essentials, I think I'm very much the same. But I like to think I'm easier to live with. I hope my wife would agree. I did not expect to find this—perhaps not ever, certainly not at this point in my life."

"Quite so." Liverpool jerked his head to the side. The conversation had perhaps been sincere, but it had also been cover to get them to the substantive part of the discussion. Raoul followed him into an antechamber. "Have you learned anything?" the prime minister asked.

"George Chase was acquiring blackmail information on a number of important people. We haven't learned what he knew about the trial yet." That was true, as far as it went, though they knew more than Raoul was prepared to reveal to Liverpool. "Some of it may concern the Duke of Trenchard."

Something flickered in Liverpool's gaze. "Trenchard is dead."

Raoul's fingers tightened. Trenchard had not only been an Elsinore League member with his own agenda, he'd been Laura's lover and had blackmailed her into spying for him by controlling her daughter Emily. Who was now Raoul's daughter, though Trenchard had fathered her biologically. "Trenchard wasn't working alone." Raoul hesitated. They hadn't spoken of this directly, but Liverpool must either know already or needed to do so. "Have you heard of the Elsinore League?" There was always the chance he was a member, though Raoul doubted it, from what they knew.

Liverpool frowned. "What do you know about them?"

"You must know my son and his wife and other of our friends have been working against them."

"I've heard rumors."

"And it's perhaps best for you not to know more. Given that a number of your allies are probably members."

Liverpool gave a short laugh. "The secret, perhaps, to holding disparate groups together. I'm something of an outsider to all. I know the Elsinore League are a group of powerful men given to dissipation, but also to advancing their own interests. I'd never have expected to be part of a group like the Elsinore League. They're considerably higher flyers than I am."

"Your father was an advisor to the late king."

"And his father was a country gentleman. My other grandfather was an East India Company official. I was never part of the Glenister House Set. Or the Devonshire House Set."

"Your sister-in-law is now the Duchess of Devonshire."

Liverpool's mouth tightened. He had married his wife not many years after he and Raoul had come to Louise Doret's aid, and Raoul suspected the determined, resilient romanticism Liverpool had shown with Louise had been part of his marriage as well, for he had married his wife in the teeth of opposition from his father. Her father was the Earl of Bristol, but she didn't have the fortune the senior Liverpool had sought for his son. Lady Liverpool, from what Raoul had seen, was happy as a Tory political wife, but her sister had been the mistress of the Duke of Devonshire, lived in ménage-à-trois with him and his wife, and helped preside over Devonshire House, the heart of glittering Whig society. Upon the death of the duchess, she had married the duke. Their daughter was Caroline St. Jules, who had married George Lamb, and run off to Italy with Henry Brougham, and was now caught up in the mystery surrounding George Chase's death.

"Families can be complicated," Liverpool said. "As I'm sure you will appreciate."

"None better." Raoul hesitated. He hadn't discussed it with the others, but it seemed time to share the secret. "Trenchard wasn't acting entirely alone when he tried to bring you down."

"You mean he had the so-called League behind him."

"He had some of them. It seems to have been the start of a rift in the Elsinore League. Alistair Rannoch was his ally."

"Another enemy of yours. Gone now as well."

"So we thought."

Liverpool froze. "Thought?"

Raoul drew in and released his breath. Saying it was still fraught. "Alistair Rannoch is alive."

"O'Roarke, this is no time for trifling."

"I'm not."

"You're saying a wealthy, powerful MP staged his own death and disappeared for three years?"

"Apparently."

"For god's sake, why?" Liverpool demanded.

"Probably for the same reason that he's now seeking a royal pardon. I thought perhaps you'd know."

Liverpool caught and held Raoul's gaze. "Rannoch was in France in the eighties and nineties."

"I know. I've heard the rumors he was a spy for the French. I don't believe he was. He was working with the Royalists. Which hardly counts as treason."

Liverpool looked away. "Rannoch played complicated games."

"Plays would be more accurate. I imagine he saw himself as the power behind Trenchard."

"I would have wished him joy of that if their scheme had succeeded. Trenchard was a lot of things, but he wasn't a man to be manipulated."

"Alistair was never an insider in the Tory party."

Liverpool gave a grunt of acknowledgement. "No. He had other interests."

"And yet he founded a group dedicated to advancing power. Did he try to get political power?"

"He had no interest in working his way up. In fact, he always struck me as rather having contempt for those of us who actually worked at anything."

"Perhaps his priorities shifted," Raoul said. "But it's likely he remains your enemy."

"And yours."

"I don't think that's in question."

Liverpool stared at Raoul. "You've actually seen him?"

"I have. He doesn't seem as concerned with keeping the fact that he's alive secret as he obviously had been for the past three years."

"Why the devil not simply reemerge? He has a fortune waiting for him. I can't see Malcolm's fighting him for it."

"No." In fact Malcolm, Raoul knew, was intensely uncomfortable at the thought that the Berkeley Square house and so much else weren't properly his. "So presumably he's afraid someone will accuse him of whatever he wants the pardon for."

"If so, it's not me he's afraid of. But surely I don't need to tell you, of all people, that I don't possess all the secrets in London. What does Hubert Mallinson know about this?"

"He knows Alistair is alive and a threat. He claims not to have any knowledge of the reasons Alistair might want pardon."

"But you're not sure he's telling the truth."

"I'm never sure Hubert is telling the truth. But I do think we all have something to be allied over at present."

"While the country is falling apart." Liverpool's brows drew together. "Our current sovereign's marital difficulties have dogged me almost from the start of my time as prime minister. I'd scarcely been in office a year before he was pushing me to investigate Princess Caroline. The queen."

"You held off a long time." The Milan commission hadn't been established to investigate then Princess Caroline until 1818.

Liverpool grimaced. "The Milan commission was the culmination, not the start. We were still giddy from the news from Waterloo when the king—the regent then—got me to dispatch Sidney Newland, Bowditch's second son, to look into the queen—Princess Caroline then—more unofficially. I rather regretted giving in to pressure, but it seemed important to placate his royal highness. And from his dispatches, Newland actually thought he was on to something. Only his carriage overturned in a river on his way back to England and his dispatch box was never recovered. This whole business has been plagued by tragedy from the start." The prime minister regarded Raoul. "I seem to have a way of saying far too much to you. Save that this may be very pertinent indeed. How close are George Chase's murder and Alistair Rannoch's return likely to come to the royal family?"

"There's no way to be sure at present."

"And no reason to be sure you'll be my ally if it does." Liverpool waved a hand. "Don't prevaricate, O'Roarke."

"I wouldn't dream of it."

Liverpool gave a short laugh. "You've always been honest, I'll give you that." He regarded Raoul a moment. "I appreciate it, O'Roarke. Whatever is to come between us."

When they went back out into the passage, Raoul expected Liverpool to be the one to be claimed by those eager for his attention. But instead it was Laura who swept up to them and took his arm. "Forgive me, Lord Liverpool. I'm afraid I must claim my husband."

"By all means, Mrs. O'Roarke. I'm sure you want to dance with him."

Laura gave a dazzling smile, though from the pressure of her fingers through his sleeve Raoul suspected dancing was the last thing on her mind.

"What is it?" Raoul murmured into his wife's titian hair, flowing loose beneath her Nimue circlet, as they moved away from Liverpool.

"Council of war," Laura said. "Malcolm and Julien say they have news that changes everything."

CHAPTER 25

"Good god." Mélanie stared at her husband. He had just told them Lady Shroppington was Alistair's mother. "I have a horrible feeling I should have guessed this from the first."

"So do I." Malcolm tugged his mask off. "It's odd how one doesn't question what seem fixed certainties. Though, given my own history and my parents', it's a wonder I never thought of it." He looked at Raoul.

"No," Raoul said. "I never guessed it. Arabella never gave me the least idea she had any suspicion Alistair's parentage wasn't what it seemed on the surface. Which doesn't mean she didn't know. There's a lot she didn't share with me."

"What does it change?" Kitty asked. "I mean, it's a shock and it explains Lady Shroppington's connection to the League, but—"

"No, it's a good question," Malcolm said. "It puts Lady Shroppington firmly on Alistair's side. She created the League to push him forwards and she must now be working to reinstate him."

"Thomas Thornsby just told me Lady Shroppington was friends with Trenchard," Harry said. "It didn't make sense that she wanted Trenchard to become prime minister to help Lewis. But Alistair is another story."

"And yet Alistair faked his death before the plot came to fruition," Laura said. "I can't help but think Trenchard is tied up in Alistair's faked death and exile. Though it may simply be that it's difficult for me to feel free of Trenchard."

Raoul dropped an arm round her shoulders. "Liverpool still has a healthy fear of Trenchard. Alistair faked his death in the midst of Trenchard's plot. It has to be relevant. Much as I'd like to consign Trenchard to the past and grind him under my heel like the worm that he was."

"You don't grind worms under your heel," Malcolm said. "I've seen you rescue them with a cup and paper for as long as I can remember."

"My point precisely," Raoul said. "Worms are worth saving. Trenchard wasn't."

"If Trenchard's father was Lady Shroppington's lover and Alistair's father, she might have had another loyalty to the present Trenchard," Kitty said. "He'd be her lover's son. Which could make her like him or loathe him depending on how the affair ended."

Frances came in the room, pink-cheeked. "Give me a sip, will you?" She reached for Raoul's whisky glass. "I've just seen Alistair."

"My god," Julien said. "His daring surprises even me. He's here?"

"In a black mask and domino. Not particularly concerned about being discovered."

"You were the same towards the end of trying to keep your presence in London a secret," Kitty pointed out to Julien. "You took fewer and fewer pains to avoid being seen. We even went out to dine. With you not in disguise."

"Most of the people I might have been worried about already knew I was here at that point."

"Precisely. Though they didn't know who you were."

"Alistair's a bit different. He didn't craft a whole life under another identity." Julien looked at Fanny. "What did he want?"

Fanny took another drink of Raoul's whisky. "To warn me that the rest of you are going to be destroyed by his plans and that he'll offer me his protection."

"Good of him," Julien said.

"I don't see why he needs to destroy us," Malcolm said. "I'm perfectly willing to give him back everything he might want. And I certainly would never want to see him again."

"You can all move into Carfax House," Kitty said. "We have plenty of room. I think we still have rooms I've only stepped into once. Maybe some I haven't stepped into at all."

"I think he wanted more," Frances said. "But I'm not sure what."

"He wants you back," Raoul said.

"Possibly." She took another drink and gave him back the glass. "He's not going to get me."

"We've just learned Alistair's parents weren't who we thought," Malcolm said. "According to Beverston and Glenister, Lady Shroppington is his mother."

Fanny stared at him.

"So you didn't know," Malcolm said.

"Good heavens, don't you think I'd have told all of you?"

"Loyalties can compete," Raoul said.

"I'd have told you," Frances said. "When he came back. When it was clear his motives mattered." She snatched the whisky back and tossed down a long swallow. "At least, I hope to god I would." She put the glass back in Raoul's hand. "Alistair didn't talk about Lady Shroppington to me. But he did tell me more than once that people thinking they could chart the course of one's life was annoying. I never knew whom he meant, as his parents were seemingly gone and Bella seemed to have little interest in what he chose to do at that point. But in retrospect it makes sense."

Archie came into the room. "I just got a message from Rupert that you all wanted to see me."

"Alistair's here," Frances said, as though determined to be the first to tell him.

"I know," Archie said. "We just had a conversation in the sitting room off the cardroom. Quite like old times."

Frances's eyes widened. "Did he—"

"He made a number of commonplace comments about the past. He tried to convince me not to look further into Cyril Talbot's death. On the grounds that he was looking out for Glenister's feelings. Which is as laughable as I told him it was. Did he—"

"He sought me out tonight as well," Fanny said in a steady tone. "I didn't learn anything in particular, except that Alistair is supremely confident, which isn't surprising. But Malcolm's learned Alistair is Lady Shroppington's son."

Archie's gaze skimmed past the worry about Alistair's presence to settle on the startling information. "That explains a lot."

"You didn't suspect?" Raoul said.

Alistair shook his head. "I was never in the inner circle. But it explains a lot about Alistair. His sense of being an outsider. His determination to gain power and position."

"One rather wonders how much of that came from Lady Shroppington," Julien said.

"A lot, I imagine," Malcolm said. "Though I'm not sure I can claim to be a keen judge of Alistair."

"On the contrary," Frances said. "I think you understand him very well indeed."

Malcolm met his aunt's gaze for a moment. "I'll never be sure if I'm taking personal bias out of it. Though I must say, Glenister's readiness to tell the truth about Lady Shroppington and Alistair strikes me as another attempt at distraction. So what the devil is Glenister trying to conceal?"

~

"Rannoch." James Fitzwalter, Duke of Trenchard, extended his hand, then hesitated, as though the political situation had fallen over him like the restraining folds of a cloak. "It's good to see you. It's been a while."

Malcolm clasped his hand. "Things seem a bit more fraught now, don't they? Don't worry, I haven't come to ask for your vote. All other things aside, I know you couldn't be persuaded to go against your conscience. Which is more than could be said for many in Parliament."

"That's a compliment that's much appreciated, Rannoch." James grimaced. "In truth, I haven't yet decided what my conscience dictates when it comes to the queen's case."

"And you're too astute a politician to ignore political realities."

"Perhaps. But I can't always be sure where those realities direct me."

James could be a valuable ally and would be a valuable convert to the Whig party. Or even to the occasional alliance. Something to explore later. Malcolm knew better than to tackle too many projects at once. Talking of political realities.

James was watching Malcom with an appraising gaze. "If this isn't about the trial—it's George Chase's murder?"

"What do you know about it?"

"Only that he was stabbed on the stairs. But I assume you're investigating."

"Jeremy Roth is."

"Which means you are. Good thing for Roth you aren't in the Lords." James cast a glance about. "What was Chase doing back in London?"

"We aren't entirely sure. But apparently attempting to rehabilitate himself."

"As if he could—" James grimaced. "It must be hell for Cordelia and Davenport."

"It's challenging, but they're coping. Chase seems to have stumbled upon information about the trial. But he also seems to have been investigating past events. Some of it may go back to your father's activities right before he was killed."

James's jaw tightened. "You mean my father's attempts to wrest control of the prime minister's office."

"With the assistance of my putative father."

James turned away. "I didn't know anything about that."

"I know," Malcolm said. "You told me so when your father was killed, and I believe you. But Alistair Rannoch's involvement is suddenly more significant." Malcolm hesitated, as he always did when it came to putting it into words, though he had known when he sought James out that he would have to. "Alistair isn't dead."

James stared at him with the look of one who isn't an agent and wasn't accustomed to changing loyalties, let alone to little things like those supposedly dead coming back to life. Which, come to think of it, was fairly unusual among agents as well, though somehow it fit the general unexpected nature of life. "Your father—"

"Faked his death. Like Julien. That is, my father didn't, Alistair Rannoch did."

"And now he's back? But I haven't—"

"He's trying to get himself pardoned. For something we aren't yet sure about. But I've also just learned his parents weren't who we thought they were." That should surprise James less, given the nature of the lives they were used to from the older generation. "His actual father may have been the father of one of the other League members."

"And you think my father—that is, my grandfather—"

"Do you think it's possible?"

"Do you—forgive me, Rannoch, ordinarily I'd never ask such a thing, but do you know who his mother was? Is?"

"Lady Shroppington."

James coughed.

"Yes, it startled me too. Perhaps more than it should have done, given her connection to the League."

"She's—Good god." James shook his head. "All right, knowing what I do about my father—and my late brother—I suppose I shouldn't be surprised. My grandfather—I don't remember him well. I certainly didn't know details about his romantic exploits. I didn't know he had romantic exploits. Though I suppose now I assume he did. People generally assume it. My wife assumed I did until we managed to talk about it. Until we managed to talk properly at all. But I haven't heard anything to connect him to Lady Shroppington in particular."

"What about your father's relationship with Alistair, in retrospect?"

James shook his head. "One doesn't study one's father and his friends."

"*Were* they friends?"

James frowned. "I'd have said so, as a boy. They rode together and drank together. Alistair Rannoch dined with us. Occasionally with your mother. Lately, knowing what I know about my father —it's difficult to imagine his being friends with anyone."

"I could say the same about Alistair Rannoch."

James gave a wry smile. Then he frowned. "There is one thing. Not about my father, but about my grandfather. Not relating to Alistair Rannoch or whether or not he—fathered—Alistair Rannoch." James blanched at the words. "But given the circumstances, it could be relevant."

"Anything that could be relevant is important. What?"

"He couldn't abide Lord Carfax. Not the current Lord Carfax. Not his—not Julien's—father. Julien's grandfather. Apparently he wouldn't allow him into Trenchard House."

RAOUL STEPPED into a salon off the ballroom and found himself face to face with a woman in a crimson velvet gown from a century ago. Her back was ramrod straight despite the walking stick she carried. Behind the beaded black satin mask, the keen eyes were unmistakable. And somehow the meeting now seemed inevitable. "Lady Shroppington."

Lady Shroppington regarded him as though from behind stone ramparts. "I don't believe we've been introduced."

"No. Though I believe you're well acquainted with my son."

Her brows rose. "The fact that you can call him so so easily should explain why it is not possible for me to accept any sort of acquaintance between us."

"I should have thought that would prohibit your acquaintance with half the beau monde. Or is it the acknowledgement that renders the acquaintance inappropriate?"

"Don't be difficult, Mr. O'Roarke. You know the rules of the game as well as I do, for all you may be dedicated to tearing society down. There are certain things one doesn't mention." Lady Shroppington stepped to the side, where they were half concealed behind a potted palm, though the buzz of conversation was loud enough no one could have overheard them. "But it's not so much your acknowledgement of your relationship to Malcolm Rannoch that puts you beyond the pale as your divorce and your remarriage weeks before the birth of your latest child. You really are untidy about these things."

"Life is often untidy. As I imagine you have found." Raoul surveyed her. He'd have sworn an hour ago that he could never feel anything resembling fellow feeling with her. "It's Malcolm though who represents the tie between us. Of a sort. Given that his putative father is your son."

He saw the start in the depths of her eyes, but on some level she must have been ready for it. One always was with that sort of revelation. Though no amount of preparation could make one ready for it.

"It's extraordinarily painful," he said. "Not being able to openly parent one's child."

Lady Shroppington returned his gaze, her own as hard as the diamonds round her throat. "Don't make the mistake of thinking we're all as sentimental as you are, O'Roarke."

"I wouldn't presume to know what you feel. But I know I was aware of it every moment once Malcolm was born. That my child was growing and learning and I couldn't always see him, couldn't openly claim him. Feeling like a parent but being childless to the world."

"Don't bamboozle me, O'Roarke. Men don't think of themselves as childless."

"All men may not. I imagine a number of women don't see it in those terms either. But I did. To own the truth, I didn't even think about children until I had one I couldn't openly parent. But I at least got to see him. I hope you got to see Alistair at times."

She tapped her walking stick on the ground. "I doubt you hope anything of the sort. Whatever side you show to your family now, I know perfectly well what you've been and what you've done. What you still do."

"I have few illusions about myself. But I have no desire to see anyone made unhappy." Raoul hesitated a moment, watching her, seeing echoes in her sharp gaze. "Thirty years ago I confess to little sympathy for Alistair. Now I have more of a sense of what he went through. And my own part in it."

Her gaze stayed hard on his own. "You can't tell me you'd do anything differently."

"I think the question is more if I'd do anything the same. We make choices. We have to live with the consequences. There's little sense in refining upon them. But one doesn't play a hand the same way twice."

She gave a short laugh. "I warned him not to marry her. He needed a brilliant marriage, but it was clear she was going to drag him down more than advance his prospects. And when it comes to marriage, love can be a great distraction."

"That rather depends on what one wants out of the marriage."

258

"You've been married twice, Mr. O'Roarke. What would you say based on your experience?"

"The first time we wanted different things and didn't realize it soon enough. The second I hope we want the same things. I was in love both times, and I believe the same could be said of both the women I married."

"But the first time it didn't last."

"As I said. Love doesn't guarantee anything."

"And in your second you're still in the besotted stage. I'll be interested to hear your answer in a year or two. It's folly to base anything as permanent as marriage on anything as transitory as love. As I imagine you and your current wife will discover. The stronger the emotions, the more tumultuous the marriage. As I imagine you could attest. As Alistair certainly could."

"You'd have to ask Alistair about that."

"You're fair game considering you were in the middle of his marriage."

"A palpable hit."

"Marriage should secure one's advancement. Given your desire to tear down all the edifices that support civilized life, I'm surprised you believe in marriage at all."

"I imagine we define it quite differently. For a long time, I couldn't imagine ever doing it again."

"I imagine not, considering you were married at the time."

"Another hit. I should perhaps have said I couldn't imagine risking the commitment."

"Hrmph. There are different types of commitment. You jumped back into it soon enough once you were free. Within days it seems. I suppose a child on the way dispels all strategy whatever one's politics."

"Children have a way of changing everything. It always seems to come back to this, doesn't it?"

Lady Shroppington shot a look at him. "I'd never have fussed over a child the way you did over Malcolm. But I wouldn't have done to any child of mine what you did to Malcolm."

"I expect few parents would. Hopefully. I make no excuses for myself."

"And yet your son appears to adore you."

"Malcolm is far too analytical to adore anyone or anything. But I know full well I have no right to what I have with him."

"Fine words. And yet it doesn't stop you from enjoying it."

"As I've said to others, guilt is a singularly useless emotion. It doesn't stop me from feeling it. But for better or worse I'm not going to dwell on it."

"You're a cat. O'Roarke. You appear to have more than nine lives. When Alistair first told me about you, I assured him it was even odds whether Arabella would tire of you or you'd lose your life to folly first, but one or the other was bound to happen before two years were out."

"Not a bad analysis." He regarded her, realization washing over him. "Arabella was remarkably like you."

Her shoulders jerked straight, pulling at the full sleeves of her gown. "Arabella and I were nothing alike."

"You're both shrewd. You're both ruthless in pursuit of what you want. You both didn't believe in letting emotions get in your way or play a leading role in determining how you should act."

Lady Shroppington twitched a ribbon on one her sleeves smooth. "Arabella had no sense of priorities."

"Arabella was willing to sacrifice everything to achieve what she wanted. Would you disagree that the same is true of you?"

"She had no sense of the reasons for marrying."

"She married Alistair to spy on him. You—"

"I didn't marry Shroppington to spy on him. The very idea is absurd."

"But like Arabella you married for pragmatic reasons that had nothing to do with emotion."

"Alistair was a fool. He walked into the situation with Arabella.

I blame her for a number of things, but I can't blame her for taking advantage of him."

"It's a matter of priorities. Bella had her priorities clear. One can quarrel with them, but she wasn't going to let emotion get in her way any more than you were."

"Arabella's priorities—"

"Weren't entirely what I'd agree with either. But one can't fault her determination."

Lady Shroppington's mouth tightened below her mask. "She had no sense of the future."

"On the contrary. I think she had a very clear sense of the future."

Lady Shroppington's gaze settled on Raoul's with the gleam of a polished rapier. "If so, she'd understand the disaster the people she cared for face now. Good evening, Mr. O'Roarke."

CHAPTER 26

"We know a great deal more than we did," Mélanie said.

"Enough to set us reeling," Cordelia said.

"But not enough to put the case into any sort of perspective," Malcolm said, moving to the decanters. They were back in Berkeley Square, in the library, sharing drinks, as they all often did after a party. Save that tonight it seemed more like a strategy session than the convivial end to an evening. Not for the first time, Malcolm thought as he refilled whisky glasses.

"I talked with Lady Shroppington," Raoul said. "A seemingly chance encounter that I rather suspect she orchestrated. She didn't openly admit she is Alistair's mother, but nor did she deny it. She's a formidable woman."

Malcolm set down the decanter. "Did she say anything else?"

Raoul met Malcolm's gaze. "She said Alistair made a mistake in marrying Arabella because love is no basis for marriage. I can't say I agree. Though I do agree Bella made Alistair vulnerable. Perhaps she still does."

"Could Lady Shroppington have had George killed?" Cordelia asked. "She had Lewis Thornsby killed because he threatened her plans and the League. Which makes a bit more sense now we know Alistair is her son. In protecting the League and Alistair, she was protecting her son. Even at the cost of her great-nephew's life. So if George was also threatening Alistair—"

"It's certainly a plausible theory," Mélanie said. "She hired someone to kill Lewis. She could have hired someone to kill George. And we know she's ruthless enough."

"Edith told me she saw Alice Wilton today," Laura said. She described Edith account of Sidney Newland's death and missing dispatch box and Sir Toby's suspicions that Newland had been killed because he had information about the queen.

"Odd," Raoul said. "Liverpool mentioned Newland's investigation and death tonight as well. Not surprising perhaps for it to come up now with the queen's case before the Lords, and it's difficult to see how it ties into the present investigation. But it is intriguing."

"Lewis Thornsby had an affair with Lady Wilton," Cordelia said. "We've wondered if Lady Shroppington orchestrated it. Perhaps she—or Alistair or both of them—thought Sir Toby might have the missing information about the queen from Mr. Newland's dispatch box."

"Alistair has certainly been focused on anything that could give him royal influence. If he got wind of Newland's investigation, he and Lady Shroppington might well have tried to make use of it." Malcolm perched on the arm of Mélanie's chair and turned to Fanny and Archie. "Did Cyril take a mistress from Glenister just before the duel?"

"I think so," Fanny said. "I remember gossip about an opera dancer. But I wouldn't think it would have provoked a duel."

"Her name was Thea McCandless," Archie said. "Lovely young woman and quite a talented dancer. But I never had the sense either of them was more attached to her than to a score of other mistresses. Not more than any of us—" He broke off. "We all took for granted we'd have mistresses. We all, for the most part, took affairs lightly. In retrospect, as a husband, as the father of daughters who I hope find better relationships, as the father of a son who I hope finds better and does better—not to mention as the uncle and adoptive father of a nephew who *does* do better—it sounds distinctly despicable. At least as far as the mistresses we supported. The others—"

"For the others, it was mutual." Fanny said, "And perhaps equally tedious for all of us. I don't begrudge or judge anyone for going on like that, but it does feel rather tiresome these days."

Archie took her hand and pressed it between his own. "Whatever Glenister's feelings about Thea McCandless, his anger over once again being the dupe of a bet might explain the duel. But I heard nothing about Thea or any other mistress or a bet that night. Unless, when Cyril said, 'Take care of her,' he meant Thea McCandless rather than his daughter Honoria."

"Did Glenister take care of Thea McCandless?" Malcolm asked.

"Not that I heard of," Frances said. "But then, I wouldn't necessarily have heard."

Archie frowned. "I never heard that Glenister did anything for her. She moved on to another protector quickly."

"Who?" Malcolm asked.

Archie hesitated a moment. "Trenchard."

"That's not surprising," Laura said. "I wouldn't be surprised if he was the one who bet Cyril to get him to take his brother's mistress as well. Assuming that part of the story is true."

"All of which still leaves us with the question of what really provoked the duel," Malcolm said. "Even if there was a bet, I'm quite sure there was more to it."

"Alistair wouldn't talk about it tonight," Frances said. "Except to say to stay away from it, and that it couldn't hurt him. But he would say that."

"Did you sense anything else?" Malcolm asked.

Frances hesitated. "That something about it frightened him."

Malcolm looked at Julien. "James says his grandfather disliked your grandfather. So much so he wouldn't let him into Trenchard House."

"Yes, that was interesting." Julien leaned back in his corner of the settee and took a sip of whisky. "Especially given Beverston's interest in my grandfather's snuffbox."

"And Lady Shroppington's friendship with James's father," Laura said. "And the possibility that James's grandfather was Alistair's father."

There was a great deal to speculate on, but little more to be learned that night. As the company rose to gather their things, Malcolm crossed over to Cordelia.

"You can't blame yourself, you know."

Cordelia shot a quick look at him as she wrapped her shawl round her shoulders. "For George's death? I'm not. Perhaps I lack imagination, but I don't see how I could have stopped it."

"That's a start. But I meant for mourning him. It's taken me over a year to admit I'm mourning Edgar."

Cordelia looked straight into his eyes. "Edgar was your brother."

"And you'd loved George since childhood. They'd both done unspeakable things. But learning that doesn't wall off the memories. I tried to pretend it did. I can't exactly say I'm sorry I'll never see Edgar again. But I still feel his loss."

"You learned the truth about Edgar just before he died. I've had five years to come to terms with George."

"It's different knowing he's gone from the world perhaps."

Cordelia twisted the fringe on the shawl round her fingers. "Harry and Mélanie tried to tell me the same thing."

"Then I'm sadly redundant."

"No. It's different hearing it from you. Because you've been through it yourself. That changes things." She reached out and pressed Malcolm's hand. "Thank you."

The two Davenport couples left, and Malcolm, Mélanie, Raoul, and Laura were in the hall saying goodnight to Kitty and Julien when a knock sounded at the door. Malcolm opened it to see Emily Cowper, swathed in a black velvet cloak. Emily hurried into the hall and threw her hood back. She was still wearing her gold Amazon combs, but her dark hair was coming loose from the combs and pins. "Thank heavens I've found you at home."

"What's happened?" Malcolm asked. "Was your carriage set upon?" Emily, he knew, had been concerned about the mob outside Parliament.

"No, it's Harry." Emily took a step into the hall and looked round at the group but made no attempt to move to the library. Her hands were locked tight with urgency. "My Harry, not Cordelia's. That is, he hasn't been set upon, but someone's broken into the war office." Her gaze darted among them. "We stopped by on the way back from the masquerade. Harry needed to pick up some papers, and I said there was no need for him to walk at this hour, it was silly to worry about gossip, no one would notice. Even if they did, all I was doing was giving a friend a seat in my carriage, and in any case, I could say with all the unrest I felt better having a gentleman accompany me. But as it was, we didn't encounter any mob or even any lone protesters on the drive to Whitehall or in front of Horse Guards. I didn't like the idea of sitting alone in the carriage, though, and neither did Harry, so I went into the war office with him. It's rather—well, I rather like seeing that side of him. I don't get to often. And at night, empty, it was quite—a bit mysterious. And one might say romantic, in its own way. It's not the first time I've been there with him. In fact—well, never mind about that. But this time we opened the door and nearly tripped over a stack of files. They were all over the floor. Along with the wreckage of a chair. I've never seen anything like it."

"No sign of the intruder?" Malcolm asked.

"Not from what we could tell. We didn't stay long. That is, I didn't. Harry didn't want to leave things alone, so he asked me to come to you. He walked me back to my carriage and then went back inside." Her brows drew together. "Do you think whoever did this could still be there? Is Harry in danger?"

"Highly unlikely," Raoul said. "Ransackers don't usually linger unless caught in the act. But we'll go to him at once."

"All of us," Julien said.

"Thank you," Emily said. "Nervous as I've been all these months, I confess this frightened me even more. It was so—unexpected. I'm coming with you."

"Are you sure?" Mélanie said. "That is—"

"Oh stuff scandal. I'm not going to leave the man I—I'm not going to leave Harry alone. If Caro can go into a lodging house with Henry Brougham in broad daylight, I can certainly do this. And yes, I know I wasn't happy with Caro, but for heaven's sake, do you really expect me to take my own advice? Let's go."

THE HORSE GUARDS building in Whitehall was usually a scene of bustling activity by day. The smell was the same late at night—ink and paper, the dust that accumulates on books, old leather. But there was no click of boot heels, no rustle of turning pages. The building was in silence. Mélanie felt the tension running through Malcolm as they negotiated the corridors.

Palmerston met them at the door, holding a lamp. "Thank god —" His gaze went past Mélanie, Malcolm, Raoul, Julien, and Kitty to Emily. "I thought you were going home, Em."

"Do you imagine I could go home and sleep in the midst of all this? What a poor creature you must think me, Harry."

"I don't think you're anything of the sort. You're reckless and loyal and have the courage of a lion." Palmerston lifted her hand to his lips. He looked from Malcolm to Mélanie to Raoul and Julien and Kitty. "I've touched as little as possible. I know just enough about investigations to want not to destroy evidence."

"You're sure we're the ones you want here?" Malcolm asked.

"Instead of whom—Bow Street? With word getting straight back to the home office and Sidmouth, who already isn't too enamored of me? I need to know what's going on and who is behind this before I decide where to take it."

"Even if it means turning to a Radical?"

"Who is far less likely to stab me in the back than members of my own party and government."

Palmerston opened the door and lifted the lamp. Emily hadn't exaggerated. Papers littered the floor. Sheaves of foolscap gaped open. Books appeared to have been pulled from shelves and tossed about. A ladder-backed chair was smashed to bits. Another lay on its side with cracked slats and one leg dangling drunkenly.

"Do you have any sense of what might be missing?" Malcolm asked.

Palmerston shook his head. "These are accounts. Why would anyone care? Unless they wanted fodder to make me look foolish in Parliament. In which case, I suppose it might be some of your friends behind it."

"My friends would just stick with the truth." Malcolm stepped into the room. "My real friends, anyway."

"Could it be to do with the trial?" Emily asked.

"The queen has a complicated history, Em," Palmerston said, "but I don't see how anyone could think to find evidence about her in army accounts."

"Not about her directly, perhaps," Mélanie said, "But we found Hubert's payments to agents hidden in accounts. There could be records of payments to agents spying on the queen. We certainly know the king had them."

"It's hard to see how those payments could influence the trial, though," Palmerston said. "As you say, no one would be surprised the king had agents spying on the queen."

They moved further into the outer office and glanced round. "Your office is in there?" Julien asked, nodding towards a door.

Palmerston nodded. "It's even worse in there."

Julien moved softly towards the door. Mélanie saw the dark blurs of files and books on the floor, drawers pulled loose, an overturned chair. "The window's ajar," Julien said.

"Yes, I think the intruder went out that way when we came in," Palmerston said.

"It looks as though he—or possibly she—dropped something on the way out." Julien came back into the outer office holding a file.

"Hard to imagine why anyone would care about this," Palmerston said, holding the lamp so the light fell on the file. "It looks to be from the last century at least."

"The last century is rather of interest just now," Malcolm said.

"Besides not seeming so very long ago to some of us," Raoul said.

They all settled on the floor round the lamp and spread the file out in the light. Even Emily seemed quite unconcerned about sitting on the floor. Mélanie had almost forgot she was still in fancy dress except when she shifted and the boning in her bodice poked her.

"This is interesting," Palmerston said. "It's from Benjamin Howland. Notes on an investigation. The French agent in British society in the sixties."

"The one Fortinbras found?" Malcolm asked.

"Who on earth is Fortinbras?" Palmerston asked.

"Supposedly one of Benjamin Howland's agents. George Chase had Fortinbras written on a scrap of paper we found. Hubert told us the story was that Fortinbras had uncovered a French agent who was a British aristocrat."

"There's nothing here about Fortinbras," Palmerston said, scanning the pages quickly. "But there are reports of an investigation into a possible French agent. No names, though. At least not yet." He passed the pages to the others.

"Wait a bit," Palmerston said, "here's something. Not a name. Benjamin Howland seems to have been too careful to commit to names. Which one would expect. But he mentions a snuffbox, of all things. That the agent was using as a seal. There's a sketch of it." He held the paper out.

Malcolm took it, but it was Julien, leaning forwards over the lamp, who went still. "Well, that's interesting. And it explains a lot."

"What?" Kitty asked.

"The snuffbox. It's actually as good as a name. It's my grandfather's. The one you found Beverston trying to steal at our ball. The one we were looking at tonight with the distinctive filagree. No explanation we could come up with ever accounted for why Beverston would care about it. But this makes sense of it. Apparently my grandfather was selling secrets to the French."

CHAPTER 27

"Well, well," Julien said. "It seems to be a family habit. I don't know why I'm surprised."

"I don't know about you," Emily said, "but I need some brandy. Harry, surely you have some. Don't worry about glasses. At this point I'll drink straight from the decanter. Or from a bottle. Don't they do that in gin mills? You should take me to a gin mill some time. God. I'm prattling."

"With good reason. We all need to take this in." Palmerston pushed himself to his feet, produced a decanter of brandy, five glasses, and two teacups. He poured the brandy and passed it about with Emily's help. Mélanie took a deeper sip than she intended. It was quite good. And she was far more in need of steadying her nerves than she would normally admit to.

Kitty took a thoughtful sip. Her gaze was fixed on Julien. "I wonder if Hubert knows," she said.

"If he does, I wonder if he's proud of his father or disgusted with him." Julien tapped his fingers on the floor and took a drink of brandy. "My money's on proud. Hubert may be devoted to his version of Britain, but he has a solid appreciation of good spycraft."

"He might feel both," Malcolm said. He looked at Raoul.

"No," Raoul said. "It was before the Revolution. It was before I was born. The players were different. Or at least playing different roles."

Julien looked down at the drawing of the snuffbox again, and then ran his gaze over the documents. "Reading between the lines in Benjamin Howland's careful reports, my grandfather doesn't seem to have been as good a spy as Hubert."

"He didn't get caught," Mélanie said.

"Not that we know of," Malcolm said. "He wasn't publicly disgraced. But what do you think Hubert would do if he learned a powerful nobleman was a foreign agent?"

"Have him killed," Julien said. "Probably task me to do it, in the old days."

"Good heavens," Emily said. "Is this the way you always talk?"

"Only sometimes," Kitty told her. "A lot of it's boring code breaking and papers passed back and forth."

"Hubert might have a French agent killed," Malcolm agreed. "Unless he thought he could put the person in question to use."

"You think Benjamin Howland turned my grandfather?" Julien asked. "Or Fortinbras did? Or Hubert did later on?"

"It would be an obvious ploy," Raoul said. "If the spymaster could pull it off."

"It's interesting," Julien said. "It sheds light on the family I have the ill luck to belong to. But I don't see what it really does for us now. While it's interesting and possibly embarrassing to the Mallinson family, I don't care, and I doubt Uncle Hubert would that much either. He's put up with losing the title. He's put up with my having it, god help him. I don't think he'd be that worried about his father's disgrace. David might mind more, but I don't think even he would that much these days. I can't see any of us paying to keep the information secret. Or agreeing to any political concessions to do so. I can't see any of our enemies being stupid enough to think the information was worth anything to use against us."

"And I certainly can't see how Alistair could use it," Malcolm said.

"Alistair—" Emily stared at Malcolm. "Your father's alive?"

"My father is sitting across from you drinking brandy. But yes, Alistair Rannoch is alive as well. It hardly seems worth keeping it a secret anymore. Especially as if anyone benefits from its being a secret it's Alistair."

"But that means you're—" Emily shook her head, sending her warm brown ringlets tumbling about her face free of their pins and falling to the shoulders of her gold Amazon dress.

"Not the rightful owner of much of what I possess," Malcolm said. "I offered to vacate the Berkeley Square house at once. Alistair seems not to want it back right away. Largely because he doesn't want the world to know he's alive."

"Why on earth not?" Emily asked.

"Presumably for the same reason he faked his death. He wants to rehabilitate himself. He wants a royal pardon." Malcolm looked at Palmerston. "You wouldn't happen to know why?"

Palmerston shook his head. His gaze, serious and intent, was fixed on Malcolm's own. "I never had the least idea your fath—Alistair Rannoch—wasn't truly dead. Though I do know he was tangled with that business of Trenchard's. Which never became public knowledge. I'm not quite sure how it could be considered treason since it never succeeded, though. Unless it went further than we thought." He glanced round the company. "Does Liverpool—"

"He knows." Raoul said. "As of today."

"All of which is much more dramatic than these revelations about my grandfather," Julien said.

"And yet someone broke in here tonight," Mélanie said. "And it stretches the bounds of belief to think it doesn't have to do with the other events of today."

"What if someone else was involved in spying along with your grandfather," Kitty said. "Someone who could still be hurt today. We know George Chase was gathering blackmail information to try to reinstate himself. He seems to have been casting a wide net in doing so. Perhaps he was trying to blackmail someone else over this."

"And that person is suddenly worried there's evidence in dusty war office records?" Palmerston said. "I'll own I'm shocked myself there's such interesting evidence in there. But surely this person would have been worried long since?"

"Perhaps not if it was his father or grandfather who was involved," Malcom said. "Perhaps they only learned about the espionage because Chase tried to blackmail them."

"And this same person killed Major Chase?" Emily said. "Or had him killed?"

"They'd certainly have a good motive," Malcolm said. "Though so would others George could threaten. Including Alistair."

"It would be convenient, wouldn't it?" Emily said. "If he were guilty and would just go away."

"My god, you're bloodthirsty." Palmerston said.

"I wouldn't call it bloodthirsty. Someone is obviously guilty. I'd far rather it was Alistair Rannoch, who is causing a lot of difficulty for some of our best friends, than someone I care about more. Like my brother. Or his wife." She looked round the suddenly silent group. "You can't deny they both have motives. You can't think I'm so foolish as not to see it. Of course, Mr. Brougham has a motive as well. And provoking as he is, I find I'd really rather he didn't prove to be guilty of murder."

"So would I," Palmerston said, "though I suspect some of my colleagues would disagree with us."

"Beverston thought the information was significant too," Kitty said. "Enough to try to steal the snuffbox, in any case."

"James Trenchard told Malcolm his grandfather forbid my

grandfather from Trenchard House," Julien said. "Which could mean the late Trenchard knew the truth about my grandfather."

"What if he was Fortinbras?" Kitty said. "Trenchard, I mean. Not James's father, his grandfather."

Malcolm frowned. "Interesting thought. He wasn't known to be particularly political, I don't think, but then from the sound of it, Fortinbras was under deep cover."

Emily took a sip of brandy. "Given what we know about his father now, you don't think Carfax, that is, Hubert Mallinson—"

Julien gave a whoop of laughter. "Lady Cowper, I love you. Who else would have the audacity to suggest my uncle might be a French agent. I wouldn't disagree on moral grounds, and while he gives an excellent impression of believing in Britain—or his version of Britain—I'd be prepared to entertain the idea that he's deceived us about those beliefs. After all, he's deceived us about so much else. He might even have come up with some elaborate scheme where he actually thought it benefited Britain to sell information to the French. Sort of a Talleyrand in reverse. But I've worked with Uncle Hubert enough that I'm damned if I can see anything he did that benefited the French. More's the pity. I'd love to tweak him on his own hypocrisy."

"Spies can be an embarrassment," Raoul said. "It's possible that whatever your grandfather uncovered spying for ancien régime France would embarrass British officials. British officials who are still alive today."

"Who in power goes back that far?" Emily said. "Even Sidmouth wasn't in Parliament until the early eighties."

"We don't know how long my grandfather kept this up," Julien said. "Or whom he worked with."

"Yes, but surely he stopped before the Revolution," Emily said.

"For something that sounds so absolute, the Revolution's a bit hard to pin down," Raoul said. "At first it was within the government."

"Alistair was a British agent in France in the eighties," Malcolm said. "Along with Harleton. And Horace Smytheton. I wonder if there could be a connection."

"You mean they were working against Julien's grandfather?" Emily asked.

"Or with him," Kitty said.

"It's tempting to consider," Julien said.

Mélanie took a drink of brandy. She had always hated the idea that Alistair Rannoch had been a French spy. That he had ever been anything that close to what she was. Which was absurd, but she couldn't make the thought go away. She looked at Raoul and knew he understood.

"It would explain why Alistair wants a pardon," Malcolm said. "And perhaps why he would have tried to take the information about Lord Carfax tonight. Assuming he was behind it."

"And why he'd have hired someone to murder George Chase," Palmerston said. "Assuming he was behind that as well."

Mélanie glanced round the group. They hadn't precisely admitted anything. They hadn't said that she or Raoul had been a French agent. They hadn't said precisely what Julien had done or whom he had worked for. Yet they had spoken to Emily and Palmerston with a candor they had not hitherto allowed themselves. Something had shifted. Emily and Palmerston had gone from friends with whom they still had to be slightly wary to allies. Without any words being uttered, she could tell the others, including Emily and Palmerston, felt it as well. It was a risk. But also a profound relief. Who would have ever thought she'd find allies in a Tory government minister and a patroness of Almack's?

"For all the answers we're finding, we seem to keep coming up with more questions," Julien said. The five of them had said goodnight to Emily and Palmerston and were walking back to Berkeley Square.

"We need to talk to a number of people," Malcolm said. "Including my sister."

Mélanie cast a sharp glance at him.

"I sent word to her," Malcolm said. "When we first got back from the Beverstons." He and Gisèle had long since established emergency routes of communication. "She and Andrew may be in Berkeley Square by the time we get back."

Kitty looked from Malcolm to Julien, who had been Gisèle's mentor as a spy from when she was a teenager. "Do you think she knows Lady Shroppington is Alistair's mother?"

"That," said Malcolm, "is the first thing I'm going to ask her."

CHAPTER 28

anny looked at her husband across their candlelit bedchamber. The bedchamber that had been her sole province for years after her first husband died. It was still decked out in her favorite violet and lavender—striped silk wall hangings, coverlet embroidered with sprigs of lavender, Aubusson carpet in just the shades she'd wanted. Archie hadn't asked for any changes when he'd moved in. But nor had she asked him if he wanted any, she realized. Just as they'd both taken it for granted he'd move out of his house and into hers, because her daughter Chloe was already settled there and it seemed the least disruptive for everyone. Archie had been scrupulously careful not to be disruptive to anyone's life. Not Chloe's. Not her puppy's. Not Fanny's grown children's. Not the servants'. Not Fanny's herself.

"Are we fools, Archie?" Fanny asked, seeking her husband's gaze in the candle-warmed shadows. "Am I a fool? Did I learn what love was too late? Too late to recognize it? Too late to act on it properly?"

"That assumes that the young can act on it properly." He spoke lightly, but she could hear the tension beneath. Like a singer straining for the right note.

"No, but they can blunder through more readily than we can. They can damn the consequences and get away with it. At our age, the consequences come back to bite." She watched her husband. "I thought we had a chance."

"So did I. I still do." Archie's voice was rough, as she had never heard it before. "My love, if there are second thoughts, they aren't on my side."

"I don't think I appreciated how damnably hard it must be for Malcolm. And Laura. To love someone knowing they have loved someone else. Who is right there beside one."

"And yet they're muddling through." Archie watched her. "With their partner's former lover living in the same house. Which Alistair isn't, thank god. Is it because they all got to make a choice and you didn't?"

Fanny had been staring at her bracelet, but at that, her gaze shot to her husband's face. "I never would have chosen Alistair."

"And now you can't *not* choose him? Would it be easier if I stepped back and offered to stay out of the way for a bit? Let you make the choice. I've said I would. I meant it."

From his tone, they might have been discussing going to a dinner party. Yet a chasm had opened at her feet. "Archie, I wouldn't. We have children." Just minutes ago they'd looked in on Chloe and the twins when they got back from the ball.

"And that's what's keeping you here?"

"Past time I prioritized my children, don't you think?"

"Perhaps. But for myself, I don't want a wife who only wants to be with me because of our children. If that's the issue, we'll find a way round it."

A noose of her own making bit into her throat. "I want to be with you."

"And you want to be with Alistair."

"No. Yes. Sometimes."

"Honesty, Fanny." His smile was sweet and sad and cut through to her soul. "Thank god we still have that."

"I'm not going to leave you for him, Archie. But I can't promise he'll go away. So I'm afraid you'll leave me."

"To literally make him go away, I think we'd have to resort to murder. And I don't think even Julien's prepared for that. At least, I don't think he'd recover from it."

"So we're going to have to live with him. And I'm not sure I can ask you to do that."

"Let me worry about what I can handle, Fanny. I've been far from incapable, if I do say so myself."

Frances forced herself to look straight into her husband's eyes and confront hard truths. "You keep asking me what I want, Archie. Is that what you want?"

"I want you, my darling. However I can get you, scarring as it is to admit that."

"Archie, you can't think I don't want you."

"As the father of your children?"

"No! Well, yes, of course. I mean, that's part of it. But not all. You can't think that's all."

"No. Not most of the time. Though I do confess to doubts. I'd have said doubts were a schoolboy business. But they are just as keen at fifty-plus. I imagine the only way to avoid them is not to care. And having tried that in prior relationships, I can say it's not very comfortable either."

Frances blew her nose. "I'd have said we were past the age of illusions. But I think we're more prey to them than ever. The only difference is perhaps we know they're illusions. And we need them anyway."

"How I feel about you isn't an illusion, Fanny." He watched her a moment. "If I help destroy him, will you be able to forgive me?"

"Better to ask if I'll be able to forgive myself. I'm trying just as hard to destroy him as the rest of you. And I may have the power to fire rather keener darts. Talking of illusions, as I said to Mélanie, those of you who've been agents seem to labor under the delusion that we non-spies don't know what betrayal is. The truth is I've been intimately acquainted with at least seven forms of betrayal since the age of twenty. If not nineteen."

"I almost planted Alistair a facer tonight."

"That would have been foolish." Fanny put her hands on her husband's chest. "But not because I'm not worth it."

Archie grinned and pulled her closer. "That was never in question."

∾

GISÈLE STARED at Malcolm with a gaze that looked stunned and bruised. "I didn't know. You have to believe I didn't know."

"You never suspected?" Malcolm asked.

Gisèle shook her head. She hadn't looked so much like a schoolgirl since Malcolm had learned she was undercover against the Elsinore League. "I knew Lady Shroppington had a hold on him. I knew she seemed to have started the League, as I told you. I couldn't be sure why or what their connection was. I thought she might have been his mistress. This—makes much more sense."

"It does," Malcolm said. "It was staring us in the face and yet neither of us saw it."

Gisèle hugged her arms round herself. "I know Alistair isn't anything to us in biology. So I suppose it doesn't really matter who Alistair's parents were biologically. But I feel a bit as though the ground has been cut out from under me."

"It's a certainty we grew up with," Malcolm said. "A seeming certainty. And now it's gone. It makes one question other certainties."

Gisèle gave a lopsided smile. "As if we didn't have reason enough to do that."

Andrew had been staring anxiously at Gisèle, but now he looked at Malcolm. "And Alistair's father—"

"Could be anyone."

"But is likely the father of a member of the League."

"It's a plausible theory."

"Including possibly Lord Glenister. The late Lord Glenister. Who is also my grandfather." Andrew swallowed.

"It's one scenario that makes sense," Malcolm said. "It's not the only one."

"And the present Lord Glenister—who is my uncle—killed his brother—who was also my uncle—in a duel."

"That seems to be the case. We still don't know what the duel was over."

"What the devil does this have to with their sister—my mother. At least in biology. I know who my actual mother is and I won't give anyone else that title. What does it have to do with my birth?"

"Nothing that we've worked out as yet," Malcolm said. "Just as we haven't worked out who your biological father was."

"But he could have been another member of the League."

"Possibly."

"Probably, surely. Who else but her brothers' friends would have been about Georgiana Talbot when she was young? I mean, trusted enough and with enough freedom to—" He grimaced and shook his head.

"It's plausible," Malcolm said. "We still don't know how all the pieces fit together or why they would matter to Alistair or anyone else, or what George Chase was trying to do with them. Chase may not have known himself. He was grasping at straws to try to get himself reinstated."

Andrew leaned his head in his hands and ran his fingers through his hair. "If Glenister senior was Alistair's father, then Alistair's my uncle. At least by blood. Which—"

"Would make him closer by blood to you than to me," Gisèle said. "Not that blood matters. But it is an odd world we live in." She looked at Malcolm. "Julien's grandfather was a French spy?"

"So it seems. Which is fascinating and rather mind boggling, but it's hard to see how it matters now."

Andrew looked up. "Surely someone's—a powerful man's being—a French spy matters."

"It's significant," Malcolm said. "It sheds light on the past. It's hard to see who in the present would care."

"Sandy Trenor," Gisèle said. "I know he matters to Alistair. I wonder, though, how much it's also that he's Lady Shroppington's grandson."

"I don't envy Trenor," Andrew said.

"Has Alistair said anything to you about Chase?" Malcolm asked his sister.

"Only that he had nothing to do with it," Gisèle said, fingers digging into her elbows. "And that suspecting him was sending everyone in the wrong direction, which he seemed quite pleased about. But Alistair would say that in any case."

Andrew looked from Gisèle to Malcolm. "This is all coming to a head, isn't it? Whatever Alistair is after, whatever his plans are. We may not understand it yet, but it's going to unravel in the next few days."

"It seems that way," Malcolm said.

"Then—shouldn't Gelly stay here? For the longest time, everything seemed to be in check, so it seemed we had time. But is it really safe for her to be with Alistair when everything unravels?"

"If I don't go back, he's likely to suspect we know more than we want him to realize," Gisèle said. "And the time when things unravel might be just the time when I can learn the most."

Andrew turned to Gisèle with a mixture of love and pride and desperate fear that Malcolm well recognized from times when Mélanie went into danger. "It also might be just the time when your masquerade falls apart."

"If I were that wary of danger, I wouldn't have got into this in the first place," Gisèle said, much as Mélanie would have done.

"You aren't in this alone," Andrew said.

Malcolm was quite sure he had used the exact same words in the past.

Gisèle jabbed her dark gold ringlets behind her ear. "All right, you have a point. A good one. You and I and Ian can go to Judith's." She glanced at the settee where their two-year-old son was asleep. "I don't think that will rouse Alistair's suspicions. Or at least, it's less likely to than our staying here."

"So you won't see Alistair again?"

Gisèle gripped her husband's hands. "I can take care of myself."

"Every spy I've met says that. But I think all of them would agree it's not always true."

CHAPTER 29

*J*ulien looked at Gisèle. They were alone in the Berkeley Square library while Malcolm, Andrew, and Raoul readied one of the carriages to take them to her cousin Judith's. Mélanie, Kitty, and Laura were packing food and spare clothes, as Gisèle and Andrew hadn't arrived expecting to be gone for days. Kitty had sent Julien a look that strongly suggested he stay with Gisèle.

Gisèle's gaze was steady but more uncertain than Julien was used to seeing it. "Do you keep things from Kitty?" she asked.

Julien studied the woman who had little more a child when he first met her. A very clever precocious child. "Gelly, my sweet. You can't imagine I don't. Just as Kitty keeps things from me. Our life would be unthinkable otherwise."

"But how do you decide—Are you ever afraid she won't understand?"

"I'm constantly stunned that Kitty puts up with me and agrees to share a life with me. But I don't think she ever expected me to tell her everything." Julien considered a moment. "I don't think she'd want me to."

"But there must be things—"

"Yes, all right. There are moments I wonder. About certain things. I imagine it's the same for her. But we both knew we'd have those moments going in."

"It's one thing to know it. It's another thing to actually go through them."

"An excellent point."

"And? How do you get by? How do you face her day to day?"

"I focus on the moment. On what I can share. I rely on the instincts that got me by for decades."

"Yes, but she's your wife."

"My dear girl. I didn't say it was easy. In fact it's damnably uncomfortable."

"And when you think she's lying to you?"

"I try to pretend I don't know. I pride myself on how adult I'm being. While all the while my feelings are distinctly schoolboyish. A mix of jealousy and puppy love and fear of losing the object of my affections."

Gisèle glanced at her son, sound asleep on the settee, then looked back at Julien. "So that's the key to making a marriage work? Pretending?"

Julien thought of multiple challenging moments he and Kitty had managed to survive. "I wouldn't say it's the key. But I certainly wouldn't underestimate how much it can help."

"I CAN UNDERSTAND if you don't want to talk about it," Gisèle said. She kept her voice steady. Because she should know, better than anyone, how there could be things one didn't want to discuss with one's spouse. And yet the fact that he didn't want to talk to her cut like a dagger thrust.

How damnable that only now was she properly seeing what she'd done to Andrew when she went to work against the Elsinore League.

Andrew straightened up from the cradle where he'd just settled Ian in the room her cousin Judith had shown them to without questions when they arrived in the middle of the night. Judith was like a sister, but she was blessedly on the fringe of family intrigues. Gisèle and Andrew were alone and they had a few moments to talk. Away from Alistair. Away from Malcolm and Aunt Frances and the rest of the family. People who meant well, people they were deceiving.

"It's not that." Andrew twitched Ian's blanket smooth. "Or not just that. It's true I need to think about what it means to me. But it's more how much it changes everything. I used to think I was on the outside of all this. It was your fight. I couldn't really understand it. I couldn't understand the world of spies and missions and plots and counterplots. I knew I was an outsider the first time Malcolm came back to Dunmykel from the Peninsula and we sat down for pint at the Griffin & Dragon. I looked at him over the table and asked questions and got evasive answers, and it slowly dawned on me that he couldn't talk to me about half the things he'd been doing. We were in different worlds, and geography was the least of it. We could recapture a bit when we saw each other. Mostly talking about the past, but sometimes sharing bits of our lives. But only bits. Most of his world I couldn't understand. Then two years ago, I realized my wife was in that same world. And I wanted to keep up. I understood—understand—-the threat the League pose. I want them stopped. But it wasn't my fight. I still don't understand it. Yet now I'm in the midst of it."

"More than I am." Gisèle moved to stand beside her husband and adjusted a fold of blanket over Ian's shoulders. How on earth could she have left her baby for weeks not knowing when she'd come back? It was something she'd forever question. While at the same time she couldn't be sure she'd make a different choice if she faced the same circumstances again.

"Not really." Andrew turned from the cradle for the first time and met her gaze. "You're still linked to Alistair in a way I never will be. Whoever my father is, I don't think his identity will put me so closely in the midst of the League and their plots as you are. And he won't be my real father in any case. I know who my father was. I know the man I'll describe to Ian as his grandfather." Andrew looked down at their son for a moment. "But I appear to be more tangled up in the League's history and their plots past and present than I realized. As more than just your husband. I'm going to have work out what that means and how I proceed."

Gisèle tucked her hand through Andrew's arm. "It doesn't change who you are. I realized that when I was quite young, when I realized Alistair wasn't really my father in the biological sense."

"No. But it changes how people see me. You have to have felt that as well. And you can't say learning Hubert fathered you didn't change anything for you."

"Well, no. It changed my view of the past. And I suppose—it created some sort of—I'm not even sure bond is the right word. Connection perhaps. I never particularly thought not knowing mattered. But now I do know I'm rather glad I do." Gisèle turned, still gripping his arm, so she was facing him, and studied her husband's familiar face. The eyes their son had inherited. The tender mouth. "Do you want to know, Andrew?"

"I'm not sure. But I think I need to. To keep us all safe."

She dropped her hand from Andrew's arm. "Oh, please don't do that, darling."

"What?"

"Decide you have to protect us and go off and try to learn things on your own and keep them from me for my own good. Malcolm occasionally has those tendencies, though I think Mélanie is very good at dealing with them. But it drives Mélanie mad from what I can tell. Julien knows better than to try." Gisèle frowned for a moment. "Come to think of it, I think it would be more likely Kitty would keep things from him to protect him. But even she knows better than to do that now. Not for his own good anyway, for all he admitted tonight they have secrets. We're all too tangled in this not to trust each other when it comes to Alistair and the League."

"You kept things from Malcolm. And certainly from me."

Gisèle didn't flinch away from her husband's gaze. "Yes, and I wouldn't do so now."

"No?"

"Well." Gisèle shifted her weight from one foot to another.

"Can you honestly say so, Gelly?" Andrew asked.

"Honestly? No, I suppose not. I was too worried about both of you. I still think if Malcolm had known about Alistair sooner things would be worse."

"Precisely."

"But now we all know it's different."

"That assumes we all know all the facts. Which we most certainly don't."

Gisèle folded her arms over her chest. If she'd been wearing a shawl, she'd have tightened it round her shoulders.

"You can't seriously think we do," Andrew said. "Did you really think you were the keeper of all the secrets? Even if you did, surely the revelations about my parentage changed that?"

Gisèle's fingers dug into her elbows. "No, of course." But a part of her acknowledged that she was used to being the one with knowledge no one else had. Not Malcolm. Not even Julien when it came to some things. Not Alistair. It kept her on a knife's edge, but it gave her a certain feeling of control of the situation. A situation that now seemed to be unraveling. It had always been dangerous. So dangerous it terrified her. But at least she'd felt she could control the outside boundaries.

Andrew set his hands on her shoulders. "It's all right, darling. I don't know how you've done it for so long. But the board is changing. As I'm sure Malcolm would say. It's more complicated than you could ever have imagined. And we're all going to have to sort our way through it. Including me."

"Andrew." Gisèle reached up and put her hands over his own. "We'll only get through this if we do it together."

"My darling. You did it without me for months."

"But—"

"Don't say that was different. I know I don't have your brilliance or your talent for spycraft—-"

"I wasn't going to—"

"Gelly. With both know you can run rings round me. But it looks as though I'm going to have to sort my way through this."

"Just don't do it without me. Yes, I know I deserve that you would, but don't do anything foolish just to prove how foolish I've been."

Andrew kissed her nose. "My love. You put things very aptly. Believe me, I'm well aware of the value of a partnership. Our partnership. But it would be folly to think there won't be things that we have to keep to ourselves. I don't think I understood that properly until I realized what you were doing."

"That's a sad lesson to have taught you."

"Not really. We're husband and wife. We're Ian's parents. But we're still ourselves. Once I realized you had to be able to be the person you were and pursue the things that were important to you, the corollary was obvious."

"You sound as though you've got it all worked out."

"Not really. Not at all. I don't have the least understanding of any of this. The ground's been cut out from under my feet. And I'm standing in a mire. Which is a mix of metaphors I'm sure Mélanie and Laura and Simon would abhor. But I have to find my own way out of this. I'll make sure you and Ian aren't caught up in my tangles."

"But we're part of them, darling."

"You're part of this elaborate game. How I feel about the truth about my parentage is for me to work out."

"And you don't want to share it with me."

His gaze was steady on her own, the gaze of the man she loved, and at the same time the look of a stranger. "I need to sort out how I feel for myself first. I imagine it was the same for you when you learned Alistair was alive."

"No. Yes." Gisèle tightened her grip on Andrew's hands as though she could meld him to her. "I knew where I stood with Alistair. That is, I knew he both was and wasn't my father."

"Which doesn't begin to scratch the truth."

"I—" Gisèle swallowed. Hard. "I know where my loyalties lie, Andrew. There was never any question in my mind. From the moment Tommy told me Alistair was alive."

"But you had to decide how you were going to act on your own."

"I had to see what Alistair wanted. I had to see how much of a threat he posed. To Malcolm. To you and Ian. To Aunt Frances. To everyone I loved."

"Malcolm, Frances, and I could have helped."

"But could you have kept it secret?"

"I might not have been able to. But Malcolm and Frances—"

"Aunt Frances isn't a trained agent any more than you are. Malcolm's brilliant, but if he'd known Alistair was alive and that everything he thought was his might not be his—that would have been asking a lot. And I was the only one of us Alistair might trust. I had to act on that. I had to learn what I could. And then in the midst of it I learned Hubert was my father. Biologically. And I couldn't even really take time to think about it. I still haven't in a lot of ways. And I suppose like you I know who my real father is."

"Alistair."

Odd to admit it, yet it had always been true. "Yes. It doesn't mean I'm not dedicated to destroying him."

"My darling. I don't doubt that. I just worry about what it may do to you."

She put her hands on his chest. "Don't worry. I'll manage. This isn't easy for any of us."

"And I'll manage too. But you have to let me sort this out for myself. Can you do that?"

"Of course." Gisèle managed a bright smile, the sort of smile she'd given Andrew when she agreed to be his wife.

As Julien had said, pretending could be invaluable in a marriage.

CHAPTER 30

$\mathcal{T}$he Contessa Montalto's maid opened the door of her rooms in Wardour Street and regarded Malcolm and Mélanie through narrowed lids.

"We are hoping for a word with your mistress," Malcolm said.

Mélanie more than half-expected them to be denied, and she and Malcolm had discussed what to do in that case. But a clear, faintly accented voice sounded from further back in the room. "Show them in, Luisa."

The contessa was sitting in a chair by the windows. She was simply dressed, but her gown of fawn-colored lustring was cut on lines that suggested a Parisian modiste. And her earrings gleamed with real gold and pearls that were not nacred glass. "I've been expecting you again. But is it the custom in England for people to simply barge into a lady's rooms?"

"We have no desire to do anything of the sort," Malcolm said.

The contessa's gaze shot to Mélanie. "I was expecting you to have your other friend with you. Colonel Davenport?"

"He is otherwise engaged," Malcolm said. Harry had gone to speak with Thomas Thornsby and then to update Roth on the investigation. "May I present my wife, Mélanie Rannoch?"

The contessa inclined her head. "Mrs. Rannoch." Her gaze moved back to Malcolm. "You thought bringing a woman would make me feel more comfortable and inclined to talk?"

"In part. But Mélanie and I investigate together."

The contessa's gaze returned to Mélanie. "You intrigue me. Pray sit down. I'm afraid I don't have a great deal to offer you. A glass of wine? I know it is early in the day, but pray don't refuse. I have far too few callers."

"We know you had two fairly recently," Malcolm said, seating himself beside Mélanie. "Mr. Brougham and Mrs. Lamb."

The contessa froze in the midst of pouring a pale yellow wine from a decanter. "They told you."

"They had little choice, given the circumstances. Though Brougham tried to keep it secret."

"I hope poor Mrs. Lamb won't be exposed to scandal. She risked a great deal by coming to see me. She is a kind friend."

"We'll do our best to keep it secret," Mélanie said. "There's no reason the news should become widespread. But unfortunately, Mrs. Lamb's husband had already seen them coming into the house."

"Merciful heavens." The contessa handed a glass of wine to Mélanie. "It was too bad of Henry—Mr. Brougham—to involve Mrs. Lamb in this. I never thought he appreciated her properly, even when I first met them in Italy." She gave another glass of wine to Malcolm and returned to her seat with a third glass. "I'm sure my connection to the queen's trial intrigues you, but I fear it will be a distraction. I don't see how it can have anything to do with the gentleman who lodged next door's meeting with an unfortunate accident. Or rather, being murdered. There's no sense in wrapping it up in softer words. I am very sorry for him. But I don't see what it has to do with me."

"He lodged in the same building."

"I scarcely spoke with him. I told you the truth about that. I live very quietly. I told you the truth about that as well. I hesitated to even exchange greetings with a gentleman to whom I had not been introduced. I only acknowledged him at all because we lodged in the same house. To suggest otherwise is a gross insult, Mr. Rannoch."

"My apologies, Contessa. I had no intention of implying any insult. But you might have noted people who called on him, or even overheard something, without of course trying to do so."

Her lips narrowed to a thoughtful line. "You're a tactful man, Mr. Rannoch. I don't gossip. I have the average person's curiosity about my fellows, I suppose, but in truth I've been too concerned about keeping my own presence in your London a secret to have much attention to spare for others."

"I understand. But you strike me as a very discerning woman. Who would notice things simply because you are careful of your surroundings."

"You're a flatterer, Mr. Rannoch." The contessa took a sip of wine. "Henry Brougham didn't tell me that. Though he did warn me you were clever and had a way of seeing the truth. And that your mind could shoot past prevarication like a horse sprinting home."

"Talk about flattery. I'm not sure anything of the sort applies."

The contessa sat back on the sofa. "I begin to regret agreeing to come to London. It seemed rather a lark at first. The trial may be the talk of London, but a fair amount of that got to the Continent as well. I'd lived very quietly since my husband died. The thought of being at the heart of things—I confess I found it alluring. I didn't realize at the time it would mean day in, day out in a small suite of rooms pacing up and down like one of those lions at the Tower of London—which I still haven't been able to escape and see."

"And yet you've stayed," Mélanie said.

The contessa shrugged, a simple gesture that took Mélanie

back to the Continent merely from the flutter of her full gathered sleeves. "I don't like to give up on something I'm committed to. And I can't but feel sympathy for the princess—the queen. My own husband was hardly a paragon, but she is far more ill-used than I was, poor lady. And far more maligned. A calumny can cling to a woman far more than a man, but in her case it has been elevated to an art far beyond the aria in the opera about the barber. Someone needs to set the record straight. If no one else is willing to do so, I can hardly abrogate my position. And I confess perhaps I like the notoriety that may come with it, as quiet a life as I am now compelled to live. Your king was a monster—keeping his wife from her daughter. I don't have children of my own, but I can scarcely imagine a more hideous thing."

"Nor can I," Mélanie said. When Malcolm had not yet known the truth about her, that had been her greatest fear. Odd now to think she could have believed he'd try to keep Colin and Jessica from her.

"It's no wonder she wanted to flaunt her supposed infamy in his face. The man deserved to be embarrassed. He deserved to be far worse. And so I agreed to stay here and keep out of the way—I didn't quite realize until I arrived in England what a fuss was being made over the trial and how much I would have to stay in the shadows. Mr. Brougham is clever, I liked him when I first met him in Italy, for all I thought he was likely to treat Mrs. Lamb shabbily. He does have a way of charming one into agreeing to things. After all, he charmed Mrs. Lamb into running off with him."

"So he charmed you into coming to England to testify for the queen?" Malcolm asked.

"I wanted to help. As I said, she'd been ill-used. Bergami is a fool. A decent looking man, but Princess Caroline, as I knew her, was only interested in him as a way of getting back at her husband."

"She told you she only began the affair to get revenge on her husband?" Mélanie asked. Princess Caroline—the queen's—relationship with her courier was at the heart of the trial, and no one truly seemed to understand it, for all the salacious stories.

"She never began an affair at all. She told me she only pretended to an affair to embarrass her husband. I can't swear that Caroline of Brunswick never took a lover, but Bartolomeo Bergami was most certainly not her lover."

Malcolm set down his glass. "I understand why Brougham is so determined to have you testify."

"I didn't realize at first what it would mean. I suppose having heard Caroline—the princess—the queen—speak, it seems absurd to me that anyone would even think they were lovers. And the British do seem to place such a great emphasis on the appearance of certain things. It was a scandal that Mrs. Lamb ran off to the Continent with Mr. Brougham, though I believe it was the first time she'd looked at a man other than her husband. And her own parents' history seems far more scandalous, though they apparently didn't openly run off together. Yet everyone knows they *were* together. No wonder the queen was lost in the British court."

"It's a challenging world," Malcolm said. "Mélanie is French and Spanish, and I think she often still feels lost here."

"Only a bit about the edges," Mélanie said, with a smile designed to hide how truly lost she sometimes felt.

The contessa took a drink of wine. "The queen has shaken things up. From what I have observed, Britain needs to be shaken up."

"I won't quarrel with that." Malcolm regarded the contessa. "We talked about what you knew about Major Chase. What might he have learned about you?"

The contessa adjusted her heavily embroidered shawl. "I don't see how he could have learned anything of interest about me from our few encounters."

"He may have overheard some conversations."

"You think he was listening at keyholes?"

"Or the equivalent." Malcolm sat back and regarded her. "Can you think of what he might have overheard? The most damaging thing?"

The contessa's fingers locked together. Her topaz ring flashed in the autumn sunlight from the windows. "Henry—Mr. Brougham—does not call on me often. He is most desirous of keeping my presence in London and my testimony secret from the prosecution. It all seems like something out of a novel, which I confess I found quite exciting at first, until I realized how restricted it would make my life. But he has come once or twice. And we've discussed the queen's case and my testimony." She looked from Malcolm to Mélanie. "You think Major Chase knew of it?"

"He was trying to give information to the prime minister," Malcolm said. "So it seems likely."

"But now he's dead—" The contessa put her hand to her mouth. "Oh, no. Mr. Brougham is a number of things, but he's no murderer."

"That's probably been said at some point of almost everyone who ultimately proved a murderer," Malcolm said.

The contessa's fingers tightened round her glass. "And I suppose you think I have a motive as well. Having gone to all the trouble of coming here to testify, I would not have liked to see my testimony upended. I certainly wouldn't have killed over it, though. I'm sure you don't believe me. But while I sympathize with Queen Caroline, my sympathies don't motivate me to that degree." She took a sip of wine. "I imagine I've now made you dislike me without convincing you of my innocence."

"By no means," Mélanie said. "You are to be applauded for your frankness."

"But you can't be sure of my innocence. Or of Mr. Brougham's. Or Mrs. Lamb's. Or Mr. Lamb's, I suppose. He might not have wished his wife's activities to become public knowledge. Or Major Chase might have tried to blackmail him."

"It's an unfortunate side effect of an investigation that to examine the situation one has to delve into a number of paths that prove not to be relevant. And unearth secrets in the process. Any investigator with a conscience would keep those secrets as secret as possible if they have no bearing on the investigation."

The contessa took a sip of wine, her gaze on Malcolm. "And you plainly have a conscience, Mr. Rannoch. But secrets have a way of getting out. I believe this is what is called collateral damage."

"You don't mince words, Contessa. And yes. Unfortunately, it is one of the most regrettable parts of the work of an investigator."

"Or a spy. I've heard about your work, Mr. Rannoch. Under other circumstances it would quite intrigue me."

"You flatter me, Contessa. My wife is an accomplished agent as well."

It wasn't the wisest thing to say, given in whose service Mélanie had been employed as an agent. But she appreciated Malcolm's determination to include her. More than she would ever be able to say. "Can you remember anything else about Major Chase?" she asked. "Anything you saw or heard?"

The contessa's delicately arched brows drew together. "As I told you, I didn't even know his name until after he was killed. But there was a lady I saw once who must have been calling on him."

"Golden ringlets?" Malcolm said. "We know he had a mistress who visited him here."

"No. I saw that woman as well, as I mentioned when I first spoke to you. If this lady was also his mistress, it was a different person. She was taller than the first woman, taller than average, and she wore a veil over her bonnet. The hair beneath her veil was quite plainly blonde, a paler shade than the other woman's, smooth and elegantly done up. And her features looked as though they could adorn a cameo."

Mélanie shot a quick look at her husband and saw the description fall home in his eyes. Because while it could undoubtedly belong to a number of people, it quite clearly fit the former Honoria Talbot.

CHAPTER 31

*M*élanie tightened her hand on Malcolm's arm as they descended the steps of the house in Wardour Street. "The description could match a number of people, darling. You know how deceptive descriptions can be."

"Don't humor me, Mel." Malcolm glanced up and down the street. "We both know damn well it sounds like Honoria. And given that she's already tangled in this, it's stretching belief to imagine it's someone else."

"Stretching belief, but not necessarily beyond belief. But obviously you need to talk to her. And in this case I think I'd be a hindrance, not a help."

Malcolm looked down at her as they paused at the base of the steps. The October sun fell across his face, but the curly brim of his hat left his eyes in shadow. "I'd never have married Honoria, you know. Whomever else it may have occurred to, it never occurred to me."

Mélanie looked into her husband's familiar deep-set gray eyes. A few years, even a few months ago, she couldn't have said it. But now she could. "Never?"

Malcolm flushed, but didn't look away from her gaze. "Only in extraordinary circumstances."

"Oh, well," Mélanie said. "It was extraordinary circumstances that got you to propose to me. What a fortunate thing that they occurred in my case and not the former Miss Talbot's."

∾

MALCOLM HAD NEVER CALLED on his own at the house in Upper Brook Street where the former Honoria Talbot lived with her new husband, Carlisle Atwood. He and Mélanie had attended a few parties Honoria and her husband had given. They'd called together once, and he thought Mel had called once or twice more on her own (it occurred to him that he should have paid better attention, especially as those calls probably hadn't been easy for Mélanie). It hadn't seemed appropriate for him to call on his own, and in truth he hadn't wanted to. But as Mélanie had said, at this point he plainly needed to talk to Honoria alone.

He paused at the base of the stairs to the portico, contemplating the unvoiced parts of his conversation with his wife at the base of another set of stairs. Odd, after almost eight years of marriage and innumerable secrets revealed, what things one still couldn't discuss.

The liveried footman who opened the door punctiliously in response to his ring took him up without hesitation. Honoria was in a sitting room done up in her favorite blue. She got to her feet at his entrance and nodded to the footman to withdraw. "Malcolm. I confess I've been hoping this case would bring you here."

She was wearing her hair differently, piled high on her head with ringlets framing her face. He had a vague sense that that he had seen the style lately on other ladies, though his own wife had taken to letting her walnut-brown hair simply tumble down her back much of the time. Having watched Mélanie with her curling tongs, he found himself wondering what effort it took Honoria—

or her maid—to create so many curls from her smooth hair. Perhaps she had dressed her hair herself, without the ringlets, when the contessa had seen her call on George Chase. But her eyes were the same clear blue. And her smile was the same, cool and restrained but with an irrepressible hint of mischief.

A year ago, even a few days ago, he might have taken her hand, might even have kissed her cheek. But given the reasons he had called, that didn't seem right. They both hesitated, both aware of the uncomfortable awkwardness of greeting an old friend whom one could no longer regard in quite the same way.

"It's so long since you've been here," Honoria said, gesturing him to a chair. "And of course when one sees friends in a crowd one never really talks. I think I caught a glimpse of you last night across the room at the Beverstons', but at a masquerade it's so hard to be sure."

Malcolm seated himself on a pale blue chair that was as stiff as it was tasteful. "Yes, we were there."

"You don't go out much these days. But I suppose things are different with the queen's trial."

"To a degree. We're both very busy. And we've found we like being home with the children. Or rather, we always knew we did, but it's occurred to us we can do it more often."

"Dear Malcolm. You make what might be dull sound so agreeable." Honoria got to her feet and moved to a side table. "Do you mind? I think we could do with something stronger than tea." She poured two glasses of a pale gold Tokay from a Venetian glass decanter. "Of course, Mélanie must be very busy with her plays. I quite admire her, striking out like that. And you're a very forbearing husband not to worry that she doesn't have time to tend to your career."

"I'm perfectly capable of tending to my own career." Malcolm took the glass Honoria was holding out to him.

"If that isn't just like a man. To assume all the work of being a political hostess is something he could do just as well himself."

"That's a novel way of putting it." Malcom took a sip of wine. Superbly smooth, if a bit sweet.

"Are you saying I'm wrong?" Honoria returned to her chair.

"Not in the least. It's a fine art and I have the greatest respect and appreciation for Mélanie's skills as a political and diplomatic hostess. But I don't want to build my career on her doing something she doesn't want to do. Not constantly. And I'm never going to be that sort of politician in any case. I'll always be on the fringes."

"Don't sell yourself short, Malcolm. You might be things you haven't even dreamed of, were circumstances different."

If he had a different wife, she meant. But she wouldn't put it into words. Honoria was far too well-bred to do anything of the sort.

"If circumstances were different, I doubt I'd be happy. We don't all measure success in life the same way, Noria."

"Nor happiness, it seems." Honoria studied him with a rueful smile. "If you'd asked me when I visited Lisbon with Uncle Hubert where we'd be now, I'd never have guessed this. Odd, the places life takes one."

"Odd and often quite agreeable."

Her gaze held echoes of moments neither of them would talk about. "As I recall, you told me then you'd never marry."

The memory of those moments was seared in his brain. Some secrets between him and Honoria he doubted he'd ever be able to share with anyone. Which made an odd sort of bond. "It wasn't the first thing I've been wrong about," he said. "And I'm sure it's not the last. And in that case, I was fortunate to be proved wrong."

Honoria shook her head. Her blue eyes were shot with humor but also a trace of regret. "It's odd. You were sure then that you'd never be able to love anyone, and you told me that I was sure to find love. And yet, of the two of us, you seem to be the one who's found it."

He felt his fingers tighten round the stem of his glass. He saw

Honoria in white satin and lace in St. George's, Hanover Square. "My dear girl. I'd say you had as well."

"Oh, yes." She smiled again, but the ruefulness had a bit of an edge. "My life is very agreeable. Just the life I wanted." She twisted her glass between her fingers. "At least, the life I thought I wanted after I realized I couldn't have you."

Malcolm drew his breath and discarded a number of platitudes. "I wouldn't have made you happy, Honoria. As I said, all other things aside, I don't have the ambition to be the sort of man you want."

"But perhaps I was wrong about the sort of man I wanted." She looked away. "After you sent Julien, I made sure I wouldn't see you, at least not until the investigation was over. Not to mention the trial. I know how busy you must be." She smiled, the rueful affectionate smile that took him straight back to childhood. And to moments later, when they hadn't been children and he hadn't behaved as sensibly as he should have done. "And lately you haven't seemed to have time for me."

"I'll always have time for you, Honoria. But it is indeed a busy time. And as you said, we don't go out in society as much."

Her gaze shifted over his face. "So if you're here, something must have changed."

Malcolm regarded Honoria in the golden autumn light as she sat across from him. The rose gold gilded her hair with the warmth of a past memory. "You saw George Chase recently."

Honoria drew back in her chair. For a moment, he thought she was going to deny it. But Honoria had always had exquisite instincts for how to play social games. And that was what an investigation was, after all. "He called on me. I was shocked. But would you expect me to deny someone I'd known since childhood?"

"Not in the least. But I would have expected you to be honest about it after he was murdered."

Honoria fingered the corner of her shawl. "I might have done if you'd come to see me. Julien always sets me on edge. Not to mention the new Lady Carfax."

"Kitty is a very good friend of mine. So is Julien, if it comes to that."

"Yes, well, neither of them imbues me with a desire to confide. My instinct was to protect myself and say as little as possible. I should have known you'd tumble to the truth." She put a hand to her mouth. "Oh, god, perhaps I did. Perhaps without realizing it, I was trying to persuade you to come and see me."

"If so, you could have simply called on me and confided the truth."

"The truth? That sounds so simple."

"Why did George Chase come to see you?"

"He told me he wanted to come back to England. To live with Annabel his children again. It was hard not to sympathize. I know he was rather beastly to Cordy Davenport, but you have to admit she played a role in that as well. Why on earth are you all so set against him? Why didn't Wellington and Uncle Hubert want him back? George implied he'd got on your bad side."

"George got on my and Wellington's and Hubert's and a number of people's bad sides because of some very real things he'd done. Which you didn't know about."

"Well, you can't expect me to have denied him over something I didn't know about and you won't tell me about. He wanted to talk to me about the past. He had questions about my father. The same sort of questions Julien asked. And as I told Julien and his wife, I scarcely remember my father or the circumstances of his death." She frowned. "I hope this isn't going to bring on a family scandal."

"So do I."

"You alarm me."

"That isn't the reason for my visit. But I do need answers."

"I've explained why George called on me."

"But not why you called on him."

Honoria's eyes went wide with shock. And reproach. He hadn't played fair. He'd let her give her story without letting her know how much he knew. But then, he wasn't the person he'd been a decade ago.

Honoria took a quick sip of wine. "I wasn't—"

"You were seen."

"So you knew all along. Malcolm, you might have just asked me to begin with."

"I wanted to see what you'd say."

She twisted the stem of her glass between her fingers. "George called on me, as I said. He asked about my father, as I said. I told him I couldn't provide him with more information. I promised to keep his presence in London a secret. He left. A few days later he sent me a message entreating me to call on him."

"And you went."

"Why wouldn't I?"

"Uncertainty about what he wanted. Fear of scandal."

"You think that should have stopped me?"

"No, but you play the social game more closely than I do."

"To put it mildly, my dear. I did go veiled. But I was concerned that George might have learned more about my father. I didn't like the questions he was asking."

That at least was plausible. "And had he?"

Honoria took a sip of wine, set her glass down, pleated a fold of her gown between her fingers. "He said he thought my father and Uncle Frederick had quarreled over a woman."

"We've heard that suggestion as well. Apparently there was an opera dancer they were both involved with."

"So that explains it?" Honoria's eyes widened with a sort of relief.

"We're not sure. From what we've heard, neither of them took the affair overly seriously. But surely George didn't ask you to call on him merely to tell you that?"

Honoria frowned at a loose thread in the fabric clutched

between her fingers. "George wanted my help. He wanted me to look through Uncle Frederick's papers for any letters from my father. He made some beastly threats."

"To reveal the duel?" Which apparently Honoria knew about. "Surely he'd have gone to Glenister with that?"

"No, he—"

Malcolm stared at his childhood friend. Who once might have been more. Mélanie was usually the one who made intuitive jumps. But sometimes he could do the same. "What was George to you, Honoria?"

Honoria's spine shot straight. "That's a dreadful question, Malcolm."

"We don't have time for finesse."

"Just because I once wanted to be your lover, you think I'd have taken any man."

"Of course not. But something made George come to you. Something made you call on George alone. Something gave him the ability to threaten you."

"It's not any of your—"

"It's not any of my business. That's very true, in the general run of things. But we're in the middle of a murder investigation."

"George and I aren't relevant—"

"George was murdered. Anything to do with him may be relevant. If you won't tell me, I'm going to have to learn another way. To ask Quen or Val or your uncle or Evie—"

"Malcolm! You wouldn't."

"We aren't playing by the rules of society, Honoria. I would."

Honoria glanced away. "It was when Atwood and I went to the Continent last year. We saw George in Venice. You know how it is when one sees an old friend abroad. The connections somehow seem stronger. I confess I felt sorry for him. Atwood was busy with his diplomatic mission. George and I talked about England. I was charmed. One thing led to another." She looked at Malcolm, gaze steady. "Don't judge me."

"My dear girl. You can't imagine I would."

"People judge people all the time." She took a sip of wine. "It would have been different if I'd married you. Don't deny it."

"I won't deny it. I suspect you'd have been miserable."

Honoria set her glass down. "Is Mélanie miserable?"

"You'd have to ask her. I don't think so. I hope not. But marriage to me hasn't been easy. We've learned to make it work."

"Are you saying I couldn't have?"

"It's not a question of that. I think you could succeed at almost anything you put your mind to."

"Well, then."

"Mélanie and I think alike."

"You come from very different worlds."

And Honoria didn't know the half of it. "We understand the life of an agent. We're comfortable with an unconventional life. And we've shared a great deal now."

"So you're together because you have children and shared adventures?"

Conversations with his wife and unvoiced fears echoed in his head. "No. That is, not entirely."

Honoria watched him in silence for a few endless seconds. "You're a good person, Malcolm. You stay true to your commitments."

"I hope so. My marriage to Mélanie isn't a commitment. That is, of course it is. But that isn't all it means to me."

She was silent a half beat longer. "I could have stayed true to you, Malcolm. Don't you believe that?"

"It's not for me to doubt it."

"Then are you saying you wouldn't have been true to me? I can't imagine your being unfaithful to anyone."

A person, a cause, one's own ideals. "There's more than one kind of fidelity, my dear. And fidelity doesn't necessarily guarantee happiness."

"That sounds remarkably cynical coming from you."

"I've always been more of a cynic than most people realize. My wife is the romantic in the family."

Honoria's brows drew together. "Malcolm. You take relationships far too seriously to be a cynic."

"But I don't tend to have illusions."

She shook her head. "You're no Julien."

"No, I'm not. Julien's much more of a romantic than I am."

Honoria gave a laugh of disbelief. "I doubt he'd agree with you."

"So do I. But then, there's a great deal Julien won't admit about himself."

Honoria glanced away. "I don't think George could ever have made me happy. But I trusted him. More, perhaps, than I should have done. I never thought he'd use what we shared against me."

"What did you say to him?"

Honoria's shoulders hunched. "At first, that he couldn't possibly ask me to do anything of the sort. I couldn't believe he really meant it. A man I trusted enough to share myself with him in that way—" Her gaze went across the room to a painting of water lilies. "I'd never have thought George's face could go so hard. That's when I found myself thinking that he was a soldier. That he'd killed people. And that he meant every word of his threats. I had the clearest sense I was looking at a killer."

"You were right. George was a killer. Not just in battle. He murdered two people."

Honoria stared at him. "That's why he couldn't come back? Who?"

"Julia Ashton. And Amy Beckwith."

"And he was free—"

"There was no way to prove it. But Wellington and Carfax— your uncle Hubert—both know."

"So how in god's name did he ever think he could come back?"

"An excellent question. He'd have needed to checkmate both of them, at the very least."

Honoria shuddered. "Perhaps that's why—He frightened me. I

told him I'd try to do as he asked. Mostly to give myself time. I found myself desperately wanting to get out of the room." She reached for her wineglass and clutched it. "I don't think I'd realized what danger I was in. But a part of me must have sensed it."

"I'm sorrier than I can say you went through that. I don't think any of us anticipated George's coming back."

Honoria gulped down a drink of wine. "Once I got home, I wasn't sure what to do. Something in me rebelled at assisting George. I don't like being given ultimatums. But I was afraid of him. And I was also curious about what information Uncle Frederick had that George wanted. What George was trying to uncover about my father and his death. And then, while I was still paralyzed with uncertainty, I learned that George had been killed." She stared at Malcolm with wide eyes. "Which means I have an excellent motive to have had him killed, doesn't it?"

"You have a motive. Along with a number of other people."

Honoria hugged her arms round herself. "That's rather harsh, Malcolm."

"It's the truth. I don't think you had George killed. But I also know you. I can't let that interfere."

"I wouldn't even know how to hire an assassin."

Given that her cousin Louisa had done precisely that and that Louisa was Hubert Mallinson's daughter and Honoria was his niece and had spent holidays in the Mallinson household growing up that was not as convincing as it might have been. "Did you see anything else when you were in Wardour Street?" Malcolm asked.

"I passed a woman in the hall. Quiet but rather elegant. I didn't recognize her, but I was grateful to be veiled. Is she important in this?"

"I'm not sure," Malcolm said. "But she may be very important indeed."

CHAPTER 32

*H*arry found Thomas Thornsby in the Classicists' Society Reading Room. He seemed to be at the society more than home these days—which was understandable, given what he faced at home. It was early in the day and the room was empty but, given what he had to relate, Harry suggested they walk. Thomas gave him a measured look but agreed without protest. Harry waited until they were in the quieter reaches of Green Park before relating the previous night's revelations about Thomas's great aunt.

Thomas stopped dead in his tracks and stared at Harry. "You're telling me Aunt Letitia—"

"Apparently."

Thomas put up a hand and tugged at the brim of his hat as though it could order his thoughts. "But—"

"At least now we seem to know your aunt's interest in Trenchard's scheme. She was trying to put her son in power."

Thomas released his hat brim and passed a hand over his face. "She's—"

"Complicated. Like most people." Harry studied Thomas. "We can get locked into seeing our parents and their generation a certain way. Locked into the roles they've always had. It can be a shock to realize they're people making their own choices. Changing and facing challenges and keeping secrets just as we are. I confess it was a shock when my uncle married and became a father after I did."

"Yes, but your uncle—I mean no offense, Harry, I have the greatest respect for Mr. Davenport. But he'd led a—varied romantic career."

"So he had." Though Harry now knew that at least some of that had been cover for Archie's espionage activities.

"Aunt Letitia—"

"Was obviously more discreet."

Thomas blanched.

Harry studied his friend in the shade of the golden-leafed branches. "Do you have any idea who?"

"Who?"

"Who might have been your aunt's lover. Under ordinary circumstances it's the last thing I'd ever ask anyone. But given that your aunt's lover is apparently Alistair Rannoch's biological father, it's a matter of some urgency."

Thomas swallowed and started walking again, gaze on the path before them. "She wasn't—she didn't—doesn't—live in that world. The world of the Devonshire House Set and the Glenister House Set and the Carlton House Set."

"The world my uncle belonged to. I quite understand. But you can't believe love affairs only occur among those who flaunt them."

"No, of course not. But she wasn't—she moved widely in society. She still does. She has a great many friends. But I've never had the least indication she had a lover. If she did have a lover, presumably they'd both have been at pains to keep the relationship secret. And this all would have happened long before I was born. At least, Alistair Rannoch was born long before I was born." Thomas drew another breath, gaze now on the line of trees ahead.

"I've met him a few times. I wouldn't say our families are in the same circle, but he's a Tory, like my father. We've been at the same events and shaken hands. I can't claim to know him. But—I suppose this news makes us cousins."

"Don't get sentimental about him. He's one of the most dangerous men I've ever encountered. And thoroughly ruthless."

Thomas stopped walking again and turned to Harry. "Has Aunt Letitia—she saw him growing up?"

"Apparently. Enough to build some sort of connection. She obliquely admitted as much to O'Roarke last night. We don't know how much she saw him as a child, but she seems to have begun trying to guide his life at least by the time he was at Oxford. The point of the Elsinore League appears to have been to create power for him. Or for her through him."

"And you think who his father is—"

"Might shed some light on her actions. Or Alistair's. Or both. Or I suppose could be entirely unrelated. But it could be valuable information."

Thomas frowned as they began to walk again. "I never saw Aunt Letitia so much as flirt with a gentleman. Even Uncle Shroppington. Especially Uncle Shroppington. The very idea of her flirting would make me laugh were this situation not so serious and my feelings about Aunt Letitia not so far from any sort of humor. By the time I was going about in society, I don't even recall her dancing."

"Do you recall anything unusual about her? Anything you noticed out of the ordinary?"

Thomas's frown deepened. "She wasn't the sort to spend much time about the nursery. Until I was at Oxford, I mostly saw her when we were brought into the drawing room after dinner. But I do remember—I think I was about seven, I hadn't started at Eton yet. We were at a house party at her country house. I ran down a hedged walk after a stray cricket ball and I found her walking with a gentleman. Not unusual. But they went quiet all of a sudden as I approached. Aunt Letitia gave me a sharp look as though she was wondering how much I'd heard. I scrambled to get the ball and murmured an apology and ran off. I just thought it was grownups not liking children about, and talking about dull grownup things they didn't want us to hear. But I could feel her gaze boring into the back of my head the whole time I retreated down the walkway." Thomas shook his head. "Odd, I haven't thought of that in years. But I can't imagine they were—I mean, there was nothing the least bit romantic about their attitude towards each other. Even at seven I could tell that. And he seemed quite old. Even granted I was seven, he must have been two decades her senior."

"Who was he? Do you know his name?"

"Sir Benjamin something."

Harry felt his pulse quicken. "Benjamin Howland?"

"Yes." Thomas scanned Harry's face. "Is that significant?"

Harry drew a breath of the autumn air. It held an unexpected chill of oncoming winter. "It may be."

"ARE you saying Alistair Rannoch's father was a spymaster?" Cordelia looked at her husband across the Berkeley Square library where they were all once again gathered. "Given everything else, I suppose perhaps that isn't surprising."

"Possibly," Harry said. "So far, he's the only man of the right age connected to Lady Shroppington. But given her role later with the League, it did occur to me to wonder if she might have had a very different association with him."

Malcolm set down his coffee, but it was Mélanie who spoke first. "You think Lady Shroppington was an agent?" she said. "Not that only agents are capable of scheming, but it would explain a number of things."

"She seems to have been looking for something to put her

talents to use in," Kitty said. "She wouldn't be the first woman to find a refuge in espionage."

"But whom was she spying for?" Cordelia asked. "I mean, whom was she spying against? It was before the war with France. At least, it would have been when she started."

"There was always tension with France," Raoul said. "And countries always have agents in other countries, even allies."

"And as someone told Julien and me recently, spying on France didn't start with the Revolution." Malcolm turned his coffee cup in his hand as the possibility settled in his brain.

"You think Lady Shroppington is Fortinbras?" Laura asked.

Mélanie leaned forwards to refill the coffee. "It would explain how the Elsinore League got its name."

"Bloody hell." Malcolm leaned his head in his hands.

"You don't think it's likely?" Harry asked.

"No, I think I should have seen it sooner."

"Does that mean the League was a spy ring after all?" Kitty asked. "She had them all gathering information?"

"Interesting thought." Raoul took a drink of coffee. "She might even have done without their knowing it. I can certainly see her as a spymaster."

"If she's Fortinbras, she was attempting to expose Julien's grandfather." Kitty looked at Malcolm.

Malcolm nodded. "I need to see Hubert."

"BENJAMIN HOWLAND WAS a clever man stuck in the last century." Hubert took a drink of coffee and regarded Malcolm and Julien across the private room at Bellamy's refreshment rooms in the Palace of Westminster where they had cornered him during a break in the trial after Malcolm had slipped a note to Julien.

"He did his work in the last century," Julien pointed out.

"You know what I mean. He quite failed to see that we

faced a new enemy with the Revolution in France and the currents of ideas sweeping across the Continent. By the time I knew him, he was trying to fight by the old rules even though the battlefield had shifted. You can't fight dangerous new ideas with moves drawn up for conflicts between monarchies."

Julien leaned against the paneled wall and folded his arms. "One could say the same about a number of your colleagues who feel they can use tactics from before the Revolution on the world we've been left in the wake of Bonaparte's defeat."

Hubert sat back in his chair. "It's not really the same at all. The field has shifted again."

"Yes, but not back into what it was before. And you'll never be able to force it into the old pattern."

"Edifying as this conversation is, and much as I'm in sympathy with Julien," Malcolm said, "it doesn't help us with the present question. Was Lady Shroppington working for Benjamin Howland?"

Carfax clunked down his coffee. "For god's sake, Malcolm. Do you imagine Howland confided those sorts of things to me? Or turned over neat files listing his agents? Even if he'd been fool enough to keep such files, he'd hardly have given them over to me."

"You worked for him," Julien said.

"Originally. When I first went into the army and went into intelligence. I went off on my own more and more as I saw how antiquated his ideas were."

"But then when he died, you took over," Malcolm said.

"To a degree. There were still layers of command to deal with. I don't think either of you will argue with me when I talk about the challenges of dealing with the military bureaucracy. As I said yesterday, one of the advantages of becoming Lord Carfax—temporarily—was being able to set up my own network outside of military intelligence."

Julien tapped his fingers on the desktop. "As justifications for your actions go, that's quite impressive, Uncle."

"I'm not trying to justify anything. But it was perhaps the most useful thing about the earldom. It gave me a certain freedom."

"Ha," Julien said. "That's the last thing I'd say of it. Or that David would."

"You're not doing badly, from what I've seen." Hubert tilted his head back and regarded his nephew over the top of his spectacles.

"Lady Shroppington," Malcolm said.

Hubert tented his fingers together. "She could have been working for Howland. He saw society as a place to gather information. For a military man, he saw a lot of work taking place in ballrooms and drawing rooms."

"He wasn't far wrong," Malcolm said.

"Perhaps not. If Letitia Shroppington was working for him, she wouldn't be the only aristocratic woman to do so. There were one or two in my time. No, don't ask me for their names. But I will say both were married to diplomats and primarily gathering information abroad. Which would make Lady Shroppington —interesting."

"Did you hear any rumors about her?" Julien asked.

"No. I've told you—"

"I know what you've told us. Don't insult all of us by asking if we believe it. Did you hear any rumors?"

"No."

"Oh, for god's sake, Uncle—"

"Damn it, Julien, don't you think I'm kicking myself for not having got wind of this? Assuming it's true. The fact that I didn't hear any rumors is what makes me doubt it more than anything, to be frank. But a lot of this would have happened before I went to work for Howland. All of it, perhaps. Even if she was working for him, we don't know how long it went on."

"Thomas remembers seeing them together," Malcolm said. "They were apparently sharing secrets years later."

Julien stepped forwards. "You were investigating the League. You've been obsessed with them since university. You can't tell me you didn't know more about Lady Shroppington."

Hubert met his nephew's gaze. "I should have known more. Which isn't the same thing."

"If she wasn't working for Howland," Julien said, "—or even if she was—do you think he could be—"

"Alistair's father?" Hubert reached for his coffee. "Howland annoyed me. Almost from the moment we met. So, given that, his being Alistair's father would make a certain sort of sense."

"There's one more thing," Julien said. "Did you know your father was a French spy?"

The cup of coffee spattered over Hubert's cravat and waistcoat.

"My god," Julien said. "I've wanted to see you do that since I was four years old."

Hubert clunked his coffee cup on the table. "Did Chase know?"

"We aren't sure. We learned it from some papers at the war office that someone was trying to break in and steal last night. Fortunately, Palmerston scared them off."

"So Palmerston knows."

Julien folded his arms. "No comment."

Hubert grunted. "I don't suppose it matters. It's old history now."

"So you knew?" Julien said.

Hubert tugged a handkerchief from his sleeve and pressed it over his coffee-soaked cravat. "I learned. After my father died. From old papers."

"Did my father know?" Julien asked.

Carfax reached for the pitcher of water on the table, splashed water on his handkerchief, and pressed it to his cravat again. "We discovered the information together."

"So you and my father both knew your father had been spying

for the French when my father wanted to turn me over to British justice to face charges of treason."

Hubert scrubbed at a spot on the cravat. "Your father's hypocrisy was one of the many reasons charging you with treason struck me as a sad waste."

"Thank you, Uncle Hubert. Your family feeling never ceases to amaze me."

"Benjamin Howland knew." Malcolm spoke up for the first time, intruding on what had been a family scene. "Fortinbras apparently investigated him."

"Meaning Lady Shroppington," Hubert said.

"If we're right."

Hubert dropped the handkerchief on the table and tossed down the coffee left in his cup. "If she was Fortinbras, she's more dangerous than ever. But given whom the two of you married, I shouldn't have to say anything to you about dangerous women."

CHAPTER 33

"It's good to see you, Malcolm." Evie Cleghorn smiled. She smiled more openly these days. On one of Malcolm's visits home from Lisbon, when Evie had been drawn and anxious over her lack of a dowry (and, Malcolm now suspected, the fact that her cousin Quen had been entangled with a governess fifteen years his senior who was now his wife), Malcolm had wondered vaguely if offering Evie marriage would solve her problems and perhaps give his own life a focus. Fortunately, before long he'd realized Evie was, in fact, desperately in love with a penniless curate. Malcolm had had the conversation with Glenister that Evie couldn't have, Glenister had given her a generous dowry, and Evie was now comfortably settled in the country.

Odd now to realize she was Andrew's half-sister. One could see it a bit in the dark hair, the blue eyes, the wide, generous mouth.

They turned and walked along the Serpentine while Evie's children ran ahead. When Julien and Carfax returned to the proceedings in the House of Lords, Malcolm had called at Evie's husband's parents' house, where Evie and her husband were staying in London. Evie's mother-in-law had told him Evie had taken her children to the park. "I couldn't believe the news about George Chase," Evie said. "I thought the queen's trial had brought enough shocks."

"I assume you had no idea Chase was back in London?"

"Good heavens, no. I hadn't heard of him in years. Do you know why he was back?"

"He was trying to return to his old life. And in doing so he was gathering information on a number of powerful people. Including your family."

Evie shot a quick look at him, gaze alert beneath the straw brim of her bonnet. "About what?"

"Nothing concerning you. About your uncle Cyril's death before you came to live at Glenister House."

Evie nodded, gaze fixed ahead. "Have you talked to Honoria?"

"Today. It seems she'd seen George. And he'd made some threats. I'm hoping he didn't also threaten you."

"Oh, no. Nothing like that. I hadn't seen him. I had no notion he was here, as I said. But that's not surprising. He and Honoria—" Evie bit back what she'd been going to say.

"It's all right," Malcolm said. "Honoria told me she and George had been close recently, in Venice."

Evie looked up at him, eyes wide beneath the straw brim of her bonnet. "Is that what she said? Perhaps it's true."

"You have reason to think it isn't?"

"No. Not precisely." Evie turned her gaze to the path ahead. "But they were also—close—years ago. Before Waterloo."

Before Honoria had been married. Which shouldn't be a total shock. But—

"I wouldn't talk about it," Evie said. "But you're investigating a murder. I think it's probably better you know everything. You're likely to learn it in any case and maybe in a more public manner."

"Sound judgment. Evie, are you saying Chase seduced Honoria?"

"I'm not sure," Evie said. "It may have been the other way round."

Malcolm stopped walking.

Evie turned to face him and folded her arms over her blue spencer. "Malcolm, Honoria and I grew up in Glenister House. Oh, I know Uncle Hubert likes to think he shielded us from the goings-on. And I suppose he did with me, in a way. I mean, I never actually did anything. But I certainly was aware of more than he realized. Even before I came to live at Glenister House, I knew I was born five months after my parents eloped, for heaven's sake. But Honoria—Honoria and Val were daring each other to all sorts of things before Honoria even made her debut."

Malcolm had a feeling he was being very slow. But it was difficult to accept what he was hearing. "You mean—"

"I assume you've read *Les Liaisons Dangereuses?* They were like a younger version of Valmont and Merteuil."

When it came to Lord Valentine Talbot, Honoria's cousin and Glenister's younger son, that was not surprising. There had been stories about Val as a confirmed rake when he was still at Harrow. But Honoria—

Evie's blue gaze flickered across his face, embarrassed but also remarkably candid. "I know. It's probably hard to believe. But I can understand. I'm a married woman now. I'm not saying I ever would have—but I do understand the impulse. Honoria was bored, I think. For all she reigned so easily over society, I think it was almost too easy for her. Life, I mean. The life we lived on the surface. So she had to find something else beneath the surface."

"That's remarkably insightful."

"I've had a lot of time to think about Honoria. And Val and Quen. They used to be my life." She glanced ahead at her sons, who were clambering up a tree. "Now my own family are." Her gaze shot back to Malcolm. "I'm sure it's hard to accept about Honoria, knowing what you know—"

"No, that's the thing." The image of Honoria sitting up in his bed in Lisbon, fair hair spilling over her bare breasts, shot into his mind. It had perhaps been flattering, but her blatant attempt to provoke a relationship between them had never really rung true. When he'd walked into his room to find her in his bed, he'd been embarrassed and confused and desperate to get them both out of it. But later, when he'd let himself remember the awkward encounter, he'd struggled to reconcile it with the contained woman Honoria seemed to be. A bet with Val accounted for what he hadn't been able to otherwise make sense of.

Evie's gaze flickered over his face, probably seeing more than he wanted her to. "I don't think it means Honoria doesn't genuinely care for people."

"Do you think she genuinely cared for George Chase?"

"Not the way she cared for you." Evie drew a breath. "I'm sorry, but we both know she cared for you."

"I confess I'm questioning everything at this point. But I'm surer than ever that it's a good thing nothing progressed between Honoria and me. What happened between her and Chase?"

"It was just after the scandal with Lady Cordelia, I think. That is, I remember knowing about the scandal already when it happened, and it was before Waterloo. And I can't really be certain of what happened. But I do know Honoria slipped outside with him at Lady Jersey's ball and another time at the theatre, because she asked me to cover for her both times. I don't think it went on for very long. But I imagine it left a—connection—between them."

"Yes, to say the least."

"Malcolm, you don't think—Honoria plays games, but she wouldn't—you have to understand what it was like in Glenister House. All sorts of things that make me ill now seemed perfectly logical. Everyone played those games. Well, almost everyone. I didn't and Quen didn't, not precisely, though goodness know he had his adventures. It seems like a dreamworld now. There are so many things from that part of my life I'll never tell Max. He's not naive, not precisely, but he'd be shocked and worried about me, and there's simply no need for him to know. It was a different life. I'm sure it's like that for Honoria now. She's married to Atwood and happily settled."

"I'm not sure she's as happily settled as you are."

Evie wrinkled her nose. "I'm not sure Honoria has it in her to be happy in that way. She always seemed to want something that's out of reach. But I think she's too sensible to go on playing those games." Evie scanned his face. "Do you think she's in danger?"

"In danger? No, not now."

Evie drew a breath, glanced at her children, looked back at Malcolm. "But you think she might be behind Major Chase's death?"

"What I think doesn't matter. She has a motive. As do a number of others. But her motive is stronger after our conversation."

"Then I haven't helped at all."

"Oh, no, Evie." Malcolm squeezed her hand. "You've helped immeasurably."

∼

"Nerezza!" Bet ran to the gate of the Berkeley Square garden as her friend came into view along the side of the square.

Nerezza stopped and waved to the children, who were playing in the garden. "Has everyone deserted you?"

"Sandy's at the Lords taking notes for Malcolm, and the rest of them are about on different parts of the investigation."

Nerezza came into the garden, exchanged greetings with the children, and then settled on one of the black metal benches beside Bet when the children went back to their game of hide-and-seek. "You're lucky you didn't have to go to the masquerade last night. It was tepid beside a real Italian masquerade."

"I didn't want to go," Bet said with a steady gaze. "But—"

"If you're worried about Sandy, I doubt he wanted to go

either."

Bet glanced away.

"You've won," Nerezza said.

Bet folded her hands in her lap. Sometimes the reality of what she had washed over her and left her stunned. At the possibilities. And also the risks. "I'm not quite sure what we've won."

"We have to enjoy life." Nerezza said. "There's not much point if we don't. Even when it seemed a hopeless muddle and I thought we couldn't possibly make it work, I believed that. You have to snatch joy where you can find it. God knows there's precious little of it to be found if one doesn't snatch it."

"No." Bet rubbed her arms. Despite the sun on her face, she could feel an autumn chill through her gros-de-Naples spencer. "But one can't build a life on snatched moments."

"One might. If one could string enough moments together. I thought I had to be hardheaded and practical. But I realized I didn't really want that if it meant not having Ben. And Ben finally convinced me he wouldn't be happy without me." Nerezza frowned. "It was probably appallingly selfish of me to let him persuade me of it. But then, I've always been appallingly selfish."

"I don't think so. Or you'd have taken advantage of Ben from the first."

"Who says I haven't?"

"Ben for one, I'm quite sure."

Nerezza watched Jessica and Emily chase each other round a tree. Berowne raced after them with Emily holding his lead. "I used to think celebrating the moment was all that mattered. I suppose now I'm thinking of the future, in a way."

"That's what marriage is, isn't it?"

"I used to think marriage was deadly dull. If I thought of it at all."

"God knows I never thought of it. And once I was with Sandy, I tried not to think of the future because I thought it meant a future without him."

Nerezza shot a look at her. "It seems to me you thought of the future too much."

"Maybe. Sometimes." Bet looked down at the shiny moss green of her sleeves. "Mostly it was something I couldn't contemplate. Now I'm trying to figure out how we're going to make it work. And I have to think of the future. Because I don't think Sandy's really thinking of it. At least, he's not facing how difficult it will be."

"I'm not sure Ben is either. Although we may be underestimating both of them. And of course it won't ever be as hard for them as it is for us."

"Nerezza!"

"Oh, I don't mean I don't want to be Ben's wife. Or that it isn't in many ways a much easier life than the one I had. But they won't be given the cut direct and not invited places, the way we will be."

"Because it's their world."

"And because they're men. Lamentable but true. And they won't be gossiped about. Not that I mind being gossiped about. In fact, Ben minds it more on my account than I do. So in that sense it will be harder for Ben. It may be easier for you. You're much more domestic than me."

"I'm not!"

"You look after your brother and sister. I imagine even when you only had one room in St. Giles it was far tidier than any room I've ever occupied." Nerezza grinned and squeezed Bet's shoulders. "It's not going to be easy, but I'm trying to get used to the prospect."

"Of what?"

"Being happy."

"Sofia!" Emily's voice caught the air, as she and Jessica ran to the gate to greet Sofia Montagu.

Sofia came into the garden, hugged the girls, Colin, and Clara, petted Berowne, and then came over to join Bet and Nerezza. "You both look very serious."

"Just talking about the complications of life," Nerezza said. "Marriage was simpler for you than for either of us."

Sofia wrinkled her nose as she dropped onto the bench beside them. "It didn't feel simple. Kit had to extricate himself from his betrothal. And we both felt horribly guilty until he realized Elinor Dormer actually seemed relieved. And then—well, it's odd to think about being a wife. I used to think I never wanted to do anything so confining."

"Kit's not in the least confining," Bet said.

"No, thank goodness. But the institution can seem as though it is. Of course, growing up with a mother who had to flee it didn't help. And don't let me alarm you. I quite like being married. Far more than I expected. But I'm not sure I'd have risked it if I hadn't known I couldn't get Kit on any other terms."

Bet laughed. "You don't mean it."

"I do honestly," Sofia said. "Well, at least I did at first. I couldn't imagine myself as a wife."

"Neither could I," Bet said. "But you were brought up expecting to be a wife."

"Which is precisely why I couldn't imagine being one. Well, that and my parents' example." Sofia looked from Bet to Nerezza. "Does that sound horridly complacent, in a way? I hadn't really thought about it, but I suppose it's a sort of privilege to be able to reject marriage on principle. Some women need to do it for security."

"And some of us don't think it's a possibility for us at all," Nerezza said.

"Yes, well, now it's possible for all of us," Sofia said. "Thank goodness, because now that I'm actually married to Kit, I have to admit it's distinctly agreeable." She looked at Nerezza. "Do you remember how nervous I was about it when we traveled to England together?"

"Nervous in between mooning about Kit Montagu," Nerezza

said with a smile. "Which I was less sympathetic to than I should have been."

"Mummy!" This time the cry came from Jessica. Mélanie came into the garden and scooped her daughter up.

"Where's Daddy?" Jessica asked. "In Parl-ment?"

"I'm not sure. He had calls to make. The trial should be over for the day soon if it isn't already, so I imagine Julien will stop by and perhaps Daddy will be with him."

Colin set down his ball and ran over to his mother. "Didn't you both go to call on the contessa?"

Mélanie smoothed Jessica's hair and looked at her son. "Where did you hear that?"

Colin grinned. "I listen. The Contessa Montalta or something."

"The Contessa Montalto?" Sofia pushed herself to her feet. "Anna Montalto?"

"Yes," Mélanie set down Jessica, who was wriggling, and walked over to the bench. "Do you know her?"

"Yes. She took a villa on Lake Como one summer. I was fifteen or sixteen. She lived very quietly, but she came to some of our parties. I think she liked that they were informal. She didn't seem to mind that Mama and Uncle Bernard weren't married. In fact, I rather think it was easier for her that they were on the fringe of society, because she didn't want to mingle with society. I was very young, but I remember her once telling me to take great care in choosing a husband. That not all women could escape from it as my mother had done. She said, dreadful as it was, she'd never been more relieved than when her husband died."

"That sounds like her, from what I've seen," Mélanie said. "She's a realist."

"I liked her," Sofia said.

Mélanie regarded Sofia. "I think you could help us with her. I'm quite sure she knows more than she's telling and she isn't inclined to trust us. Sensibly. Perhaps you can persuade her to talk."

Sofia smiled and tightened the ribbon on her bonnet. "Thank goodness. I've been feeling quite sidelined. Kit will be so jealous. "

~

THE PORTER LET Mélanie and Sofia into the house in Wardour Street without question. "You know the way," he said, gesturing to the stairs.

Mélanie rapped on the door of the contessa's rooms. Her maid opened the door and inclined her head. "It's Signora Rannoch," she said to her mistress.

"Show her in. I have a surfeit of visitors today. It almost feels as though I am not living in seclusion from society."

The contessa was sitting by the windows with a gentleman beside her. Brougham. Perhaps as well. Though Sofia might not be able to draw the contessa out as well with him present. Both Brougham and the contessa got to their feet when Mélanie and Sofia stepped into the room.

"I've brought a visitor to see you, Contessa," Mélanie said.

"Anna!" Sofia said, and then went still.

The contessa went still as well, her gaze wide and wary. Which was not in itself surprising. She had reason to be cautious and to question the sudden appearance of someone in England whom she had last seen years ago in Italy. What was surprising was the utter blankness in her gaze.

Sofia's spine went straight in a way Mélanie had seen when danger threatened.

The contessa broke the silence first. She gave a smile, easy, warm, and quite clearly practiced. "How delightful. Do come and sit down."

"Thank you." Sofia's voice was steady but with an edge of broken glass beneath. "But before I do so, may I know whom I am addressing?"

CHAPTER 34

or a moment, something that might have been fear
broke across the contessa's face. Then her features
settled into admirable control. "It's been some time since we've
met, my dear. And I fear the years may not have been as kind to
me as I would like to think."

"In that case," Sofia said, in the same steady voice, "since I do
not recognize you and you seem to recognize me, perhaps you can
tell me who I am? No, Mr. Brougham"—she put out a hand as
Brougham made to get to his feet. "I should like to hear it from
this woman who calls herself the Contessa Montalto. Though she
is certainly not the Contessa Montalto I met on Lake Como at my
parents' home six years ago."

"Ah," the contessa said. "Perhaps there is the confusion. I was
not on Lake Como six years ago."

"Don't be absurd, Donna Sofia—Mrs. Montagu," Brougham
said. "Mrs. Lamb and I met the contessa four years ago. I can
assure you the lady we met is the woman before us now."

Sofia folded her arms across her chest. "Then it is quite clear
one of us met an imposter."

"How dreadful," the contessa said. "To imagine someone impersonating me."

"Yes," Sofia said. "But what's troubling me is that while I can quite see someone's impersonating the Contessa Montalto to gain Mr. Brougham's attention and play a role in the queen's case, I can't for the life of me see the point in anyone's impersonating the Contessa Montalto to get close to an exiled family living quietly outside of society."

"I'm sure there's an explanation," Brougham said. "Perhaps we could all sit down and discuss this. Contessa, it seems you are not acquainted with Donna Sofia Vincenzo—that is, now, Mrs. Christopher Montagu."

"I am delighted to meet you, Mrs. Montagu," the contessa said. "Despite the distressing circumstances. Do sit down and have a glass of wine," she added, moving to a decanter and glasses.

Sofia accepted a glass, though her gaze remained armored. "Can you think of why anyone would have chosen to impersonate you all those years ago?" she asked. "The contessa I met lived very quietly. And she had letters of introduction from friends of my mother's. Elena Vincenzo."

"Vincenzo." The contessa set down the decanter and returned to her seat with her own glass. "I knew I recognized the name. Your mother—"

"Left her husband and ran off with Lord Thurston. They're now married, because his wife agreed to give him a divorce after my father died. And I'm married to Lord Thurston's son. Which is all rather complicated, and admittedly it was a great scandal, but I don't see why anyone would have gone to such elaborate lengths to deceive us."

"Nor do I," the contessa said with great cordiality. "Perhaps this woman simply wanted to make use of a respected name to secure a villa and to go about in society on Lake Como."

"But she didn't really go about in society. She lived very

quietly. She would come to see us because we lived quietly as well."

The contessa took a sip of wine and smiled at her guests with the ease of an accomplished hostess. "You're obviously gently bred, my dear, but one never knows what sort of scheme such a person may be involved in. Perhaps she needed a place to hide after some other scheme put her at risk. Perhaps she gained some financial advantage from your parents."

"I doubt that last. Even though I was young, I suspect I'd have heard about it. And most people who know me well would say if I was gently bred, I've quite got over it in recent years." Sofia took her own sip of wine and gave a decorous smile. She had been working for the Carbonari and breaking Elsinore League codes before she turned twenty. "The Contessa Montalto—at least, the woman who called herself the Contessa Montalto—has written to my mother regularly through the years and my mother has replied. Odd that she could have taken the trouble to keep up such a correspondence long after her masquerade."

"I imagine she might have thought it could be useful to maintain the masquerade for a future scheme," replied the contessa. "A clever person might set such a scheme up years in advance."

"Yes, I can well see that," Brougham said. He was sitting beside the contessa, giving every indication that he was her ally, but Mélanie caught the faint question in his tone.

"If so, I hope it wasn't anything that will disrupt your plans in London," Sofia said, in a sweet voice that was quite unlike her usual tones.

"I very much doubt it," the contessa said, in equally dulcet tones.

Sofia took another sip of wine. "Did you ever meet my father? The Conte Vincenzo? He mostly lived in Milan and I was with my mother more than with him."

"I know the name," the contessa said, "but I don't believe we ever met. Is he in Milan now?"

"No, he died two years ago," Sofia said. "Or rather, I should say, he was murdered."

"How dreadful. I'm so sorry."

"It was a difficult time. I'm very sorry for his death, of course, but he had got himself involved in some quite unsavory schemes. It's amazing how that can happen to all sorts of people."

"Sad, the world we live in," the contessa said. "You have encountered a great deal in your young life, *cara*."

"And yet I've never had anyone try to impersonate me."

Brougham tossed down the last of his wine. "I'm glad you called, Mrs. Montagu, and that we learned that someone else may be using the contessa's name. I have business for the queen to attend to, so I fear we must take our leave. May I escort you, ladies?"

"That would be delightful," Mélanie said.

They finished the wine and made their farewells with no one trying to prolong the situation. No one spoke until they turned down Wardour Street. Mélanie saw a coffeehouse on the corner. The thick glass of the windows did not show a large crowd.

"I think we're all in need of fortification," she said. "I suggest we repair there."

Brougham frowned. Ladies did not generally frequent coffee-houses. "Are you sure—"

"Believe me, Henry, I have long stopped caring about society's opinion. And I don't think Sofia did to begin with."

Brougham nodded without further speech. No one said more until they were settled in a booth at the back of the coffeehouse with cups of strong coffee. Mélanie scribbled a note in the mean-time and gave it to the waiter with a coin.

Brougham took a drink of coffee. "Until an hour ago, I thought the worst challenge of the day was the new Lord Bowditch telling me he's not sure how he'll vote because his younger brother was looking into the queen and he has questions about his brother's death. As though whatever happened to Sidney Newland has anything to do with me or with her majesty. Newland's investigation is ancient history at this point. But that's positively tame compared to this."

Sofia blew on the steam from her cup. "I'll grant that it may be slightly possible that an imposter came to Lake Como and ingratiated herself with my family in the guise of the Contessa Montalto. Uncle Bernard is involved in a number of schemes, and my father was an Elsinore League member, so I suppose she could have been sent to spy on us. But I'm not aware of any follow-up actions that indicate she was a spy. Or an imposter." Sofia took a sip of coffee. "And given that she is obviously here to testify on the queen's behalf, I think it is far more likely that your contessa is an imposter, and someone set up an elaborate plot years ago to introduce her to you."

"So do I." Brougham grimaced and clunked his cup down on the table. "But if so, it was a very careful plot. I vetted her for years."

"How were you introduced?" Mélanie asked.

Brougham frowned at a nick in the tabletop. "Someone sent Caro a letter. A marquesa something or other who had been introduced to Harriet and Granville when they were abroad." He looked up. "At least, that's what Caro told me. That's what this woman claimed. We weren't expecting schemes and imposters. I pride myself on anticipating plots, and I knew the queen's case was delicate. But I certainly wasn't thinking of a trial at that point. Or if I considered it, it was only one of a number of possible eventualities. Truth to tell, when we got the letter of introduction to the contessa, Caro and I were both growing a bit restive." He coughed and cast a quick glance at Sofia.

"Pray don't have qualms on my account, Mr. Brougham," Sofia said. "I grew up in a household with my mother living with a man who wasn't her husband or my father. And I am quite convinced that if she hadn't left my father, my mother would have been miserable."

"Er—yes." Brougham took a drink of coffee, as though seeking refuge in the cup. "In any case, Caro and I were both in need of distraction, and we went to call on the contessa. She and Caro got on, and I was happy Caro had found a friend. It was only on our second or third visit that I even spoke at length with the contessa —the woman who called herself the contessa—about the queen. Princess Caroline, then." He looked up at Mélanie. "If she is an imposter, what the devil is her endgame?"

"I don't know," Mélanie said. "It could be to change her testimony on the witness stand. It could be to be exposed and discredited and embarrass you and the queen. It could even be to help the queen, assuming she can get away with the masquerade. It rather depends on whom she's working for."

Brougham stared at her. "Oh god. Of course she's probably not doing this on her own. Not if she's an adventuress. But who the devil—"

"Henry," Mélanie said. "If she is an imposter, she knows we may be on to her. What do you think she'll have done the moment we left?"

"Christ." Brougham scraped his bench back. "She'll be out of there like a shot—"

Mélanie gripped his wrist before he could leave the table. "I sent word to Malcolm the moment we got here. He already had a Bow Street patrol watching the house because of George Chase. He'll update the patrol. We'll know if she leaves. Or if she sends for whomever she's working for."

Brougham subsided onto the bench. "I think of myself as a good strategist. But I'm no agent. I forget sometimes what you and Malcolm are." He ran a hand through his hair. "Who could be behind this?"

"Someone laying an elaborate trail to embarrass you. Most likely someone supporting the king and the government. Or possibly someone supporting the queen, assuming they thought they could get away with it." She took a drink of coffee.

Brougham froze, his own cup clutched in his hand. "You think I might have set all this up, don't you? That I planned it four years ago and introduced her to Caro for verisimilitude?"

Mélanie set down her cup. "I think it's a possibility we have to consider. Not the likeliest possibility. But a possibility."

Brougham clunked his cup down on the table, spattering coffee on the scarred wood. "But I'm sitting here with you. Questioning her motives. Admitting she's likely deceiving us. Trying to figure out why. Why the devil would I do that if I were behind her deception to begin with?"

"To throw us off the scent." Sofia reached for her own cup. "Just a suggestion."

"Oh, Christ." Brougham stared into his coffee. "I'm not that adept. I can think through a case, but not—"

"This is part of your case," Mélanie said.

"Yes, but I didn't plan it to be. I mean yes, I was thinking about the princess—the queen—four years ago. But I didn't know where things would end up. To have set something up, to have involved my mistress—whom I was already sure would not be my mistress that much longer—for god's sake, don't waste all your time suspecting me. We have to catch whoever is behind this."

"We do," Mélanie agreed. "I'm hoping the supposed contessa makes a move. But we also should search her rooms."

Brougham blinked. "How?"

"If she doesn't go out on her own, you need to get her out. And her maid."

"But won't she be suspicious? I mean, I tried to act as though I was still on her side, but she's no fool. She has to know I'm wondering."

"I expect she is," Mélanie said. "So we need to give her a good excuse. And her maid. Or we need to hope she leaves on her own." Mélanie took a drink of coffee, then set the cup down as she saw her husband come into the room. "Oh, good, darling. Did you get the message?"

"I've alerted the guard." Malcolm dropped down on the bench beside her. "The contessa just went out."

Brougham frowned. "Shouldn't you—"

"Harry's following her." Malcolm took a drink from Mélanie's cup of coffee, which she had pushed towards him. "We need to get her maid out of the way."

Mélanie drew a paper from her reticule. "I took this from the contessa's rooms."

"What is it?" Brougham asked. "Does it tell us—"

"It's a note to her modiste and it reveals nothing. But it should allow me to forge her hand well enough to get her maid out of the rooms."

"So the two of you are going to search?" Brougham asked.

"We need all the help we can to get this done efficiently," Malcolm said. "I've sent for Kitty and Raoul as well."

Brougham stared from her to Malcolm. "I don't have the least understanding of what you do. I mean, I knew you were agents but—good god."

"Don't worry, Mr. Brougham." Sofia touched his arm. "You'll get used to it."

CHAPTER 35

*M*élanie flipped through a stack of letters she had taken from a green leather writing case embossed with the contessa's initials. "Letters from friends in Italy, from a modiste in Milan, a milliner in Venice. Here's one from her late husband's aunt complaining that she doesn't visit often enough. If this is a deception, it's carefully orchestrated."

"We know that." Malcolm was turning over the supposed contessa's linen without any of the qualms he would normally have shown at invading a lady's privacy. "If it's a deception, she was planning it for years."

"Her handkerchiefs are all embroidered with her initials," Kitty said. "And her jewels are tasteful but aren't paste. If nothing else, this effort is well-financed."

"No hidden compartments so far." Raoul was tapping the walls. "Wait a bit." He tapped the paneling again, then pulled a knife from his coat and pried off a piece of paneling. He reached behind it and pulled out a stack of folded papers. They all gathered round the lamp on the writing desk to examine them.

"Travel documents," Raoul said. "In the name of Bianca Falconetti."

"But wouldn't she have traveled here as the Contessa Montal-to?" Sofia asked. "Surely Mr. Brougham arranged for her travel."

"These are probably in case she needed to leave under her own name." Raoul turned them over and pulled out a scrap of paper from underneath.

The Red Lion. Bedford Square.

"What does it mean?" Kitty asked.

"I don't know," Malcolm said. "Perhaps a place to send word in case of emergency. But I recognize the hand. It's Alistair's."

"Well, that proves she's an imposter," Sofia said.

"I suppose it shouldn't be so surprising," Malcolm said. "We already suspected she was an imposter. We knew Alistair was plotting something to do with the trial. But what the devil is he up to?"

"We know he was in Italy most if not all of the time he was absent from England," Raoul said. "He attended Carfax's meeting in Milan about British interference against Italian revolutionaries. He had a long time to set this up."

"He started setting it up before he faked his death." Mélanie said. "Brougham and Caro were in Italy and met the supposed contessa in '16. A year before Alistair disappeared."

"Could the plot be part of why he disappeared?" Kitty asked.

"Possibly," Malcolm said. "Though it's difficult to see why. Presumably he's planning to use it to embarrass Brougham and damage the queen's case by having the contessa exposed as an imposter. And I suspect now he hopes to use it to secure the king's favor and a pardon. But four years ago, he wouldn't have known he'd need a pardon."

"He might have," Mélanie said. "Whatever made him run might have already happened. He just didn't know how bad it would get. But he might have known he could have to run long before he did."

"He wouldn't have even known there'd be a trial yet," Malcolm said. "Though he could certainly have seen the value of having leverage in the queen's case." Malcolm looked at Sofia. "When did you last hear from the actual contessa?"

Sofia smiled. "I'm quite relieved I can think of our Anna as the real contessa. I haven't seen her in years. But I think—yes, Mama mentioned her in a letter over the summer. Anna had written to congratulate Mama and Uncle Bernard on their marriage. She said she looked forward to seeing them, but it wouldn't be for a time, because she'd be traveling. And that she might have news of her own when she got back."

"Interesting," Malcolm said. "It could be a coincidence, but one can't but wonder—"

"Could one witness change the trial?" Sofia asked.

"We've seen the trial shift so often," Malcolm said.

"It's brilliant," Raoul said. "Prove a star witness is a fraud and cast doubt on all the other legitimate witnesses in the process."

"But to prove she's a fraud, wouldn't he need the real contessa?" Kitty asked. "I mean, we wouldn't have questioned her if it weren't for Sofia, and even then we wouldn't have been sure. Just having someone challenge the contessa might raise questions, but it wouldn't prove anything."

"If the supposed contessa is working for him, as she seems to be, she could fold on the witness stand," Malcolm said. "But you're right, Kit, it would be stronger with the real contessa." He looked at Sofia.

Sofia grimaced. "I hate to think of Anna caught up in something like this. She was so kind and she seemed so sweet. I know one can't tell, and I certainly can't be sure of my instincts, but—"

"We don't know how it seems to her," Raoul said. "Alistair Rannoch can be very persuasive."

"But she's sympathetic to Princess Caroline. The queen, that is," Sofia said. "That is, she was." Sofia frowned and chewed on her lower lip. "Given how much has changed in the past years among people I know, personally and politically, I don't know how I can say I'm sure of anything. It sounds laughable."

"Alistair could have spun all sorts of stories," Malcolm said. "He could have—"

"Seduced her?" Sofia asked.

"It's possible. In a number of ways. Not necessarily the obvious construction we usually put on the word."

"If Alistair's planning to use her to discredit Bianca Falconetti, she'll be somewhere in London," Raoul said. He looked at Sofia.

"Of course, I'll help you look for her," Sofia said. "I wouldn't forgive you if you looked without me."

"Thank you," Malcolm said. "Harry will let us know what Bianca Falconetti does next. Meanwhile, I have something else I need to follow up on." He met Mélanie's gaze and Mélanie caught an unexpected apology in her husband's gray eyes. "I need to see Honoria again."

～

"MALCOLM!" Honoria got to her feet as the footman showed Malcolm into her sitting room. "Have you learnt more?"

"You could say so." Malcolm paused a few feet inside the door and looked across the room at Honoria. She had changed into a different gown from the one she had worn this morning, a blue-and-gold-striped silk that shimmered when she moved. "I've learnt you and Val were playing at Valmont and Merteuil for years."

Honoria went white above the square neck of her gown. To her credit, she didn't look away. Or feign denial. "Who on earth— Evie or Val?"

"That's for you to discuss with your cousins. But thank you for not trying to deny it."

"I know you, Malcolm. You wouldn't accuse me of such a thing without proof." Honoria folded her arms. "Given the world we both grew up in, are you really surprised? Are you going to accuse me for doing what my father and Uncle Frederick, and both your parents, and your aunt and her new husband all did? I'm sure Julien's done far more beastly things than I have."

"I'm sure Julien would agree with you. I'm not accusing you of anything. As far as I'm concerned, people should be free to do as they like, provided no one gets hurt."

Honoria glanced away for the first time since he'd confronted her. Her wrought gold earrings stirred beside her face. "Women have more to risk in these things than men. You can't tell me men don't know what they're getting into."

"Perhaps. Most of them. What about the women Val dallied with?"

"Now I'm going to get a moralizing lecture."

"On the contrary. It's not my business to judge one way or the other. Your life is your own to live. Though it does make sense of certain things in our past."

Honoria's gaze shot back to his own. "You can't think— Malcolm, that wasn't what went on between us."

"Val didn't dare you to climb into my bed?"

She glanced away again, chewed on her finger. "Val liked to give me challenges. You were a challenge. But you were a challenge I wanted. If you'd—I know you'd have offered for me if things had progressed between us. And I wanted that. You must believe me, Malcolm. I wanted to be your wife."

"I am more and more convinced you'd have been bored."

"The games would have stopped. I wouldn't have needed diversion if we'd been together."

"That's a lot to ask of anyone, don't you think? That they can make your life complete and end your restlessness? I'm sure I'd have disappointed you."

"You underrate yourself. We could have been happy. Val would laugh at that, of course. But Val is hardly an expert."

"When it comes to what makes a relationship work, I don't think any of us is an expert. But I think honesty helps."

"So you and Mélanie started with honesty?"

Caught. "Mélanie and I are honest with each other now."

"Of course, one has to take the other's word for what honesty is."

"An excellent point. Tell me about George Chase."

Honoria retreated to the blue satin settee and sat, hugging her elbows. "It never meant very much. Val dared me with George because he thought George would be a great challenge as he was still getting over Cordelia. But George was willing enough to tumble into an affair. He did have a tiresome habit of talking about Cordelia, though. He did the same thing in Venice years later. More, perhaps. I mean, I had no illusions we had a deathless love, but one doesn't like to hear a lover go on and on about someone else. I never went on and on to anyone about you."

"George threatened to reveal your affairs?"

"Both of them. I always made sure my lovers had more to lose from the truth's coming out than I did. But George was already facing scandal. He was willing to go to great lengths to restore his reputation." She loosed her hands and folded them in her lap. "The rest is as I already told you. George threatened to reveal our past if I wouldn't look through Uncle Frederick's papers. I was still prevaricating about what to do when I learned he'd been killed. And quite honestly, when I learned he'd been killed, my first reaction was intense relief."

CHAPTER 36

"*P*robably good for Malcolm to have something else to focus on, hard as this is," Frances said. "I mean, something besides Alistair's return, despite Alistair's being caught up in this. Is Malcolm—"

"Matter-of-fact," Mélanie said. "He doesn't talk about Alistair except when we need to. I wouldn't expect him to. He shares more than he used to with me. But I wouldn't expect him to share that." Just as he hadn't shared precisely what he was doing after they left the supposed Contessa Montalto's rooms, save to say that he needed to talk to Honoria again. Mélanie had returned to Berkeley Square to check on the children, to find them in the garden with Laura and Mary Laclos, the former Duchess of Trenchard. Frances had called a few minutes later, clearly wanting to talk.

Frances took a sip of tea. "Give him time, my dear. Malcolm's come an amazing way since he married you. And even more in the past two years. You can't push these things."

"Of course not," Mélanie said, perhaps too quickly. "I firmly believe everyone needs privacy. And it can be very hard to maintain in a marriage." And she truly believed that. One always needed to have those places that were yours alone. But the times he retreated still stabbed at her.

Frances's gaze continued steady and shrewd on her face. "Archie and I still have things we don't talk about. I suspect we always will. We began our affair accepting that both of us had tangled pasts. We talk in bits and pieces. Of course, we haven't been married as long as you have. We didn't really talk about Alistair until we had to. And there are still things we haven't said. I don't suppose we ever will. But that doesn't mean there aren't things I wish he'd say to me. Sometimes the hardest thing is knowing that if I ask for those things, it will make it worse."

"Yes, precisely," Mélanie said. "I can't imagine anything ghastlier than someone demanding emotional confessions. That would destroy us."

"When Alistair returned, I thought it would force a great deal into the open between Archie and me. Or else destroy us. I'm still not quite sure which it will do. Though so far we seem to be muddling through. Muddling through day to day can seem a great victory. Though it does rather pull at one's nerves." Frances set down her tea. "I've been wracking my brain for anything Alistair might have said to me that could be relevant. I keep thinking about the night after Cyril died. The night I spent with Alistair. Archie was matter of fact, but there was a limit to what I could say in front of him. At least, in my mind. I've gone over all the details in the privacy of my thoughts since. But I'm afraid there's not a great deal that's relevant. At least, not so far as I can tell. Except, perhaps—" She frowned into her silver-rimmed teacup. "Alistair and I were lying together, neither of us able to sleep. I'd asked if he wanted to talk, and he quite obviously didn't. Which both relieved and distressed me. But then quite suddenly he asked me if I thought it was possible to pawn a heart. I actually sat up in bed, because the words were so odd. I said, in our world we gave hearts away and gambled and sold them, so I didn't see why pawning should be so different. Alistair got an odd look on his face and said 'Just so.' But thinking back, I can't help but feel that moment meant more than I realized at the time. Perhaps it's just my desperation to latch on to something. But—"

She broke off as the door opened and Valentin showed Simon Tanner into the library.

"I'm sorry to interrupt," Simon said. "We had a break in rehearsals. David is still at Westminster. I wanted to see if you'd learnt anything. Or, I suppose, I really mean if there's anything I can do."

"We have more bits of information," Mélanie said. "But it doesn't add up to anything yet." Or rather it did but not to the full story. And Alistair's mother's identity seemed something for Malcolm to share.

"I'm afraid all I have to talk about is theatre, which I doubt you're in the mood for."

"On the contrary," Fanny said. "I think Mélanie and I could both desperately use distraction."

Simon dropped into a chair and accepted a cup of tea from Mélanie. "I've been rehearsing *Hamlet* with Brandon and Manon all afternoon. I'm glad we're doing the new version again. Or perhaps I should say the old version." Two and a half years ago, Simon had first staged an alternate version of *Hamlet*, which had also been used as an Elsinore League codebook. And had been part of the investigation that had led to Mélanie's own spying being exposed.

"Is Jennifer called for the rehearsal?" Mélanie asked.

"She'll be there after the break. Do you need to talk to her?"

"No, but I should talk to Sir Horace," Mélanie said. Jennifer Mansfield's husband, Sir Horace Smytheton, had been an Elsinore League member, and Lady Shroppington had attempted to have him killed at the opening of Mélanie's play the previous January. They still weren't sure why but given what they had learned in the past few days (god, it was still only a few days since Alistair had appeared in their library?), it must concern Alistair.

Simon nodded, but didn't ask questions. "Sir Horace wouldn't miss a rehearsal. He still loves to comment on the differences between this *Hamlet* and the version we all know. Brandon says after playing this version, he can never do the traditional version without thinking of Claudius as Hamlet's father, even if it's not in the script. I told him I was once in a production that the director insisted on staging as though Laertes had an incestuous passion for Ophelia, which has as much or as little textual justification." He broke off, staring at Mélanie. "What is it?"

"Nothing," Mélanie said. "Or perhaps everything." Mélanie looked at Fanny. "Alistair asked you about pawning a heart? You're sure those were his words?"

"Yes," Fanny said. "They were odd enough I'd hardly have imagined them."

"Christ," Simon said. His gaze met Mélanie's.

"What?" Fanny asked.

"'I have killed a love, for whose each drop of blood I would have pawned my heart,'" Mélanie said. "From *'Tis Pity She's a Whore*. Set in a decadent society in which perhaps the purest relationship is the incestuous love between a brother and sister. I need to go out."

"To see Malcolm?" Frances asked.

"No. To see Lord Glenister."

∽

"I THOUGHT NOTHING COULD SHOCK ME." Glenister's face was like bleached linen as he stared across the sitting room at White's. Mélanie had got word to Malcolm and Julien, who were at Brooks's. Malcolm had had Palmerston bring him into the Tory White's while Julien and Mélanie slipped in through the service entrance, flattening themselves against walls and darting behind doors. It was not the first time Mélanie had been in a gentleman's club, though on other occasions she'd been dressed as a man.

Glenister passed a hand over his face. "You know I've done things I'm not proud of. I've done things I'm not ashamed of—that I scarcely even think about—that I should be ashamed of. I've boasted about my own sons' exploits. But this—"

"It's interesting," Julien said. "The limits we all have."

"For Cyril to take advantage of his sister—"

"Is that what happened?" Malcolm asked.

"My god—"

"There's still an issue of choice."

"He claimed he loved her." Glenister glanced away. "I never guessed. Not until after Georgiana went away. I guessed that she'd had a baby. I demanded to know who had taken advantage of her. I was determined to call the fellow to account. Father finally told me. He said, for god's sake, I couldn't fight my own brother." Glenister drew a hard breath. "One of the few times I knew him to lose his temper. I could scarcely believe it. I stalked out of the room and found Cyril just come back from a ride. I pulled him off his horse and threw him to the ground. We both fought. But at a certain point I realized he'd stopped fighting back. Both our noses were bloody. But I cracked Cyril's jaw. He knew. Without my saying anything. He had the gall to claim he loved her."

"You don't think he did?" Mélanie said.

"You can't call that—"

"There are many different forms of love. Did Georgiana say she loved him?"

"My God, you can't imagine I asked her."

"You never spoke about it?" Malcolm said.

"Of course not." Glenister drew a breath. "Cyril swore he wouldn't go near her again. He went abroad. He married. Father saw to it they were apart. I thought—I believed it was in the past. When Georgiana eloped with Mortimer I was concerned, but I believed she did it because she loved him. And I suppose—to be honest, I should have paid more attention. I was at Ascot when I learned about the elopement. I tried to convince Father not to cut off her dowry. Father wouldn't hear of it. I realized soon, of course, that she was with child when they eloped. But that would hardly shock me. I'm not quite such a hypocrite as to be shocked by my sister's indulging in something I indulged in so freely myself. It wasn't until the house party at Dunmykel that Cyril said something and I realized. He'd gone back to her. I could still scarcely believe it when I confronted him. Cyril didn't even try to deny it. He said that when he and Susan had come back from the Continent and he saw Georgiana again, he couldn't resist. She couldn't resist. He claimed she loved him too. But he was older. He should have—"

"Did you know Alistair knew?" Malcolm asked.

Glenister drew a rough breath. "Father told me after the first— after the baby was born. I think he thought Alistair would keep me in line. He said we were indebted to Alistair."

"Did he tell you he'd paid Alistair?"

"Not in so many words. But I can piece things together. Alistair told me not to waste time on Cyril. And that if I wanted to avoid a scandal, I wouldn't let the world see that Cyril and I had fallen out. Which was later true of Alistair and me." His jaw hardened. "And at times the pretense became so real I'd forget I was angry with both of them. For long stretches of time. Perhaps the majority of the time."

"Being undercover is like that," Mélanie said.

Glenister stared at her. "I never thought of it that way, but— yes, I suppose you're right, in a way. We were certainly all living a lie. After Cyril—after the duel—Alistair told me not to blame myself. He sounded as though he really meant it. It was perhaps the most genuine I've ever heard him sound. I'll never forgive Cyril. But I'll never forgive myself for killing him."

"I understand," Malcolm said.

Glenister met his gaze. "You didn't kill Edgar."

"No," Julien said. "I did."

"And he's still gone," Malcolm said. He looked at Glenister. "Did Alistair tell you what happened to Georgiana's first baby?"

"Only that the baby was well provided for." Glenister's eyes widened. "Do you—"

"He was given to the estate agent at Dunmykel and his wife, and raised as their biological daughter's twin. His name is Andrew Thirle. He's married to my sister."

Glenister's eyes squeezed shut. "Does he—"

"He only just learned Georgiana is his mother. He doesn't know who his father is. We didn't, until just now." Malcolm hesitated. "Does Evie know?"

"My god, no. But you can see why I took her in. I've done everything I could to protect her. She seems happy, thank god, with Cleghorn. Though I could have wished to see her more comfortably settled. Cleghorn's a decent fellow but he hadn't a feather to fly with. I tried to set them up with her dowry, and I help more when I can. Difficult with a growing family. Just this past week she sweetly asked me for assistance because Cleghorn got into a bit of trouble with cards. Not used to town life, poor fellow." Glenister gripped the back of a chair, fingers white on the scrollwork. "Do you think Chase knew? About Cyril and Georgiana?"

"I think he was close to discovering the truth," Malcolm said. "He'd been asking Honoria for information."

Glenister's gaze shot to Malcolm, suddenly sharp.

"They knew each other better than I realized," Malcolm said. "If Chase had known the full truth, you'd think he'd have realized it couldn't hurt Alistair. Though it's possible he uncovered the truth just before he was killed."

"And you think that's why he was killed?" Glenister said.

"I think it's one possibility," Malcolm said.

CHAPTER 37

*T*he autumn light washed over the Berkeley Square
garden, still warm but tinged with the coolness of
oncoming winter. Mary Laclos smiled at her older daughters and
Emily, Colin, and Jessica playing tag through the plane trees and
then at her toddler daughter and Clara investigating sticks on the
ground. Her hand went to her stomach, already slightly rounded
with her new child.

"It's amazing to think about doing this again. I mean, it's not
really novel in any way. And yet this time it isn't connected to
Trenchard. Even superficially." She drew a breath and smiled at
tiny Marie Louise. Who was theoretically the Duke of Trenchard's
daughter, but in fact the child of Mary's second husband, Gui
Laclos.

"I can imagine that's a huge difference," Laura said.

"As you would know better than anyone."

Mary turned her head to meet Laura's gaze, and Laura felt
herself go still. Her first husband, Jack Tarrington, had been the
son of Mary's first husband, the Duke of Trenchard. Laura and
Mary had become friends, but there was so much of the past
Laura still kept to herself, and for all secrets had a way of unrav-

eling there were certain things she had counted on continuing to hold secret. That she couldn't quite bear to imagine being in the open air. Yet she wanted to talk to Mary about Trenchard for the sake of the investigation.

Mary pulled the skirt of her pelisse closed round her legs, gaze still on Laura. Her clear blue eyes were steady and unflinching but held no hint of judgment. "It's all right. You didn't give yourself away. I think sometimes with one's husband one has a sense about such things. Which is funny, really, because Trenchard could hardly have been said to have properly been a husband to me in the way I understand the term now. But I put the pieces together. Things I knew about Jack. Things I'd heard. Things Trenchard said."

"What things?" Laura's voice was rougher than she intended.

"Nothing that could have been meant to betray you. But when he talked about you—that is, Jane Hampson, who I know is you, though it always seems rather like a different person—"

"Jane is a different person, to all intents and purposes. Though I can't deny the connection. I can't not lay claim to her." Laura cast a quick glance at Emily. She had been Jane when she got pregnant with Emily and gave birth to her, but Laura before she could properly be a mother to her daughter. "I certainly can't not take responsibility for her actions."

Mary met her gaze, fingers frozen on the sapphire silk taffeta of the pelisse. "Mary, Duchess of Trenchard, seems like a different person to me now as well. A person I'd quite like to disown at times. Except for my children." She cast a quick glance at them, then looked back at Laura. "But I'm learning to make peace with her. In any case, when Trenchard talked about Jane, which he did rarely, there was something in his voice—I couldn't put my finger on it, but it lingered in my mind. I didn't make sense of it until I met you and learned your story. At least, some of it."

Laura smoothed her fingers over her skirt. Warm coral, embroidered with copper-colored silk round the hem, more the colors she had worn as Jane Hampson than those she had sought refuge in as a governess. Her fingers were trembling. The wedding ring Raoul had given her caught the late afternoon sunlight. "I doubt I was significant enough to Trenchard for much to show."

"I don't think so. He was a first-class bastard. But when it comes to you, I think his feelings were complicated."

"He tried to have me killed."

"I think he was capable of having anyone killed who he thought was in his way." Mary's voice was cool and level. But then, she was Hubert Mallinson's daughter. "I thought my father was ruthless, but he has limits of a sort, even if I'm not sure I've ever seen the end of them. Trenchard didn't have them at all. Not that I ever saw. I can't believe I was ever mad enough to think being a duchess made up for all that."

"You were a girl." Laura and Mary were much of an age, but for a moment Laura felt as though she were talking to Bet or Nerezza. Or Emily or Jessica. "And you didn't know him."

"I was over twenty and I knew him enough I should have been more wary." Mary gripped her elbows, fingers digging into the taffeta. "He hit me. More than once."

"He only hit me once." The memory still stung. "Much later. But it made me feel more powerless than anything he'd done before. I'd have cheerfully—"

"Killed him? It's all right." Mary smiled with unexpected warmth. "We know now that you didn't. And truthfully, I wouldn't blame you if you had done."

"I was far more than twenty. There were all sorts of reasons I should have been more wary."

"He could be charming in a way, when he chose to. I didn't entirely marry him to be a duchess. There were moments—I can understand how it happened."

"I'm not sure I can."

Mary cast a glance at the children. The tag game had paused

and her older daughter was spinning Emily in a circle. "There's so much I don't know how to address with my children from my first marriage when it comes to their father. I rather envy you—" She broke off.

"Yes," Laura said. Emily was giggling up at her supposed aunt. Who was her half-sister. And Mary deserved to know the truth of the connection between their children. "I don't want Emily ever to know."

"I'd never have asked."

"No. But I'd rather tell you outright than have you wondering. And it seems some things we should be open about. We are a family, after all."

Mary smiled. "So we are." She fingered the braid that edged her pelisse. "It's an odd thing, family. It matters so much to some people and yet some of it is an accident of biology."

"It matters to some people," Laura said. "Having a father. A blood father. To a lot of people. To men, in particular."

"They're told it's so important," Mary said. "All their lives. Most men, that is. To own the truth, from the stories I've heard, Papa grew up in his elder brother's shadow." Her brows drew together in consideration. Before she had been Duchess of Trenchard she had been Lady Mary Mallinson, and she would always be very much Hubert Mallinson's daughter. "I don't know that Papa exactly envied Julien's father, because he had ten times the under-standing, but it must have rankled. His less brilliant brother's being the heir to so much and wasting it so much. I mean, until he married Aunt Pamela and made use of her fortune."

"I've never heard the rest of the family talk quite that way."

"I'm not sure David and Bel are as aware of it, and I'm quite sure Lucy isn't. I remember our uncle better than any of them. I can even remember Aunt Pamela. I don't think even David can at all. She was lovely. Exquisite, but more than that, one of the kinder people in the family. I quite understand why Julien can't forgive his father. He was a shocking profligate. Oh, that's not something I remember, but I've heard the stories. Of course, Grandpapa had run things into the ground before he inherited."

"Do you remember your grandfather?"

"No, he died before I was born. Before Arth—Julien was born. But Papa's quite blunt about him, even to us. Papa doesn't seem to care about sons so much as heirs. I don't think he gives a damn about bloodlines so long as he has what he wants."

It was a remarkably astute analysis of Hubert Mallinson from a young woman who had once seemed to want nothing more than the trappings of the world he was so determined to preserve.

Mary smiled as the thoughts flitted through Laura's mind. "People can change. More than Papa would like to admit, I think, though he's changed himself." She hesitated. "We're both fortunate. To have escaped Trenchard and found something a world better. You have an enviable life. And yet there was a time when I'd have looked at what you have and not been able to imagine how you could endure being denied vouchers to Almack's. Now it seems rather agreeable."

Laura laughed. "I never had them. I only went once. After I was revealed as Jack's widow. When Mélanie and Malcolm still attended occasionally."

"Before you married Mr. O'Roarke."

"Before I was his lover, as well. At least—" Laura thought back to the dates. "Before I was openly."

Mary laughed. "We would have got on very well, you know. If you'd ever had to live here with Jack. We could have kept each other amused. Though I expect we'd both have been equally miserable." Her fingers tightened. "George Chase was asking questions about Trenchard, wasn't he? About his plot to become prime minister?"

"George Chase was asking questions about a lot of things and people." Laura looked sideways at Mary. "Thomas Thornsby said Trenchard was friendly with Lady Shroppington."

"Lady Shroppington?" Mary frowned. "Is she important in all of this?"

"Possibly very important."

"Good god, was she his mistress?"

"We have no reason to think she was. But she may have taken an interest in his plot to become prime minister."

Mary's frown deepened. "He knew her, of course. I mean, it seems everyone knows her. I can't say they were particular friends. Trenchard wasn't the sort of man to have women friends. But I do remember his speaking with her more than most. I asked him once if she'd been friends with his mother. He looked a bit surprised that I'd noticed his connection to her and simply said his mother had had a wide acquaintance. He had a way of ending the conversation when he didn't want to talk. Is she—Laura, how serious is this? Is there any risk to the children? Because of the questions being asked now?"

Laura felt her own fingers tighten. "There's no risk to the children that we know of. But I'm not sure what Major Chase's questions may unearth. It's possible there's more risk to us. If anyone thinks we know anything more about Trenchard's plot."

Mary gave a short laugh. "At least in my case, if anyone thinks I knew anything, they have no notion of the sort of marriage we had."

"And yet you knew more about the plot than any of us realized."

"After the fact." Mary studied Laura. "I imagine you're more at risk. I don't mean to pry, but he had you spying for him, didn't he?"

Laura felt herself flinch inwardly. Not from sharing the truth with Mary. From confronting it herself. Though it was a truth she lived with every day. "Yes. For years."

Mary's gaze shot to the children. They had settled down with dolls. Jessica had her doll riding Berowne—who as usual was putting it up with it very well—while Emily held his lead. "I imagine he was controlling Emily."

Laura's nails bit into her palms. "How on earth do you know?"

"Emily was away from you until you supposedly recovered your memory. It would have taken something very strong to compel you to go against your principles and instincts. And it's just the sort of thing Trenchard would have done. Although that shows just how great a monster he was."

"On the contrary," Laura said. "Monsters can have humanity—think of Mary Shelley's. Trenchard was all too human, but quite devoid of humanity. That makes it worse somehow." She hesitated. But Trenchard's possible connections to Lady Shroppington and Alistair Rannoch were at the heart of why she had wanted to talk to Mary. "There may be more to Lady Shroppington's connection to Trenchard, or at least to his father," she said. And she told Mary about Alistair's being alive and being Lady Shroppington's son. And the key question of who Alistair's father might be.

"Good God," Mary said. "You think Trenchard's father was Lady Shroppington's lover? That Trenchard and Alistair Rannoch were brothers?"

"It's one possibility," Laura said. "Did Trenchard ever say anything that might suggest he knew it?"

Mary frowned at her hands. "Trenchard's father died long before we were married. Trenchard didn't talk about him a great deal, but I do know from rumors that the late duke's romantic exploits were as varied as my husband's. As for Alistair Rannoch—he and Trenchard were friends, I suppose. To the extent Trenchard had friends. They certainly spent time together. But I always sensed—they respected each other, but there was a rivalry despite it."

"Or perhaps because of it," Laura said. "There's no sense in trying to outdo someone if one doesn't think they're your equal."

Mary nodded. "I can't say it was a brotherly rivalry. But I can imagine brothers acting that way." She waved to Marie Louise, who was holding up a leaf, then looked back at Laura. "I don't have much of Trenchard's. James told me to take anything I wanted from Trenchard House, but I was only too happy to see the last of all of it. But there was one box of his papers. He kept it in his study, and I'd seen him locking it once. I took it when I left. I knew just enough of what Trenchard was not to want James to have to face more of it. Not to want his secrets to hurt my children." Her hands locked together in her lap. "I know spies ferret out the truth, but can you understand feeling there are some secrets that are better left unexplored?"

"All too well," Laura said. "What did you do with the box?"

"Took it with me and locked it away. I was ready to get on with my life. I wanted to look ahead. I couldn't bear to look at secrets that might open old wounds. Part of me wondered if it was about you and Emily. There was no need for me to see that. Part of me feared it might be something even worse that I had no inkling of. Either way, I didn't want to know and then have to pretend to my children and James and everyone that I didn't. Trenchard was dead. I thought it was all in the past. Which I suppose was completely foolish of me."

"It's understandable. I thought it was in the past as well. At least Trenchard's part. Or I tried to tell myself it was. But those papers could be important now."

Mary nodded. "You'd think growing up with Papa I'd manage these things better." She turned as Mélanie, Malcolm, and Julien approached the square garden. "I never thought to find myself saying this," she said, as they came through the gate, "but it seems we need to move your investigation to my house."

∽

MARY WENT to a trunk in a corner of the room she shared with her second husband, Gui Laclos, in a house far more modest than

359

Trenchard House. And far more comfortable. The sofa was elegantly striped in red and cream, but it was piled with cushions, and toys and books overflowed a basket beneath it. "I had to find a hiding place my maid wouldn't look in. I haven't even told Gui I had this. It's not that I don't trust him—I just didn't want Trenchard to intrude on our life together. You'd think by now I'd have learned that one can't escape the past. Not completely." She took piles of letters bound in red ribbon and two sketchbooks from the chest, then lifted out a dispatch box. She stared down at the age-worn brown leather and ornate tarnished brass. "I know he's gone. I know he can't touch any of us anymore. But I don't want to open this."

"I understand the feeling." Laura exchanged a quick glance with her husband. Raoul had returned to Berkeley Square just before they left, so he was there along with Mélanie, Malcolm, Julien, and Kitty, who had also just returned to Berkeley Square. "Though I confess I'm also distinctly curious about what it contains. Information is power. This information could give us power over Trenchard."

"Quite true." Mary opened the drawer in her night table, took a key from the back, and carried it to the table where she had placed the dispatch box. Without further hesitation she unlocked the box and pushed back the lid.

Piles of papers tied up with buff-colored ribbon met their gaze. Mary lifted them out but then stepped back. "Do you mind? I can't quite bear to."

"They appear to contain information about various people," Raoul said. "If George Chase was acquiring blackmail information, Trenchard had turned it into an art. There's a file on Liverpool."

"He seems to have kept these as ammunition to use against Lady Shroppington." Julien spread a stack of papers out. "Some are letters from her. But this one isn't her hand."

"No, it's Trenchard's," Laura said. "It looks like a draft of a letter." She stared down at it and felt all the blood drain from her head.

You can't escape Carfax. You wouldn't be the first agent to seduce an enemy agent. But having a child with him complicates things.

She read it through three times, one word at a time, not quite able to take in the implications.

Raoul had gone still beside her. But it was Julien who put it into words.

"Well. That answers two questions. Apparently Lady Shroppington was Fortinbras and exposed my grandfather as a French agent. And apparently my grandfather was Alistair Rannoch's father."

CHAPTER 38

*T*hey were all silent for a moment, staring at the dispatch box as though it were a portal disgorging secrets— which it was, in a way, Mélanie thought, the revelations still reverberating in her head.

"Good god." Julien's voice was low and slightly breathless, tinged with both shock and bemusement. "I feel singularly stupid for not having seen it or at least wondered. After all, we got as far as thinking Alistair's father might have been the father of a League member."

"One doesn't care to think such things about one's parents," Mary said. "Let alone one's grandparents."

Julien shot a smile at her. "That they're having love affairs or that they're spying for another country?"

"Both," Mary said.

"You'd think in this family—which by now encompasses all of us—we'd be used to both by now. But I confess our grandfather was always a shadowy presence to me. I never knew him. The main thing I know about him is that he left my father with debts that caused him to marry my mother. Which wasn't very good for my mother but was good for me, in that otherwise I wouldn't have been born. I should have thought that the lack of funds might have driven him to something like spying."

"It's not generally one's first thought of how someone would seek to get out of debt," Raoul said.

"Not unless one is a spy oneself."

Kitty reached for Julien's hand but didn't say anything.

"I can't believe I didn't see it," Mélanie said. "Lady Shroppington has all the skills of an agent. If anyone should have known—"

"Perhaps that's it," Laura said. "I can imagine not wanting to find any common ground with Lady Shroppington."

"Not surprising that she was cleverer than he was," Julien said.

"Yes, that's rather a pattern," Malcolm murmured.

Mélanie met his gaze. They had always used humor to deflect the harsh truths of their life, but she realized much of the bitterness was now gone.

"If nothing else, this may explain the name Elsinore League," Malcolm said. "Alistair never seemed to much like Shakespeare. Perhaps his mother does."

Mary was looking at Julien. "Alistair is our uncle."

"In biology. Yes. And more to the point, he's Uncle Hubert's brother. I think that's shaped a lot."

"So do I." Malcolm was studying the dispatch box as though mentally extracting pieces of the past from it and fitting them together. "I'm quite sure the jealousy was there on Alistair's side. As to Hubert—" Malcolm shook his head. "He once told me *Lear* wasn't about Edmund and Edgar. He was talking about my brother Edgar and me. But in some ways, he was acting it out with Alistair."

"Which one of them is Edgar in the analogy?" Julien demanded.

"Perhaps the analogy doesn't hold up. Perhaps they're both Edmunds. But still. A legitimate brother and an illegitimate."

"And yet Alistair had the League," Mélanie said. "In that,

Hubert was the outsider. Determined to bring him down. In that case, he's more the Edmund."

"I wonder if Hubert knows," Kitty said.

"Yes. Given his attitude towards Alistair, I rather suspect he does." Julien was studying the papers. "Interesting to contemplate how much Alistair knows. I'm inclined to think he knows my grandfather is his father. It makes sense of much of his attitude towards Hubert. I'm less sure if he knows his father was a French spy."

"Trenchard did," Laura said. "And Trenchard was working with Alistair. Of course, that might have been something he held over Lady Shroppington—revealing that part of the truth to her son."

"And yet for all the shock," Malcolm said, "it still doesn't explain why Alistair had to leave Britain. Or why he wants a pardon."

"I need to meet Sofia," Raoul said. "We have some ideas for how to trace the real Contessa Montalto."

"Simon says Sir Horace will be at the Tavistock," Mélanie said. "We still haven't talked to him since Alistair returned."

"I should update Brougham," Malcolm said. But even as he turned to the door, it opened and Cordelia stepped into the room with Danielle Darnault.

"I'm sorry to barge in, Mary," Cordelia said. Mélanie hadn't seen her all day, though she knew Cordelia had meant to call on George Chase's sister Violet. "Your footman told me to come up. Harry sent word. He said the contessa—the woman who calls herself the contessa, I seem to have missed a lot while I was at Violet's, but I gather she's an imposter,—went to a modiste's in Bruton Street and was inside for half an hour. Harry thinks she delivered a message. She then returned to Wardour Street, but she and her maid left with bandboxes and got in a hackney. Harry is following them and says he'll keep us updated. But when I went to Berkeley Square to tell you, I found Mademoiselle Darnault looking for Julien. Oh, I don't think you've met," she added, turning to Mary.

"Never mind the formalities," Mary said. "Mademoiselle Darnault clearly has important news to impart."

Danielle glanced round the room. Her gaze was steady and yet unsettled. Given what she had lived through, in the past and in recent history, that was alarming. "I haven't been able to find Étienne Lémieux. I think he may have left England."

"That would make sense if he'd been hired to kill George Chase," Julien said.

"Yes. But I think I've learned the identity of the man who hired him. The man who was at Les Trois Amis looking for an assassin and who talked to Antoinette—Anne. I spoke with Anne and got a good description and I found one of my old contacts. Someone who—well, never mind about that. But he said he'd seen the man Hugo told Julien and me about at Les Trois Amis. And that his name is Joseph Eden. He's—"

"An agent who works for Hubert Mallinson," Malcolm said.

Julien met Malcolm's gaze and moved to the door. "Uncle Hubert has a lot to answer for. Including—" He glanced at Mary and didn't say the rest of it, but the implication lingered in the air.

Including, apparently, George Chase's murder.

CHAPTER 39

*M*alcolm slammed his hand down on Hubert's desk. "You didn't think we'd trace Joseph Eden?"

Hubert tugged a paper loose from under Malcolm's hand. "Joseph Eden hasn't worked for me in months. What's he done?"

"Hired the assassin who killed George Chase." Julien moved to the other side of Hubert's desk.

Hubert scraped his chair back and pushed himself to his feet. His face held rare alarm. "I didn't engage Eden. We need to find whoever did so immediately."

"You almost convince me, Uncle," Julien said. "At least, enough for me to make inquiries. I'll get Kitty to help. Malcolm needs to talk to Brougham. But first, did it ever occur to you to warn me that Alistair Rannoch was my uncle?"

Carfax dropped back into his chair.

Julien held his uncle's gaze. "How long had you known?"

Hubert spread his hands on the ink blotter. "After my father died. Your father and I found the information in his papers at the same time we learned he'd been spying for the French. My father was a number of things, but he was hardly the most adept in the family at a number of things."

"I assume you also knew who Alistair's mother was," Malcolm said. "And that she was Fortinbras."

Hubert tented his fingers together. "Let us say I strongly suspected. And while my father was gone, the fact that Lady Shroppington had information that could make things difficult for our family was one of the complications in dealing with her and the League."

"Did it occur to you to tell us when we asked you if she might be Fortinbras earlier today?" Malcolm asked.

"I confess you took me by surprise." Hubert glanced down at his still coffee-stained cravat. "I needed to think through how much to share. And in any case, I wasn't sure. It was quite helpful to have you prove it. I imagine you did that with more energy without my sharing what I knew."

"Does Alistair know that you're his brother?" Julien asked.

"We've never spoken of it. But then, I haven't seen him in years."

Julien continued to regard his uncle. "I think he knows."

"What makes you so sure?"

"Because I think he knows Gisèle is his niece. I think he may have known it before you knew she was your daughter."

"Ah." Hubert glanced down at his fingers for a moment. "At this point we should all be aware a person may have parental feelings without a biological connection to the child in question. But you have a point."

Malcolm stared at his former spymaster. "You knew Lady Shroppington's connection to the League before we'd ever crossed paths with her. You knew she was Fortinbras. You knew your father was the French agent she exposed. Why the hell tell us as much as you did and not tell us the whole?"

The slanting early evening light from the windows bounced off Hubert's spectacles as he returned Malcolm's gaze. "While the truth about my father would hardly lead to anyone's arrest at this point, it would undoubtedly be an embarrassment for our family and weaken my position. I saw no point in giving you something you could use as leverage against me in a number of ways. At the same time, as you got closer to the truth, I knew I had to give you something."

"You must have known we'd work it out," Julien said. "Or at least that Malcolm and Mélanie would."

"Very likely. I wasn't sure how long it would take. As I just said, I was considering telling you more. But I saw no reason to rush things."

"That's bloody rich."

"My dear Julien. You can't tell me you haven't withheld information from me. But right now our family's tangled history seems of less interest than the question of who engaged Joseph Eden to find an assassin to kill George Chase. And why."

⤳

"MÉLANIE, MY DEAR." Sir Horace kissed her cheek as she came into the green room at the Tavistock Theatre where he and Jennifer were helping themselves to tea before the rehearsal got underway again. "Come to watch the rehearsal? Love seeing this *Hamlet* come to life again. So many nuances I missed the first time. Do you know, I now think Ophelia suspects Claudius is Hamlet's father? When she says—"

"Horace, dear." Jennifer gripped her husband's arm. They had been a couple for a quarter century and married for over a decade, though they had kept the marriage secret until recently. "Devoted as Mélanie is to the theatre, if she's here today I suspect it's something to do with her current investigation." Jennifer had been more concerned than her husband ever since the assassination attempt on Horace.

"I confess that's true," Mélanie said. "Much as I love rehearsals. It's about Alistair Rannoch."

Sir Horace frowned. "I've told you everything I can about him and the old days in the eighties and nineties."

Jennifer cast a quick glance towards the hearthrug, where their eleven-year-old daughter was entertaining her toddler sister. "Are you any closer to knowing why they tried to kill Horace?"

"Possibly." Mélanie accepted a cup of tea and settled beside Jennifer and Horace on the comfortably worn green room sofa. "Alistair Rannoch is alive."

Horace blanched.

Jennifer raised her elegant brows. "I think I should be more surprised than I am," she said. "But somehow nothing about that man can surprise me."

"But—" Horace shook his head. "Alistair faked his death? Why?"

"That's what we're trying to discover." Mélanie took a sip of tea. Strong and bracing, designed to get the company through a long day or night. "He wants a royal pardon. Do you have any idea why?"

"Not in the least." Horace settled back against the faded tapestry of the sofa, a former set piece. "The things they got up to when we were all in France shouldn't have caused him to flee now. Not unless there was some new revelation about those events."

"We wondered about that," Mélanie said. "But it also seems it may be tied to his plot with Trenchard."

"Didn't have anything to do with that. Didn't even really know about the plot until it all unraveled." Horace frowned. "Is Trenchard really dead?"

"Trenchard is dead. We saw the body."

Jennifer was sitting quietly, gaze on her husband, teacup untouched in her hand. "You popped over to Paris quite a bit in those days, Horace. When I was busy with rehearsals."

"Yes, but—" Sir Horace's frown deepened. "Wasn't really part of the League at that point, but there was one thing. Took it for hyperbole at the time. But I was at the Salon des Étrangers one night. Found myself playing whist with Debenham, and then we

369

were drinking and he mentioned the turmoil in the League and said he'd heard a rumor Alistair had been trying to hire an assassin to arrange an accident."

"Those were his exact words?" Mélanie asked.

"Yes. My first thought was that it was Alistair boasting and trying to make more of himself. Or making one of his cutting jokes that someone took seriously. Then for a moment I wondered if Alistair had turned on someone else in the League. Kept looking over my shoulder on the walk back to my hôtel that night. But then before the month was out, Alistair himself was dead. Or so I thought. Since he wasn't—" The realization settled over Sir Horace's features. "I suppose he might actually have been trying to have someone killed. I mean, I wouldn't put it past Alistair. I think all of us can accept that now. But I can't imagine who his target might have been."

Mélanie set her teacup down. "I think perhaps I can."

～

"Mr. Rannoch." Queen Caroline held out her hand. "Are you looking for Mr. Brougham?"

"Yes, there are some developments I wanted to update him on. I was hoping he was here."

"Not yet. He said he had a meeting at Brooks's before he could update me on the day's events." The queen scanned Malcolm's face. "I'd have thought you'd be there as well, but I expect this investigation has diverted your attention."

"You might say so, ma'am."

"I take it you haven't yet learned who was behind the unfortunate Major Chase's death?"

"Not yet, ma'am. We've learned more about Major Chase's activities but we haven't yet determined the motive for his murder."

The queen regarded Malcolm with a shrewd, steady gaze. "I

won't tease you to tell me more. I abhor prying into information people don't wish to share openly. But I hope you are able to arrive at a solution before too much longer. For everyone's sake." Her gaze moved over Malcolm's face. "I keep looking for a resemblance, but you don't look very like him."

"I beg your pardon?"

"Your father."

Odd. Most people thought he looked like Raoul. Then Malcolm realized that many people still didn't think of Raoul as his father. "Do you mean Alistair Rannoch? Do you know him?"

The queen gave a faint smile. "It was a very long time ago."

That was not necessarily surprising given that Alistair had traveled on the Continent. And yet something about her tone . . . "Ma'am? I don't wish to pry, but—"

The queen spread her hands over the figured white muslin of her skirt. "He could be charming. I don't suppose you like hearing that, it isn't the sort of thing one likes to hear about a parent. It was all a long time ago. He was calling himself Alexander Radford, but I made some inquiries and learned that wasn't his real name. Don't look so surprised, Mr. Rannoch. I may not have my husband's resources, but I know how to employ agents. I was a bit concerned that information about my association with Mr. Radford, who I later learned was Alistair Rannoch, would get out, long before that dreadful business with the green bag, but it never seemed to, which was a great relief. And then, not much later, I learned of your father's death. I was sorry."

"Ma'am." Malcolm chose his words with the utmost care, aware that he was moving over verbal glass. "Like you, I despise prying into secrets people do not wish to share. But for the sake of the investigation—and for the sake of your case in Parliament— may I take it that information about your association with Alistair Rannoch might prove damaging to your case?"

Queen Caroline's gaze stayed steady and open on his own. "Very damaging indeed, Mr. Rannoch."

CHAPTER 40

*E*dith tossed a ball to Colin, who tossed it to Livia, who tossed it to Emily, who sent it sailing over Leo's head. Leo ran to the Berkeley Square garden gate after it. The ball thudded over the garden rail towards two ladies with the sort of fashionable bonnets Edith disdained because one couldn't turn one's head enough for a proper game of catch or tag. Before the ball could bump them, a gentleman ran forwards, scooped it up, and tossed it back to Leo with a tip of his hat. Leo seemed to be thanking him, their words carried away on the breeze.

Edith put a hand to her hat to anchor it. Given the nature of their parents' work, she was more wary with these children than she had been with other charges, but it looked harmless enough. And it was good to see Leo so self-possessed. Edith remembered being tongue-tied round strangers at the same age.

"Who's that?" Bet walked up beside her, carrying Clara. Edith had come to Berkeley Square with Cordelia and the Davenport girls and had stayed to help Bet with the children when Cordelia went in search of the Rannochs.

"He caught the ball Leo lost. Before it could trip up two ladies whose half boots are probably laced too tight." Edith was watching Leo and the gentleman exchange words but felt Bet's sudden stillness. She cast a quick look at her friend. "What? Who is it?"

Bet's gaze was trained on the man. Her arms tightened round Clara. Leo was stepping back through the gate and moving towards them, and the gentleman was following him. The fading light was behind him, but his eyes gleamed like polished agate in the shadows.

"This is Mr. Radford," Leo said. "He helped retrieve the ball. He says he knows Julien."

The gentleman tipped his hat. "Miss Simcox. It seems I owe you my felicitations."

Bet's gaze locked on the gentleman. Fear radiated from her and yet at the same time, a strength Edith had always suspected her friend possessed but had never quite seen. As though Bet was drawing in on herself and summoning up her reserves for a battle. "Thank you."

"She's going to marry Sandy Trenor," Leo said. "Do you know?"

"I had heard."

"I don't believe we've met," Edith said. "I know it's a scandal to introduce myself, but if I cared a rap for scandal, I'd live my life very differently. I'm Edith Simmons."

The man called Radford inclined his head. "Alexander Radford. As Leo said, I know his stepfather. In fact, I have past connections to a number of members of the extended family. As well as to Miss Simcox."

"What do you want?" Bet asked.

"Merely to offer my greetings," Radford said. He tipped his hat again. "You have a good arm, Leo. You just need to learn more control."

"My father throws well," Leo said.

"Indeed."

Leo looked at Bet as the gentleman walked away. "Ought I not to have talked to him?"

"You couldn't have known," Bet said. "But we need to talk to your parents."

Colin ran up to join them, holding Berowne against his shoulder. "Who was that?"

"He said he knew my parents," Leo said. "But I'm not sure he does. Or not sure he's a friend."

"I wouldn't call him a friend," Bet said.

"Should we report it?" Timothy asked. He and Emily and Livia had run after Colin.

"Our parents will know what to do," Livia said.

"Quite right," Edith agreed.

"Oh look," Timothy said. "There's Daddy!"

Julien strolled up to the gate. Timothy ran over to meet him with Genny toddling after. "Is the investigation solved?" Timothy asked.

"Not yet, I'm afraid. I was out making inquiries, and since I was near I thought I'd see how you all were doing." Julien stepped through the gate and scanned the group. "Everything all right?"

"A man stopped by," Leo said. "He said he knows you. But I'm not sure—"

"It was the man who calls himself Alexander Radford," Bet said.

Julien scarcely moved, but Edith saw the realization shoot through him. "Was it? It seems I have some long overdue business with him."

"Daddy," Leo said. "Did I—"

Julien touched Leo's shoulder. "You didn't do anything wrong at all, Leo. In fact, it's perhaps as well this happened when it did." He smiled at Edith and Bet. "If you don't mind staying with the children, I have something to take care of that should have been handled long since."

～

374

IT WAS twilight when Kitty turned into Berkeley Square, planning to check on the children and see if the others had learned anything before she made more inquiries. She neared the house to see Edith and Bet shepherding the children out of the garden.

"Mummy!" Timothy ran over to her. "Daddy was just here."

"And he left again?" Kitty asked as Genny hugged her legs . They had all agreed to meet in Berkeley Square to exchange news, but perhaps Julien had gone in pursuit of a new lead.

"A man stopped by the garden," Leo said. The gathering shadows fell across his face and settled in his eyes. "He said his name was Alexander Radford. I think Daddy went after him."

Cold that had nothing to do with the cooling evening air cut through Kitty's spencer and gown. "Which way did he go?"

"There." Timothy, Colin, and Livia all pointed to the left in the same moment, towards a narrow alley that led to the mews.

Kitty looked from Edith to Bet. "I need to find Julien." Her fingers tightened on Genny's hair for an instant. "I'll be back as soon as I can."

She ran down the alley the children had indicated, reached to the mews, and turned, heart pounding. The shadows were thickening, but she could see her husband. He had his hands at Alistair Rannoch's neck. And he was tightening a length of twine round Alistair's throat.

"Julien. No."

Julien's fingers stilled on the twine, but he didn't glance round at her. "This has to end, Kitty." He tightened the twine. Alistair was limp against him.

"Not like this."

"Kitkat." He stared into her eyes over his shoulder. "You know who I am."

"But this isn't who you want to be now."

His fingers stilled on the twine again. But he didn't release Alistair.

Kitty ran up to her husband and jabbed a knife into his arm.

CHAPTER 41

*M*élanie ran down the mews to see Alistair Rannoch on the ground, clutching his throat, and Kitty tying a cloth round Julien's arm. Seconds later, Malcolm ran into the mews from the opposite direction.

Mélanie scrambled to Alistair's side, half boots skidding over the cobblestones. "You'd best come inside, Mr. Rannoch."

Alistair jerked away from her hand.

"Julien won't attack you again," Kitty said, knotting off the bandage round Julien's arm. "You have my word."

Alistair stared at her. Kitty returned the stare. Julien, white-faced, put his hand to the bandage on his arm. "You should listen to my wife. I should do so myself."

Mélanie put out a hand to help Alistair to his feet but also gripped his arm to prevent his bolting. Malcolm moved to Alistair's other side. Mélanie looked at Julien as they helped Alistair to his feet.

"I don't need stitches," he said. "Kitty is very precise in her work. Let's go inside."

They went through the gate from the mews to the garden and through the garden to the house that had been Alistair Rannoch's and had become Malcolm's, and now might be Alistair's again. The house that Mélanie had thought could never be her home and that now was more of a home than any other place she had ever known.

A few minutes later they were settled in the library. Alistair, a towel full of ice pressed to his throat and a whisky in his hand, was seated on the sofa. Julien was on the settee, his jacket removed. Mélanie sat beside him, her medical supply box open, dressing his wound. Malcolm and Kitty flanked Alistair.

"I wouldn't run, Alistair," Malcolm said, as Alistair's gaze flickered towards the door. "Not unless you want us sharing the information we have with the world."

Alistair took a drink of whisky. "I can't imagine what you know."

"That rings hollow, considering you admit to wanting a royal pardon."

Alistair went still, whisky in one hand, ice pack in the other, uncertainty writ in the lines of his body.

"It makes sense," Malcolm said. "You and Trenchard were scheming to get him made prime minister. You were looking for whatever leverage you could find. Perhaps not surprising you thought the prince regent's estranged wife could be of use. Perhaps by making an alliance with her. Perhaps you hoped to get information against her you could give to the regent and then he'd support Trenchard's moves against Liverpool. Perhaps either. It was before you faked your death, but you used the name Alexander Radford with the princess, so you clearly wanted your dealings with her to remain secret. And given your general technique in most things, I don't suppose it's surprising that your efforts to get close to Princess Caroline led to your ending up in bed with her."

Alistair's gaze clashed with Malcolm's own like crossed swords. "You can't possibly have proof of that."

"I have the word of the one other person who was involved."

Alistair went still.

"But I think someone else knew," Mélanie said. "There was evidence about you and Princess Caroline in the papers Sidney Newland was bringing back to London. You hadn't counted on there being anything in writing. Perhaps it was worse. Perhaps you had said things to the princess about your plot with Trenchard that could be damaging. So you had to stop Mr. Newland. And, as Malcolm said, given other things you had done, perhaps it's not surprising that you hired an assassin to eliminate the evidence."

Alistair lifted his chin. "I can see you are a former actress. Your delivery is superb. But you can't prove that."

"That depends on what you mean by prove. A plausible case would get you in trouble. Especially since your fellow Elsinore League members got wind of what you did, and Mr. Newland's brother has come into the title and is now asking questions. And because Mr. Newland's dispatch box disappeared and has never been recovered."

Alistair tossed down another drink of whisky. "If—"

He broke off as the door opened. "We have visitors," Laura said. "They all arrived at once."

Harry and Cordy followed her into the room, the supposed Contessa Montalto between them. Raoul and Sofia were just behind with a slight, fair-haired woman in a lavender gown.

Sofia glanced round the room. "This is a bit awkward. May I present Anna Vaselli, the Contessa Montalto?"

Mélanie got to her feet. "You are very welcome, Contessa. As are the rest of you."

Sofia stared at Alistair. "I suppose you are—"

"Alistair Rannoch," Malcolm said.

The contessa—the real contessa—flew across the room and dropped down on the sofa beside Alistair. "*Caro!* You are injured."

"Anna, my dear." Alistair set the icepack on the sofa table. "I am unhurt, I assure you."

One had to give Alistair credit for sangfroid. He had nearly been strangled and he must be wondering how much Sofia and Raoul had told the real contessa, but his gaze could not have appeared more sincere.

"This," Harry said, turning to the woman who had come into the room with him and Cordelia, "is Signora Falconetti. Some of us formerly met her as the Contessa Montalto."

The real contessa's gaze shot to Signora Falconetti. "You were impersonating me?"

The woman now called Signora Falconetti lifted her chin. Whatever had transpired when Harry and Cordy found her, her allegiance had apparently shifted. "I was. On the orders of the gentleman beside whom you are now sitting with such an appearance of intimacy."

The contessa turned to look at Alistair, the look of a woman regarding a man she loves and trusts. "Nonsense. Alexander would not do anything of the sort."

"I assure you, madam," Malcolm said, "a number of us met Signora Falconetti presenting herself as the Contessa Montalto."

"That makes no sense," the contessa said. But in the angle of her head and the faint lilt of her voice, Mélanie caught the first hint of uncertainty.

"He had you staying secretly in London," Sofia said.

"Yes, because he didn't want anyone to disturb me before my testimony. Alexander, tell them these are all lies."

"My dear Anna," Alistair said. "I assure you, I don't trust anyone in this room."

"And yet it's our word against his," Sofia said. "My word, and the word of my closest friends. You know me, Anna. You knew me long before you knew him."

Alistair set down his whisky glass. "Anna. I think we should take our leave."

"Anna," Sofia said, "surely you aren't going to leave without answers."

The contessa drew back slightly against the sofa cushions. She might believe herself in love with Alistair, but she had known Sofia longer. She looked at Signora Falconetti. "These people say you were impersonating me. But I see no proof that it was on Alexander's orders. When do you claim he hired you?"

"Four years ago," Signora Falconetti said.

"Four years ago? That proves it. I did not even meet Alexander until last spring."

"I believe that's because the man you call Alexander originally hired Signora Falconetti for a different purpose," Mélanie said.

"You're very clever, Mrs. Rannoch," Signora Falconetti said. "You are quite right. Mr. Rannoch—not your husband, Alistair Rannoch—first engaged my services to secure Mr. Brougham's trust. I do not know his full motives at the time, but I do know the situation changed. Indeed, I heard Mr. Rannoch had died."

"So had a number of us," Julien said. "Heard that is. Though some of us were already presumed dead."

"You intrigue me. But in any case, I had been living quietly. I am a former actress, but I gave up the stage some time ago. Which was perhaps a mistake. But I was at loose ends in the spring when I heard from Mr. Rannoch wanting to engage my services again. Asking me to reach out to Mr. Brougham and offer to testify."

"But that is an absurd story," the contessa said. "I was going to testify. There would be no need for an imposter."

"I believe," Malcolm said, "that Mr. Rannoch's plan was to have Mr. Brougham call a supposed Contessa Montalto to testify in the queen's defense and then have you step forwards to expose her as an imposter."

"But—" The contessa spun towards Alistair. Mélanie saw the doubt in her eyes.

The door opened. "Forgive me," Valentin said. "But you have a caller. Lady Shroppington."

Lady Shroppington swept into the room in a stir of vermilion taffeta and surveyed the group in the Berkeley Square library. Her gaze went to Alistair and settled on him for a moment. His collar and cravat were damp and there was still a red mark round his throat. Something shifted in her eyes. It was subtle, but it might have been fear.

Mélanie got to her feet. "Lady Shroppington. I think you know most of those present. Though I'm not sure if you've met the Contessa Montalto or Signora Falconetti."

Lady Shroppington inclined her head, though her gaze narrowed and her lips thinned. "I won't pretend this is a social call, Mrs. Rannoch. Needless to say, there are distinctions that would prevent my calling in this house in the normal run of things."

"Being known to be a murderer might be considered one," Harry said.

"I won't bother to refute your nonsense, Colonel Davenport." Her gaze swept the room. "There's been a great deal of nonsense talked in the past few days. I came to insist you all put an end to it."

Alistair got to his feet, swaying slightly. "I believe there has already been enough said tonight. I suggest you allow me to escort you home, Lady Shroppington."

"No!" The contessa seized his hand. "You are not leaving until things are settled between us."

Alistair looked down at her. "Anna, my dear—"

"Do not speak to me like that. Who is this lady? What is she to you?"

"She's his mother," Julien said.

The words, though they expressed a truth known by almost all those present, acted like an incantation that breaks a spell. For a moment, everyone in the library went still.

Lady Shroppington took a step forwards. "That's a preposterous accusation and, needless to say, quite untrue."

Julien tilted his head back. "Come, Lady Shroppington, there's no need for prevarication. We are practically family, after all. Your son is my uncle, and my grandfather was your lover."

"Damn it, Julien—" Alistair said.

"I really don't think you want to challenge him, Mr. Rannoch," Kitty said. "I can't promise to stab him again. In fact, I don't think I would."

"I feel as though I've stumbled into a play," Signora Falconetti said.

"I know the feeling," Harry told her.

The contessa pushed herself to her feet and moved to Sofia's side. "I considered myself betrothed to Mr. Radford—Mr. Rannoch," she said.

"Nonsense," Lady Shroppington said. "He already has a wife. You're standing in her drawing room."

"Not Mr. Malcolm Rannoch, Mr. Alistair Rannoch. Whom I met as Alexander Radford. Who they say is your son. Which I suppose makes you Mr. Malcolm Rannoch's grandmother."

"No," Malcolm said. "It doesn't. Alistair is not my father."

"More and more like a play," Signora Falconetti murmured.

"I do not care about that," the contessa said. "I came here to speak at this trial before your House of Lords. But it now appears Mr. Rannoch has been using me to embarrass the queen."

"He's been using you to get himself a royal pardon," Julien said.

"*Nome di dio*, why would he want a pardon?"

"That's something we would all like to know," Raoul said.

"Fascinating as this is," Alistair said, "I should have taken my leave long since. If—"

The door burst open. Mélanie looked round in surprise, for Valentin was not usually so abrupt. But it was not Valentin. Nerezza and Ben ran into the room.

Nerezza stopped abruptly, staring at Alistair. Then her back straightened. She was clutching a sheaf of papers. "It's probably as well you're here." She looked at Malcolm and Mélanie. "Mr. Rannoch asked me to take some papers from Lord Beverston last night. He promised me his support if I complied. But all he managed to convince me of was the importance of looking at those papers. So I found them. It wasn't easy, but I managed it this afternoon. Then I told Ben." She glanced over her shoulder at her fiancé. Ben met her gaze and smiled. Nerezza smiled back, then held the papers out to Malcolm.

Alistair tensed as though to lunge forwards. Julien got to his feet and moved to stand between Alistair and Malcolm. Mélanie wondered if their library was going to become a scene of violence again, but really there were enough of them to overpower Alistair. And Lady Shroppington, if it came to that. Not to mention the Contessa Montalto, whichever side she ended up on.

Malcolm looked down at the papers. "Beverston always tended to play both sides. You had Sidney Newland killed, but Beverston managed to get the papers Newland had been carrying that reported on your and Trenchard's activities with the queen."

The reality settled in Alistair's eyes. He hadn't been fully sure that Beverston had Sidney Newland's papers until now. And that realization was a cut that struck to the bone.

"So now we have the papers. And you've lost your chance of a pardon," Julien said.

Alistair surveyed the group for the length of several heart-beats. He gave a faint smile. "One expects such things to end with a grand struggle. But perhaps Julien and I have already had that. Though when one man jumps another it can hardly be said to be a struggle. It's surprising how often these things end in council chambers or drawing rooms." His gaze went to Raoul. "Don't you find that, O'Roarke, for all your high-flown adventures?"

"Very true," Raoul said. "I'm sure Malcolm could tell you that from Vienna."

Alistair turned to Malcolm. His gaze was steady and opaque but held a weight of history. "It seems this house will continue to be yours."

"Alistair—" Lady Shroppington said.

Alistair raised a brow. "Mother."

For a moment, Lady Shroppington turned to a creature carved from ice. It occurred to Mélanie that this was perhaps the first time Alistair had ever called her that.

Alistair took a step towards the woman he had just publicly acknowledged as his mother. "Signora Falconetti said this seemed to be a play. And I think we can all tell when the curtain has come down."

CHAPTER 42

"That's it?" Ben stared at the door through which Alistair Rannoch and Lady Shroppington had just departed. "He's gone?"

"For the present," Raoul said. "His scheme for a pardon fell through, and the crimes he wanted the pardon for have come to light. Alistair is a number of things, but he knows when to cut his losses."

Ben swallowed. The Contessa Montalto and Sofia had moved to two chairs at the other end of the room and had their heads together. Signora Falconetti was still observing the scene with interest beside Harry and Cordelia. "But if these papers my father had make things so dangerous for Alistair Rannoch, why didn't my father simply use them again him?" Ben asked. "Take them to the prime minister or something?"

Nerezza started to speak, then bit her lip.

Ben looked from her to Malcolm to Raoul to Mélanie. "Because the papers implicate my father too, is that it?"

"I think so," Malcolm said in a steady voice. "We know Beverston played both sides in the League before opposing Alistair. I suspect he was working with Alistair and Trenchard and then turned on them. Glenister implied something of the sort last night. But there must be something in the papers"—he glanced down at them—"that could implicate your father enough that he didn't want to use them. So he held on to them and was hoping we could find another way to check Alistair."

"Lady Beverston talked about the time he spent in Italy last night," Nerezza said.

Ben nodded, gaze ruthlessly steady. "I always knew Father was —I didn't have illusions. Or I haven't had for a long time."

"He helped us, in the end," Mélanie said. "And he saved Nerezza's life."

"There's one thing I don't understand," Cordelia said. "The regent—the king—has wanted to divorce Queen Caroline almost from the moment they married. So why was Alistair so desperate to conceal his affair with the queen—Princess Caroline then. Proof of her affairs was just what the king wanted."

"The king might have been able to make use of the proof," Malcolm said, "but being a queen's lover is hardly the way to rise to power. Alistair might not have been executed like Mark Smeaton and the rest of Anne Boleyn's supposed lovers, but he'd have been disgraced, at the very least. Then and now. And then in his effort to cover up the affair, he committed murder."

"So often it's the coverup that brings someone down," Raoul said. "If—"

The door library door opened again. Mélanie half expected Alistair to have returned, but it was Valentin. "Mademoiselle Darnault and Mr. Blayney," he announced.

Danielle and Edmund took in the group with a quick glance but wasted no time on greetings or introductions. "I'm sorry," Danielle said, "but we have news. Perhaps—"

"It's all right to speak," Malcom said. "Everyone here is part of things, one way and another."

"Edmund's been helping me make inquiries," Danielle said. Amazing how her flexible voice could be so clipped and to the point. "We haven't found Joseph Eden, but we found someone who saw him in Green Park three days ago." She hesitated. "He was meeting with a lady."

"Was there a description?" Malcolm asked.

"Slight," Edmund said. "Not overly tall. She was veiled, but her hair appeared to be dark. And the thing is, I had a talk with Bill Cauford. He's an actor who was involved with Abby Clifton when I interviewed her. Apparently he and Abby have been involved for some time, with interruptions when she finds a gentleman with more to offer financially. Bill took this last break up hard and he was hanging round Wardour Street. He saw a gentleman I was assume was Mr. Brougham. But he also saw a woman call. A slight, dark-haired woman. It sounds as though it could be the same woman who was meeting with Eden in Green Park. I know it doesn't prove anything, but—"

"No." Malcolm was already halfway to the door, and in his gaze Mélanie caught a flash of horror. "It makes sense of everything."

~

"MALCOLM." Evie Cleghorn looked at him across the sitting room of her husband's parents' house in Marylebone. "I didn't think I'd see you again until the trial was over. Or at least your investigation."

"The investigation is coming to a close. That's why I came to see you."

"You've learned more?"

"A great deal. But I'm still piecing some of it together." Malcolm studied the woman he'd known since she was a bright-eyed toddler. "Did Chase demand something of you? Or did Honoria say something that made you realize he knew the truth or was close to it?"

"The truth about what?" Evie's gaze was steady but he caught a telltale flicker in it. "Malcolm, I told you I hadn't seen George Chase."

"You were seen going into his lodgings."

"I don't even know where he lodged."

"Honoria knew. And George could have sent word to you. Did he want you to go through your uncle's papers like he did Honoria? Or did he demand something else? Whatever it was, it caused you to engage Joseph Eden to find someone to kill him."

"What? Malcolm, that's absurd. I don't even know who Joseph Eden is."

"An agent who works for Hubert Mallinson. You visited Carfax Court with Honoria when you were growing up. You're practically part of the Mallinson family."

"But I'm not a spy."

"No, but you're observant enough to have figured out how to use a spymaster's agents." She wouldn't be the first one. Hubert's daughter Louisa had done much the same. To tragic effect.

"But why on earth would I have done?"

"To protect your family. Your children. Your mother. Perhaps even Honoria."

"From what? It makes no sense. Even if I had the least idea how to reach a man like this Joseph Eden, I haven't the resources—"

"Glenister gave you funds because your husband had got into debt over cards. Or so Glenister thought. Shall I ask Cleghorn if those debts are real?"

"Keep Max out of this!" Evie's voice cut the air. And the layers of pretense.

Malcolm regarded her in the silence that followed. "How long have you known who your parents really were?"

Evie glanced away. The lamplight etched her profile against the soft cream walls. She held her chin as steady as a rifleman holds a weapon. "I told you, I've always known my mother was pregnant when she and my father eloped."

"But not pregnant by the man who is now your father."

Her gaze shot to him. "You can't possibly prove that."

"No. And I have no wish to do so. But I think you killed George Chase to prevent the secret from coming to light."

Evie turned away again for a long moment. The lines of her back were taut beneath the slate blue of her gown. But when she looked back at him, her gaze was steady and secure. The gaze of the girl Malcolm had known all her life. And yet at the same time, he felt he had never seen her properly before. "I admit nothing, Malcolm. But you know better than anyone what George Chase was. What he did to Cordelia was bad enough. But David told me after Waterloo. That George killed Amy Beckwith and Julia Ashton. George had no conscience and he didn't care whose lives he smashed. If I had stopped him from smashing more—can you really imagine I'd be sorry? And can you honestly tell me the world isn't better off without him?"

CHAPTER 43

*A*listair got to his feet as Gisèle approached the table at the back of the tavern. "Thank you for coming to see me."

"I was afraid you'd have already left."

His mouth twisted. "Malcolm won't do anything. I don't think even O'Roarke would. I'm not even sure Julien would, for all he nearly choked the life out of me. But the evidence is there. Time for me to leave England again."

"I don't suppose you'll tell me where you're going."

"Better not, don't you think? For both of us." He poured her a glass of wine and pushed it across the table. "It was always a desperate gambit, you know. My return. Like Napoleon's leaving Elba. Only I like to think I know when to cut my losses better than the former emperor."

"So you can return and fight another day?"

Alistair took a drink of wine. "Possibly."

"And the League—"

"Can fight it out among themselves. I have little interest in who controls something that isn't mine anymore." Alistair set his glass down. "You may hear stories about Lady Shroppington."

"You mean that she's my great-aunt? Or my grandmother, depending on how one views things?"

Alistair inclined his head. "She's quite proud of you. But I wouldn't suggest you trust her."

"Oh, don't worry. I have no intention of doing so." Gisèle picked up her glass and tossed down a swallow of wine. Her throat was tight for reasons she couldn't have possibly explained. Or didn't want to. "Father—"

Alistair turned and gave a smile that was surprisingly without bitterness. Every moment since she had run from Dunmykel and gone undercover to supposedly work with him hung between them. "No, Gelly, don't. I'd honestly rather not know."

~

"So ALISTAIR'S LEFT LONDON?" Hubert asked.

"Or will shortly," Malcolm said. "He may not be checkmated, but he knows this gambit has failed."

Hubert grunted. "We were all so shocked to see him again, we didn't quite realize how desperate a gambit it was. But I'm grateful to all of you for checking him."

"Thank you, Uncle." Julien's voice could have cut glass.

Hubert frowned at his nephew over his spectacles. "What happened to your arm?"

"Kitty stabbed me." Julien pushed himself up on his uncle's desk with his good arm. "Alistair knew you were brothers. You knew it. In many ways your interests align more with him than with us. I'm surprised he didn't reach out to you."

"He did, as it happens." Hubert took a drink of coffee. "No harm in saying so now. I kept him talking. One never knows when someone will drop something of interest. He claimed he could influence the trial."

"Did he tell you about the Contessa Montalto?" Malcolm asked.

"Not the full story."

"Even if he only told you part of it, I'm surprised you didn't consider an alliance with him," Julien said. "If his plot had worked, it might have shaken the trial and turned things against the queen."

"You think even that would have prompted me to make an alliance with Alistair?"

Malcolm held his former spymaster's gaze in the lamplight. "Yes. I do."

Hubert set his cup down. "Doesn't really matter at this point, does it? Alistair's plan failed. And momentum seems to be moving in the direction of Brougham and the queen."

"I hope it is," Malcolm said.

"You two aren't going to claim you've told me everything either, are you? I'm still not sure why Alistair wanted a pardon."

"That doesn't really matter at this point, does it? Alistair's gone. For the moment." Malcolm exchanged a look with Julien and moved to the door.

"Malcolm," Hubert said. "Are you any closer to learning who hired Joseph Eden to engage the man who killed George Chase?"

"No." Malcolm looked back, one hand on the door handle. "And I don't expect we ever will learn."

LAURA LOOKED at her husband as he turned from pulling the covers over Clara in her cradle. "We've never talked about him. Trenchard. Beyond the necessities."

"No." Raoul's voice was easy, his gaze steady. She knew that gaze and tone from when he was confronting a particularly touchy agent situation. "It's for you to discuss if you ever need to. Want to. There's no need to otherwise."

"Unless it impinges on an investigation. Which it seems to have done."

"Quite." Raoul leaned against the wall. "I hate Trenchard on a level that is difficult for me to put into words for any number of reasons, but just now not least for intruding on your peace and forcing his way back into our lives."

"We should all be used to the past intruding by now." Laura locked her arms over her chest. "I wouldn't say Trenchard ever confided in me. But he did talk to me. That was one of the—one of the things that drew me to him, for want of a better word. At the start he would talk about India. About the politics there. We disagreed about so much and had some rather intense quarrels. But he would listen when I challenged him. It was rather intoxicating to be able to argue ideas after Jack, who had little taste for ideas at all."

Raoul gave a faint smile that tugged at her heart from halfway across the room. "I'd never have guessed arguing ideas appealed to you."

She looked into his gray eyes and felt the memory of their—debates? verbal duels?—when she was imprisoned in Newgate tighten the air between them. "It was nothing like that with Trenchard. But he'd ask me my opinion. Even later, when I was spying for him. When I was giving him reports on Mélanie and Malcolm." She kept her gaze on her husband's face. They all had their regrets, but the memory of how powerless she had been and what she had done under Trenchard's compulsion still brought bitterness welling on her tongue. "He wanted the details, but he'd still ask me what I thought. He asked me once if I thought you and Mélanie were lovers."

Raoul raised a brow. "What did you say?"

"That I was sure there was nothing between you. That I was quite sure of Malcolm and Mélanie's marriage. But it did make me realize there was something different between you and Mélanie. I realized there was constraint between Malcolm and Mélanie. And though I'd met you before, the constraint had started round the time you began spending more time in Berkeley Square."

He grimaced. "So it did."

Laura hesitated, but they were at the point now where she could say it. Or they should be. "I remember a moment. You and Suz—Mélanie and Malcolm crossing the street from the square. You almost touched the skirt of Mélanie's gown and then pulled your hand back. Sometimes restraint can show a lot."

He met her gaze and gave a faint smile. "You don't miss much. It was harder in those days. Things were shifting."

"You don't owe me an explanation. But it was disturbing. Because I didn't like to think of anything coming between Mélanie and Malcolm. But also because I was starting to feel jealous about you. Before I'd even have admitted I had any reason to be jealous."

"Did Trenchard—?"

"Suspect I had any interest in you? I'm not sure. There was that Christmas. The dinner you gave at Mivart's on Boxing Day. I ended up sitting next to you."

"I rather strategized that."

"How on earth—"

"I'm not a spymaster for nothing. It's almost second nature to learn to arrange seating the way one wants it."

"So you were spying on me?"

His mouth curved in a smile. "You intrigued me. Because I thought you weren't what you seemed. I was concerned on Malcolm and Mélanie's account. But that wasn't the only reason you interested me." He watched her for a moment. "Were you spying on me?"

"By then, I was telling Trenchard as little as I could. So I was afraid of what you'd see about me. But at times you'd make me laugh and I'd forget everything. I didn't say much about you to Trenchard at all. But he'd ask about you. I think he read into my silences. He was a lot of things, but I can't claim he wasn't perceptive."

Raoul crossed the room to her and took her hands. "The investigation's over. Alistair's gone and the questions about their plot with him. We can put Trenchard back in his box."

Laura studied her husband. They might be done with Trenchard, but—"Do you think Alistair will stay away?"

"Permanently? No. But we have time. Which is perhaps the most we can hope for."

~

CORDELIA LOOKED at her husband across their bedchamber. "How did you persuade Signora Falconetti to turn on Alistair?" Somehow, with everything they had all discussed tonight, she hadn't leaned the truth of that. The real Contessa Montalto had left Berkeley Square with Sofia, but Bianca Falconetti had departed for a hotel that Cordelia was quite sure her husband had paid for.

Harry gave a faint smile. "By making it clear we could offer her considerably more than Alistair could. Including an introduction to Simon. She's interested in returning to the theatre. She already knew her masquerade was exposed by the time I tracked her down. Alistair would have no incentive to pay her further."

"You're brilliant, Harry. Not to mention compassionate."

Harry shrugged. "I like her. She's pragmatic. And tough. I find it hard to blame her much for looking out for herself."

Cordelia nodded. She undid the ties on her cloak and dropped it on her dressing table bench. "Alistair's really gone."

"For the present, at least."

"And George—" They knew who had killed George, from Malcolm, though he hadn't shared it with many. Cordelia gripped her elbows. "I'd never have thought—" She saw Evie Cleghorn, as a bright-eyed little girl, bending over her children by the Serpentine, smiling up at her husband. "I'm glad we know."

"So am I." Harry had gone still. She could feel his gaze on her. "Even George deserves to have the truth discovered."

"I'm not sure what George deserves." Cordelia felt her nails bite into her arms. "But I don't think I'll ever be able to look Evie Cleghorn in the face again."

"I'm not sure I will either."

Cordelia stared into her husband's eyes, polished agate in the lamplight.

"It's not an answer. And it robbed us of ever being able to resolve anything with George. Herculean as that would have been."

"You mean he'll always be between us?"

"I don't see how he couldn't be." Harry's gaze stayed steady on her face. "I suppose the question is how we deal with him."

Cordelia went up to her husband and put her hands on his shoulders. "Without George we wouldn't be where we are today. We wouldn't have the girls. Either of them." She swallowed, but didn't let herself look away from Harry. "So I can't wish him out of our past and our lives. But I can say he's irrelevant to our future. I love you, Harry."

Harry's gaze stayed steady and appraising, but his mouth curved in a smile as he bent his head to hers. "I know."

CHAPTER 44

"*H*ow's your arm?" Kitty asked, as Julien closed the door of the nursery on the sleeping children.

"I'll live. It's quite clear my attacker didn't aim to do serious damage."

"It was dark and I was moving fast."

"You're an expert. It's ingrained." Julien moved to the chest of drawers and picked up a glass of whisky he'd poured earlier. "I was hesitating when you stabbed me."

"Yes. I know. But I wasn't sure you'd stop. And I wasn't sure how long Alistair would last."

"It's a fair point." Julien took a drink of whisky. "I'm not sure I'd have stopped either. And now there's always the chance he'll come back. That we'll find him talking to Leo again."

"I don't want Leo to grow up with the burden that his father killed his grandfather to protect him. You should know better than most how the past can burden one."

"Leo may never know."

"Julien. You're talking to me."

"Alistair isn't his grandfather in any meaningful sense of the word."

"But he'll know. Someday. And at some point, he may see it that way."

Julien swung his head round, his gaze hard on her own. "If he sees Alistair as his grandfather, he'll have to face that I killed his father."

"I don't think he'll see Edgar as his father. But it's one thing that you killed Edgar to save Malcolm. It would be another if you killed Alistair to protect Leo from something that hadn't happened yet."

"Not just Leo."

"Leo's what drove you to attack Alistair tonight."

"Kitty." He stared into her eyes. "You're the last person to ever try to tame someone."

"Of course not. But I don't want this on Leo's conscience. I don't want it on your conscience. Because I know you have one, whatever you say. I know how Edgar's death weighs on you, and that was justified." She drew a rough breath. "I don't want it on my conscience. And I wouldn't have thought I'd say that. But I can't take another."

He took a step forwards. His hand came up to cup her cheek. "Edgar's death shouldn't be on your conscience."

"If I hadn't come to England when I did, he'd still be alive."

"Not necessarily. He wouldn't have died precisely when he did. Maybe. He didn't attack Annabel Larimer because of you. At some point, that was going to unravel and he was going to move against her. It all might still have happened. In any case, Malcolm would have worked out the truth sooner or later. He'd have confronted Edgar or Edgar would have attacked him. I likely wouldn't have been there. I only was because you called me in. Malcolm might have killed Edgar or Edgar might have killed Malcolm. If Malcolm had killed Edgar, he'd have an intolerable time living with the guilt of it. And if Edgar had killed Malcolm—that's a world none of us wants to live in. And you and I would both feel the guilt of it."

"Well, then."

"And Malcolm loved Edgar, whatever he says."

"Gelly loves Alistair."

"You think that should have stopped me, given the stakes? It didn't with Edgar."

"But Alistair wasn't threatening to kill anyone."

"He's—"

"He wasn't the moment you attacked. It's different. It's a line I don't think you want to cross anymore. I don't want to see what that will do to you."

"My love. The damage has already been done."

"People can change, Julien. Our whole relationship is built on that. If it's not true, our marriage has no hope."

Julien's gaze fastened on her own, open and raw and unyielding. "Are you saying it can't survive if you hate me?"

"I don't think I could hate you. I'm saying it can't survive if you hate yourself."

Julien rested his forehead against her own. "The fact that there is an 'us' is the opposite of how I was in the past. I wasn't responsible for anyone. I'm trying to learn to be responsible to those I love. I owe that to Leo or I'm not much of a parent."

"There are different ways of being responsible to him. We need to be there for him. And give him the tools to cope with this. Part of being responsible is showing children how to handle a situation. Is this what you'd want Leo to do?"

Julien drew in and released his breath. "Caught."

She slid her hand down his uninjured arm and slid her fingers into his own. "It didn't occur to me until Leo was born. I wanted him to be proud of me. That started to change me."

"You've always been someone Leo could be proud of."

"I thought about myself differently. I thought of how he'd feel about me. And more than that, how I'd feel about myself." She squeezed his hand. "We'll get through this, Julien."

"You sound absurdly optimistic."

"Oh, that's another thing being a parent teaches you. You spend so much time being optimistic for them that it bleeds over into your own perspective." She pressed her forehead against his own. "We're always going to live with threats. We both know that. Malcolm and Mélanie know that. God knows Raoul knows that."

Julien nodded. "It was easier. When I didn't care about the consequences for anyone else. Or for myself."

"Maybe." Kitty ran her free hand over his hair. "But I don't think you've ever done what you almost did tonight."

"Kitkat, whatever you think of me, we both know—"

"You've killed under orders. You've killed in a fight. I don't think you've ever, on your own initiative, killed someone just because they were in your way."

His gaze settled on her face. "I'm not sure that's a major distinction. I could have refused the orders."

"And you would now. But I think it is a distinction. And I think it would haunt you." She tilted her head back. Their eyes were level. "What would you have done if, when you found Edgar and Malcolm, Edgar hadn't been about to kill Malcolm?"

Julien's gaze slid to the side, the way it did when he didn't want to let her in. "Given what I knew about him, I'd have been hard pressed not to kill him even if Malcolm hadn't been anywhere near."

"Malcolm said the same thing. But I don't think either of you would have done. I don't think you've ever killed out of emotion. I don't think you'd like yourself if you did."

"You're assuming I like myself."

"I think you do. I don't think you could not like the man I love."

He lifted her hand and kissed her knuckles. "That's either sound or appalling logic, Kitkat."

Kitty slid her arms round her husband and put her mouth to his. "Take your pick."

∾

400

MALCOLM SCRAPED his hands over his face. "I knew," he said in a low voice. "I didn't want to admit it, but I knew."

"What, darling?" Mélanie kept her voice level, because she felt as though she were stepping on glass.

"That somehow the conclusion of this investigation was going to touch on someone we knew. It touched on so much of our past. So many people we knew. Even more than other cases. I was worried about what it might do to Harry and Cordy. I was worried about where it might push Julien. I was worried about what it might dredge up for Laura. I was worried about Raoul—god knows, I'm always worried about Raoul. I've been desperately afraid for Gelly and Andrew. I've been worried about Frances and Archie ever since Alistair reappeared. I've been worried about Sandy and Bet and Ben and Nerezza and lately Sofia and Kit. I was worried about Glenister and even Beverston, for all one could say they've sown what they may reap." He drew an uneven breath. "I was worried about Honoria—I was quite sure she was lying. I was worried how it might spill over to touch Quen and Aspasia and even Val. So many of our family and friends are tangled in the espionage game. And tangled with the Elsinore League or fighting against them. But Evie was the last person I thought would be at the heart of it."

"She thought she was pushed against a wall," Mélanie said. "And she made a desperate choice."

"She hired someone to kill someone else." Malcolm's voice had the precision of rifle shots. "Strip away the details and that's what it comes down to."

"The details include who George Chase was and what he'd done."

Malcolm shot a look at her. "Would you have done what she did?"

"I've done a lot of things, darling. A lot of things I'm sorry for. A lot of things I wouldn't necessarily do differently, but perhaps should."

"But would you have done this?" Malcolm's gaze held her, as inexorable as his emotional examination could be.

Honesty was its own sort of ruthlessness. "I don't think so. Not even to protect you and the children from scandal. But then, I didn't grow up believing in appearances."

Malcolm nodded. "I can't pretend to be sorry Chase is gone. But I wouldn't have either. I hope Evie goes on to live a happy life. I hope her marriage thrives and her children flourish. I don't think she's a danger to the world. I don't worry about what she'll do. But I'm never going to be able to forget."

"I doubt Evie will either. But I don't know what the memory will do to her."

Malcolm's mouth tightened. "From what I saw today, not as much as I'd have hoped it would."

"If Kitty hadn't stabbed Julien, Alistair might be permanently gone from our lives."

"And I think that would have weighed on Julien more than George's murder will weigh on Evie. Which is one of many reasons I'm glad Alistair is still in the world."

"He's out of our lives."

"For the moment." Malcolm glanced round their room in the house that was once again theirs. His gaze lingered on the theatrical prints she had hung on the walls. "And we're living a lie."

Mélanie went up to her husband and put her hands on his shoulders. "I, at least, am used to it."

"What self-respecting spy isn't?"

"So you admit we're still spies?"

His arms slid round her. "I may be slow, but some things do dawn on me. Not that spies are the only ones who live with lies. The king and queen's marriage has been a lie from their wedding day."

"Unlike ours, which only began with a lie."

"That's my Mel. Never afraid of honesty." He pressed his lips to her forehead. "*Doubt truth to be a liar*, sweetheart."

"Do you think Brougham can prevail? Without the star witness he thought he had?"

"I wouldn't bet against him." Malcolm bent his head to kiss her. "Life is going to stay interesting."

Mélanie pulled him closer. "I wouldn't have it any other way."

HISTORICAL NOTES

The Contessa Montalto is fictional. So is the conspiracy to make the Duke of Trenchard prime minister in place of Lord Liverpool. Though the Milan commission was very real, Sidney Newland's investigation into Caroline of Brunswick is fictional, as is Alistair Rannoch's involvement with her.

Henry Brougham and Caroline (Caro George) Lamb did go off to Italy together in 1816. Emily Cowper, Caro's sister-in-law, did follow them to Italy to persuade Caro home. In her letters chronicling the amazing months of Queen Caroline's trial, Emily mentions that though the affair is over, Caro still cares about Brougham and admires him. See Mabel Airlie's *Lady Palmerston and Her Times* (London: Hodder and Stroughton, 1922); Tresham Lever's *The Letters of Lady Palmerston: Selected and Edited from the Originals at Broadlands and Elsewhere* (London: John Murray, 1957). For further insights into the months surrounding the trial, see the letters of Caro George's half-sister Harriet Granville: Edward Frederick Leveson-Gower's *Letters of Harriet, Countess Granville, 1810-1845* (London: Longmans, Green, and Co., 1894). Kenneth Bourne's *Palmerston: The Early Years 1784-1841* (New

York: Macmillan, 1982) has excellent information on Palmerston, his relationship with Emily, and the Brougham/Caro George affair.

A READING GROUP GUIDE

The Whitehall Conspiracy
About This Guide
The suggested questions are included
to enhance your group's reading of
Tracy Grant's *The Whitehall Conspiracy*

.

1. As Julien says, they'll never know if he'd have killed Alistair if Kitty hadn't stabbed him. What do you think would have happened if Kitty hadn't stopped Julien?
2. Evie says she wouldn't be sorry for killing George Chase given what he'd done. How do you feel about what she did? Do you think any of the other characters would have done the same?
3. Harry and Cordelia acknowledge that George will always be between them. Do you think it will easier or harder for them to cope with George's memory after the events of this book?
4. What do you think Alistair Rannoch will do next?
5. Mélanie and Lady Shroppington were both agents who

had affairs in the course of their espionage work. Compare and contrast them.

6. What do you think Lady Shroppington will do next?
7. What do you think lies ahead for Edith and Thomas?
8. How do you think Evie will cope with what she's done going forwards?
9. Do you think Alistair and Lady Shroppington are closer or further apart by the end of the book?
10. Harry and Cordelia confront the past in this book, but so do Archie and Frances, Laura and Raoul, Gisèle and Andrew, Malcolm and Mélanie, and Julien and Kitty. Which couple do you think has the most challenging road going forwards?

ALSO BY TRACY GRANT

Traditional Regencies

WIDOW'S GAMBIT

FRIVOLOUS PRETENCE

THE COURTING OF PHILIPPA

Lescaut Quartet

DARK ANGEL

SHORES OF DESIRE

SHADOWS OF THE HEART

RIGHTFULLY HIS

The Rannoch Fraser Mysteries

HIS SPANISH BRIDE

LONDON INTERLUDE

VIENNA WALTZ

IMPERIAL SCANDAL

THE PARIS AFFAIR

THE PARIS PLOT

BENEATH A SILENT MOON

THE BERKELEY SQUARE AFFAIR

THE MAYFAIR AFFAIR

INCIDENT IN BERKELEY SQUARE

LONDON GAMBIT

MISSION FOR A QUEEN

GILDED DECEIT

ABOUT THE AUTHOR

Tracy Grant studied British history at Stanford University and received the Firestone Award for Excellence in Research for her honors thesis on shifting conceptions of honor in late-fifteenth-century England. She lives in the San Francisco Bay Area with her young daughter and three cats. In addition to writing, Tracy works for the Merola Opera Program, a professional training program for opera singers, pianists, and stage directors. Her real life heroine is her daughter Mélanie, who is very cooperative about Mummy's writing time. She is currently at work on her next book chronicling the adventures of Malcolm and Mélanie Suzanne Rannoch. Visit her on the Web at www.tracygrant.org

Cover photo by Kristen Loken.

facebook.com/tracygrant
twitter.com/tracygrant
instagram.com/tracygrant93

CPSIA information can be obtained
at www.ICGtesting.com
Printed in the USA
LVHW081730170822
726162LV00009B/297

9 781641 972208